Murray

A Novel

Melanie Senn

Murray: A Novel

"Up to the present I traveled the opposite way of the sun; henceforth, I travel two ways, as sun and as moon. Henceforth I take on two sexes, two hemispheres, two skies, two sets of everything. Henceforth I shall be double-jointed and double-sexed. Everything that happens will happen twice. I shall be as a visitor to this earth, partaking of its blessings and carrying off its gifts. I shall neither serve nor be served. I shall seek the end in myself."

--Henry Miller, *Tropic of Capricorn*

"Should women mount the political platform or amputate limbs, let her remember there are laws controlling the social structure of society, the operations of which will disrobe her of all those qualities now the glory of the sex, and will cast her down in the dust of the earth."

--Dr. D. Hayes Agnew

That you are here—that life exists and identity,
That the powerful play goes on, and you may contribute a verse.

--Walt Whitman

Prologue

June 11, 1900
Census Records, 145 Sixth Ave. Manhattan, New York.

Surname: Hall **Given**: Murray H. **Sex**: M **Born**: Feb. 1840 **Status**: Widow

Place Born: Scotland **Father Born**: Scotland **Mother Born**: Scotland

Immigrated: 1846 **Occupation**: Employment Agt.

January 18, 1901, ***New York Times***

"He was a shrewd, bright man, in my estimation. He used to send people from his intelligence office to room here for a day or two, and often came himself to see somebody stopping here. He played poker and was sweet on women. I knew him for years. He could drink his weight in beer and stand up under it."

--John Bremer, owner of the Fifteenth Ward Hotel

January 19, 1901, ***New York Times***

"Why, I knew him well. He was a member of the Tammany district organization, a hard worker for his party, and always had a good argument to put up for any candidate he favored. He used to come to the Iroquois Club to see me and pay his dues, and occasionally he would crack a joke with some of the boys. He was a modest little fellow, but had a peppery temper and could say some cutting things when anyone displeased him.

He never sought political preferment for himself, but often said a good word that helped along a deserving friend. And he could say nice things and some bad things about a man too, just as cleverly as any one of the big politicians. Why, when the County Democracy was in the heyday of its glory, Murray Hall was one of the bright stars in that constellation."

--New York State Senator Bernard F. Martin

January 19, 1901, ***New York Times***

"He used to come in here and buy papers and books, but never tobacco. His wife used to come in, too. She was a large, good looking woman, almost twice her husband's weight. She did most of the business in the intelligence office up to the time of her death. Last week, Wednesday, Mr. Hall sent a servant around here with a message that he was very sick and for me to call without fail between 2 and 3 o'clock next afternoon. My husband was very bad from the grip at the time, and I didn't get a chance to go. He didn't send for me again. He thought a great deal of me and used to come in and sit down and read for hours. On my last birthday he gave me a cake for a present."

--Johanna Meyer, who kept a newsstand at 109 West Tenth Street.

Friday, Jan. 18, 1901

"I must positively refuse to give any information about this case. It would be a violation of professional confidence. I have made my report to the Coroner to avoid the possibility of any trouble, but I will say nothing whatsoever about the matter."

--Dr. William C. Gallagher of 302 West Twelfth Street

Part One

1900

Chapter One

There it is again before me, the painting. I've thought of it so often—what a scandal it caused. Poor Eakins, so misunderstood. I saw it in person once and only once, with Celia. We took a special trip to Philadelphia to view it, a rare trip out of Manhattan, but I wanted to see it, felt I needed to see it. A small gallery was showing Eakins' work and there it was, *The Agnew Clinic*. The painting was large and glorious, though utterly disturbing. The commissioned portrait of Doctor Agnew was paid for by his students, and any one of them who contributed got to be in it. Eakins was famous for his portraits—my favorite was of Walt Whitman in Camden, New Jersey, where the poet spent his last years. *The Agnew Clinic* was grand, though, and Eakins finished it in just ninety days. Imagine the focus, the obsession. Nearly thirty students are rendered in the operating theatre audience (including Eakins himself; his wife, also a talented artist, painted him in it). Dr. Agnew is highlighted on the left, and on the right foreground are the anesthesiologist with his ether cone, the assistant surgeons, including the one making the incision, the stoic nurse, and, of course, the patient with her right breast exposed. The other, the left breast, is undoubtedly the one with the cancer, the one being cut into. Here was evidence and celebration of Agnew's radical mastectomy, a surgery with very little success that often resulted in terrible deformity, life-long pain, but, more often than not, death.

Celia was so patient when we went to see the painting. I stood before it for more than an hour until she finally encouraged me away. And now in my dream I find myself standing before it again.

And then I'm in it—in the painting. It's not the first time I've had this nightmare.

It's no longer a two-dimensional piece of art but rather an actual operating theatre, and I the patient, lying there cold and exposed. I can hear the students shifting in their seats; I hear the whispers of the man sitting next to Eakins himself, but can't make out the actual words. As the patient, I feel utter helplessness and terror, but also the humiliation of being sick, of having cancer. I wonder if they scorn me, find me deserving of the disease? Punishment for my sins. I'm at the mercy of those on this operating floor. Do they see me as human? They cannot know my thoughts, don't know my struggles, can't feel my pain. I look around at the students. All men, some mustached, some bearded, some spectacled. They're dressed so nicely, these students of medicine, in their suits and hats, though someday they hope to wear the clean white surgical scrubs that Agnew and his male posse have donned. When you choose a profession, that might be a consideration. Look at the uniform, the clothes you will wear every day to do your work. I personally loved mine, though how wonderful it would have been to wear a coat that fit me properly rather than one that was three sizes too large.

Most of the students look curious, though some, typical of any school setting, look slightly bored, resistant to humbling themselves to the act of learning. They are the ones with hubris. Agnew, for his part, appears almost benevolent. He gestures to the class, explaining the procedure. I have read about it so often, I could probably perform one myself, and in fact, had of late considered doing it to myself, though I couldn't get around the thought that I would likely pass out and bleed to death. You would need enough ether to take away the pain and get the job done, though not so much that you couldn't perform. Anyway, as I said, the surgery didn't have much of a track record.

I think I see my brother among the students, young and handsome as he was when he enlisted in the war, more alive than the last day I saw him. Usually I relish dreaming of my brother, but in this setting, it seems too macabre, as if I am about to join the dead. Will you be there, James, when I do finally die? If only I had been able to volunteer and fight alongside you; to die by your side would have been a worthy death, for losing you was the most terrible thing that ever happened to me—dare I say, even worse than losing Celia, for whom I had tremendous love. But my devotion to you, James, trumped all.

Dr. Agnew himself, I read, honed his own surgical prowess removing bullets and mangled and infected limbs during the Civil War. Perhaps he performed on you, James, though if he did, I know that the environment was more frantic, dirty, and slipshod than this antiseptic surgical theater. Now, with bombastic gesture, Agnew concludes his introduction in such a way that I realize the impending operation is more a demonstration for the students—more a scene to be captured by an artist—than an opportunity for healing. Does he despise women? I heard that he would rather resign from the Philadelphia Medical School than allow women into his classrooms. Indeed, he speaks to the audience and not to me; and I wonder: to him, am I a mere specimen, a pile of flesh he can and will cut into for the purpose of furthering the field?

The nurse appears, her back to me, and my eyes lock on the back of her black dress and move upward to the top of her white nursing cap. A man approaches the head of the operating table; he's the anesthesiologist and holds an ether cone in his hand. Ah, thank goodness itself for ether, a truly remarkable advance in surgery.

"Hang tight, Murray," he says in a soothing voice. "We're going to make sure this doesn't hurt a bit."

But then the nurse, upon hearing his words, turns toward us. I gasp, sucking in air with true shock at the sight. Not only am I face-to-face with my first wife, Mollie, but her face is a hideous blue and yellow hue, her eyes bulging slightly from her skull. Horribly, blood seeps out from a slice in her neck, dripping down like red tears onto her white nurse's apron.

"Oh, that won't be necessary," she says, and bats the cone out of his hand, her grimace menacing. I hear a dissonant clang as the cone crashes to the operating room floor.

So I'll be awake for this.

I try to move but I'm strapped in. Then Dr. Agnew says, "Scalpel," and approaches. But instead of the lancet, Mollie hands him a wood-handled pen knife with a rusty blade. He frowns at her and then shrugs. He stands next to me.

"I will now remove the tumor as well as the infected area," he says to the air. He doesn't make eye contact with me; this is nothing personal. Then he jabs me hard and I feel the pen knife go deep. He's sawing my tender flesh, and I feel each awful, piercing cut.

Chapter Two

Every day begins the same for me: first the bandages, then I dress. This morning, I put on a machine-sewn undershirt. In winter, I wear wool, but it's still summer, so this one is a light cotton-silk blend. Then I put on cotton drawers, also machine-made. I pull on my garters and then my dark socks and attach them. A button-up shirt with a built-in collar, cotton trousers, suspenders. Black leather shoes that would fit a young boy. I choose a tie—the only thing that ever varies. Today, a dark blue one with a pattern of little white birds. I don and button a too-large dark wool coat; I wear it always outside this room, no matter the weather. I glance in the mirror, place my favorite felt derby hat on my head. I think I look younger than my sixty years—I have few wrinkles and my hair has barely begun to gray—but what does it matter? I'm near the end.

When I emerge from my room this morning, my daughter Minnie is sitting at the table, her long dark hair down and a little wild, unbrushed. She's still in her sleeveless nightgown, white cotton with ecru lace. Her arms are thin and pale, and I wonder, as I have in the past, what her actual father looked like, but she would not know since she never met him. She's been in my life since she was six and considers me her true father.

A cup of coffee sits on a saucer in front of her. A plume of smoke rises from the cigarette in her hand. She took up smoking when her mother fell ill and the habit stuck.

"Morning," I say.

She has been lost in thought but now looks up at me, taps the ash into a saucer.

"Are you really going to wear that coat today? It feels like 100 degrees already." When I don't answer but just smile, she says, "Want some coffee?"

"Sure, thanks."

I sit down at the table. She puts a cup and saucer in front of me, places the cream within my reach. I ask her what she's doing up so early. Lately she sleeps in.

"I had a dream about Mom."

I nod, sigh too audibly. I too dreamt of Celia last night, as I do most nights. It's been three years since diphtheria strangled and took her from us. I should reach out to Minnie, hug her or something—I don't know—but I resist even though I love her so much it hurts. When her mother was alive, she was our glue; Celia bound us together. Now, without her, the once-easy affection we were able to express has become awkward.

"I'm going to get some money together, get her a proper headstone," I say.

"I could help, you know. You could get me a job. You do run an employment office, after all."

We've had this conversation before. I shake my head.

"You don't need to be out there in that jungle. There's plenty for you to do taking care of this place and the boarders. You're a tremendous help to me here."

"Ester and Louisa don't require much. They're women. They clean up after themselves. Now you..." she teases. Then she leans in toward me and lowers her voice. "You know, Dad, don't you sometimes think they're a couple? I hear them sometimes early in the morning..."

I cock my head at her. "Wouldn't that be scandalous?"

"I think it's kind of nice—two old ladies, never married, caring for each other to the end."

I think but don't say: *Until one of them dies and leaves the other lost and lonely.* I finish my coffee and stand up.

"Where you off to?"

"Just a walk up to Pratt's." I whistle and my dog, Walt, who's been asleep at our feet under the table, springs to life. He circles around me, eager for the excursion. We got him in 1890 when Minnie turned eleven. He's as full of vitality as the poet I named him after, though that man, sadly, has been dead now more than eight years. Such a shame he didn't make it to the turn of the century.

"Going to spend the morning there reading, aren't you?"

"There are worse ways to kill time, you know." I reach out for her cigarette, bring it to my lips. "No, I just have to pay Pratt for a book she lent me. I've got an appointment later on this morning. Croker's sending someone over for a job."

"Maybe that's who I need to see. Surely the Tammany boss himself could find a use for me."

"Shirtwaist factory's always looking for women. Only nine hours a day, six days a week."

"What's it pay?"

"Ten dollars."

"A day?"

"A week."

"And I thought slavery was outlawed." She takes a drag off her cigarette. "You're lucky you're a man."

I smile, but then she asks, "Don't you want to know what the dream was about?"

Do I? It's going to hurt to hear, and I've got my own nightmares. But she seems like she needs to tell me, so I nod.

"Mom's fallen overboard on a ship and I throw her a life preserver, but she can't reach it, and I watch her go down. When it's over, you and I are just standing on deck, alone."

We stare at each other for a long moment, until she says, "Do you know what day it is?"

Then it dawns on me: It's July 7, 1900. Celia died two years ago today.

I nod, clear my throat. "I'll work on that headstone," I say, and head to the door, Walt at my heels. I don't trust myself to say anything more without breaking.

On the street, I see that Minnie was right: it must be a hundred, which wouldn't be so bad if the humidity weren't bearing down on me in my coat. While I walk up the block to Pratt's, I try not to think about Celia and her death, try not to think about how alone Minnie feels, how alone I feel. We should be there for each other, but we aren't. I can't. Women can comfort one another, bear their souls. Not men, so not me. Vulnerability on that level would require honesty too, and as much as I love Minnie—*because* of how much I love Minnie, I can't tell her the very thing that would break down the barrier between us. I can't risk it. I won't.

So we're at an emotional impasse, a dead-end which may only end, ironically, when I'm dead, when she learns the truth about me. But then it won't matter—I won't know how it affects her because I'll be gone. That's what I tell myself: It won't matter. But it's affecting us now, widening that chasm between us, isolating us both and making us unbearably lonely.

The miserable heat makes my sadness worse. I turn my thoughts to the East River. I fantasize about going down there, disrobing, and plunging into that cool water with the other young, supple-bodied bathers, almost chuckling to myself as I imagine their repulsion at the naked Tiresias come to bathe with them! I haven't swum there since I was a teenager, and I never will again. Swimming is done. Celia is gone. Loss all around me—loss and shut doors.

But ahead lies an oasis: Pratt's Bookstore.

The door chimes when I enter. Pratt, sitting at her gorgeously carved mahogany desk reading a book, looks up. She grins when she sees it's me. A couple of things I like about Pratt: she knows what kinds of books I like; despite her name, she doesn't prattle on with small talk; she's not nosy; and she's not a gossip. I live at 145 Sixth Avenue and Pratt is at 161, half a block away. I love this shop. The tall windows let in natural light, and the shelves, all painted a clean white, are lined floor to ceiling with books on every subject. Pratt herself is one of the most well-read people I know. And she lends me books—lets me take them home to see if I want them before I buy them. When she gives a price, I don't squabble. I have too much respect for her. She's not rich—not with money, anyway.

"Good day, Murray!"

"Good day to you. I've come to pay you for the Agnew book."

"Ah yes, *The Principles and Practice of Surgery*. How did Volume 3 hold up?"

"Even better than the previous two." I hand her the money. A disproportionate amount of my income goes to books, but I cannot help myself.

"I've got a new Havelock Ellis in."

"Oh, you terrible temptress. Don't you know I have to work today? Well, maybe just a peek."

She finds the book on the shelf and hands it to me. I settle into my favorite chair in the back corner and open *Studies in the Psychology of Sex*, Volume 2. Within seconds, Walt is asleep at my feet.

Havelock Ellis. How interesting it would be to talk to the man in person, to sit down and have a drink and hear his thoughts spoken aloud. Reading them can at times be amusing or even infuriating, but I enjoy the way he approaches the world and how he puzzles out the conundrums of life. He writes about sex, yes—about men and women and their differences. He writes about sex as a physical act. But he is so learned and philosophical, and the authors he has read and analyzed—Nietzsche, Saint Francis de Assisi, Zola, even my own beloved Whitman—have become some of my own favorites. All the things we think and feel about sex and intimacy and love—he ponders them and then articulates his theories. He's open-minded and un-shy. In the preface, I come across this line: "There are very few middle-aged men and women who can clearly recall the facts of their lives and tell you in all honesty that their sexual instincts have developed easily and wholesomely throughout."

An unintentional sound of approval issues from my throat and I look over at Pratt, but she is buried in a book herself.

Havelock Ellis goes on to explain that his friends are reticent about sex and tell him he should be too. But he refuses. He compares sexual instinct to eating, wondering what it would be like if no one ever discussed food or drink, because it was considered immoral and immodest to reveal the mysteries of this natural function. This is what I love about Ellis: he refers to sex as natural, not an abomination, not something to be ashamed of. *Is it wrong to eat fruit, which I like?* he asks. When I first read him a few years ago, I felt as if I'd been exonerated, set free, even blessed.

I borrow the Ellis, as Pratt knew I would.

I head back to our apartment at a quarter to eleven and climb the stairs to the second floor and enter my employment office. I open a window even though there is no breeze, and sit at my simple desk, which is nothing like Pratt's antique. The whole office, in fact, is plain, utilitarian. I have electric lights in here which to me are so much more glaring than the soft light of oil lamps I still use in our apartment. I have a few books piled on shelves, but I keep my reading collection in my bedroom. The people who come here for work, most of them recent immigrants from Ireland or Germany or even Italy, don't need a display of erudition; they just want employment, and they'll take anything you can offer them. Their options are quite limited and often they have many mouths to feed.

A man is coming by at eleven A.M. for a job, construction work near Jefferson Market. Apparently, he's a cousin of a friend of an uncle of one of the Tammany captains.

Tammany has been good to immigrants, including me. I've watched the organization change over the decades, especially since William Tweed died. The bosses have built the reputation back up, after the millions that Tweed and his Ring looted from the city coffers. Hard to believe Sweeny was part of it.

Me? I'll never be rich; it was never even really a desire. I like books too much I guess, and books generally don't give you money-wealth. All that time wasted on reading when I could have been speculating, rising in the ranks like Plunkett or Croker. Plunkett, in fact, likes to brag that he's never even read a book. He's scornful of anyone who's gone to college. I never attended a university, though I think I would have liked it very much. Instead, I learned to read and didn't stop. Almost everything I learned about the world I learned from books—books of science, medicine, poetry. But much of what I learned about politics—and about men—came from my experiences with Tammany Hall.

I was never going to be rich, but neither could I stand being poor. When I was finally able to move out of Five Points, I considered that progress. But I experienced for years what it meant to live there, to be that poor. For decades, I never even wanted to look back, but now I'm grateful for having lived there and known that struggle. And so I help people get jobs now, help them to escape that kind of crushing indigence, if they're willing to work.

But don't get me wrong—it's not all altruism. On election day, we round up the people we've helped and lead them to the polls; we pat them on the back and look them square in the eye as they cast their vote for Tammany.

I hear a knock and look at my pocket watch—eleven on the dot. Not bad. I call out "Come in."

The man who enters is a man I have seen countless times in this office. Irish, red hair, long beard, but clean. A slight tremor in his hand, which I don't shake, suggests that he hasn't had his morning whiskey. He takes off his hat and I can see he's sweating. Me, I don't sweat much, which is lucky; even wearing my coat I don't.

"John O' Conner?"

He nods, obsequious. I don't offer him a seat.

"Lucky day. Only job opening at the site right now. Take this slip of paper, go to the corner of Hester and Mott, find the boss on the job, a big guy named O' Hara. He'll put you to work. Have you done brick work?"

His hesitation tells me he hasn't, but he says, "Yeah, I have. I know bricks and brick laying!"

It's not surgery—he'll figure it out.

John O' Conner reaches out his shaky hand and takes the paper and slips it into his pocket. He looks me in the eye and I see a glimmer on his face, see that he is trying to make up his mind about something now that the transaction is over. I take a cigar out of a drawer and light it, blowing a plume of smoke toward him. I don't offer him one.

"That's it. You can get the hell out of here. Good luck with the job—and come election day, don't forget who provided it."

"Oh, I won't Mr. Hall," he says and makes his way to the door. I can see from his look now that he's made up his mind. The cigar always helps.

I stub it out after he leaves. I'm wondering if Minnie has lunch ready when someone bangs on the door and then opens it.

A man is standing there, unruly hair down to his shoulders, dirty jacket and trousers, a gaunt look. My heart often softens for the downtrodden, but there is something in his eye I don't like. Plus, he barged into my office.

"Yes?" I say.

"I'm here for a job."

"Do you have an appointment? Did someone send you?"

"This is an employment office, right? Well, I'm here for work." I can smell the whiskey on his breath. Definitely not obsequious.

"I gave out the last job I know of to the fellow who just left."

"Well, can't you tell him that it was a mistake?" He crosses his arms.

I want to laugh. He thinks he's going to bully me into giving him work? I pick up my cigar and re-light it. I take my time.

"What's your name?"

"William Reno."

"Well, William Reno, do you have any skills?"

"I can do any work. But the trade I know is needlework."

"Needlework?" I choke out the question. Tough guy sews lace. It almost makes me soften to him.

He pulls out a piece of fabric from his pocket, with, I admit, very pretty embroidery.

"It's Oriental. Chinaman taught me." He pulls two other pieces out of his pocket. "See how the lace patterns are all different? This is quality—it's original. People will pay for it."

"Well, whether they will or not isn't for me to determine. I'm told of jobs and send people to fill 'em. Most of the needlework jobs are all women." The irony of this isn't lost on me. "Can you work a machine? I know a shirtwaist factory needs someone. But like I said, it's all women. I doubt they'd have a man." Especially not one as surly as William Reno.

"Goddam machines. Taking jobs is what they're doing. Everyone thinks faster is better."

"So if I'm understanding you, the answer is no—you don't know how to work a machine."

He shakes his bitter head.

"Where did you learn that needlework?" I ask him. But instead of answering, he puts both hands on my desk and leans forward. "Doesn't seem to me that you need to know that. Now, I know you know people. I know you're connected—you're all connected. And something tells me that you could get me a job if you wanted."

I take a puff off the cigar and blow the smoke toward him. "I don't have a job for you, Mr. Reno. And I don't appreciate you bursting into my office demanding one." I sit back, feigning calm. He's making me a little nervous, which makes my blood boil. Some people say I have an irascible temper, and I can feel it percolating just below the surface. "You don't have many friends, do you? I don't mean to make this personal, but if I were looking for a job, I'd try to be a little more gracious. It's just social skills, Mr. Reno. You treat people kindly and with respect, then they're likely to reciprocate. I don't have a job for you, but maybe the next person you see about one will and may even offer it to you, if you take my advice and try to behave with more decency."

"Who the hell you think you are? All your big words? You think you're so smart?"

"I'm just a person who runs an employment bureau, Mr. Reno, just one of many. But if you don't get the hell out of my office right now, I'll see to it that you never work in this town again."

He is visibly shaking and I can see that this is a person whose whole life has been marred with uncontrollable ire. He's a nasty, pathetic soul. I'm relieved when he turns and walks out, though a little irritated when he slams the door. I thought my advice to him was sound, though I doubt he has the self-control to take it. It's true, I could have sent him to someone with a recommendation, but no way was I going to endorse William Reno.

I stub out the cigar to save for later.

That evening I head up to 10th and Greenwich and enter Skelly's with my own thirst for whiskey, but unlike William Reno or his brethren, I generally wait until the day's work is finished, so I feel like I've earned my drinks. Nothing, though, like that first sip going into your mouth, dropping into your belly, its effect migrating slowly up to your head. That truly is one of the best feelings I've had in this life, and much as I pity the drunks who need to start the morning with drink, I also feel sorry for the teetotalers who never get to experience the intoxicating warmth rising up in me. The day is done. Except for a round of poker or two.

I scan the room. I love Skelly's—it's been my home away from home for years. The usual crowd is here. Most of the guys work at the Jefferson Market Courthouse—police, lawyers, clerks; the rest are Tammany men, all of them people I've known for years. I see John Bremer at a table playing poker with a couple of fellas. Bremer runs the Fifteenth Ward Hotel. I send him people who have come to my agency and who need a temporary place to stay. He calls my bureau the "Intelligence Office," and chuckles when he says it.

Skelly pours me a second whiskey and I put some coins on the bar. He never charges me the full price and always gives me a generous pour. When I have enough money, I buy people drinks. But right now, I'm saving for Celia's headstone, so I can't be as generous as I'd like. I have enough, though, to buy in. I approach Bremer's table.

"John Bremer, boys."

Bremer looks up from his hand. He'd been scowling—never quite learned not to show his cards through his face—but he brightens when he sees me.

"Murray! Pull up a chair." He's ahead of me, whiskey-wise. The other fellows I know but can't remember their names, which always happens to me. But they're friendly and deal me in.

Poker is not a game of luck. It's a game of psychology and money management. If you play well, you'll come out ahead—not every time, but you can prevail if you follow a certain methodology, don't get too intoxicated, and walk away at the right time. It takes a degree of discipline most people simply don't possess, especially when you add alcohol. You have to be capable of and good at bluffing, which is my forte. You have to act counter-intuitively on occasion, and never get greedy. Much of what poker demands goes against human nature. But there's a certain thrill to the game I relish: reading a man's face, trying to guess what he's holding, anticipating his move. I'm naturally good—or perhaps I've trained myself to be good at both reading other people and not letting them see my truth.

I throw in a quarter for my buy-in. The guy to Bremer's right, a pipe clenched between his teeth, deals, five cards to each player. I've got three spades—a four, a six, and a queen, and a pair of threes, diamond and club.

"Wild cards?" I ask.

"Nah," says the dealer, taking the pipe out of his mouth. "Why—need one?"

"Nope."

It's Bremer's bet and he throws in a quarter. The guy to Bremer's left, his bright blue eyes piercing his hand trying to produce better cards, reluctantly throws one in too. It's my turn. I put in a quarter and raise a quarter. They all look at me. I shrug. My cards are fairly lousy, but they don't know that. The dealer puts in two quarters, Bremer puts in another quarter, and bright eyes considers folding but then throws in one too. Now we have a chance to give up cards. Bremer gives up two, bright eyes four, and then me: none. Now that really throws them. I don't want one fresh card. The dealer takes two new cards and puts his pipe back in his mouth and lights it.

I say to Bremer, "You should have seen the guy in my office today, John. I don't think you can refer to it as the Intelligence Office anymore."

"Oh yeah? Looking for a job?"

"More like demanding. And get this—wants a job doing needlework. Whipped out some hand-sewn samples from his pocket, ecru lace, all different patterns. Said a Chinaman taught him."

"What did you tell the dandy?"

"Well, more than a dandy, he was an ass, so I threw him out, but not before I told him that if he was gonna do women's work, he ought to try to be a little sweeter."

Bremer chuckles. It's time to bet so he throws in another quarter. He's got nothing, I figure, just hanging tight. Probably a pair. Likely better than my pair of threes. Bright eyes must've gotten something in the exchange. He throws in a quarter, hesitates just a moment, and then raises a dollar. Yep. Got something. My turn. I put in the quarter and a dollar coin and then raise five dollars. The dealer with the pipe coughs.

One by one they fall out. And when I'm pulling the money toward me, Bremer says, "Come on, Murray, let's have a look." And when I lay my measly pair of threes out, they're all beside themselves. "You've got balls, Murray!"

I put a cigar in my mouth but don't light it.

We continue playing. It's Bremer's deal. Curious, bright eyes asks me the name of the needle-work guy. I've got to think back a moment but then it comes to me.

"William Reno."

"Nah, really? You know the story of that bloke?"

I shake my head.

"Ah, this is a good one. It's been all over the courthouse."

"You work there, yeah?" Bremer asks.

He nods. "Court clerk. Okay, so Judge Newburger gets a letter from this Reno fellow. Turns out he's spent the last 22 years in prison from some trouble he got in when he was a youth, convicted on five different indictments for grand larceny. He's a bugger all right. But he served his term and was let out of prison and signed the papers and was discharged, free for the first time in more than two decades. Then before he even gets down the street, he's re-arrested on an older larceny charge and thrown into City College."

City College is slang for The Tombs. I picture the prison in my mind, having spent a few days within its dank, dark walls on more than one occasion myself. I shake my head, imagining Reno's shock and dismay at being re-arrested within minutes of being released after more than two decades in prison. "Terrible luck."

"Yeah, so he took it upon himself to write this weepy letter to the judge about how he was a reformed man even though no one believes that a man in prison can repent and emerge to lead an honest life and would the good judge take mercy on him, and 'I beg you, Sir, for a chance to redeem myself' and all that rot. I was there for the case last December when the judge read the letter to the court as Reno sat there with his head hanging low and his hands folded on his lap. Some members of the jury were clearly moved by it."

"What about the needlework?"

"Oh, that was another thing—the prison representative, man named Kimball, came forth and said that he believed Reno to be deserving of mercy—that he had learned embroidery in Clinton Prison and thought that he should be able to earn four- to five-thousand a year with his designs."

At this I laugh. Any woman with that skill could scarcely earn $15 a week, let alone hundreds a month.

"Then?"

"Then the judge set him free and he cried like a baby in front of the whole courtroom. An article about the whole thing ran in the *New York Times.*"

"Wonder how I missed it." I sip my whiskey. "Well, I saw William Reno today and the man doesn't look like he has a dime—empty life, save for being full of piss and vinegar."

I feel someone's eyes boring into me, and when I look around, I see only a man in the corner, his face obscured by a newspaper. It's my turn to bet so I focus back on the game, but I don't like the feeling I get. Is that William Reno? After the hand is played, I lean toward Bremer.

"John, you see that man in the corner?"

He glances over. "Who?"

When I look, the seat is empty, and so is the glass and whiskey bottle on the table.

It's just after eight when I leave Skelly's that evening. The sun has only just set and the sky is ablaze with pink streaks. I glance over at the courthouse, its gorgeous, imposing façade basking in the dusky glow. I remember when they leveled the Jefferson Market to build it in 1875. Calvert Vaux, one of the Central Park's master planners, designed it. A panel of architects voted it the fifth most beautiful building in America. If you're going to be arrested and tried, at least you get to go through it in style. I'm feeling nostalgic about the city tonight…that happens sometimes when it dawns on me how much I've seen it change over the decades, how it will go on, changing and growing. How I won't be there to see it.

I consider stopping by my other cherished place to get books: Johanna Myer's newsstand, just around the corner on Tenth. It's like a vice I can't control. Or I could head over to the Iroquois Club to drop in on the Tammany big wigs. Skelly's is more for the middle-men, like me, but about once a month or so I drop by the club just to keep my face fresh there and to pay my dues to the General Committee. Senator Barney knows me by name. Croker would recognize me. I helped the last election along quite a bit. I'm in good standing, which is the way I like it.

But I'm too content with the company of my own mind at the moment to go to the Iroquois. Instead, I decide to head home, but I take the long way; rather than a straight shot down Sixth, I head over to Fifth Avenue so I can walk through the stone archway at Washington Square.

My thoughts turn back to Havelock Ellis. I'm so impressed with this man. I've read almost everything he's written and he writes about everything—literature, medicine, disease, and of course, sex and sexuality. He coined the term "sexual inversion" for men who love and desire other men, women other women….

That's the thought going through my head when someone crashes into me at full force.

I'm thrown several feet forward, sail through the air. I hit the ground with a thud, my wrists fling out to break my fall. When I look up, everything feels spotty and dark. I see that I'm on the sidewalk at the entrance of an alley-way between buildings, but I can't remember what the buildings are: I don't know where I am. I'm lying on my stomach and reach up to feel a scrape on my head. There's not much blood coming from the wound, but my wrists feel like they might be sprained or even broken. I'm about to look around to see who hit me, to see if the person is hurt from the accident, but before I can turn over, someone grabs my ankles and begins dragging me into the alley. From my awkward position and damaged wrists, I can't turn to look at the person. I wonder if I'm being pulled away from danger, but before I can speak, I feel a kick to my side so hard that all hope of speaking is lost. I gasp from the pain. And then another kick comes. My face is down and I'm forcing myself not to scream. He doesn't make a sound either. I assume it's a man: the force of the kicks tells me so. Men are simply stronger than most women, and, in general, more ruthless when violent.

My arms brace against my side and I instinctively fold into a ball, as much from pain as self-preservation, anticipating another blow. It comes, cracking my left elbow. I stifle a shriek and try to tuck the busted arm under me, but my assailant will have none of that. His boot slides under me and flips me over as you would a lifeless animal. This leaves my face and front exposed, which makes me feel even more terribly vulnerable: if he kicks my head or face with the same brute force, I will die. But from this position, I do finally get a look at him. And it is he, of course it is—William Reno.

At least I think I recognize him in the split second I glance at his face before he raises his boot above my chest and stamps with such fury and force that everything goes black.

I hear voices, feel movement. Am I alive? Consciousness slowly returns, and with it pain—dull and sharp—which makes me grimace. I'm lying flat, being carried. To where? To heaven? To hell? My eyes flutter open. A man at my feet and another looks down at me from above.

"You're going to be all right," says a voice the one behind my head. Apparently, they are ambulance drivers and carrying me on a stretcher.

When they get to the carriage, the one at my head starts to slide me in head-first. He speaks again, his voice not unkind. "We'll have you to Bellevue in just a few minutes."

Foggy as my head is, I'm still able to foresee the consequences of that happening, and I know it can't. Hell would be better than the hospital.

"No," I garble from my prone position. "Not to Bellevue. To my home."

"'Fraid we can't do that."

"You don't understand. I don't want to go to the hospital. Take me to 145 Sixth Avenue."

"Sorry, but rules are rules."

"Listen," I say with assertion, "I am Murray Hall of the 13th Senatorial district. If you don't take me to my apartment, I'll see to it that you lose your jobs. Every officer from the Jefferson Market Courthouse will know your name personally and will do everything in their power to make your life a living hell."

They look at each other.

"Look, I'm no doctor," says the one at my feet. "But you've no doubt got some bad injuries, maybe even broken bones. The hospital's the best place for you."

"I have a personal doctor I will call for. Now—145 Sixth Avenue. And five dollars for each of you if you get there quickly." I know they are paid per delivery at the hospital and will lose that money if they take me home. I also know they earn nothing near it from Bellevue. But I did well at Skelly's that evening.

If I thought the jostling on the stretcher was bad, it is nothing compared to a ride in a horse-drawn carriage, though I'm quite lucky the sandbagging happened on Fifth Avenue, whose street is better paved than almost any other in Manhattan. Perhaps I shouldn't have told them to get me there quickly—the horses practically gallop through Washington Square.

When we pull up to my apartment, I am wholly relieved, though when I try to find money in my pocket, it's not there.

So, William Reno robbed me too.

"My daughter should be home," I say.

In a moment, Minnie comes running out. "My God, Dad. What happened to you?"

I shake my head. "Minnie, pay these men five dollars each, please."

"He didn't want to go to the hospital," one says.

"Why not, Dad?"

"They can carry me to my bedroom." I cough and blood spatters onto my hand though I don't know whether it's from a wound inside my mouth or from deep inside my body. "Then I want you to ring Dr. Gallagher and ask him to come immediately. Make sure he brings morphine."

I wait until she nods to make sure she understands, and then I allow myself to finally faint.

That's when I dreamt about Eakins' painting.

My own scream, finally released, wakes me. I am sweating with terror and infection, both real; indeed, I can smell both emanating from me. I instinctively reach out for Celia, but she is of course not there and my heart sinks as it does every time I wake in our bed alone. Somehow the part of me that still longs for her comfort convinces my somnambulant self that she is still alive and ready to hold and soothe me. She was supposed to be holding my hand when I died—not the other way around.

For the last few years, I often felt that I was killing time just waiting for my own death. Until, ironically, William Reno tried to hasten it. Now I find myself burning with a desire to live, as if when he was kicking me as I lay there on the sidewalk, he awakened my being, albeit with pain. At least it made me feel alive.

But I need help if I'm going to live. I use my right hand to push myself up, and, wincing and perspiring with pain, gingerly pick up the tumbler of whiskey off the nightstand and bring it to my lips. I drink it in one gulp. I try to move my left arm and feel a moan escape from deep inside me. The arm might be broken; it certainly feels broken, along with a couple ribs on the left side. William Reno could not have known I was sick, but still, if his goal was to maximize damage, he succeeded. I'll need something stronger than whiskey.

"Minnie!" I cry out.

She opens the door almost immediately, as if she'd been standing guard outside. She enters with Gallagher behind her.

"How are you feeling, Dad?"

"Not great," I answer with a raspy voice.

Gallagher speaks: "The morphine has worn off, Murray. I'll prepare another shot."

Minnie removes a washcloth from a basin of water, wrings it out and tenderly pats my face with it, her brows furrowed with concern.

"You had me worried," she says. "Why didn't you let them take you to the hospital?"

"Too dismal. Better to be in my own bed with my daughter and physician friend tending me."

Gallagher returns to the room with his black bag from which he removes a syringe.

"Hold on a second, Gallagher," I say. "I'd like to talk with you before I'm out again."

"Good. I'd like to examine you anyway, see what we're looking at here."

I nod though I'm not ready. Gallagher is a good friend and I trust him for the most part. He is the only doctor who's treated me for the last twenty years, albeit for minor ailments. He treated Celia, too, and tried to make her as comfortable as possible at the end.

Before she died, Celia said to me that if one person knows your secret, you will not be so alone. "You have to confide in someone," she said. Then she took my secret to her grave. But could I really trust Gallagher? Did I have a choice at this point?

Celia was on to something, because for the last two years, I have felt dreadfully isolated and alone. Even surrounded by my Tammany friends, even with Minnie here at home with me, I feel utterly lonesome and something else I never expected to feel as deeply as I do: afraid. And the fear of ceasing to exist—of dying truly alone—almost supersedes my other fear, the fear of being found out. The scale has finally tipped.

And this girl by my side, this twenty-one-year-old woman tending to me so tenderly—no, I can't leave her, can't just abandon her. And if I am going to die—I mean *when* I die—I don't want her to discover that I deceived her. I realize, lying on this bed, that it's the last thing I'd want. And yet—even though we are all each other has left now that Celia is gone, I'm still not ready for my daughter to know. Will I ever be?

"Can you leave us, Minnie?" She looks at me, and then nods with reluctance. She closes the door behind her without a sound.

Now alone, Gallagher asks me why I didn't allow the ambulance to take me to Bellevue.

"Don't trust 'em."

In a way, it's true, but not for the reason he thinks.

"You're so funny, Murray, reading all these books about modern medicine—you probably know more than most medical professionals. But you don't have any faith in them."

I love Gallagher's gentle baritone, so rich and deep compared to my own naturally higher pitch. I tried for years to train myself to speak with more masculinity, but in the end, a voice is a voice and I grew tired of the contrivance.

When I don't speak, Gallagher pulls up a chair and sits down next to my bed. "A bicycle accident, eh?" I give him a wan smile.

I'm very fond of Gallagher. He is one of the most intelligent men I know. His office is just a few blocks away, up Sixth Avenue and down 12th. Today he's dressed as impeccably as ever in a charcoal wool suit and bowtie; his beard and mustache are trimmed and combed, neatly but not too meticulously; tufts of his wispy salt and pepper hair take off from his head in several directions. The bags under his eyes make him look both tired and learned. He is an averagely tall man, which means his height reaches a foot above my own. And unlike me, he doesn't have a temper, but exudes self-possession.

"Looks like a whole bicycle parade went over you."

"It was a disgruntled ex-convict I wouldn't find a job for. William Reno. He took his pitiful, frustrated life out on me. He'll pay, though—I've got to get better if only to assure it."

"Well, before you devise your revenge, I should examine you to see the extent of the damage. May I turn up the lamp?" The lamp he's referring to is a low-burning oil lamp that's sitting on my dresser. At the moment, it's casting a soft light on Gallagher, making him appear almost saintly.

"I—I'd like to wait a moment, if you don't mind." I let out a cough and wince. The pain coursing through me is almost nauseating. I'm stalling. It's a big decision. Shine the light on the truth?

"I'm in no hurry, but you're going to feel progressively worse as that last dose of morphine wears off."

"There's something I want to show you first—that I need to show you."

"All right."

"We're friends, aren't we, Gallagher?"

"Course we are."

I use my right arm to sit myself up and push the blankets back and carefully swing my legs around and land my feet on the floor. Minnie has taken off my shoes, but other than that, I remain completely dressed; in fact, I'm still wearing my oversized coat.

"Can you help me stand?"

Gallagher places his hand behind my back and carefully pulls me up. At the foot of the bed I turn away from him and begin to unbutton my coat with one hand: top button, second one down, third. I'm sweating, not just from pain but anticipation. My fingers tremble and I can feel my heart thumping in my chest. I slip the coat off my right arm and then with great care take it from my left. I loosen my tie and then begin to unbutton my shirt. Then, with my back toward him, I begin to unravel the bandages that I wrap my chest with every morning, something I have been doing for the last few decades. Only two people in my adult life—my wives—had ever seen me without them. When they are completely removed, I reach for the oil lamp and raise the wick, flooding the room with light.

I look down at my marred torso and take a shallow breath, which is all my wrecked ribs will allow. Then I turn to face Gallagher.

I watch his eyes widen, his mouth agape and silent for a moment before he finally speaks, and when he does, he utters only three words:

"Dear God, Murray."

Chapter Three

Gallagher is standing there, his hand covering his mouth, speechless now, as I just revealed two truths to him at once: I have cancerous tumors in my left breast. And I, Murray Hall, at least in my physical body, am a woman.

"Gallagher…"

"Murray…"

"I can explain….I didn't mean to shock you. I just—"

"You have indeed shocked me, Murray. You are…you are a woman?"

"As you can see, I have breasts, but the rest of my anatomy is female too."

"And those tumors in your left breast—how long have they been there?"

"They've been steadily growing for a few years."

I cover myself then, pull my shirt closed. The tumors are ugly, and I see that one has a ruptured lesion because of Reno's attack on me. I have never liked my breasts and now the one is horrible looking. "I'm sorry, Gallagher."

"What are you sorry for, Murray? For being in pain, for suffering with cancer of the breast?"

"For lying to you about my sex."

"I won't take it personally since it seems that no one knew. Did Celia?" I look at him for a moment and don't answer. "Yes," he says sheepishly. "Yes, of course she did."

I find myself blushing.

"What about Minnie?" Gallagher asks.

"No, she has no idea. About either—the breast cancer or…"

"Are you going to tell her?"

"I might tell her that I have some kind of cancer. That seems fair."

"And the other?"

"No, Gallagher. I cannot tell her that, and she's not to find out under any circumstance."

Gallagher looks at me pensively, then says quietly. "There's one circumstance that will reveal you, Murray. She'll know then."

Now I turn pensive. "I know, Gallagher. I'm just afraid."

"Afraid of what exactly?"

"I'm her father—it's all she's known me to be—her *father*. Celia wanted me to tell her and I promised to. We were going to—had planned to tell her together when she turned 16. And then Celia…two years ago today, did you know that?"

"I didn't realize today was the anniversary of her death, Murray. I'm sorry…"

"Yes, well. Minnie is very sad; she misses her mother so much. We both do. And of course, she does deserve to know about me. But Gallagher, if I tell her, what if she decides she hates me? Then I will have truly lost everything."

"But if you don't tell her…"

"Right, if I don't tell her, and she finds out…afterward…she'll feel like her whole life was a lie, a deception. It will tarnish her memory of me—and imagining that she might despise me when I'm gone is unbearable."

"Yes, I see." He takes a deep breath, shakes his head. "That is quite the conundrum."

"Yes, well." I try to take my own deep breath then but the pain in my ribs prevents anything but a shallow sip of air.

"All right, Murray. I can't imagine how you went undetected all these years, and I have so many questions for you, but they can wait. I'm going to give you another shot of morphine and examine you."

I nod and limp to the bed. Gallagher helps me lie down.

"Besides the tumors, what hurts most?"

"My ribs, my left arm at the elbow, both wrists."

He administers the shot, and the morphine courses through my blood, swirls to my head. I feel my limbs go limp, my eyes close, my mind calm to the point of not caring. It feels wonderful—so, so wonderful I could weep, but I'm too relaxed.

"I'm going to examine you now, Murray," I hear Gallagher say from somewhere far away even though he's right by my side. Then I feel his soft, cool fingers on neck, feel them gently palpitating my armpits. And then they touch my left breast, feeling around the tumors. And then the right one.

I'm grateful for the morphine. I trust Gallagher completely, but no man has ever touched me so intimately.

I awaken not knowing how many hours have gone by. Minnie is asleep in a chair next to the bed. I watch her sleep, remember all the times when I sat by her bed when she was ill. Now she is here, tending me. I never thought it would come to this—that the day would come when I was convalescing and she was the caregiver.

She opens her eyes and smiles at me. "Are you all right?"

"I think so."

"Dr. Gallagher set your elbow and taped your wrists. He said that a few of your ribs are likely broken but that for those, you'll just have to rest. He expects you'll be in pain, however, and he wanted me to call for him when you woke so he could come with more morphine. I'll call for him now." She rises up.

"I'm—Minnie—I want to talk with you." I'm groggy from the drugs but determined.

"Shall we talk after I call Gallagher?"

"No, I have something I want to tell you first."

"All right." She sits back down, brushes the hair from my brow. She does this so casually, so tenderly, I nearly choke up. I was never very physical with her. I stopped hugging her early on when we had a close call, though it pained me to not be more affectionate with her. So her gesture moves me. Plus Celia used to pet my hair.

She's looking at me expectantly. Can I tell her everything? Is now the time? I decide to start with the easier information.

"Minnie, I think you should know that I have cancer."

"What?" Her smile crumbles. She's crestfallen.

When I repeat the statement, she looks away from me, stares at the bedroom door as if she's heard a knock. Finally, she looks at me.

"What kind of cancer is it?" She says, matter-of fact.

I should have anticipated that question but stupidly I did not. I rack my brain. "It's lymphoma, a kind of blood cancer that affects the lymph nodes."

"Is it curable?"

"Well, not really. Mine has…spread."

"How long have you known?"

"I…I suspected for some time now, but Dr. Gallagher has confirmed my suspicions."

She considers this, then crosses her arms. "Why didn't you tell me? How could you keep that from me?"

"I—I didn't want to worry you. Especially after your mother died. I—I didn't want to face it myself."

"Is it very serious?"

"I'm afraid so."

She considers this a moment. "So you must get treatment," she says. "There's that new Cancer Hospital—where is it?"

"Central Park West."

"So go there." She's young—she wants to solve it, overcome it, beat it.

"Minnie, I'm too far along. There's nothing that can be done. But Gallagher will come regularly—he'll do what he can for me."

"So that's it? You're just giving up?" At this point her voice is breaking and she begins to cry. She is twenty-one, and the idea of dying is unfathomable to her, but I am sixty. Some would say I have lived past life expectancy, and few would be surprised to hear that a sixty-year-old is dying of cancer.

When I don't answer, she says through her tears, "Do you know how long you have before…?"

"I don't know. I'll talk to Dr. Gallagher about it." I try to sit up, but the pain in my tender wrists makes it difficult. Minnie begins to lean down to help me, and I say to her, "No, it's all right. Just please ring Dr. Gallagher now."

"Yes, of course, Dad."

"And Minnie? I'm sorry—I'm sorry I didn't tell you sooner."

"So am I." She is still crying when she leaves the room.

This exchange does not give me confidence to reveal my other truth, which I don't even like to think about let alone say aloud.

I raise my right arm and whack my chest, which makes me yelp in pain, but I'm more angry and frustrated at my decrepit vessel than I have been for a long time.

I must have drifted off again because I'm awakened by a knock at my door, and the announcement: "Murray, it's Gallagher."

"Come in," I call out.

He enters and sets his bag down next to the bed. "How are you feeling today?"

"Not too bad. My arm is starting to throb a bit. Thanks for fixing me up."

"Let's get you some morphine," he says.

"I told Minnie," I say. "About the cancer, that is."

"How'd she take it?"

"Not good. She was angry I hadn't told her sooner."

Gallagher nods. "Celia knew about it?"

"Yes. I first noticed something around 1895. Then the growth got steadily larger, and then another appeared, and then another. But even as Celia was dying, she was more concerned for me than for herself."

Gallagher smiles but sadly. "She was just like that, wasn't she?" I nod. She was a better person than I am, for sure. "Terrible disease, diphtheria," he says.

"I heard the vaccine is nearly ready."

"It will save many lives."

"Will there ever be a breast cancer vaccination?"

"That would be a medical miracle. What treatments have you tried?"

"Oh, you know—everything that's out there that makes a claim to mitigate it. Arsenic, iron, poultices. I went through six bottles of Swift's Specific—the 'blood purifier'—to no effect. I considered leeches and bloodletting but couldn't bring myself to do it. I even tried to quit drinking for a spell to see if that would help, until I realized that teetotaling would make life not worth living."

Gallagher grins. We have shared many a whiskey together.

"And the radical mastectomy?" he asks.

"It seems like radical butchery to me."

"You've read many books on the topic."

I nod. It's true. I have read dozens of theories; have read, for instance, the infuriating opinion that the heart of a woman is in her uterus, but that disease is born in the brain, born of impure and lascivious thoughts and that the body simply becomes a conduit for them, evil suppurating from the tumors' lesions. I read that women who exercise often bring on breast cancer. I read that a woman who rebels against the natural course of her life as deemed by the creator—motherhood, sacrifice, marriage, and obedience to one's husband—that those are the women more often than not afflicted. It would be the opinion of many physicians, not doubt, that the cancer I suffer from is payment for sinning, that with my rejection of what is considered genuine, wholesome womanhood, I brought disease upon myself. I read that vice—referred to by one surgeon as "dance, drink, obnoxious laughter, and a lack of piety"—also would trigger tumor growth. All right, guilty as charged. Except for dance. I never liked dancing.

But as ridiculous as I find these theories, neither can I wholly dismiss them. In my darkest moments, I sometimes wonder if my breasts, hidden for nearly three decades, have, in fact, finally retaliated.

But a radical mastectomy….

I read that if she survives, a woman often loses use of her entire arm on the side where the breast was removed. That the itch from where the skin is grafted to replace the breast is absolutely maddening. I read of gynecologists castrating women to cure irregular periods or nymphomania. Until women become doctors for women or at least highly educated spokespersons, none of this seemed likely to change. Women are seen as weak and nervous, as "delicate," but the one thing that really gets my bonnet is the tendency to say that women exaggerate pain—the pain of menstruation, of childbirth, of cancer. Most of our ailments are chalked up to neurasthenia, a psychological disorder.

Gallagher, I know from our past conversations, has studied up on it to. I ask him, "Do you think it's unfair of me to refer to the surgery as butchery?"

"In medical circles, I've heard awful stories," he says.

"I read in the *New York Times* a couple years ago of a woman in Ohio whose breast surgery was actually deemed successful, until the nurse, thinking she was giving the woman pepsin, accidentally gave her a dose of carbolic acid."

"Which killed her." Gallagher shakes his head.

"I remember reading about Marion Sims," I say. "The doctor who started the first women's hospital here in 1855?"

"Ah, the father of modern gynecology, yes."

"Is it true that he purchased black slave women to practice his surgeries?"

"Not only that, but it's said that he would perform up to 30 procedures—on the same woman."

"Sometimes when I think of the scope of human cruelty, I feel ready to let this world go."

"One doctor I knew performed the surgery on several of his patients even though he knew—knew with absolute certainty—that it wouldn't help and in fact could only hurt, would only hasten death."

Now I shake my head. "Why?"

"He said he thought he was giving the women hope, a sense that some action was being taken, since they all felt so helpless with the disease."

"That is what infuriates me—this idea that women have to be lied to, that they can't handle the truth."

"Well, Murray, not all women are like you." He offers a smile but then it fades. "But seriously, friend, you've not much time. The tumors will reach your heart one day soon. In the meantime, I'll continue you on regular doses of morphine to keep the pain at bay."

"Did the attack on me make the cancer worse?"

"It's likely," he says. "Life expectancy for untreated cancer is about three years from the first detection. So if you discovered the first tumor about five years ago, it seems that the cancer might be slow-growing. The sandbagging, I'm sorry to say, made a bad situation much worse, especially since, as you said, the lesions appeared afterward."

The blows that fell on my body by William Reno have opened the tumors, and pus and blood now seep from them, as well as from my nipple. Gallagher tended to them the first time when he examined me, but I tell him I can clean them and put on fresh bandages myself.

"I don't mind doing it, Murray. But when you take care of it, be sure to keep the area sanitary and as dry as possible. Otherwise, you'll get an infection."

"No, I'll do it." It hurts me to see the subtle transition on his face, when he goes from talking to me as the same old Murray to perceiving me as a woman, and, more specifically, a woman with breast cancer. I wish I were not either.

"You're going to need to put your affairs in order, Murray. Do you have a will?"

"I have to file it."

"Have you given more thought to Minnie?"

It's all I think about. I try to picture—to hear—the words coming out of my mouth, watching as they enter her ears, see as she tries to make sense of what I'm telling her. I imagine bracing for her reaction. And I realize I cannot tell her.

But then it dawns on me. I can do something else.

"You know what, Gallagher? I could write it down, explain it. I can't say the words to her face, but if I could tell the whole story, maybe, just maybe—"

"An autobiography."

"More like an apologia."

"It's an excellent idea, Murray." He is giving me my shot as he says this.

I want to get some paper and a pen, start right away, but now the drug is entering my bloodstream. I lose the logical thread of my thoughts and let the pain be covered with the heavy blanket of morphine. I drift off into a sweet, euphoric trance where nothing, none of it, at least temporarily, matters anymore. Maybe tomorrow…

Part Two

1846 – 1869

Chapter Four

My mother was an angel. By day she wore her braids pulled back and tucked into a bun, but I liked her hair best at night, cascading in waves around her shoulders. She would sit between my brother and me, the oil lamp casting a glow on her face as she read to us. We liked Robert Burns, of course, our Scottish poet, but she also read us Wordsworth, whose words put ideas into my head. In fact, I blamed his poetry for the intense fondness I felt for my brother. He was older than me by eight years, and although just fourteen, already taller than our father. My mother was an angel, you see, but it was my brother whom I tried to follow, entertain, emulate.

But first, how do I describe that beautiful land where I was born? I would need poetry to do it justice, but I was no poet.

Our little village of Govan, once known as Meikle Govan, was quite near Glasgow, a little less than an hour's walk away along the River Clyde. The village was known for that river and the spectacularly tall ships built there. My father was one of the builders—he worked on those great ships. They were world-famous, my father bragged. Everyone wanted a Clyde ship.

The work, however, wasn't regular, and when he wasn't building, my father drank. Most of the men drank and could be quite funny and lively, but when my father imbibed, his mood plummeted. And so the work of running their household, of growing food and making bread and cooking and cleaning and washing our clothes—all fell to my mother, who also taught school so that we would have at least some steady income and not be evicted from our little thatched cottage. Thus when my father was working, my mother was more kind and patient; it's when my brother and I saw the best of her. But when he wasn't working, his dark mood settled over our entire little house, and I could only stand by and watch as sadness and worry and frustration befell my mother.

I somehow knew from a very young age that his black mood would worsen if I sang or laughed, so when he drank, I'd leave the house and roam. But my mother did not have that luxury; after teaching, she'd work relentlessly the rest of the afternoon and collapse in bed at night without the energy to read to us. We tried to help. My brother cut and stacked wood and I harvested and weeded the garden. But I was young and not much help really.

Mary Anderson was my name, and I was not a delicate girl. From a young age, I refused dresses and proper shoes, opting for the clothes my brother had outgrown and his brogues (though I was generally barefoot when I could get away with it, except in the coldest days of winter). I did not think of myself as pretty—indeed it was unlikely that anyone did—but that didn't concern me. Agility, speed and fearlessness were the characteristics my brother seemed to value, and so they became the ones that I strove to accentuate.

James, in fact, was the beautiful one. He got our mother's looks, her lush auburn hair, smooth skin and high cheekbones. They both shared eyes that in the morning seemed golden as hayfields and in the evening hazel as the waters of the Clyde. They had long, slender bodies, an effortless gracefulness. I, on the other hand, had apparently inherited my father's stout figure, not fat really, but thick—baby fat I never outgrew. I shared his sensitive, blotchy skin, which seemed to always have a slight rash whether from wind or cold or heat or soap or lack of soap, who knew? But I didn't care. As a child, the only things that mattered were James, my mother's affection, and bread. I could have lived on fresh, hot bread.

Everyone thought the Scots all loved haggis, that "great chieftain o' the puddin' race," according to Robbie Burns, but my dad was the only one who relished it; my mother downright despised it, saying it was the bane of Scotland to suffer the reputation of being haggis-lovers. We ate it only on occasion and my mother never, though she would indulge in tatties and neeps. Still, my dad's real craving wasn't for haggis but Scotch whiskey, and as long as he had the latter, he didn't care what else filled his belly.

Let's return to William Wordsworth, whose poetry fueled the passion I had for my brother, James. The poet Wordsworth and his sister, Dorothy, lived in a cottage called Grasmere. He wrote verse, she kept a journal, and the two of them, sometimes accompanied by their poet friend Coleridge, walked for hours over hill and dale, immersed in nature. And even though William married, his true companion remained his sister. I remembered reading that Dorothy and William left to take a six-month walk when his wife had just given birth to a baby. I knew in my heart right then and there, I wanted to be the beloved sister, not the wife stuck at home with the children!

I was just a young girl in 1846 when my father and mother said we were going to America. Many, many people were going there, especially from Ireland, my mother told me, because their crops were failing and people were starving.

"But we aren't starving, Mama," I stated.

Her sigh belied the patience with which she answered. "No, we're not. But we won't have our house much longer, I'm afraid. The work is too unsteady with the ships and I cannot support us with my teacher's pay. Your father knows people who have gone to America. They have written to us about a place called New York City and say there are many jobs there."

"Will we go on a ship?" I grew excited, hardly caring at all that we'd be leaving Scotland. As long as I could be with James and my mother, I was up for adventure.

"Yes, we'll go on a ship."

"One that Dad built!"

"No, not one that he built, but one like it. But we won't be able to bring many things."

I thought of Dorothy and William Wordsworth then, of their long walks. Surely they didn't bring a lot of stuff.

"Can I pack tonight?"

My mother smiled. "No, we won't go for another month or so. It's time for bed, anyway."

James came into the room then.

"James!" I yelled. "We're going to America!"

"Shhhh," said my mother. "Don't yell."

James was in his nightclothes already. He nodded. "I know, Grice." That was my brother's nickname for me. It referred to a kind of swine that was popular in the Highlands. He meant it affectionately; I knew he did.

"James, don't refer to your sister as a little pig."

From under his covers he oinked. I oinked back. He oinked again. Our mother sighed again and then said, "It's time to read." Meaning time for us to listen.

"Mother, please, please read 'To My Sister'."

James groaned. "Mother, please don't. Read Burns' poem about the louse he sees on a lady's bonnet at church. *'Ha! Whare ye gaun, ye crowlan ferlie!'*"

Another long, audible breath from our mother. And then instead of reading, she closed her book and then her eyes and starting singing with her sweet, tender voice. "*For fame and for fortune I wandered the earth, and now I've come back to the land of my birth, I've brought back my treasures but only to find, they're less than the pleasures I first left behind.*"

She sang on, and before she finished, I fell fast asleep.

I was too young to know that my mother had no desire to leave Scotland, but felt that she had no other choice than to follow her husband, our father, who thought the grass would be greener in New York City and who probably hoped he could become a new person and shed whatever it was that held him back there in Scotland.

My brother had just turned fourteen, and instead of with me, he'd recently begun walking home from school with a girl, an awful thing who offered a dumb giggle for everything he said on some days, but on others, acted haughty or wounded or just simply ignored him, and I could see the effect it had on him. Since they wouldn't let me walk with them, I followed closely behind, picking up small rocks along the way that I'd throw periodically at the back of the girl's bare calves, and if I was on target and she turned around to glare at me, I would simply put my hands behind my back and stare at the sky. I developed quite a good throwing arm and some good precision too with that activity. The girl's name was Lexine MacCrumb, stupid name, but fitting, I thought. As I walked behind them, hurling pebbles, I tried to recite Tintern Abbey in my mind:

For thou art with me here upon the banks
Of this fair river; thou my dearest Friend,
My dear, dear Friend; and in thy voice I catch
The language of my former heart, and read
My former pleasures in the shooting lights
Of thy wild eyes. Oh! yet a little while
May I behold in thee what I was once
My dear, dear Sister! and this prayer I make,
Knowing that Nature never did betray
The heart that loved her…

I yelled the last three lines aloud. I didn't really understand Wordsworth's words, but I had learned them like a prayer, my prayer. I would understand it all too well someday.

My brother and Lexine ignored me as best they could, until the pebbles hit too hard, and then James would chase me. When he caught me, he'd give me a drubbing, and just to extend the attention I was getting from him, I would hit him back. You may think it unseemly, a young man boxing his little sister, but these fights proved useful for many future occasions. It was how I learned to receive a punch and to return a decent one.

I was a tomboy, a scrapper, and my mother was tolerant of this because I was young and she probably did not have the energy to keep me in line and try to make me behave in a more lady-like manner—or maybe she just loved me and let me be myself. But I was not totally ignorant. Looking around at older girls, I saw my fate. Most were prim and reserved, spic and span. And the women, mostly house-bound with chores that never finished, the same tasks over and over, day in and day out: milk the cow, tend the garden, wash and mend the clothes, clean the hearth, prepare the meals. The relentless chores of women never changed. That life seemed like drudgery to me, a fate to try to escape, if possible, but I had no idea how. I observed that men, in contrast, went out into the world. There was simply more variety to their lives, more opportunity. They had the option of all the different trades and businesses open to them. And then the possibility of going to university, all the subjects a man could study, all the things he could become! Men practiced law or became doctors or professors; men ran shops and had businesses; they built things, like roads, buildings, ships.

That's what I learned early on: men lived one life, women another.

Maybe it would be different in America, I thought. Maybe women had more opportunities there.

Anyway, I was a child, what did I know?

My parents packed our belongings, almost nothing, really. Just a trunk of clothes, toiletries, blankets, food, plates, silverware, and pans. I chose a few of our poetry books to include in my own bundle. We did not really know what we would need in America.

It seemed that we had not paid our rent the last couple of months and were being forced out. This didn't make sense to me at the time; I thought our house was our house, and I had no understanding that we didn't actually own it or the land but rather had rented it from a landlord. After all, I had been born in that cottage. I thought it belonged to us.

On our last morning there, I skipped around the periphery of our hovel, singing a made up song, essentially "Guidbye wee hoose," over and over, until I saw my mother emerge. Something about her made me stop and observe. She looked so dreadfully sad and was dabbing her eyes when my father approached and tried to put his arm around her. She swatted it away like you would a bothersome mosquito.

I went up to her and to my relief she let me her take her hands and kiss them.

"Don't worry, Mama."

She blinked her eyes and looked at me. "Where is your brother?"

"He's saying goodbye to Lexine."

"It's time to go."

Our things were all loaded on the wooden cart, which my father would pull to the port of Glasgow as we had no horse, had never had a horse.

We started off. My mother turned and took one last look at our humble dwelling and then turned forward and began walking, determined, it seemed, not to show any more emotion, but I could see that something in her was altered, and when she gave me a smile, it was the falsest I'd ever seen from her.

But ahead was James. He was leaning against a tree in front of Lexine's house, which was substantially nicer than ours (as were most of the cottages). As we approached, I saw that Lexine was standing there with him. Our father called to James and he looked toward us. Then he and Lexine embraced for nearly a minute. He finally tore himself from her, and once he was at our side, our walk resumed. I knew Lexine was watching us, so I turned and stuck my tongue out at her.

Whenever I got tired of walking, I thought of Dorothy and William and their walks that lasted for months. I tried to see the world as a poet but saw only pretty hay fields and barns that needed to be shored up. I saw scrawny horses in the field and wished I had some apples for them.

James was silent and sullen most of the walk, despite my efforts to engage him. Our father took nips from the bottle in his knapsack throughout the day. Our mother kept offering that unconvincing smile. I ran ahead and then lagged behind. I picked flowers and tried to place them in my brother's hair. I begged my mother to let me take one last swim in the Clyde, but she said no. I sang songs she had sung to me my whole life, but no one sang along.

Glasgow harbor was a mess of ships, giant sails flapping in the wind, men walking up and down ramps loading cargo, lumber stacked to outrageous heights, ready to be shipped to some part of the world, barrels full of who knew what.

Then I saw them: droves of the thinnest, poorest souls I'd ever seen, gaunt, skeletal faces, threadbare clothes that were more like rags, shoeless children. I myself preferred to be unshod, but this, I could tell, was not by choice but from lack. They looked mad with hunger and desperation. It was my first glimpse of real human suffering and it made me feel humble and helpless. There were so many…

"Who are they, Mama?" I whispered.

Her face showed immense pity and something else. Perhaps it was fear. Perhaps it was the awful gratitude one feels in witnessing the terrible suffering of a fellow human being—that one's own lot in life had not yet fallen so low. My father looked defiant and defensive, as if trying to communicate that anyone considering asking us for help would not receive it. He stood taller, I could see, and puffed out his chest. He told my brother to walk behind our cart to keep watch.

"They're Irish, Mary," my mother said.

"What's happened to them?"

"It's like I told you before, their crops have failed, and the British abuse them. They had to leave Ireland to avoid starvation. Many have already died."

"Where are they going?"

"Some will stay here in Scotland to look for jobs."

My father cut in: "And make an already bad situation worse, no doubt."

"The rest will leave as we are leaving," she continued, ignoring him. "And head to America, I imagine, like we are."

My father left us to inquire about tickets. I wandered along the docks stealing glances at the groups of Irish families and especially the children, thinking I could entice one of them into conversation or perhaps a game. But whether from fatigue or shame, they wouldn't look me in the eyes, and so I turned my attention to the ships. I had a sparse vocabulary for describing what I saw, but during my six years on earth, terms like paddle propulsion and iron hull and steam-powered and secondary masts had been spoken so many times, they were part of my lexicon, though I wouldn't have been able to explain to anyone just what they meant. I tried to look now at the army of ships in my sight and distinguish one from the other.

I heard my mother's voice, sounding nervous yet firm, calling for me. I found my way back to where they stood, all of them together, holding the tickets—Passenger Contract Tickets they were called—that would determine our fates. Our ship was the *Charlotte*, which I thought was a very fine name. I couldn't wait to board her.

"It says to Quebec. I thought we were going to New York City," my brother said.

We all looked at my father.

"The fee into America has gone up. It's three times the amount Canada's charging."

"Are we going to stay in Canada then?" I asked, not knowing where Canada was in relation to New York. I remembered a map my mother had shown me and knew, at least, that Canada and America were touching.

"We'll make our way to New York after we arrive. Fellow I worked with on the Clyde told me to look him up—Neil Buchanan. Said the entire tip of New York City is a harbor, ships as far as the eye can see."

My mother was looking more closely at the ticket. "It says steerage, John. I thought we said that we weren't going to do that, that we were going to get a cabin."

"You can see they were already more than five pounds each. Not to mention the fee head-money they might charge when we land. And we'll need money to get to New York and get started."

"It's not going to matter, John, if we don't make it."

"Why wouldn't we make it?" I asked. But my mother just glared at my father.

He looked down at the ticket. "It says each adult must have less than ten cubic feet of luggage. Do we have more than that? Are we going to have to leave something behind?"

My mother shook her head.

I asked to look at the ticket and my mother handed it to me. I read the food rations aloud: "3-1/2 pounds of biscuit; 3-1/2 pounds in all of flour, oatmeal, rice or a propor…proport…"

My brother took the ticket from my hand and read, "rice or *proportionate* quantity of potatoes; five pounds of potatoes being computed as equal to one pound of other articles the above enumerated. Per week—issued not less often than twice a week. Plus three quarts of water per day."

Which made no sense to me. "What about food and water for children?"

"I think they share with the adult accompanying them," my mother answered.

"But what if there are a lot of children? What if a family has six kids and only one adult parent. Will they get extra?"

My mother sighed but said nothing. I wasn't sure if she didn't know the answer or was just tired of my questions—or both. I decided to stop asking since I seemed to be making her feel worse.

We slept in a crowded inn that night. In the modest dining room, my dad, James, and I ate as much cod and bread and cheese as we could stomach. I tried to give my mother bites, but she said she wasn't hungry; she seemed terribly homesick and we hadn't even left yet. She surprised me by ordering a whiskey and drinking it in one gulp.

That night, I was jittery with excitement and couldn't sleep. There were two little beds in the room, and my mother and I took one and my father the other, while James opted for just a blanket on the floor.

Instead of reading poems, my mother sang a famous Robbie Burns song we usually sang on Hogmanay: "*Should auld acquaintance be forgot and never brought to mind? Should auld acquaintance be forgot and days of auld lang syne…*"

I was tucked under my mother's arm, my head nestled on her breast, our bodies pressed together in the small, single bed.

I was finally drifting off to sleep when I heard an unfamiliar sound come from my mother, a quiet whimper. I felt her body begin to quiver and I held still, holding my breath and keeping my eyes closed as her warm, wet tears fell from her face and onto mine.

Chapter Five

In the morning we trudged up the gangway onto the ship, each of us carrying our own belongings, the only things going with us to the New World. A throng of passengers boarded with us, though many more stayed on the dock, waving goodbye. I wanted to stay on deck until the ship sailed, but we were encouraged toward our lodgings—herded, really. Down the stairs we went, our luggage bumping and sliding downward. I tried to keep a hand on the railing and solid footing, but the stairwell was packed and I was little. The light was waning and the air thickened with a stench I couldn't identify. My mother was right behind me and my brother and father behind her, so I just followed the threadbare coat of the stranger in front of me, until we arrived at the bottom of the stairs and entered a large room: steerage. Long wooden benches ran the length of it, though it was lined on either side with bare wooden berths made of wooden slats and stacked two or three high. They were already filling, with families of four or five occupying the double berths that seemed only meant for two. My mother nudged me toward a set of them that were still near the door. We would share the single on top; James and my father the single on the bottom.

"We'll be safer up here," my mother said.

"Safe from what?" I asked.

She knit her brow. "More comfortable is all I mean." She hoisted me and our things up into the bunk. We had a blanket each in our bundles and lay them out, though no pillows or sheets.

The room seemed at capacity, but impossibly, more people filed in. Babies cried. People spread their things out on the benches to claim extra space but then reluctantly gave it up as more and more men and women and children came through the small opening until we were bursting at the seams.

Even so, I was still excited about the journey—it sounded thrilling to be at sea for forty days. Until, that was, I asked where the bathroom was, having to go quite badly.

"That's the bathroom," my father said, pointing to a sheet hanging from a hook with a bucket next to it.

The thing I looked forward to: we were allowed on deck for an hour every day. Groups of steerage passengers would take turns, going up on deck to make their fires and make tea and cook oatmeal or potatoes or rice. But mostly, I relished the fresh air and light, which was so bright when we emerged, I would squint the whole time, looking out onto the horizon of the glistening sea, no land in sight.

What I least looked forward to: my mother would fill our small pail with sea water and take a rag and dip it in and then scrub my skin raw in an effort to keep me clean. We had no fresh water with which to rinse—the little we had was reserved for drinking and cooking—and so my skin itched from the salt.

Eleven days into the trip a storm came upon us, and the crew on deck battened the hatches. For three days, the ship was tossed about as if a giant sea monster were toying with it.

"Will the ship sink?" I asked my mother as I clung to her that first night. We slept on our sides as we would not fit if we laid flat. She was to my back, cupping my body to her, her arm draped over me. The ship would summit a wave only to crash down over its peak and when it did, she would hold me tight.

"No, I don't think it will," she said with feigned resolve and stroked my hair. "Your father says these storms are common and that most ships survive." I did not sleep that night, terrified that we'd be one of the rare ships that wouldn't.

I lay awake listening to people retching with seasickness. The smell was worse than the sound—and people had no way to clean themselves.

While the storm lasted, we couldn't go on deck and cook of course. So for three days, those who could keep them down ate nothing but hard-tack biscuits. The buckets filled and soon overflowed with vomit, urine, and excrement, and the unstable ship, rising and crashing down with the waves, soon had that vile mixture sloshing about and migrating across the floor. I had never smelled anything so awful. It was a horrendous, nauseating smell, vomit-inducing itself, and there was no escaping it; the stench seeped into the floor, permeating everything. It would stay with me for many, many years, that horrid olfactory memory.

Then the storm went away, almost as suddenly as it had come on, and the seas were calm again. I burst out the top of the stairs onto the deck and breathed deeply, relieved that we had survived, that the worse was over.

But it wasn't.

Some people continued to vomit and suffered dysentery as well. This time, it was not just that the buckets overflowed, it was that there was a dearth of them, and when people needed them suddenly for one end or the other, there were not enough.

Many people were coughing, sweating or shaking with fevers. Everyone was thirsty.

And then on day twenty-six, the first among us perished.

It was a baby who had wailed loudly for two full days and three nights, its cry maddening, so much so that I had at one moment wished the baby dead. And then the crying stopped, only to be replaced by the mother's wailing, truly the saddest sound I had ever heard. Then I would have given anything to hear that baby cry again. After two more days, the father pulled the baby's body from his wife's grasp and carried it up to the deck and returned some time later without it. Though he shed no tears, grief seemed to have permanently planted itself on the man's face.

Days passed. The little drinking water we had left turned putrid. Our meager rations were reduced even further. Families that were already living with hunger when they boarded now looked even more emaciated. I had been watching a girl who looked to be around my age since the first day; their family huddled on one of the benches about ten feet from our bunk. Her dress hung on her ever more—she seemed mere skin and bones. On day twenty-nine, I went up to her and said hello. Her mother was sleeping next to her.

"Hello," she said quietly and met my gaze and then stared at the ground. I reached out my hand to her, my palm open, and offered her a biscuit. She reached her too-thin arm out and took it, her fingers just grazing my hand. "Thank you," she whispered, and then placed the biscuit into her dress's front pocket, her grey, listless eyes flashing with life for a moment. Her health had declined since the first day of our journey. I was witnessing someone deteriorate, a child like me. I was in fact about to ask her how old she was when I heard my father call my name and wave me over once he got my attention.

"Did you give her food?" he asked me and glared at the girl.

I just shook my head, unable to lie aloud.

"If I see you giving food away, I'll beat you in front of everyone."

I didn't say anything but just looked at him.

His voice softened. "It's a long journey," he said. "We don't know what's going to happen. We have to guard everything we have."

"She needed it more than I did."

"You say that now. But if the ship runs out of food, you'll be missing that biscuit all right."

I looked back over at the girl. She was focused on nibbling the biscuit, but her mother looked my way, and though she had a terrible look of worry and suffering on her face, she smiled at me.

One day my brother and I slipped away from the area on deck where we were corralled so that we could explore some of the ship.

We ducked into another stairwell and hid when we saw one of the crew coming our way. Then we emerged again and crept along the side of the ship until we came to a window and took turns peeking inside. It was a dining room, I realized. Several people were seated around a table with filled glasses and plates of food in front of them. They raised their silverware nonchalantly, drank from glasses filled with water and wine. These passengers were clean; their lace and jackets and shoes were not soiled with human waste. We smelled the delicious meat they were consuming; we heard music. Then a deckhand grabbed us by the necks and roughly escorted us back toward our doom.

I learned a few things on that ship, things about the world and human nature and the human body. It was a lifetime of lessons I learned during that forty-one-day journey.

I did not know or understand the word "disease" until then. I knew nothing of typhus or cholera. I had never seen anyone die. I had never experienced loss of a loved one. I hadn't seen what people who are depraved and desperate will resort to. I did not know yet that one's own survival might require selfishness. I had not considered myself someone who would fight for my own comfort and survival over that of another's. On that ship, I learned that and more. I came to realize, for instance, that money, as in the possession of it, could determine whether you live or die. Money could keep you safe, keep you sanitary, keep you healthy, keep you alive. Money meant that you didn't have to sleep a few feet away from someone whose body had aqueous matter coming from both ends. Money meant cleaner water, better food—even just some food.

It was unbelievable to me that the captain of the ship would allow the conditions that existed below. After my brother and I had stolen away above deck and seen that others were not suffering—indeed, they seemed to be enjoying the journey across the Atlantic—I began to think of those of us in steerage as animals in cages.

When I spoke this thought aloud to James, he answered: "No, worse, Grice. Because animals would have more value and their cages would be cleaned. They wouldn't have to spend the trip living, eating, and sleeping in their own filth and that of their fellow animals. The captain has been paid. He doesn't lose money if people suffer or don't make it."

"You can't call me a pig anymore, James. Not when there's so little to eat."

He pulled a handkerchief from his pocket and opened it. There were three pieces of tablet sitting there, their caramel color and buttery smell already making my mouth water. He handed me one.

"Where did you get it?"

He smiled. "Lexine."

I didn't care that it was from my brother's beloved; in fact, the candy made my heart soften toward my arch nemesis. It was the most delightful thing I'd ever eaten, the creamy sugar coating my tongue, the flavor lingering for hours.

My mother held and caressed and sang me to sleep every night. And then one night she didn't. She seemed already asleep when I crawled up to our berth, but as I lay down next to her, I felt her body hot as bread just pulled from the oven. I sat back up.

"Are you all right?" I asked her.

She shook her head without opening her eyes. Her fingers found her face and covered her mouth.

Then she vomited.

Now it was I who used our small pail and filled it with sea water and took the rag and tried to clean her. But she vomited again, though barely anything since she had hardly eaten or drunk, a bile-like substance, the sight of which evoked more fear than disgust.

I still believed in God then and I prayed. I tried to sing to her but the fear of losing her closed up my throat and I wound up weeping instead. I went to find her clear water and begged a cup off a family that had a small bucket of rainwater they'd saved. My mother's temperature rose even more, her forehead burning hot, her sheet drenched with sweat. In the middle of the night, she began to shake with chills. The next day she wouldn't eat, even when James tried to share a candy with her.

"Mum," I cried. "Mum."

"I'm all right," she mumbled, but I could see the fear in her eyes when she opened them to look at me.

A couple of days later, there appeared in her eyes something worse than fear: an emptiness now took over her gaze. She lay with her eyes open, her mouth agape, not saying anything. Except for her warmth and the rise of her chest with each breath, she may as well have been dead. I refilled the pail with seawater and cleaned the vomit from her hair and face, from the boards of the berth. I wanted to keep her as clean as I could, clean as she had tried to keep me. That's when I noticed the rash: dark red spots like rubies appeared on her stomach.

I called to my father and showed him.

He stood on the bottom berth and peered over ours to examine her stomach.

"What is it?" I asked.

His face grew cross and he wouldn't answer. Then he ordered me down from the berth, away from her.

"You are not to touch her!" he said to me in a quiet, yet firm voice I could not argue with. He told me to stay down in the lower berth with my brother and hoisted himself into our top one.

He took over tending my mother. I could hear him speaking to her in a low voice, but then, as if deranged, he suddenly lashed out at those around us.

"Beasts!" he yelled. "Couldn't you have stayed in your own country? Did you have to bring this scourge to us?" As if they were responsible for my mother's illness and not the dire circumstances we all found ourselves in.

No one responded. Everyone was so tired and hungry and beaten down. It seemed that each group of families had at least one ill member. I looked around then and saw the mother of the girl I had given the biscuit to, and I saw that she had her daughter's head in her lap and was pressing a linen cloth to her head. She looked at me, not with anger at my father's harsh words, but with a look of pity, worry, and deep sadness.

He lay with my mother all day and night, not moving from her side. James and I brought what water and food we could find, which amounted to little. Then, four mornings after she had first fallen ill, I heard my father singing to my mother in a low voice. I had never heard him sing. His voice was raspy, broken:

> *"Maxwelton braes are bonnie, where early fa's the dew*
> *Where me and Annie Laurie made up the promise true*
> *Made up the promise true, and ne'er forget will I*
> *And for bonnie Annie Laurie I'd lay doun my head and die."*

Then I heard my father cry, which was even more incongruous than the singing.

And I knew my mother was dead.

Chapter Six

My father did not move from my mother's side for the rest of the trip, which lasted three more days; nor did he allow my brother or me to tell anyone our mother was dead. He could not bear, he said, to see her body thrown overboard. By the time we reached Canada, everyone in steerage was starving and nearly half had the fever.

We docked. An official came on board; he shuffled around, taking stock of the passengers. "We will check the ship to see who's well and who's sick. The ones with fever will go to the hospital on Grosse Isle; the sick aren't allowed to go to the City of Quebec until they've made a full recovery," he said to no one in particular. "The rest of you will be quarantined on the island for 10 days. If you do not develop any illness, you'll be transported to the immigration center at Quebec City."

I clung to my brother's hand. I had not cried yet for my mother and neither had James. Does that sound strange? Heartless? We were half mad with hunger and thirst, numb to everything. It was the most awful feeling: helpless, filthy, useless to anyone. But *alive*. Still, we couldn't feel relief—we had no idea what would happen to us.

James and I waited on deck where the sun was warm. The murky water of the Saint Lawrence River swirled by, bobbing with detritus from the ships. I could see some of the island from the dock: dirt, rock, some trees and brush. I saw an area lined with plain wooden sheds and beyond them a large whitewashed building. A nurse all in bright white like an angel brought us water and dried pork. We watched as helpers carted sick passengers away. A priest came aboard, his face resigned and tired but still kind, and I considered asking him to bless my mother before she was buried. But I didn't see the point, really. God had abandoned our ship and I wasn't about to invite him back on.

Our father was being carted out. We stopped the assistant and peered down into his blank face. He was still alive. I could hear his shallow breath, smell the fetid stench of it. The assistant, whose strength and tanned skin almost felt like an affront, stepped back, letting us have a moment.

"Father," my brother said, and put his hand on our father's shoulder. "They're taking you to the hospital on the island. Mary and I will wait for you until you're well."

Our father's eyes flickered open. He shook his head. "Take the money and address," he said. He tried to put a hand in his pant pocket but lacked strength. James reached in and took out a cluster of money and a piece of paper with some writing on it.

"Go to New York City. Find Neil Buchanon. He'll help you."

"We'll wait for you, Dad," I said. "Here or in Quebec."

He shook his head again and closed his eyes. I leaned down to kiss his head, but the assistant stopped me.

"Best not," he said. "Probably got the fever." He looked at our father and then us.

"Will he…" I began but stopped, unable to say the words. I did not have a tremendous love for him, but he was my father. And his death would mean we would be alone in the world. His presence in our lives, however difficult and volatile, still tethered us to this earth. If he ceased to exist, our fates would be even more precarious; we might as well just float up into the sky and disappear.

"If he has the fever, he still might survive. Some do," the assistant said.

My brother nodded at him with solemnity, perhaps grateful for the honesty, and the assistant carted our father away from us.

Just then the girl I had given the biscuit to was removed from the ship. Though there was no cloth covering her face and though her eyes were closed, I knew she was not asleep, but dead, her long, too-thin arms draped across the front of her black smock, her red hair fanned out behind her head, her face no longer flushed with fever, but bluish-white and eerily calm. Her journey was over; her story had ended right there. And here I was, still breathing, still apparently without fever, holding the hand of my brother. The sight of the girl's lifeless body and saintly visage took me over the edge. I would not say that it was only the girl, even more than my own father, who moved me to tears. It was the relief of being on deck after weeks down below and knowing we didn't have to go back down there. It was the remorse I felt that this girl had died while I myself lived on for now. It was the loss of my mother, the most caring, loving person in my life. Who would hold me? Who would read to me and kiss me goodnight? I let go of my brother's hand and crumpled to the ground.

Chapter Seven

They quarantined us in sheds on the west side of Grosse Isle. It was a miracle to be free of the ship and not sailing on an open, irreverent ocean. We had food and fresh water. Nearly every day, a new ship or two arrived at the island dock with more wretched souls. My brother and I did not veer far from the sheds—we were not allowed to walk about the island—but we could see the hospital and the forest beyond it where the dead were carted for burial. All day we heard the sound of nails being hammered into wood: sheds to accommodate the ever-growing number of those with fever; coffins for those whose bodies succumbed to it. Every day we inquired about our father. We were not allowed to see him.

We heard that the ghosts of the dead inhabited the island, that the assistants and nurses had seen them, white shadows in the forest. I wondered if my mother were among them, if her disembodied spirit lurked about or if it was stuck forever in the berth of the *Charlotte*. I had been unable to cry on the ship, but I wept all the time now—woke crying, walked about crying, ate crying, tears mixing with the butter on my bread. I fell asleep crying, exhausted. James on the other hand, was contemplative but stoic. He lay on his cot totally awake, staring at the ceiling, as if reading it for clues, as if it were a puzzle he needed to solve. While I was pure emotion, he didn't allow himself to feel too much or at least to show it if he did.

Then, on our sixth day on the island, my father's ghost joined the others. I overheard that they had ceased to bury bodies individually in coffins as there were too many—and so I imagined him dumped into a large grave, his body mingling with dozens of others. I listened carefully and thought I could hear the scoop of the shovel gathering the loose dirt, hear it rain down upon the dead, slowly covering them until their thin limbs and spotted flesh were no longer visible. There was no funeral, no goodbye prayer at his grave—only the macabre imaginings of a young orphan girl, and tears, tears, tears that seemed to never end. I wondered if his spirt found my mother, and then I decided that I hoped it had not. I wanted her to be free of him, wherever she was.

Four days after that, the officials let our disinfected ship sail up the St. Lawrence to Quebec City. The journey was mercifully short, about an hour or two, and they did not make us go down into steerage again, into that sepulcher of lost souls. If they had forced me down there, I would have gone mad.

We took stock of our luggage, including the cumbersome trunk our parents had brought. In the end, we left the pots and pans and all our father's and mother's clothing, except for a nightgown which I kept for her scent. I took two books of poetry, one by Wordsworth and one by Burns, and put them in a knapsack with the nightgown, a blanket, and a few pieces of my own clothing.

"You're going to have to carry that yourself. I'm not going to carry it for you," James said.

"I've got it," I said. But it was heavy.

We had little money, no parents, no support. We were all alone in the world. It seemed that every few moments I would start to cry and then look at James and stop myself. I wanted to be big for him, to be strong, but inside I was frightened. The fear of not knowing what would happen to us finally overtook the sad fact of the loss of our mother and father. It was a very young age to be faced with death, to have experienced first-hand that death was very real and that life was fleeting and worse, random, that whatever forces were at work on our lives, they were wholly indifferent, disinterested, impartial. Life felt both precious and precarious. Death could come unexpectedly for me, without reason or remorse. Death could take James and leave me utterly alone in the world. I found myself physically clinging to him. To his credit, he let me.

All around us were people in the same or in a worse situation: families torn apart—children, siblings, parents lost. All of us were broke. None of us knew where to go. And even as we disembarked from the ship in Quebec City, we were checked again by immigration officials. Many more had unknowingly sickened in the few days since they'd arrived at Grosse Isle, their latent fever finally emerging en-route to the port of Quebec City, and those who had were taken to another over-flowing hospital. I was ordered to stick out my tongue, something I had been good at, and thought of Lexine and the last time I saw her. It had been more than a month, though it felt like years. I no longer felt like that bratty, petulant child. I had sailed the seas of Hades, had suffered terrible loss. I knew, at that tender young age, that my childhood, and my light-hearted attitude and approach to life, were gone. My mother was right: we should have stayed in Scotland. We would all still be together, even if we had been evicted from our house. Maybe James and I could go back, I thought for a moment. And then I realized there was no way I would board another ship as long as I lived.

We stood in a line, awaiting an interview with the immigration intake officer. He had before him an enormous leather-bound book with hundreds of pages of entries. The top of the page was organized with columns. I peered at it. Even upside down I could see that it was written in another language other than English. A nun stood by and translated. The officer needed our date of entry; our names and ages; our parents' names; our country and county of origin; the dates and cause of our parents' deaths (if applicable). My brother answered for us. Then there was a column for the adopted parents' names and another for their address. Finally, the date of adoption.

"So you are orphaned," the nun said, her nun habit giving her an authority even I couldn't argue with. "Do not worry, children. You'll be adopted with the help of *Les Sœurs de la Charité d'Quebec*."

I looked at her quizzically and she said warmly, "The Sisters of Charity of Quebec will make sure you find a loving home here."

"No, that's impossible," I said. "We're going to New York." It was the first time I had spoken and the officer looked up from his book with surprise. I glared at James, desperate, but he had no answer and appeared as bewildered as I was.

The nun answered firmly but with patience.

"I assure you, they have placed many orphans coming through Grosse Isle. You may even be able to keep your surname of Anderson when you go to live with your new family."

"I don't want to be placed with a family here!" I began to cry.

I felt someone place a hand on my shoulder and turned to see a woman from the *Charlotte*. She was alone.

"My daughter died on our ship," she said to the nun. Then she looked at me. "You were kind to her—you shared your biscuit." Then I understood who this too-thin and broken-hearted woman was: the mother of the red-haired girl.

"I will adopt these children if they need a guardian."

And so it was. My brother and I were released under the care of Anne O'Grady.

* * *

Gallagher turns out to be more of a friend than I believed. Every day he shows up to administer a bit of morphine, each time a tad less to keep me from gaining too much dependency. I see it in myself—I always want twice as much as he gives me and twice as often, not to dispel the pain of my still-healing contusions and cuts—not to mention the cancer—but because of the marvelous feeling that opiate brings me: a relaxation deeper and more complete than I have ever known, until it wears off and I slowly become painfully conscious again of the sharp edges of reality.

Gallagher asks about the writing and so I share with him what I have down so far.

"So they died of typhus?" he asks.

"Yes," I answer. "You know how typhus spreads? Whereas the bubonic plague requires fleas and rodents, typhus relies on body lice and thrives in cramped, filthy environments. The poor are twenty times more likely than the rich to be infected." I had eventually read quite a bit about it.

Gallagher nods. "Those ships, especially steerage, were the perfect breeding ground. The lice live in the clothing, but they emerge, go to the body and bite it, and then return to the clothing, like a wolf going out for the hunt and then returning to its den nice and full."

"But it's not bite that infects the person."

"That's right, it isn't—the excrement of the lice does the job. When the louse bites the human, it produces droppings, and when the human scratches the bite, he essentially rubs the excrement into the bite, thus infecting himself."

"But that doesn't explain how it spreads." I realize Gallagher knows more on the topic—on many topics, in fact—more than I do, which is one of the reasons I value our friendship. He is a bottomless well of knowledge.

"That's the interesting thing," he explains. "When the infected human becomes too feverish and therefore too hot, the louse looks for a more mild temperature—in another host."

"So in a sense, my father may have saved us by lying with my mother and not letting me near her."

"He may have, yes," he says.

"That makes me feel a little bit better toward my father. You see, it took me years to really comprehend that the only real reason we left Scotland was because he couldn't support us—because he didn't work hard enough and drank too much. But supporting a family is a lot of pressure too, especially when the work isn't steady. He thought America was a way out—a solution to his problems. But he wouldn't have changed in America; I know he wouldn't have. We take our problems with us, wherever we go."

"It's true a change of geography doesn't change a person's core."

"But my mother didn't want to leave Scotland. She certainly wouldn't have chosen steerage, and if she had known that was all we could afford, she wouldn't have agreed to the journey. She must have heard the rumors of those coffin ships, as we refer to them now. But in the end my mother deferred to her husband. Because that's what wives do."

I can hear the bitterness in my voice and grow silent for a moment. It's a lifetime of frustration rising to the surface. Not angry at women, not angry at my own sex, but angry at the conditions that dictate their lives, and nearly dictated my own. Angry at a society that has always tried to keep women down, has made it difficult for them to own property or go to university or advance in a profession or run for office or even vote. Resentful that men in so many cases dominate their wives—control them, beat them, and sometimes kill them. I think of my first wife, Mollie, and feel myself fill with revulsion and remorse.

Gallagher checks my breasts. At first I close my eyes, as if to give us both privacy as he examines the tumors. But then I open them, and watch his face, which I have been afraid to look into. I am nervous when the conversation stops, a conversation between two friends, indeed, two men, and I become a female patient with a ruined, scornful breast that will eventually see to my demise. But his face is calm and caring without being pitying. I let him take care of me—let him redress the bandages. Then he gives me a shot of morphine.

Once I am covered again, he speaks. "Are you going to keep writing?"

"Yes, at least as long as I can. It's not easy, re-visiting these memories, but now that I've started, I feel inclined to go on."

"Good. And thank you for reading me what you have thus far."

"Thank you for listening."

"When are you going to share it with Minnie?"

I look at him, then shake my head. "Not now, Gallagher. Maybe not ever."

"Do you mean to say that even after you're gone you wouldn't want her to read it?"

"Maybe then. But I also realize that if I'm going to be completely honest about my life, I can't write it with her in mind, or anyone really."

The morphine is doing its trick. I close my eyes then.

"I'll be back tomorrow, Murray," I hear Gallagher say, but I can't respond. The morphine's lovely tentacles are spreading through my physical body, making my mind feel too complacent to care about the past—or future.

Chapter Eight

We were led to a church run by the Irish, the Notre Dame des Victoires. There we were fed and then taken into the chapel where we would spend the night sleeping in the pews. My brother and I were to sail with Anne O'Grady two days hence to Montreal. We would all stay on with her sister's family who had come the previous year, at the beginning of the blight in Ireland.

That evening, Anne O'Grady came and sat by me in the pew. She asked me about Scotland and our family. I began to cry when I tried to tell her and so she lay my head on her lap and stroked my hair and told me what she knew of Montreal and of her sister and her family until I fell asleep.

When I woke, she was lying near me in the same pew and I stayed very still, watching her shape under the blanket rise and fall with her breath. I sat up in the pew, stared through the darkness at the elevated statue of the Virgin Mary holding the baby Jesus at the front of the church. I looked for James. He was gone.

My heart sank. I looked in the pew where he had laid down to sleep. Neither he nor his bundle were there.

I picked up my own bundle and began to tiptoe out of the chapel, listening closely to the snoring mounds of human bodies, wondering if I would be caught by one of the nuns. I knew I wasn't supposed to leave, but I had to find James.

Outside, the stars were bright and the moon shone on the tall steeple. The night was not cold. I willed myself not to cry. And then I saw a figure walking in the shadows and saw that it was my brother. I ran down the cobblestone street toward him.

"What are you doing?" I whispered.

He looked surprised to see me.

"Mary—you should be asleep."

"But what are you doing?"

"I'm going to leave. I'm going to go to New York."

"But you can't. We're going with Mrs. O'Grady to Montreal. It's been settled."

"You're going, Mary."

I shook my head. "Not without you."

He let out a long breath. "She wants you, Mary. You can be her daughter. She doesn't want a son, and frankly I don't want a mother. But you're young—and she'll take care of you."

I thought about this. One thing was for certain: I could not bear to part with James.

"No, James. You have to come. She'll be kind to you—she'll be kind to both of us. We can have a home with her."

"No," he shook his head with determination. "I'm going to New York."

I put my hands on my hips. I could be determined too. "Then I'm coming too."

"You can't."

"Why not?"

"Because, Grice. I can't take care of you. I'm not old enough—you're just a young girl."

I started to cry.

He said, "You see, you're too sad. You're too little. You can't do it. I can't do it with you."

He was right, but that only made me cry harder. A light went on in the church.

"OK, shush, shush," he said gently. "Listen, Grice. You're right—I'll come to Montreal. We'll try it out."

"I don't want to go there either, but I don't know what else to do."

"I know. We'll go. We'll go together. It will be fine."

One of the nuns came out of the church then.

"Children!" she whispered harshly.

We went back into the church, but I could not sleep for a long time. The next morning when I woke, James was gone again, but I was not too upset, as his bundle was there, and I knew he wouldn't leave without me.

The daughter Anne O'Grady had lost was named Dana. This morning when I woke, Anne O'Grady was sitting before the trunk of her belongings, holding a dress, tears streaming down her face.

"Are you all right, Ma'am?" I asked her. I should have known she was grieving. I suppose I did know. I just didn't know what else to say.

"This is her only other dress" she said. "It was my dress when I was a girl and I saved it, because I hoped I would have a little girl I could give it to. It only just began to fit her," she said between tears.

"It's very beautiful," I said to be kind. It was white and lacy, a rose-colored bow at the collar.

"It would make me so happy if you would wear it," she said. "I think it would fit you just right."

Now what to say to that? I was wearing an old pair of my brother's brogues, a pair of his old pants, and shirt with buttons. I had no desire to wear that dress. I was going to say, *No thanks, Ma'am*, but she looked at me with sad, pleading eyes and I could not deny her that which she desired. I took off my outer clothes and donned the dress, trying to be careful not to tear the lace. I frowned. She smiled.

"Let's comb your hair now, and put in some barrettes."

I succumbed to Anne O'Grady for the time, but I was yearning to be back in my brother's clothes—and to be with him. She did not ask if I knew his whereabouts. I do not think she cared, and I think he knew it. I, on the other hand, kept my eye on his bundle, feeling as if it were the only thing that anchored him to me at that point.

Although I had vowed to myself that I would never board a ship again in my life, we were to take a steamship to Montreal the next morning. To my delight, James finally returned late that evening when we were already settling in for bed.

I whispered to him, "Where were you?" But he put his fingers to his lips and wouldn't speak.

I could not sleep and lay there awake until I heard Anne O'Grady's soft snoring. I snuck from our pew and went to where my brother slept. His eyes were open already and he looked at me, put his finger to his lips again to keep me shushed, and motioned for me to follow him outside.

"I asked around and it sounds like there's a two-day stagecoach ride from here to a place in Maine called Skowhegan. Tickets are ten dollars. Some people just walk instead, but it's a five hundred mile journey."

I thought of Dorothy Wordsworth and her brother William and their long walks. "I thought we were going to Montreal together."

He shook his head. "You still can, Grice. You should."

"I'd rather come with you."

"Do you really want to? It's going to be hard. Not just getting to New York City, but whatever happens once we get there. I have no idea what it's like or what's going to become of us. At least if you go with Anne O'Grady, you know you'll have a home, someone to take care of you."

I felt my heart beginning to pound harder. I thought of Anne O'Grady, how badly she wanted a daughter to replace her beloved Dana. I thought of how much I missed my mother. But Anne O'Grady was not my mother. My brother was the only real family I had left. I could not part from him. "I'm coming with you, James."

"Then no complaining."

"I won't complain."

"And you can't cry all day."

"I won't."

He looked at me a long moment very serious, and then he smiled. "Then let's get our things—and quiet. If anyone awakens and sees us trying to leave…"

"I'll be quiet," I whispered. I was ecstatic—scared and thrilled.

Though I didn't dare kiss the lips of Anne O'Grady for fear of waking her, I wanted to. She had rescued us—and I was abandoning her. I didn't want her to think we were ungrateful, so I found in my Wordsworth book one of my favorite poems, "A Slumber Did my Spirit Seal," and tore it as slowly and quietly as possible from my book. I carefully tucked it just under Anne O'Grady's pillow and placed her daughter's dress, folded neatly, beside it. Then James and I slipped away.

Yes, I thought we'd be like Dorothy and William….

Only we weren't. At least, not at first.

I was so young, only six and a half, and James was fourteen—two children in a new country, walking our way toward another. We had no idea what awaited us; we just put one foot in front of another for days on end, barely noticing the city fade into the background.

The first few days were miserable. My feet hurt, my bag felt heavy. The journey was so daunting. James could've gone much faster and covered much more ground without me. I would start to complain then stop myself, remembering my vow. I tried not to cry and if I had to, cried silently.

Something happened, though, after a few days. My shoes had given me blisters, so I took them off and walked barefoot. The dirt road was carved for stagecoaches and not too hard on my feet. I got stronger. Somehow, walking for hours each day began to feel natural.

Follow the Chaudire River out of Quebec to the Kennebec in Maine, we were told. It was a route used by the native people. When I caught glimpses of them in their canoes on the river, their long dark hair and strong, bronzed bodies, I was awestruck. The river was their road and they traveled it with deft gracefulness, their paddles dipping in unison into the water.

Once my brother and I were far from Quebec City, the vistas were taken over by pastures as far as the eye could see. When we entered Maine, the landscape morphed from pastures to hills, mountains, and forests. We stopped in the little towns of Jackman and Moose River. We slept in roadhouses or took refuge, with permission, in barns where we slept atop the hay. Generous souls fed us. Others turned us away, the fear and disgust at two disheveled young people from somewhere else apparent on their unwelcoming faces. Still, many people took mercy on us, two downtrodden but determined orphans traveling alone.

Outside of the little villages, the woods were dense on either side of the road, and in the mornings and evenings, the mosquitos devoured me; for some reason, they preferred my blood to my brother's. I could barely sleep at night and itched like a flea-bitten dog.

I was grateful for poetry, and my brother read Tintern Abbey to me when he was in the mood or had tired of my badgering and gave in. Now I found I loved this part:

And I have felt
A presence that disturbs me with the joy
Of elevated thoughts; a sense sublime
Of something far more deeply interfused,
Whose dwelling is the light of setting suns
And the round ocean, and the living air,
And the blue sky, and in the mind of man:
A motion and a spirit, that impels
All thinking things, all objects of all thought,
And rolls through all things. Therefore am I still
A lover of the meadows and the woods,
And mountains; and of all that we behold
From this green earth; of all the mighty world
Of eye, and ear,— both what they half create,
And what perceive; well pleased to recognize
In nature and the language of the sense
The anchor of my purest thoughts, the nurse,
The guide, the guardian of my heart, and soul
Of all my moral being.

I still didn't know what the words meant, not really. But if it was sublime for Wordsworth, then these woods, this nature, and our long walk would be sublime for me. It would not be the last time that poetry would carry me through a difficult time. Because otherwise, what would that time walking so many miles have been? Tedium, aching muscles, sore feet, sadness, loneliness, and irritation at the mosquitos, an endless itch. The words made me feel more deeply, gave me strength to keep going, gave meaning to what could have otherwise been a dreadful journey.

If I was lucky, if he wasn't too tired and if he had sufficient light, James read to me at night until I fell asleep, which didn't take long since we often walked all day. A stagecoach might pass, its passengers looking at us with either disdain or pity. But I felt sorry for them in their leisure. They travelled along indifferent, no doubt, while James and I earned every vista, every step. Our trip to New York City would be hard-won, and I would never forget it.

But at night I dreamt of the ship, our *Charlotte*, and all she took from us. In those days and weeks following out arrival to Canada and our walk into Maine, I dreamt of my mother so vividly that I would awaken believing she was still alive since she had just been holding me in her arms, and so I mourned my mother's death over and over and over. She was still, and would remain, the anchor of my purest thoughts, the guardian of my heart.

We came around a bend in the road just past Parlin Pond when I came upon something standing before me in the sunlight—a massive creature!

I stopped walking and breathing and watched as it lifted its giant head and stood to full height. I could not comprehend what I was seeing. This giant with antlers, brown fur, big eyes, and long snout snorted at me and then trotted off into the woods, and only then did I realize there was a smaller version behind it, its baby, who hurried after its mama. My breath came back in huge gasps and my brother clapped me on the back.

"What was that?" I asked when I could finally speak.

He laughed. "It was a moose. We're lucky it didn't charge us. They're known to."

It was the most spectacular animal I'd ever seen.

I spent the rest of the day on edge, not frightened, but no longer complacent or lost in my thoughts. Suddenly I was aware of the nature all around us, that in those dense woods, animals lived, some of them several times my size. We had seen many birds and bunnies and some deer. We'd heard wolves howling at night. But now, as I walked along, I jumped at every sound emanating from the thick woods on either side of us, and many sounds there were, but the leaves cracking and twigs breaking under the weight of some unseen animal were the ones that most unnerved me.

James wasn't afraid—or if he was, he didn't show it. He also wasn't a chatterbox like me. He spent much of his time quiet, listening to me or not listening. When I heard his audible sigh, I knew it was time to clam up for a bit so as not to irritate him even more.

When we came to The Forks and walked across the bridge crossing the Kennebec River, both of us fell silent, watching its calm, gray ripples flow. I thought of the Clyde and of Govan and our little home, now so far away.

My impending tears were interrupted by a wagon filled with hay, pulled by two horses.

"Hello," said the driver. His voice and appearance seemed familiar. He introduced himself as William Dunlop and upon learning we were Scottish, told us he was Ulster-Scot, from Antrim in the north of Ireland. He had arrived in Quebec in 1825, and had, like us, walked down the Canada Road into the United States.

"I'm heading to my farm in Caratunk if you want a ride—'bout eight miles from here. Save you some walking."

So grateful was I for this small reprieve that I fell asleep in the back of his wagon on a bed of hay, the sun my blanket, the sound of the birds and the river and the horses' neighs my lullaby.

After a good meal with William Dunlop and his wife, Cecil, and a solid night's sleep, we were fortified enough to try to walk the fifteen miles to Bingham the next day. But once we entered Moscow, just a mile or two from our destination, I felt I could barely take another step. James urged me on, but I finally stopped on the side of the road and sat, too tired to move. William and his wife had generously packed a knapsack with bread and cheese and apples and dried meat, but we had consumed all of it at lunch, and now I was ravenous. My body seemed to be quitting.

The ride in William Dunlop's wagon and his and the generosity from him and his wife had spoiled me. It seemed I no longer had the gumption to keep going.

James told me to wait there and walked around the next bend. When he came back, he said there was a farmhouse just up the road, that we would stop there and ask for lodging.

"Come on, Mary. You can make it there. We'll see if they can put us up for the night." He pulled me up from where I'd slumped and practically carried me down the road. When I saw the pretty farmhouse with its beautiful shady tree out front, I wanted to weep. I practically ran to the front door, and when I got there, knocked loudly. James scowled and put his hand up, a gesture and look that meant: calm down.

On one side of the farmhouse was a large garden, while the other was flanked with an orchard of fruit trees. The house was sturdy, large and well-built with logs that looked and smelled fresh. The swept porch had a small table with a large vase of bright flowers and two inviting rocking chairs on either side. I wanted more than anything to just sit down and rest in one of them.

When I was about to knock again, a girl opened the door. Her smooth, dark brown skin contrasted with the bright white dress and apron she wore. I looked her up and down and then just stared at her face with what must have been a dumb look. The girl spoke but the words didn't register. She seemed a little older than James, since she was a bit taller. She was also the most beautiful person I'd ever seen.

When she said, "May I help you?" more firmly this time, I blurted out, "We're looking for food and maybe a place to stay the night."

The girl smiled warmly, seemed amused at my outburst. "Just a moment. I'll fetch Mrs. Mansfield."

A tall, buxomly woman with hair the color of blended gold and silver came to the door some minutes later, and after establishing what we wanted and where we were from— "We're from Scotland, ma'am,"—she offered us a meal and a place in the barn.

Mrs. Mansfield had the girl lead us around the house. We walked past the thriving garden, tomatoes red and big as fists; cucumbers long as my arm. Then a chicken coop, with at least a dozen happy chickens pecking about and clucking. A pen held at least one pig, which oinked a greeting as we walked by. I saw three large cows grazing lazily in a green pasture. Everything was neat and tidy. The red barn stood out brightly among that bucolic setting.

"My name is Binah," said the girl.

"I'm Mary and this is my brother, James." James had become quiet, but now he looked at the girl and she at him not without curiosity.

When I saw the look that passed between them, I might have felt a tinge of jealousy, but for what or toward whom I wouldn't have been able to say. They were two young, pubescent people coming into contact with one another, and James looked at her as someone his age, someone his equal, someone who could understand him—whereas I was just his little sister.

"You can sleep here." Binah pointed to an area with clean hay. "I'll bring you some food once you're settled."

"I'm settled!" I said, but James shot me another scowl. Binah laughed and left us.

"Don't be rude, Grice."

"I wasn't being rude. I'm starving."

But I lay down my things, spread out my blanket, and within a few seconds, fell asleep.

When I woke, the sun was down and it was dusk. My brother was sitting with a bowl of soup in his lap, a chunk of bread and cheese and apples on a plate beside him. Binah was leaning against the wall of the barn, focused on him. I closed my eyes again and just listened as he told her the story of how we came to be walking on this road. His voice sounded different to me, sadder. With me he often took a tone of authority, a parental tone or a tone of exasperation. With her, he sounded open, vulnerable. And perhaps for the first time, I was hearing him speak his feelings aloud—his loss, his woe. And though he was sharing it with another person and not me, I was hearing it, and it made me aware of my own selfishness, how everything I felt was the center of my world and that I didn't consider others, didn't put myself in their shoes. It made me want to cry—for him his time.

I peeked at Binah. She was standing there silently, but her eyes were locked on him, and no wonder he was airing his grief with her: she had kind, compassionate eyes. And she didn't jump in to the conversation, didn't interrupt like I usually did. She just listened openly, nodding slightly at times. She made an occasional sound of understanding: "Mmmm." It was my first lesson in how to listen to someone with care. So I told myself not to cry—not even for James—and to just listen.

He told her how our parents died. That we had an opportunity to be adopted in Canada, but how he just couldn't do it—didn't want to go live under someone else's roof, especially after living under my father's for so long. "We had no love for each other," my brother told her, which surprised me; I had not realized how bad their relationship was.

He told her about agreeing to let me come with him, how he regretted it in a way. This made my heart sink and made me regret it too. But then he clarified: "She's just so young, and I don't know if I can keep her safe. I don't know what I would do if something happened to her. At the same time, it would have crushed me to separate from her…"

At that, I couldn't help myself: I smiled in delight at those words.

Binah caught my grin.

"Looks like Mary is awake," she said. I opened my eyes.

"I'll bet you're hungry," she said. I nodded. "I'll bring you a bowl of hot soup and some bread."

"Thank you—thank you so much," I said and she smiled and left. I sat up and turned to James. "She's so nice."

"Yeah, she is. Her parents are dead too."

And instead of saying something, anything, I just sat there and let those words, those terrible words, hang in the air and waited for him to speak again. But he didn't. And for the first time in my life, I let him be with his thoughts in peace.

When Binah did return, she gave me the soup and some wonderful warm bread and asked me if I needed another blanket. I shook my head no and asked Binah to sit down with us, but she patted me on my head and told us that she had to do her chores.

The next morning, she came out to the barn with a set of clean clothes for each of us. We changed and she took the clothing we'd been wearing, along with the filthy clothes in our knapsacks, and then invited us into the house for breakfast.

What a lovely home! From the dining room, I glanced into a large kitchen and saw another girl stirring a large steaming pot of soup, could smell the smoky, hearty goodness escaping from it. That same girl reached into the oven and pulled out not one but two pies, and from the smell I knew they were apple, the sweet cinnamon aroma making me woozy. Tea and eggs and bacon and fresh bread were on the table for us. Mrs. Mansfield entered the room and invited us to sit down, taking her own seat at the head of the table. We sat and Mrs. Mansfield said grace. I bowed my head, but peaked sideways at Binah who was standing in the doorway. Her head was bowed too, but she caught my glance and winked.

"Please eat," Mrs. Mansfield said when we hesitated after the prayer.

We dug in, but when I heard James clear his throat and looked at him, I knew I'd been eating noisily and too hungrily and so slowed down and thanked Mrs. Mansfield.

"You seem like you're very good children," the woman said matter-of-fact.

"Thank you, ma'am," said James.

"Plenty of work to be done on this little farm, and I could use the extra help. Room and board in exchange for work."

James and I looked at each other.

For a moment I tried to imagine my life there. Fresh air, food, chores, the lovely Binah. A good home. I wondered what James was thinking—was he imagining himself shoveling hay, cleaning the stalls, milking the cows each morning, building and mending fences?

He spoke: "That's a very kind offer ma'am, and we really do appreciate it." What would he say next? What did I want him to say? "But we have a family friend waiting for us in New York City, and he would be worried if we didn't show."

Mrs. Mansfield considered this. "You could go ahead and leave Mary here and fetch her once you get there and see that everything is in order."

At this I burst in: "No, ma'am, that wouldn't work. I can't be without James. I—I just can't." My mind flashed to James leaving me as he almost did in Quebec City. I couldn't bear it. All of it—the trees, the garden, the porch, the pies, Binah—all of it became in my mind these seductive lures meant to make us stray from our path. Yes, we could stay there, live there for years and be fine—I could see that. But it was a trap in the middle of nowhere, or suddenly felt like one. We had New York City waiting for us, with its harbors and tall ships. I somehow knew I would regret it if I never made it to the city.

I looked out the window, noticed for the first time a boy out in the field, digging a row for planting. I thought about the other girl, now disappeared from the kitchen and not eating with us either. Children run this farm, I thought. Orphans like us.

"You know, you really should have an adult guardian. How old are you, James?"

I saw a shadow of worry begin to cloud his face.

"I'm sixteen," he lied. "I'm old enough to take care of my sister, and like I said, there's a family friend waiting for us in New York City who is going to take us in and raise us as his own. He and our father built ships together in Scotland."

"In fact, we should get going, James," I said. I might have sounded a bit unsteady, even panicked, but I didn't care. It was taking everything in me not to grab my knapsack and James and run for the door.

"Well, you can at least wait until your clothes are dry." There was that voice again: firm but kind. An adult voice. A parental voice. A voice you don't defy.

"Thank you, we will," said James. "And if there's anything we can do to help until then."

There certainly was. For the next two hours, I worked alongside Binah doing the dishes and sweeping the floors and washing the windows while James cleaned the pig's stall. Binah sang as she worked, songs I had never heard, and I nearly broke down when she sang the line, "God's gonna trouble the water." Her voice was sweeter than my own mother's.

She handed me fresh clothes and led me into her room so I could change. It was a simple room: a twin bed with a yellow quilt, a small dresser with another vase, this one with fresh wildflowers, and on a little window, yellow curtains that matched the pretty quilt. A nightstand with a hymnal.

"You can keep the dress," Binah said. "It doesn't fit me anymore."

I folded it and set it on her dresser. "No, but thank you."

Binah smiled. "You dress like a boy," she said. "Like your brother."

Even though I was wearing my underclothes, her words made me feel naked, exposed. It was true—I did prefer my brother's clothes. But it had never really occurred to me that other people were noticing or would care.

"I can do more in boy clothes."

She nodded. "Ain't it so. Boys have it easier than girls in some ways, but harder in others."

I considered this. And what was her life like here on this farm? Was she happy? Did she have any choice? I had an idea and blurted, "You should come with us to New York."

Binah looked at me, sweet and resigned, and I had the sense suddenly that she felt like her life was done, that at her young age, she had already arrived at the end, where she would live out the rest of her days. For James and myself, everything remained yet unknown.

"Your life is yours to live, Mary," she said. "So go and live it and be brave and don't let anyone stop you from being who you want to be."

Then she kissed my cheek and went to do her chores. I wondered if she could not leave, was not allowed to, even if she wanted to. And I knew James and I had to escape that place.

Mrs. Mansfield saw us out, told us the journey to Solon was about ten miles, that there was a church there where we could sleep and people who were very kind and would help us. (I knew she was not a witch, but I also wondered if it were a trick—that the Solon church people rounded up orphans and made them servants.) Skowhegan was about another 15 miles past Solon, about a five or six-hour walk. We should plan to stay the night in Skowhegan, Mrs. Mansfield explained, and take a carriage to Boston in the morning. From Boston, we should catch a train to New York City. Then Mrs. Mansfield told us her offer would still stand if we changed our minds. She handed James a little pouch of coins and wished us luck. Binah came out to the porch and waved as we made our way down the road. I was sad for her despite the comforts the farm and home offered. They came with too large a price.

Instead of heading straight to Solon, we took a detour that Binah had suggested, a side trip to a see a nearby waterfall. Just off the road and down a meandering path surrounded by ferns that were thriving under the shade of the tall trees, we heard them before we saw them: the Houston Brooke Falls. The water cascaded dozens of feet down a tall cliff, splashing into and filling a pool surrounded by rocks.

We told ourselves we would stay only a few minutes, but we frolicked for hours there, swimming in the cool water. Standing under the waterfall, the water falling on my head like giant heavy rain, I felt alive and free.

We got to Skowhegan three days later, where we hitched a ride on the back of a wagon on its way to Boston. Staring up at a blue sky, I slowly drifted off to sleep. When I awoke, we were in front of the train station—the kindly driver had taken us all the way to it. James made inquiries, found that tickets for the train to New York City were $1.75 each, and bought two. I was so excited to ride a train, but after we boarded and found our seats, once again we both promptly fell asleep, leaning against each other, not even noticing when the locomotive started click-clackety down the tracks.

We arrived in New York having missed the entire train ride. No gradually changing landscape for us—we were just plopped into the city as if dropped from the sky.

* * *

A knock at the door, and then Gallagher's quiet voice: "Are you awake, Murray?" I set down the pen and paper and call for him to come in.

"How are you today?" He opens his bag, pulls out the bottle of morphine. My body yearns for it; I can almost feel the relief running through my vein. But I shake my head.

"No shot today, Gallagher. I think I'd like to get out of bed."

"Oh?"

"I want to walk my dog. And I want to go to Pratt's. I have to pay her for a book."

"Can't you ask Minnie?"

"She's been taking Walt out for a walk every day. But I'm ready, Gallagher. I can't spend the rest of my life lying here." *However short a time that might be.*

"Do you want me to stay? Help you around?"

"No. I want to try on my own."

He nods. "Call me if you feel pain, if you'd like me to come to give you a shot."

"It might be a good idea for me to walk to your office for it. You know, earn it." I imagine this, getting the short of morphine in his office and then walking the streets of Manhattan afterward in a state of morphine-induced paramnesia. Could be interesting.

"Well, take it easy, please. I much prefer you to wait until Minnie's home so she can help you if you need it." I nod my compliance. "How's the writing coming?"

"Do you want to hear the latest installment?"

"Absolutely." He sits down in the chair, settles in.

I read to him about Anne O'Grady, about the decision to abandon her and Canada, about the long walk and the farm and Binah and the waterfall and the carriage ride and the train trip I don't remember and our final arrival.

"No regrets, of course?" he asks.

"No. None. I can't imagine my life if I had gone on to Montreal without James. I would never have been able to let him go. It would have haunted me. Same with the farm—what if he had left me there and never returned? Now our lives almost seem inevitable."

"It's so very true—at any turn with a different decision—or a slight alteration or happenstance—your life would have been very different. You both seem like you were so impetuous, so bold and brave. I can't believe how far you traveled."

"People did it, though. Many, many groups of Irish were walking, and children among them. And many apparently stopped along the way and decided to stay and settle in those villages and on those farms. I remember reading about the Irish influx all along the Kennebec River. They became loggers, homesteaders, blacksmiths, farmers, domestics, cooks. It must have felt like a miracle after what they went through in Ireland. And when I think about the conditions of the lives of the immigrants in New York City—especially the Irish immigrants—well, it makes those forests and farms and villages look downright enchanted in comparison."

"Yes, I'm sure life wasn't easy along the Kennebec, but you're right—it probably felt like Eden."

I pull back the blankets and start to get up. He gestures to my chest. "Want me to check you?"

"No, but thank you. I'm going to get up from this bed and take a much-needed bath. Then if I'm up to it, I'm going to walk my dog."

"Good man," he says, then blushes.

After Gallagher goes, I emerge slowly from the bed. Writing has invigorated my mind, but after two weeks of convalescing, I feel my muscles have atrophied. I need fresh air, need to move. Walt raises his head when I stand up, and he too stands and wags his tail in applause. With Walt there I never feel alone, even when Minnie is out much of the day. She walks him in the morning and sometimes again in the evening, which had been my routine—Walt's and my routine for several years now—and I'm not ready to give it up yet. I feel light-headed but not enough to sit back down. When I try to stretch my arms above my head, the bandages around my chest tighten and I wince, knowing that they aren't simply obscuring my breasts anymore, but soaking in the seepage from ruptured tumors. I feel a pain that almost nauseates me but I decide to ignore it. The morphine will make me too lazy and I can take the pain. Someday the pain will be gone completely, but then I'll be gone too. Better to learn to live with it as much as possible.

I bend down and pet Walt's head. He licks my hand as I consider the state of my ribs. Much better. Like my chest, they too are taped. My left arm is stiff but movable, though the range is quite limited. Gallagher advised me to move it every day, to stretch the arm out straight in front of me and bend at the elbow. At first, I was capable of no more than a ninety-degree angle, my fingers pointed to the ceiling, but I've done that exercise every day, and this morning I am only a couple inches away from the collar bone (whereas my right fingers could easily scratch my right shoulder). Little by little, he said. There have been moments I wanted to give up, take my sickly body and toss it into the East River. But I have Minnie to think of and Walt to care for and books to read and a story to write.

It is enough.

I haven't fully bathed myself in two weeks. I move into the bathroom and lock the door. I turn on the bath water and sit on the toilet, so grateful for indoor plumbing and the water heater, I could sing. I strip my bedclothes off, remove the bandages, and stand naked in front of the mirror. I've lost weight but am still thick, and the bruises on my ribs and breasts have turned a sickly yellow. The tumor is visible, the lesions raw and red. But instead of feeling the usual disdain I feel at my breasts and the cancer, I feel instead an odd tenderness, as if they are little abused children in need of sympathy and affection.

I lower into the hot water, steam rising up in a misty haze, and I lie back and close my eyes and remember the budding of my breasts, at age twelve, the beginning of womanhood.

I think about the years before that—of how grand it was to be young, a child, before my body took over and defied me.

Chapter Nine

I opened my eyes on my new home. The city felt like madness, especially after the weeks we'd spent on the road surrounded by flora and fauna. Manhattan was man-made, dense, chaotic, unreal. I had no geographical understanding that New York City was an island—and not just at first but for months. We had no map to study and saw only what was in front of our eyes, a myopic view without scope. Endless streets, hundreds of buildings, and so many horse-drawn carriages that it seemed quite possible and even plausible that I would meet my demise under a horse's hoofs. I looked around myself uncomprehending, unable to take it all in at once. Small details began to emerge: faces, clothing, languages that were new to me. It was overwhelming. I felt lost.

We had our piece of paper with the name and address of our father's acquaintance. James had studied it so many times, we didn't even really need it anymore, except that its very existence seemed proof that we were legitimate. Neil Buchanan, 83 Anthony Street. He was not a family friend; I had never met him. But he had worked with our father on the Clyde and had written his former colleagues that there was work in America, had given his address. We didn't know how long ago that was. James stopped a tall man on the street dressed in a nice suit, and asked him where we were.

The man said, "What do you mean? You're in Lower Manhattan." Which meant nothing to us. James showed him the piece of paper and he gave us directions we didn't understand and so we just walked in the direction the man had pointed.

I was tired, so tired of walking and carrying my things. The train ride had allowed us to rest, but I felt like I wanted to lie down right where we were and just stop. The romance of the road was done for me. William and Dorothy Wordsworth got to end their long journey at their cottage in Grasmere. Me? I got a bustling, baffling city and nowhere to lay my head.

James asked another man for directions and he said it was in the "Sixth Ward." He looked us up and down with distaste. I glanced at James whose clothes and face were dusty, and then down at my own dirty clothes. My shoes were caked with mud. My nails were jagged and dirt-filled. We hadn't washed for the last few days. The way the man had looked at us—void of compassion—made me tremendously sad. Here, among strangers who made a brief and cold assessment, I was rubbish. I could see it in his eyes. "Where's the Sixth Ward, please?" I asked as kind as I could muster. "Five Points," he said. "It's that way."

We approached a part of town that felt more dismal that the rest.

I saw a group of young children and asked them where Five Points was.

"You're in Five Points," one of them said and snickered. These children were dirtier than we were. Indeed, I looked around and saw many children—some my age, some older, some younger, and all of them filthy.

But surely they must have homes! Surely they weren't all living in the streets? Surely someone was caring for them? I had an excuse: our parents were dead and we'd traveled for nearly two months to get there. Was this the existence that awaited us? I had seen people in horse-drawn carriages who looked clean and well-fed, who were dressed in fine clothes. So, if there was money in the city, why was I now looking at destitution? Why was no one caring for these children? Were they all orphans like me and my brother?

"Do you have parents?" I asked them.

"'Course we do," said the one who had first spoken. His front teeth were either chipped or only half grown in.

"I've got a mum," another said, this one a barefoot girl in a dress whose hem was torn.

Just then I saw two men spill out of a squat building. They yelled at each other in what sounded like the Gaelic I'd heard spoken by the Irish families on the *Charlotte*. One man, the larger, hit the other, landing him face down in the mud, and then walked back into the dwelling. I worried that the downed man would drown in that thick, disgusting quagmire, mud mixed with waste, though horse, human, or some combination, I knew not. Indeed, the neighborhood was a veritable swamp, everything stinking with filth. I stood frozen to the spot staring at the man, wondering how long he could survive without breath. Was he even conscious? No one helped him, though plenty walked by. Not one of the children batted an eye. Then James yanked on my arm and I followed and didn't look back.

That was my introduction to Five Points, a violent act that caused human suffering which inspired no compassion. This was where my father's friend was writing us from to encourage us to emigrate?

James approached an older woman wearing a red scarf on her head. "Excuse me, Ma'am. Can you tell me where I can find Anthony Street?"

The woman cocked her head and then took the paper from James and held it in her calloused fingers.

"Next street over," she said.

James thanked her and she grunted in response. We followed where her finger had pointed. The road curved slightly. We found the address—we had finally arrived.

The ramshackle building we stood before looked like it would blow over in a storm. It was two stories tall, with small dirty windows and no flowers, no effort at all, to cheer it up. James knocked. I didn't like the look of the place. It made me nervous.

James knocked harder. We heard screams come from inside, which could have been a baby or a wild animal, and thumping footsteps approaching the door. I hid behind James. The door flew open.

"What do you want?"

"Excuse me, Ma'am. Sorry to bother."

"A bother indeed—you woke the little one with all that pounding."

I peeked out from behind James. The woman was large, dressed simply in a brown dress and yellowing apron that I assumed was once white. Her hair was pulled back tight, which made her face look fleshy and menacing. She wore no makeup or jewelry save a simple ring that might have been a wedding band. She didn't exactly soften when she saw me.

"You see, we've come all the way from Scotland, and all we have is this fellow's name; a friend of my father's he was. He wrote and told us he could help us when we got to New York City." He handed her the piece of paper.

"And where's your father?" she asked with suspicion.

"He and our mother died from fever they caught on the ship."

She backed her big face away a few inches. "And how do you know you're not sick, not bringing the fever here?"

James shook his head. "We've been traveling for weeks, Ma'am. We're tired but fit as fiddles."

She peered closely at our faces and then looked at the piece of paper again.

"Never heard of him."

She handed the paper back to James dismissively. That was it? Our only contact in the America—and she's never heard of him?

"This is the right address?"

"It is and I've been here for five months, and I can tell you I've never heard of Neil Buchanan. Doesn't live here at least. You can ask around. Go down to the Old Brewery; they might know something."

"Where's that, please?"

"Cross Street." She gestured up the road. Her creature cried out again, a hideous sound. "Now if you'll excuse me." She made to shut the door.

"Sorry, just one more question, please, and sorry for the interruption."

"Yeah?" she reluctantly opened the door back up.

"We have just arrived. We don't know the city and feel rather lost. Seems our only person of contact here in New York City doesn't even live at the address he supplied us with. Do you know where we might find lodging?"

Again the woman scrutinized us from top to bottom and then back up to our faces as if considering a purchase of livestock.

"I might have a place you can sleep." She cocked her head. "Ten cents a night—each. Or a dollar total for a week. But you've got to pay now."

James looked at me and I at him. We were so road weary. I didn't think I'd have the energy to carry my knapsack around Five Points inquiring about our father's friend.

"May we see it?"

The woman opened the door and let us into a dark hallway. In a small kitchen, a pot of soup was simmering, greasy broth and a chicken foot sticking out of the top. A small table and four chairs were crammed into the space, and a tiny, dirty window, impossible to see out of and framed with short, tattered curtains, was cracked open just an inch.

"It's nothing special—just the cellar. And no beds, but there's room on the floor to sleep if you have blankets."

"We do," said James. The woman went to the corner of the kitchen and pulled up a door on the floor. "Here, take this," she said, handing James a candle. "You can go down and look at it and see if it's the kind of accommodation you're looking for." Her sneer and the greasy soup and lack of air were making me feel sick. I thought of the dense woods. We weren't in Maine or Canada anymore, that was for sure.

James approached the door in the floor and I followed. He started down the rickety staircase, no handrail, and I reached out and held onto his shoulder and descended with him into what felt like purgatory. I wholly expected the woman to slam the door once we were down there and lock us in. My imagination had only gotten so far in that moment, but it was enough to terrify me. At the bottom of the stairs the room spread out—a dirt floor, dank and dark, without any window at all. We were completely underground.

"I can give you a bucket to relieve yourselves," she shouted down. I thought of the *Charlotte.* Was this to be a land-based version of that hell?

There were wood beams and spider webs and beyond that, blackness. The dim candle did not allow us to see into the corners.

"Well?" she called down.

'We'd like to stay here, thank you," James answered. I glared at my brother. "We'll find something better, I promise," he whispered. "But we need to sleep."

"I'll throw in a meal for an extra half dime a day."

I shook my head so vigorously, it made James chuckle. I would rather starve, I thought, than eat that soup. We had passed many vendors on the street selling all kinds of fruits and vegetables and bread. We'd find something.

"Just the lodging for now, thank you," James called up.

"Lodging?" I asked him quietly, indicating the damp, dirt floor glowing in the candlelight.

"Just a week," James whispered back.

We took out our blankets and spread them on the dirt floor and lay down. Exhausted as I was, it took me more than an hour to fall asleep. I was in a more dismal state than I'd been in during my short life.

The apartment of the woman who rented the basement to us was also occupied by her husband, or a man we assumed to be her husband at least, and three boys, one who looked to be about James's age and two others who were bigger and older. They were not friendly with James or me. And the baby—whose unanswered cries made my head pound—seemed to know it was doomed. The man was gruff and when he was home we heard shouting from all of them. Besides the little kitchen with the stove, there was one other room where the six of them slept. A privy and water pump were outside the building in the back. The smell of sweat and piss permeated the apartment. No wonder they yelled.

James left me to go see if he could find work. I didn't want him to leave me, but he said he was asking around at grog shops and bars, since that's where the men seemed to gather. After he left, I would come up from the cellar and scuttle quickly out of the apartment through the front door. James gave me strict instructions not to wander off, so I just sat outside and observed. A lot of men walked up Anthony Street, where women stood in the doorways of the apartment buildings beckoning them. Some men went in. They didn't stay long.

Once I just went down the block no farther than the end of the street, but James came home at that time, and when he didn't find me out front or in the basement, he became frantic. When he did find me, he boxed my ears in front of a crowd of strangers and dragged me back to the apartment. My face was red with fury and hot tears of shame and frustration streamed down my cheeks.

"You're just going to have to stay down here, Mary," he said when he'd brought me back to the basement. "You can't be wandering off. You can't imagine how big this city is. If I lost you, I don't know what I would do." He put his arm around me and wiped my tears with his thumb. Still, I shook my head in defiance.

"I hate it here."

"You've got to hang on while I try to figure things out. I've met some fellows who might give me work. It means hanging out at the tavern, though, sometimes all day, but they've got to get used to seeing my face. I've got to be smart. If I can get a job, we'll be out of here sooner."

"Let me come too. I can help."

He shook his head. "No, Mary. There are hardly ever any women and certainly no girls in the tavern. It would hinder more than it would help. The best thing you can do is sit tight. You've got your poetry books. I'll make sure you have enough candles."

That hurt to my core. It wasn't that I was too young, though it was probably that too. What prevented me from going out into the world with my brother was my sex. I felt like a prisoner, trapped in a basement, trapped as a girl.

And since I was so young, I couldn't imagine a time when our lives would be different. A day felt so long, the hours dragging out; a week felt like an eternity. I was mad and frustrated—but I agreed to stay put.

"Be patient and have faith in me," James said.

James I could have faith in—he had my best interest at heart. Someone else, however, didn't.

My brother had gone out in the morning, had left me sleeping. When I awoke, I ate some of the bread and fruit we kept in a box to keep rodents out of it. Somehow I had gotten used to hearing them in the shadows, though I still jumped every time they ran across my legs at night.

On this particular morning, I lit a candle and opened my Wordsworth but found it too awful that morning to read about nature—of clouds and streams and daffodils. I was thinking of the farm where we stayed, of Binah, of the offer from Mrs. Mansfield to stay on, and wondering if we'd made a mistake. In my mind, I could put myself in Binah's room, the comfort and warmth, the sunlight and pretty curtains, a real bed with a soft quilt. I imagined laying my head upon Binah's lap. I ran my fingers through my hair and imagined it was her petting me, soothing me. James and I could have made a life at that farm, surrounded by animals and good food and the trees and the warmth of women. That's what I was thinking when I heard the basement door open.

"James," I called out.

I saw light and then a man's boots on the ladder descending. Then I saw that it was the husband, and stupidly I felt relieved for a moment—it might not be James but it was someone I knew. I didn't know enough to be afraid.

"Girl," he said when he was at the bottom of the stairs. I could make out his shape but I could not see his face.

"Sir?" I asked. "James is out."

He grunted. Stood there awkwardly.

"How's the baby feeling? It seems her cough is better." That was me—chatty, covering the awkwardness.

"Let's see what you're made of then. Stand up."

I stood, confused.

"Six, are ya?"

"Yes, but I'll be seven in January."

He reached out and touched the top of my head as if feeling in the dark for me, which was an odd feeling since I had just been imagining Binah's long graceful brown fingers in my hair. He touched my ear, then my neck. I stepped back and he stepped forward. I could smell his stench, his old sweat and oniony breath. He reached out again and held my arm with one hand so that I couldn't step back away from him. When he had a firm grasp, he pulled me toward him.

"See what you're made of," he mumbled again. I was wearing a dress and my brother's brogues. I felt his hand then on my leg trying to reach under my dress. I struggled back but he gripped me more firmly. Then he grabbed my underpants and yanked, tearing them. I kicked him and I felt a slap against my face. But he had let go of me to slap me and I fell back, stumbling into the darkness. He lunged and caught me. I screamed as loud as I could, screamed James's name. Screamed to wake my mother from the dead to come save me. He put his hand over my mouth. I felt the weight of him on me.

I felt his finger like a fat sausage in my mouth and I bit down. I bit that disgusting hand, bit it as hard as I could. I had a grip on it with my teeth and sunk them in. His blood filled my mouth and now he screamed, and I scrambled away from him and hid in the shadows, trying to hold my breath. He was yelling and holding his hand. I heard a door slam upstairs and the unhappy baby cry out.

He climbed the stairs.

I crouched there in the dark. My candle had been extinguished. I spit his blood from my mouth.

From the basement, I heard the woman upstairs say, "What the hell happened to you?"

I did not hear his answer. She said, "You better get that stitched up or you'll lose it and be even more worthless."

After the door slammed again all was quiet, I climbed the stairs and slipped out to the street, terrified that I would see him again.

I was hiding behind a broken carriage, when James came back. I came out from where I hid. "James," I tried to say, but my voice cracked. One of my eyes was swollen shut and throbbing. Reddish-brown splatters of drying blood stained the front of my clothes.

"Mary—what happened?" James ran to me, his face grimaced.

"The man—the father—" I stammered.

"Bastard—I'll kill him," said James. "What did he do?" I had never seen James that angry. He made toward the tenement,

"James, he's not there. I think I might have almost bit his finger off. I think he went to get it stitched."

"I'm so sorry, Mary." He picked me up and held me tight. I felt his body shaking with rage. My own started shaking with my sobs. He held me for a long time.

Finally he said, "I'm going to go get our things."

I nodded weakly and hid behind the carriage again. Then my brother was there again, our knapsacks in his arms.

That night, we stayed at a dirty inn, but I barely slept, reliving the basement scene over and over in my mind. James had his arm around me all night, and squeezed me gently every time I cried.

Some years later, after I became wiser to the ways of Five Points, I learned that nearly all the dwellings on Anthony Street were brothels, and that a man would pay thirty dollars to have sex with a virgin, and fifty for a virgin child.

The next day, James asked around and found a one-room shack to rent on Mulberry Street. He had to give the new landlord almost the last of our money for the room. The main tenement building was on Mulberry with outhouses behind it, and our dwelling sat in the far back of the lot, behind the outhouses. The smell wasn't great, but it was our own little place, and the door locked. The front room had two little windows that allowed in a little light, and, if opened, welcomed in the putrid aroma of urine and defecation from the outhouses. It was a small room, yes, but it had a table and chairs and a stool and a little stove. And then another little room, even smaller, was the sleeping closet, which had enough room for James and me to sleep side by side. There were no beds or mattresses. I didn't care. I was relieved to be out of that basement.

When James tried to leave me the next morning, I wouldn't let him. But he couldn't take me with him to find work either, not as a girl.

"Then cut my hair, James," I told him. "Cut my hair and I can pretend to be a boy."

I already wore his brogues and hand-me-down clothes when I wasn't wearing one of my dresses. But my hair had grown long, since it hadn't been cut since our mom last trimmed it in Scotland.

He looked at me for a what felt like a full minute and then finally said, "Stay here." And before I could interrupt and reject that command, he held up his hand. "Give me ten minutes. You can stay alone for that long. I'll be right back—promise."

He left. I peeked out from behind the drab curtains and through the filthy window and watched him go. I saw a young woman come out from the building in front and approach the outhouse. When she stepped out from the shadow of the building and into the sun she paused and turned her face toward the sky, her eyes closed. She was pretty, I could see, and in the sunlight, looked almost angelic. Then she opened her eyes and looked right at me! I ducked my head. When I peeked back out again, she smiled at me and then entered the outhouse.

James rounded the corner then, scissors dangling from his hand like a metal appendage. I opened the door for him and then sat down on the chair. I thought he might just lop my hair all off quickly, but he combed it and cut it carefully, making sure it was even. Then I put on James's old jacket, a cap, and with my hair cut short and my brother's old clothes, there was no telling I was a girl.

"We have to come up with a name for you instead of Mary," he said.

"How about James?"

"No, Grice, we can't both be James. That's stupid." He thought for a moment. "There's a place uptown called Murray Hill. How about that?"

"Murray Hill?"

"No, just Murray. It's close to your real name, so you won't forget it. And if you screw up, you can just say you meant Murray, not Mary."

It was perfect.

I'd been born anew.

* * *

It was harder to write about that than I thought it would be. I remember reading the psychoanalyst Freud who said that early experiences…like what happened or nearly happened to me in that basement…could have a lasting effect. And I remember wondering what that effect might have been on me. Perhaps it seems obvious. No man would ever have contact with my body again. Not like that.

I feel raw and sad this morning, spent. I get up from the bed and make sure my bedroom door is locked before I change my bandages. This morning the sight of the tumor in my breast makes me tear up. I am trying to be strong—I want to be tough. I am sad, though; I am dying. The pain is there, yes, and I thought I could take it, but as I re-bandage my chest and dress, I decide I will walk up to Gallagher's for a shot of morphine.

In the dining room, I find Minnie having coffee and a cigarette and reading a book. With some pleasure I realize that my daily reading may have rubbed off on her. Even though I raised her on Whitman's poetry, she prefers novels written by women. Recently when I told her she needs to think about her future, she told me she wants to be a writer, which pleased me. But most female authors do not get paid very much: their work being valued almost exclusively by other females, and so therefore lacking in merit, apparently.

She looks up from her book dreamily and I'm struck as always by her beauty and youth. Walt is snoring at her feet, more loyal to her now that it's she who walks him.

"Want some coffee?" she asks me.

I shake my head. "I'm going to head up to Gallagher's."

"I'll come with you," she says, and stubs out her cigarette. "We can bring Walt."

And so the three of us walk the distance to Gallagher's together. She is innocent and unscathed, as far as I know. I met her when she was six, the same age I was when all that happened. I don't know what happened to her before that—if anything bad did. Celia was her bodyguard, her guardian, and she never indicated that Minnie had experienced anything like what happened to me. She doesn't seem interested in having a relationship. A few men have pursued her, but she rebuffs them, which made me secretly glad since they didn't seem good enough for her. That she realized it too, since so many young women don't, thrilled me.

Minnie makes small talk, tells me about the plot of the book she's reading. I'm grateful for the chitchat—nothing deep or hard or painful, not her mother's death, for instance—just everyday life stuff and yet I'm so moved by it. She trusts me; we've known each other for years. She calls me Dad. She tells me about her nightmares or this current novel's plot. We are just together, walking down the street, yet it's so precious to me, that I nearly begin to weep.

So pleasant is our walk that I decide I don't need the morphine after all and suggest we go down to the harbor and see the ships and get oysters and beer for lunch.

"Yes!" she says. "And then ice cream?"

"Absolutely," I say.

She is a girl after my own heart. My daughter, even though her mother is gone. Even more so because her mother is gone.

She has Walt's leash in one hand, and when she takes mine with her other one and squeezes, I squeeze back.

I can't help it—my eyes start to tear up and I wipe them when I think she won't notice.

Chapter Ten

I followed James wherever he went. For several weeks, we stood outside certain taverns. James greeted the men and women entering and said goodbye to those leaving, never asking for a thing, just making his presence known. Soon, a few of them were offering a coin or two for little errands. James was prompt, efficient, friendly, and reliable, and soon he was asked to do bigger things, like delivering a message across town. In this way, we got to know little pockets of the city. I had to work hard to keep up with him, but he didn't mind or didn't show it, even if he knew he could probably work faster alone and earn more money.

At home, I finally befriended Emma. Almost the same time every morning she would come out of the building and walk toward the outhouse and then stand with her face in the sun and then wave at me. I soon stopped ducking whenever I saw her, and finally when she gestured for me to come out one day, I did.

She was about twenty, and like so many there in Five Points, had come from Ireland. I told her my name was Murray, though I felt guilty about deceiving her, she was so kind and warm. One Saturday morning she asked if I wanted to go to church with her the next day. All the Irish in the neighborhood attended mass at Transfiguration, just down the street. But I shook my head with such vehemence she laughed.

"Okay, then," she said. "How about you come to our place afterward for supper? The girls and I usually make something savory on Sunday. Your brother can come too if he wants. We eat around 2."

I washed and even brushed my hair Sunday in preparation for lunch, and so did James. At half past one, not wanting to be too early nor to arrive just when the food was being served, we went up to the second floor where Emma said their apartment was. We knocked, and a woman answered, tall, thin and Irish (I could tell from the moment she spoke to invite us in), and introduced herself as Francis.

James said, "Hello, I'm James and this is my brother, Murray." He shook Francis's hand, which reminded me just in time not to curtsy.

"How do you do," she said. I shook her hand, afraid to speak.

The room was warmly lit with gas lamps and candles. The smoky smell of simmering stew emanated from the corner of the room that was dedicated to the kitchen. Their place was about twice the size of ours, and while ours would have been filled with smoke if we had a stove fire going as large as they did, their windows were letting in a sufficient breeze. In addition to a long table and chairs, they had a little sitting area with a couch and smaller table and stools nearer the window. The fabric on the couch, a worn pink velvet, along with the lace curtains, gave the place an air of feminine taste and decor that was utterly lacking in our apartment.

Emma had risen from the couch and set her book aside when we entered. She thanked us for coming and for the loaf of bread we brought and invited us to the table, where five settings were placed. She called out, "Liz, time for dinner," toward the bedroom where she said their other roommate was napping.

"Please don't wake her on our account," said James.

"Not at all—Liz works all week sewing with us, but on Saturday nights, she likes to go dancing and she always sleeps in on Sunday and misses church. And don't think I don't know that's intentional," said Emma. "But she loathes to miss dinner and always has us wake her before we eat."

A woman emerged from the room, her face sleepy and puffy, though one could see that she was beautiful.

"Hi," she said.

"Hello," said James and I smiled.

We ate a good, thick mutton stew, which, along with the bread, made it the best meal I'd had in ages. We even had dessert: cake filled with cream and covered in chocolate! Rather than ply us with questions, the women told stories and jokes and teased one another, and by the end of the meal, I was feeling so full and happy that I wanted to cry. Or nap.

Francis, in fact, went to go lie down, and Liz suggested a card game to James. Emma and I moved to the couch where she took out her sewing. I had hardly spoken during supper. As a girl, I would not have been shy at all, but I had not been in such close quarters with people as a boy and was nervous about being found out.

"Do you know how to sew, Murray?"

I shook my head.

"Do you want me to show you?" When I hesitated, she said, "It's a handy skill for a boy or a girl. Here," she sat closer to me. "I'll teach you how to sew on a button."

She took a piece of fabric from her sewing box and threaded her needle. I watched as she poked it through the buttonholes carefully, deftly. I had watched my mother sew many times, but she had not taught me; she must have thought we would have more time, that she would teach me someday…

Emma passed the cloth to me and I practiced. Then she put a shirt on her lap and started to stitch.

"We sew with machines during the day, but I do slop work in the evenings and Sunday."

I gave her a confused look. "Slop work is clothes done by hand, piecemeal," she said, gesturing to the shirt on her lap.

I nodded. Even at that young age, I did not want to work in clothes-making, though I did see the usefulness of knowing the skill. Our clothes were starting to fall apart and with a little attention, we could keep them going longer.

"We're lucky to have the work," she said. "Lucky to have this place. The slop work pays for a few extras." I nodded again and smiled. "You and James are from Scotland, right? But you know about what's happening in Ireland?"

"Only a little," I answered, my voice barely audible.

"It was so bad over there, Murray. You can't imagine it. Your father was a shipbuilder, James said, but most of us were farmers living on rented land. Just to pay the rent to the landlord, we had to raise so much food, and all we kept for ourselves in most cases were the potatoes. The eggs we sold; the chickens we sold. We gave up the pigs and the milk and the cheese and the grain. Wages were low and jobs scarce. But an acre of potatoes could feed half a dozen people more than an acre of corn could." She shook her head. "You can't imagine how many potatoes I've eaten! Sometimes we had only potatoes for breakfast, lunch, *and* dinner. And not all slathered in butter and cream either—I mean, on rare occasions we did. But mostly we just ate those boiled potatoes with a bit of salt for flavor. That meal we just ate still feels like a feast to me."

"For me too," I said and meant it. But I didn't venture anything else. I was grateful for her monologue.

"There were about two weeks between the end of spring's harvest and the beginning of summer's, so we were used to hunger. Two weeks we knew we'd be weak from lack of food, but at least we knew relief was only days away. We lived in North Sligo, in a little rented cabin with dirt floors and a thatched roof that rained dirt down on us. And you know how it rains in Britain—puddles on the floor, everything muddy and wet and cold and never clean. Here in America," she said, patting the couch, "I have this old thing, this beat-up, beautiful couch. In our place in Sligo, we had almost nothing but a table and a few stools—no cots to sleep on even, at least not for us children. My mother and father slept on some planks of wood piled with pieces of scratchy burlap. But it was home, and even though we had no shoes and hardly any clothes, we were *alive*."

She paused and looked out the window. It was early evening and as it was late summer, the sun still shone.

"But then the blight hit, and when we dug up the potatoes, we were shocked—most were brown and rotted inside, useless. That first failed crop was the summer of '45, and it was bad, but we managed. Then the spring crop of '46 was worse. But it wasn't until that summer that folks began starving to death."

In Sligo, they didn't have outhouses where she lived, she explained. People, racked with dysentery, blood in their bowels, relieved themselves where they could. She tried to describe the maddening hunger, how she watched a neighbor fall to her knees in the street and beg; how her parents helped bury her two days later on the side of the road; how the dogs would dig up the bodies in the middle of the night, but how no one had the energy to bury the corpses deeper, nor the money or material for coffins.

"We soon learned that this blight wasn't just affecting Sligo but all of Ireland. Our landlord, Mr. Booth, bless him, tried to help us, unlike most of the landlords in other counties, like Kerry or Cork. He opened a soup kitchen and tried to feed the people of our county, but it was too little too late. So he gathered 1,500 of us from Drumcliff and paid our passage to America, though they routed us to Canada because it was cheaper."

"We landed in Canada too!" I burst out.

"Where?" she asked. "Gross Isle—and then Quebec City?"

I nodded.

"Ah, then you know." Her voice drifted off for a moment before she continued. "Well, when my family received the passenger contract tickets, it seemed I had been booked to go on a different ship, but it was all right, since some friends of ours were on that ship and said they would take care of me. Our ship was lucky—we had plenty of supplies, thanks to Mr. Booth, even a doctor on board, so we arrived with very few deaths." She dabbed her eye then with the sleeve she was sewing.

"But my whole family was on a ship named the *Carricks*, which shipwrecked on the coast of Canada in Cap-des-Rosiers. There were

200 people on the ship. About 120 of them died." She paused trying to compose herself but silent tears fell down her cheeks. "I lost everyone that day—my two brothers, my three sisters, my dad, and my dear mum."

I could feel the sadness in her core and it awakened my own. I felt my own eyes filling and the pressure in my chest rising.

"I'm so sorry for you, Emma. I lost my mother too. But you lost everyone." I began to cry. Emma held me and wiped my tears and her own. I wept and wept and wept.

Drained of emotion, I fell asleep in Emma's arms and woke only momentarily as James carried me back to our apartment.

James was so smart. Renting our little shack left us flat broke, but he wasn't worried, or at least didn't let on that he was. I think he liked the challenge of having to make money. Though we had no tub or sink, we did have a kettle James would fill with water and heat on the wood-burning stove. He insisted that we keep ourselves clean and kempt and made me wash my face every day and bathe my body once a week.

We were well-spoken and well-read, especially James, who was a good writer too. It was important not to put on airs, he explained to me, as many of the people we met had been humble farmers in Ireland without much book learning. But James understood how to talk on someone's level. He understood when to be bold and when to be humble. Most of the time I just stood behind him and observed, as I was dressed as a boy and still nervous about passing myself off as one. Even as time went on, I remained unnaturally quiet for me since I didn't trust my voice. I might have always been a tomboy, but I was convinced that people would perceive me as a girl the moment I spoke.

Every day, James took me with him into the streets. We sat outside a certain tavern like sentries and watched people come in and go out, looked people in the eye and said good day, never asked for a handout, never begged. Many of the children around Five Points were filthy and dressed in little more than rags, but we kept our clothes in good condition with Emma's help and I replaced our buttons. When I resisted bathing or grooming, James said: "Murray, we must make ourselves as presentable as possible." He was disciplined, even at his young age, and wouldn't tolerate any of my whining.

Early one morning I happened to see a boy steal an apple from a fruit vendor, and a few blocks away when we passed another fruit cart on Cross Street, I slowed down and hesitated beside it. The vendor was giving change to someone and not looking in my direction at all, so I put my hand around one of the red apples and quickly tucked it into my pocket. My heart was pounding in my chest. Then someone grabbed my arm and I almost screamed. It wasn't the vendor, but James.

He dragged me into Bottle Alley and pushed me up against a wall. An old woman, her back covered in a dirty brown shawl, was sweeping mounds of a dark, shit-smelling substance. She didn't bat an eye at James's treatment of me. Drying clothes and rags hung on crisscrossed lines above us. Small, blackened windows, encrusted with soot, lined the buildings' facades on either side. Large sacks of grain or flour were stacked outside an uneven doorway. A man emerged, sweaty and staggering and obviously drunk, though it was still morning. James waited until the man passed; his hand had me pinned by the neck to the wall.

"If I ever see you steal something I will throw you out onto the street to fend for yourself." He was spitting his words at me, his face contorted with anger. "All this work, all this struggle, and you're just going to throw it away by getting caught stealing."

"But I didn't get caught," I said, which enraged him even more.

"Yes, you did—by me. And you're lucky you did. Because getting away with an apple this morning would make you feel bolder about something bigger tomorrow. Look at me," he grabbed my small face in his adolescent hands. "I am going to take care of you, but not if you do stupid stuff that could get us both in trouble."

I swallowed the tears coming up my throat and nodded.

"We have got to be smart if we're going to survive," he said in a low voice. "You want to get out of this part of town, want to live somewhere safer, somewhere cleaner? Have good food to eat? Have a warm, safe place to lay your head?"

The underlying message was clear. This warning, this mention of the precariousness of our situation—of what an unsafe place might yield—made my tears resurface and emerge.

"Eat the apple," he said.

I was crying harder now and held it out to him, shaking my head.

"Eat it," he said. He had let go of my neck and was standing with authority in front of me, hands on his hips, voice firm.

"No, I can't." I could barely breathe.

"You're going to eat that apple. Eat it and tell me if it was worth it." When I shook my head, he yelled, "Eat it!" with such force and vitriol that I brought it to my mouth and took a small bite.

"Eat the whole damned thing," he said, as I choked it down between sobs. "I want you to remember this."

He made me eat the core too.

Then he said, "You've got to choose who and what you're going to be—what kind of person you're going to be. You may see yourself one way, believe you have every justification in the world for how you behave. But the outside world will form its own opinion of you. You might think that because you're dressed as a boy that one deception deserves another. But that's not true. You will build a reputation. People have to believe you and believe *in* you. You're going to have to work hard to get them to trust you, to employ you, to give you responsibility. And stealing is not going to help you in that regard."

I wanted to hate him in that moment but I couldn't: my love for James was fierce. I was only angry at myself for disappointing him.

* * *

"That memory of James will never leave me. Even today, I still eat the whole apple, including the core. I never again stole a piece of fruit."

Though in a way, I ended up helping steal elections. I think that, but don't say it aloud. I'm with Gallagher, in his office, which is the front room of his apartment. It's a dark wood-paneled room with beautiful bookshelves, filled with books on every subject. There is a comfortable reading chair, a couch, a large desk, and a curtained off area that has an examination table. I have just caught him up on the latest chapters of my writing.

"Seems your brother was an effective guardian."

"Well, Five Points was full of petty thieves, and James didn't want us to go that route. We were bent on survival, yes, but he also knew we had to maintain our dignity. Our situation was desperate but not dire, but it could go either way. And I think that James also understood that we couldn't isolate ourselves, that we needed others."

"Like the Irish girls…"

"Yes. My goodness, they were like sisters to me, especially Emma. But we needed work too, needed to make money. And James was smart about that. He seemed to understand that if we were going to survive, we needed to form connections with the right people."

And my brother was already laying the groundwork. Thankfully, he let me follow him like a puppy dog. Because of James I made the acquaintance of Peter Barr Sweeny, long before the man became part of the most corrupt political ring the country had ever known.

"So that's when you became Murray," Gallagher says.

"That was the first time I became Murray."

"The first time?"

Ah! So much to tell, but I don't want to get ahead of myself.

Chapter Eleven

James had the idea that we would park ourselves outside of Sweeny's saloon. My brother tried to explain the political situation of New York City but it didn't make much sense to my young brain—though someday it would. James told me about the party that controlled Five Points—Tammany Hall. They were the Democrats, he said.

"They help immigrants—at least the ones who have come here with nothing."

"Like us?"

"Yeah, like us. And especially the Irish."

"Why?"

"That's a good question. You might say they're compassionate, but others might say they just want votes. I mean, they see the hundreds of thousands of people arriving—they know those people need help and that in return, those people will vote them into office, and keep them there."

"What's an office?"

It's remarkable how patient he was with me. "An elected position—there's all different ones. Mayor, alderman, sheriff."

"Can we vote?" I asked.

"No, Grice," he said. "We're kids."

"Then they won't help us, will they? Since we can't vote for them."

"I don't know. They have a lot of jobs and a lot of power. And I hear Sweeny's name a lot. So maybe he's rising in the ranks. And maybe important Tammany people hang out at his tavern."

Every day, we perched there outside the saloon, watching men go in—an occasional woman entered, but mostly men. When I peeked in the door, I saw clusters of little tables with two or three chairs around them and a long bar where the men stood, with Sweeny himself behind it. It didn't look like anything important was happening, just groups of men drinking and smoking cigars and cigarettes and pipes, their smoke hanging about the room, wafting slowly toward the one front window and open door. Sweeny had dark, wavy hair parted far on one side and swarthy eyebrows. The men came for a beer or whiskey and a smoke after a long day of work before they sauntered back to their cramped tenements. Sweeny was friendly to them but not gregarious; instead, he seemed to engage them in long conversations in his quiet, confident voice.

Sweeny would have been about in his early twenties, but looked older. It said something about him, explained James, that young and running a saloon. He seemed to command respect. Eventually, Sweeny would go to law school, become a lawyer, be elected district attorney, and then in 1866, city treasurer. No one, not even he, a child himself of Irish immigrants, could imagine that he would eventually become one of the most prominent Tammany politicians of all time, the brains of William Tweed's Ring. Because at this moment, he was simply wiping a grimy bar in Five Points with a dirty rag.

We greeted Sweeny in the morning and said good evening at night. We were tidy, polite, alert, and eager. We didn't roughhouse. James didn't curse or smoke. He let me bring my poetry books, and I sat and read, occasionally asking him for help on certain words. I buried my face in a book rather than eye the squalor around us: pigs walking the street, rooting in garbage; dirty children dressed in torn clothing; dilapidated buildings; sewage flowing through the streets. That my father had chosen to leave our pretty Govan in Scotland was still so strange to me. I did not yet see the beauty of New York City, did not see that this was a land of opportunity. Rather, I saw poverty and sickness all around; I watched men drink whiskey until they fell down because their lives were unbearable to them. I saw exhausted women haggling with food vendors, sweeping stoops that would not stay clean, hanging endless laundry. The questions loomed for us: How long would we have to live like this? Always? Was there any way out? If so, what was it?

One day when we said good morning to Sweeny he stopped and took a good look at us. I stood up straighter and, not sure why, I hid the book I was reading behind my back.

He considered us for what felt like a good minute. We'd been parked outside his tavern for a few weeks, but I felt this was the first time he was really seeing us.

"What are you reading?" he asked me.

"Robbie Burns, Sir."

"Poetry?"

"Yes, Sir."

"You Scottish?"

This time James answered. "Yes, Mr. Sweeny. We're from Govan."

"Clyde River?"

"Yes, Sir," said James. "Our father was a shipbuilder."

"And where's he now?"

"Dead, Sir. He and our mum. She died before we arrived to Canada and he on Grosse Isle."

He shook his head. It was a story too often heard in Five Points, one that would be echoed for years. "How you get here, then?"

Here I chimed in. "We walked most of the way, Sir, hundreds of miles. But sometimes we hitched a ride on a wagon, and we did take a train for the last bit."

Looking amused, he fished in his pocket and took out a half dime. "Go buy *The Herald* for me?"

I watched James's face light up. "Yes, Sir." He took the money and looked back at me as he walked away. "Come on!"

There was a newspaper stand on Mulberry, and we bought a paper for a penny and ran back to Sweeny. He was at the bar talking to a man in a derby hat. I stayed at the entrance as James went in and set the paper on the bar and the four pennies next to it and turned to leave and Sweeny looked up and called to James, "Keep the change." James turned around and Sweeny handed him the four coins.

"Thank you, Mr. Sweeny," James said. Sweeny went back to talking to the man so James walked back out to the front. He held his hand out to me and gave me a penny and pocketed the other three.

It wasn't enough to live on, of course—wouldn't even afford us one baked apple. But for James, it was a sign that the time we had invested had a chance of paying off.

And sure enough, the next day, Sweeny had us buy another newspaper.

The day after that he approached us with a piece of paper in his hand. "You know the Old Brewery?" he asked us.

Of course we knew it; the Old Brewery was at the corner of Cross and Orange, the heart of Five Points. It was a massive, decaying old building that had been converted into apartments, though "apartments" might be a stretch. We'd never been inside, but the alley on one side of the building was referred to as the Den of Thieves, while the one on the other side was Murderer's Alley. Rumors circulated about the place.

"I want you to go there and find a man named John O'Connor. Lives on the third or fourth floor, I think. Find him and give him this."

He handed James a folded piece of paper. "Wait for his answer and then come back and tell me what he says."

James took the paper and nodded his head solemnly. "Yes, Mr. Sweeny."

This time, James didn't have to call me—I was right there beside him.

We were on a job! And I'd finally get to see inside the dreaded Old Brewery!

Hundreds of people lived there. It was rumored that the windowless basement rooms were reserved for black men who had married white women, that this was the only place they could lodge together. It was also rumored that there were children born in its cellars who had never seen the light of day. Bodies of murdered boys and girls were supposedly buried in its walls. I didn't wholly believe these rumors, but the place was so strange, I admit those thoughts were going through my mind as we approached. What if we were murdered and buried there? No one would ever know…

Outside the building, James said, "You're going to wait here."

"No I'm not!" I said too loudly. I mean, I was terrified to go in, but I wasn't going to miss the opportunity to.

A group of disheveled men stood nearby and one of them gave me a hellacious stare. I had to tell myself not to stick my tongue out. I was on someone else's territory and had to keep cool. The truth was I was too curious not to go in and too scared, really, to be left alone outside of it.

"I'm going in with you, James," I said, my voice lower but firm.

My brother sighed. He approached the group of men, all four of them in dark, dirty suits, tattered hats on their heads. I kept my gaze low and focused on their grimy nails growing out the end of their thick, tough fingers, and their dark, worn shoes caked with mud and horse manure. I heard James ask about the man—about John O'Connor. None of them said anything and when I glanced up, one of them was shaking his head and another was shrugging. They weren't going to help us—and why should they?

Then one said, "You can check inside. A few O'Connors in there, I'm sure."

Another of the men chuckled and James thanked them. I followed him to the entryway. It was mid-morning and the sun was high and warming us, but standing at the entrance of that building was like standing at the gates of hell, except hell, with its fire and brimstone, must have more light. We were looking into the heart of darkness. James went first. Immediately we were enveloped in almost a total blackness, feeling our way into a hall that then split in two. I blindly clutched James's shirt in front of me and followed him. Stairs went down, another set up. An open doorway coughed out smoky air; glancing inside we saw an oil lamp casting its greasy light onto several lumps on the floor covered in dirty burlap. I heard shouting from behind one cracked door. I was relieved when James took the stairs up instead of down and then another staircase, and then another. We must've been up on the fourth or fifth floor; I wasn't sure anymore. The place was a maze and without windows, I felt turned around, lost. My heart thumped in my chest.

Piles of old clothes and trash and empty bottles lined the tight hall, and I was making an effort not to tread on anything but also to keep up with James. Then I stepped on what looked like an old coat and when I heard a moan come from it, I let out a bloodcurdling scream. Several doors slammed when I did, but from an open one, a man' face appeared, looking at us with irritation.

"What's that?" he said.

"Sorry, Sir, my brother is a bit jumpy," said James. "We're looking for our uncle, John O'Connor. Mother sent us to find him and deliver a message."

He looked at us with skepticism but then said, "One floor down," and closed his door.

We descended one floor and James knocked gently on doors to no avail, but then, behind one that was slightly ajar, we saw a group of men sitting around a small table playing cards. In the shadow of a corner, I thought I saw two children lying motionless on the floor. The men were smoking and their cigarette smoke hung like a dense, unmoving cloud just above their heads.

"John O'Connor?" James said in a friendly but firm voice. All the men looked at us and one of them, somehow thinner and dirtier than the rest, said, "I'm him."

"Message for you, Sir."

He got up from the flimsy stool and staggered over to us. James handed him the folded piece of paper and he opened it and handed it back to us.

"What's it say?" he asked in a low voice.

Whether it was too dark for him to read it or whether he was too drunk or illiterate, I didn't know. James, who had read the note once he was out of Sweeny's sight, now glanced at me uneasily.

"Well?" said John O'Connor. He was sneering and I decided I didn't like this man. I wanted to feel sympathetic for his condition, but he had a look in his eye that made that near impossible. In Five Points, I had seen much poverty void of depravity, but here I saw a lethal combination.

"You owe six dollars and fifty cents by Friday," recited James from memory. He was looking at the note, but even I saw that it was too dark to read. "Or else," he added reluctantly, not wanting to awaken John O'Connor's wrath.

But rather than anger, the man hung his head for a moment, as if hearing a life sentence. Or a death sentence.

"You tell Sweeny this is all I have," he said, and fished a coin out of his pocket and handed it to James. "Man gives me a job and then fires me for taking a little whiskey home? When he's got a full cellar and no idea what a shit situation I got here?" He was raising his voice and the men in the room had stopped talking and were all staring at us. "Sends you two to deliver his message?" He reached out and grabbed my shirt and pulled me to him, my face right in his. "You two sprats?"

James punched him in the face. It happened so fast I fell back into the dark hall when John O'Connor let go of my shirt. As he crumpled to the ground, I saw his friends all scrambling to their feet inside the room. James yanked the door closed. Then he threw me forward.

"Run!" he yelled.

I heard the men behind us spilling into the darkened hallway. I ran and tried to remember where to turn to get to the stairwell but James pushed me into it, holding onto the back of my neck to keep pace with him, two stairs at a time, the men close on our heels. Another stairwell and then I saw the light harkening at the end of the first floor and dashed for it with all my might. I burst out into sunshine with James right behind me. He took my hand and pulled me up Cross Street toward Orange. We looked back and saw three of the men, including John O'Connor, emerge from their massive hovel. John O'Connor shook his fists at us but he and his cronies didn't pursue. The advantage of youth and sobriety had helped us escape.

I was so glad to be out of there and away from danger. And I was so glad we did it! We couldn't stop telling each other our version of what we had seen.

When we told Sweeny what had happened he threw his head back and laughed. I had expected him to be angry that we had not collected the full amount, not amused. He let us keep the dollar "for a job well done"—said we had earned it.

A dollar! We felt rich and splurged on not one baked apple, but two.

Chapter Twelve

I was shorter, of course, than James, and had more girth, while he was a full-grown, though thin man, with strong, sculpted muscles. How strange that two children born of the same mom and dad could be so physically different. He was so handsome too, ironically prettier than me. His high, carved cheekbones gave his face an elegance and he had full, sensual lips. I was always a bit pudgy, though I was in my twelfth year and had started to have growth spurts that seemed to increase my height an inch in a day, I thinned out a bit. I had continued my subterfuge for years: everyone thought I was a boy named Murray. Indeed, Mary had ceased to exist. Or so I thought.

It seemed to happen suddenly: to my dismay, small islands surfaced on the sea of my torso, with areola of pink sand around the pointy peaks. Their growth caused an ache both mental and physical. I asked Emma for some silk gauze, and she happily gave it to me, not knowing what I would use it for. Thus, I began wrapping my breasts in an attempt to both flatten and hide them.

I grew lazy, wanting to sleep in most mornings while James, who was nearing twenty, began working longer and longer days alone. He had made a number of political acquaintances—mostly Tammany men—and now helped with elections and still ran messages and did all kinds of errands. He saved our money with the goal of getting us out of Five Points.

The neighborhood had been flooded by thousands more immigrants from Ireland as the famine continued. It was horrifying to see the walking skeletons emerge from their ships. So many starving and sick arrived, with most taken to a hospital that had been constructed precisely for them. Better to keep the very sick ones from mixing with the populace was the thought. There was tension, not just between the immigrants and the native New Yorkers, but between the older immigrants—ones who had arrived when we did or before—and the ones arriving currently. The tenements grew even more crowded. Gangs formed and fought. Riots broke out.

James went all about town, had learned the island like the back of his hand, could navigate the entire city without fear or doubt, knew which neighborhoods were German, which were Jewish, knew the black dance halls, knew the shipyards, knew where the wealthy congregated. A little more money had allowed us to eat well and explore and even enjoy the city. We went to minstrel shows, and almost every week, James took me to the Barnum American Museum to see exhibits. We bought machine-made clothes and decent shoes and had good coats for the winter.

Emma, meanwhile, was still working as a seamstress, and in the years I had known her, her wages had hardly improved. James, on the other hand, made two or three times Emma's daily pay with just a few hours of work. Hence I witnessed firsthand the differences in opportunities for men and women. Her roommate Francis had moved on, taking a job as a domestic, which was one way women could improve their lot, but it meant living with a family as cook or nanny or housekeeper, or some combination thereof. Liz was still living with Emma, and still as beautiful as ever. She had quit the sewing factory and now worked at Macy's, which was then still a dry goods store. She still liked to play cards with James and sometimes they went dancing in the evenings and I would sleep on Emma's couch until they got home.

Recently a new girl had moved in with them, Harriet, a young Protestant who worked at the Reverend Pease's mission, which was right across the street from the Old Brewery and whose goal it was to save the wayward souls of Five Points. When we met Harriet one Sunday, the first thing she asked James was where he and his little brother went to church. When he told her we didn't, disappointment was written all over her face, as if by not attending church, we had assured her that we were not capable of being good, moral people.

Whereas Emma was like a sister to me and my best friend in the world besides James, Harriet set out from the get-go to be our educator, our great redeemer. She made us bow our heads before supper and say a prayer she taught us: "Oh Lord, we thank you for the gifts of your bounty which we enjoy at this table. As you have provided for us in the past, so may you sustain us throughout our lives. While we enjoy your gifts, may we never forget the needy and those in want." When I tried to just mumble the words, she made us start over and say the prayer loud and clear so the Lord could hear our gratitude.

One fateful day, we had prayed and had lunch and afterward Liz and James were going to play cards and Emma and I were going to lounge on the couch and talk and nap like we usually did, when Harriet came over with a box and sat in the chair next to the couch and called

Liz and James over and had them bring their chairs from the table. They reluctantly did, though Liz was visibly irked to have her weekly poker game interrupted by her new roommate.

Harriet waited until everyone was seated and then beaming, said, "I have a special gift for each one of you."

She reached into the box and pulled out a black book and handed it to me. It was a Holy Bible. There was one for each of us, and after she had handed them all out, she said, "I thought we could start at the beginning and take turns reading."

When no one responded, she said, "I'm sorry to presume. You do all know how to read, don't you?"

Emma took an audible breath. Her smile was a tight one and she seemed to choose her words carefully. "Harriet, I'm sure you're doing some wonderful work at the mission. But here in our apartment, we like to relax on Sunday and let the day unfold. I've already been to mass today, and now I would like to catch up with Murray and I think Liz and James would like to play cards."

"But Liz and James and Murray—you didn't go to church today, did you?" She offered a thin smile with her reprimand. "And is there any better time to read the bible and reflect on Jesus than Sunday? We're all busy throughout the week; I know I am. Sunday is a perfect time to worship. We don't have to spend all afternoon. But I thought you'd appreciate the chance to do something really good and worthy together."

My stomach had been aching since that morning, which didn't stop me from eating heartily at lunch, but now I shifted with discomfort. A little moan escaped me and I brought my hand to my belly and rubbed.

"Are you all right?" asked Emma. She felt my head.

"I think so," I said, and shifted again on the couch. I felt like I had wet my pants. "Excuse me, I think I need to use the outhouse."

When I stood and walked from the couch, Emma gasped and exclaimed, "Murray, you're—"

When I turned back to look at her, she had covered her mouth with her hand. The late afternoon light was coming in the window and shining on the couch. There was a dark stain of blood where I had been sitting.

"Well, I'll be honey-fuggled," said Harriet.

I ran from their apartment and down to the outhouses, threw the door of one open and slammed it shut. My stomach was in knots, both nerves and something else: it felt as if someone were gripping the innards of my lower belly, squeezing and twisting, a pain that almost made me moan. I reached down into my pants and felt the wetness. When I brought up my hand, I saw through the light coming through the wood slats of the outhouses, that my fingers were slathered with a muddy red substance I understood to be blood, though it wasn't as bright. I wondered if my insides were coming out—something in me was obviously broken. I felt disgusting and terrified. I heard a knock on the outhouse door.

"Murray? It's me, Emma."

"Go away."

"Murray, honey, let me in."

I wiped my hand on my pants and opened the door. She came into the tiny outhouse and shut the door. The stench was horrible as the night soil hadn't been removed for several days.

No matter—she said, "Oh, Murray," and hugged me. I put my arms around her and held her. I started to sob.

"What's happening to me?"

"Murray, you're going to be all right. It's your menses—it starts around this age."

"When will it stop?"

"It's going to last a few days. But it's going to happen every month."

"Every month!" At this I cried harder.

"Come with me, Murray. Let's go to your apartment. I can show you what you need to do."

She led me out of there and over to James and my place. She had a bag with her and once we were inside and the door locked, she removed several clean rags and pins.

"We're going to pin one of these rags onto your underwear, Murray. The rag will absorb the blood. I can show you how to do it."

I shook my head. I was so ashamed—ashamed at the mess, ashamed I'd been found out.

"Don't be embarrassed, Murray. It's just me. I'll show you on my underwear if you prefer."

I nodded and to my shock she pulled down up her dress and took off her underwear. Then she took one of the rags, folded it until it was a tidy rectangle, and pinned it to her underwear.

"When you put it on, it will soak in the blood. But you have to pay attention—the rag can become saturated quickly depending on how heavy the flow is. You can wash and dry the rags and reuse them," she said. She unpinned the rag from her underwear and pulled them back up. "Do you want me to help you?"

I nodded meekly. It was simply unfathomable to me that this would happen every month and I thought I would rather die. I pulled my pants down. They, along with my underwear, were wet as though I had peed myself and stained with dark red splotches.

"Give me your clothes," she said. "You want to wash them immediately or they'll be stained for good." The fact that she took my soiled clothing without batting an eye just astounded me. She was so good—so…loving. I took a fresh pair of underwear from my pile and my only other pair of pants and folded the rag and pinned it to my underwear as she had shown me and then put them on.

"Are you in pain—does your belly ache?"

"Yes. It's awful."

"I thought you might. Here—I brought this laudanum." She poured out a teaspoon of it and put it in my mouth. I cringed—the liquid was bitter and tasted rather awful, but the pain was getting worse and I would have tried anything to assuage it.

"Come, lie down, Murray."

She led me to the sleeping closet I shared with James. I lay down, and she covered me with a blanket. She sat down beside me and began to pet my hair.

"Does this happen to boys?" I had my eyes closed, could feel my belly relax a bit, no longer clenching as it was.

"No, just girls."

"That's rotten. Will it ever stop?"

"Only if you're pregnant—or once you're old."

We were quiet for a few moments, just Emma petting my hair. I took her hand and held it and kissed it. "Thank you, Emma. I'm so—I'm so grateful to you. And I'm so sorry. Will you forgive me?"

"I already have," she said and hugged me.

I fell asleep with her arm around me.

Chapter Thirteen

Everything changed.

I became Mary again.

And somehow, I became Harriet's project, a sinner to reform. Her mother was a founding member of the New-York Ladies' Home Missionary Society of the Methodist Episcopal Church American Female Moral Reform Society, so Harriet knew what she was doing.

First and foremost: my clothes. Harriet encouraged me to wear dresses to demonstrate my commitment to forgoing my ruffian ways. Second: religious training. I was to read the Bible and discuss it with her. She imagined a full conversion to Methodism for me eventually, but reading the Bible was a start. Third: education. James had been schooling me in reading and arithmetic—which basically amounted to me reading poetry aloud to him and him helping me with the words I couldn't pronounce or didn't know the meaning of, as well as learning math and accounting with the money we earned and saved. But Harriet thought I should have real schooling, in a classroom with a teacher and other pupils. And since she was working so closely with Reverend Pease, she knew she could turn to him for help.

Pease initially worked with the Ladies' Home Missionary Society but had since branched off on his own. His mission was to provide both education *and* work training, which would be the fourth element of my reformation: work. But not the kind I had been doing with James, not being an errand boy for saloon owners and Tammany men. No, for Harriet and the Reverend Pease, I would do work that was suited for women: sewing.

On the first day of my reformation, Harriet asked me to come to her apartment so she could help dress me and take me to meet Reverend Pease. I had hot chocolate and toast with James that morning as we did most mornings, but instead of leaving our place with him and venturing out into the city, we siblings said goodbye and parted ways. James was rather reticent about what had happened. Harriet didn't blame him per se for dressing me as a boy—she commended his dedication to me, especially since we had been on our own for so many years. But neither did she want him to interfere with her efforts to save me.

Liz, it seemed, was delighted with our masquerade and so impressed that we'd pulled it off for so long. I had been nervous about going back to their apartment, afraid of what she would think.

"It makes me love you two even more!" she exclaimed. And then she said in a low, sly voice to my brother, "Does that mean I'm going to find out you're actually a girl?"

"I'd be happy to prove my maleness to you," he said with a wink. She punched him in the arm.

They were always flirting and sometimes went dancing together, and I sometimes dreamed of the two of them getting married, a thought that both enchanted me and turned me green with jealousy. I was starting to understand the complexity of emotions, mostly because I now felt confused about everything.

First my body mutinied, and then my heart and mind followed. I didn't know what I was supposed to do. Emma was accepting and loving; Liz was amused, even titillated. Harriet, however, was motivated. But why did I acquiesce to her? In some ways, it seemed inevitable. My body had revealed that I was a girl, and, even though it's hogwash, I sometimes wondered if the painful cramping I felt during that first monthly time weren't punishment for rejecting girlhood, especially after I learned that not all girls suffer them.

Harriet was so convinced that she was setting me on the right path that it was difficult to argue against. And maybe I liked the attention; after all, in a sense Harriet was mothering me. It made me feel important, though I was still torn.

James said little. I could tell he was not a fan of Harriet's. But he had also expressed to me that he wanted to volunteer on a fire squad. All of the firemen were volunteers; it was a way to make a name for yourself. He wouldn't be able to do that with a 12-year-old "brother" tagging along everywhere he went. There was part of him that must have felt guilty for dressing me as a boy, even though I had almost always dressed in his old clothes in Scotland. But this was not only donning boys' clothes; it was not only a name-change. It was an attempt at a full denial of girlhood and all that might entail. After the close call in the basement where we first lodged, it was clear I wasn't safe as a girl orphan. And so perhaps he gave me over to Harriet because he knew that although Harriet was overbearing and sanctimonious, she was good, she was caring, and she would keep me safe—safer, perhaps, than he could keep me. On the streets, we'd occasionally be confronted by a pack of boys who would try to take our money or just bully us. James had had to teach me to fight and I was a good fighter! But he didn't feel right about it.

In fact, when I went to see Harriet that morning, I still had the yellowish remnant of that shiner from a fight we'd had with three boys who wanted to take our money. I'd socked one of them fast when he wasn't expecting it, as I'd seen James punch John O'Connor in the Old Brewery—the benefit of surprise. But one of the other boys punched me back before James could stop him. In the end, they took off from us without acquiring even a half-dime.

So when Harriet opened the apartment and said, "Come in, dear," she was smiling so sweetly, I wanted to run away and go catch up with James.

Harriet sat on the couch and gestured for me to sit too. I plopped down as I always had. Harriet, sitting erect on the edge of the couch with her hands folded deliberately in her lap, frowned. Then she smoothed her long, plain, cream-colored dress, straightened an already perfect lace bonnet. Her cheeks were a natural pink; she wore no paint and was really quite plain, I observed. That felt like another unfortunate phenomenon menstruation had triggered: I now found myself looking closely at women, noticing their physical details and how they carried themselves, found myself comparing and making judgments. If I was going to be a girl, what kind of girl was I going to be? Which was odd that I would even have to ask myself that, because masquerading as a boy did not require acting at all, but rather came completely naturally to me.

"Can you sit up taller?"

I pulled myself up from my slouching position against the back of the couch.

"Now...Murray isn't your real name, is it?"

I shook her head. "No, but I like it."

Harriet's smile was a bit forced. "What is your real name—your birth name, the name your parents gave you?"

I hesitated, then finally answered. "Mary."

"That's a beautiful name," Harriet said earnestly. She reached over to the chair next to the couch. On it was a dress, which she unfolded. It was also cream in color, and long. It had a few grease stains on the front. "I picked this out for you from the House of Industry—Reverend Pease's mission. He's expecting us this morning. I told him all about you. He's very excited to meet you."

I looked at the dress and said nothing.

"Do you want to change in the bedroom? Emma and Liz are gone off to work already."

I stood up. Should I walk to the door and leave and go find James—or change?

I took a deep breath and held my hand out for the dress. Then I went into the bedroom, pulled off my boots and trousers and shirt and stood there, my underwear bulging a bit with the pinned-on cloth. I would have to change it in a few hours. I looked down at myself. My breasts were small but a bit swollen. I was a girl. Even if I didn't want to be, I was. There was no denying it. Not anymore.

When I emerged from the bedroom wearing the dress, Harriet clapped her hands as if I'd achieved something magnificent.

I felt like a fool. I was short and stout—and my belly was swollen from my menses. The stupid dress pulled in the middle making me look even worse. I felt right in my brother's brogues and in his pants, felt tough and strong. But in this dress, I felt dopey and dumb.

Harriet stood and touched the cotton fabric, put her hands on my waist and said, "We can take that out a little, you know or find a dress with a little more give, but I think it's fine for today, don't you?"

I nodded, not trusting my voice.

Chapter Fourteen

We walked down Orange to Cross Street, me in a dress for the first time in years, though I was still wearing boots since Harriet hadn't known my shoe size—she assured me we'd find a more appropriate pair at the House of Industry, and I did not tell her that I didn't want to give up my boots. Harriet had brushed my short hair, parted it to one side and secured it with barrettes, which I immediately forgot were there, so that when I scratched my head, I inadvertently messed up Harriet's efforts to beautify me.

I was shuffling my feet, stalling. "Should we stop for a baked apple on the way?" I asked.

Harriet looked at me with sudden understanding. "Sure," she said.

We found a vender and bought two. I insisted on paying, since Harriet had brought me the dress and all. We sat on a bench in Paradise Park with the baked apples. I could see the Old Brewery from where we sat.

"Reverend Pease initially worked with the Ladies' Home Missionary Society, of which my mother is a member," said Harriet. I bit into my apple. "But there was a bit of a squabble between them, so Reverend Pease turned his attention to a different charity—the Industrial House for the Friendless, the Inebriate, and the Outcast." My eyebrows shot up and Harriet laughed. "Yes, I know—quite a mouthful. That's why he eventually renamed it the Five Points House of Industry."

"What was the squabble about?"

Harriet took a delicate bite out of her own apple and chewed thoroughly and swallowed before she spoke again. "The Ladies' Society claims to want to help the poor and destitute, and they do…but their main interest lies in converting Catholics to Methodists—and they refuse to help those who won't convert. Bible first, then aid, is their way.

"The Ladies' Society was doing charity, but it came with a price," I assessed.

She nodded. "Reverend Pease, however, saw that the people needed bread even more than religion, so he focused on feeding them—started a soup kitchen so that anyone who's hungry could get a hot meal. They didn't like that—his willingness, even eagerness, to help them if they wouldn't convert. But he didn't stop there—he knew the problem was bigger than just hungry mouths. He was determined to get to the root of that poverty. So he started a school, but then he discovered that most of his students were filthy and ill-clad. So he installed bathtubs so they could bathe, and got clothing and shoe donations so that they'd have proper attire. Many of them came to us in rags."

"Where did he get it all? Is he rich?"

Harriet smiled wistfully. "No, he's not rich. But he's got boundless energy and he's very effective at getting people to care about his cause. Do you know there are hundreds of well-to-do children all over this country who donate their old shoes to the children of the House of Industry?"

I shook my head. It did seem impressive. I could see, too, that Pease had gotten Harriet to care about his cause.

"So he fed them and got them clean and clothed and started to educate them. But he wanted to provide a means for people to support themselves, especially women. Many of them have no means to care for themselves or their children. He arranged it so that when the children attend school, the women learn to sew. He helped create an industry from it; the women sew and he sells the clothes and pays them. The women who stick to it now earn $2, sometimes $2.50 a week!"

At this I scoffed. "But that's nothing." That was the amount James and I usually earned in a day—*each.*

"It's *something,*" she said defensively. "These women are destitute, after all. At least they are learning a skill with which they can support themselves."

I couldn't imagine trying to support myself—let alone myself and my children—with that little. But I didn't want to be critical. I could see she put the Reverend on a pedestal. "When did you meet him?" I asked to divert the subject.

"I was there at the meeting he attended with the Ladies' Society—the meeting where he parted ways from them. When he said he wasn't concerned about proselytizing and that in fact he was going to move to Five Points to live among those he wanted to help, well, they were clearly affronted. They called him a socialist, an infidel. But I saw how good he was, I knew I wanted to work with him. So I moved here. My mother—she was one of the founders of the Ladies' Society—well, you can imagine: she was not happy about it."

Suddenly it dawned on me. Harriet had money—she came from a well-off family—and she was living in Five Points *by choice.* I couldn't imagine choosing to live there, especially having seen some of the nicer areas of the city.

"Getting out of Five Points is what James and I have been working toward—and you moved here."

"Well, we've got to improve the living conditions here or improve people's lives so that they can get out. That's Reverend Pease's mission." She stood up. "Are you ready to meet him?"

I nodded but then pointed to Harriet's half-eaten apple. "Are you going to finish that?"

Harriet pursed her lips with a hint of disapproval but handed it to me. I finished it in two quick bites.

We approached the House of Industry, a large building just off Little Water Street. It was smaller than the Old Brewery, for sure. Inside was a spacious classroom filled with mismatched chairs and a large chalkboard stood at the front on casters. Shelves lined one wall with a set of matching books I assumed to be Bibles. A window let in quite a bit of light. It wasn't a cheerless room, but, as it was Saturday, it was void of students. Down a hall was the kitchen where several women were working—kneading bread, chopping vegetables, washing dishes. Harriet greeted them and they dutifully responded. Beyond the kitchen was an enormous dining area, just rows of long tables and benches that someone must have built for the place; they were the perfect length and filled the room from front to back.

"We sometimes feed two- to three-hundred people in here at a time," Harriet explained.

The first room on the second floor was a large industrial space filled with bags of clothes and tables with sewing paraphernalia. Harriet said that the women would arrive within the hour and work the whole day and into the evening. The other rooms on the second floor were filled with donated goods. The third floor, which we didn't tour, had eight apartments that could house up to six women each.

At the end of the second floor sat Pease's office. The door was ajar, but Harriet gently knocked.

"Come in," a man's voice invited.

He was sitting at a desk covered with papers and books, a pen in his hand, and dressed in a dark-brown jacket, white shirt and red bow tie. He looked busy but waved us in.

"Reverend, this is Mary, the young lady I told you about."

He peered at me not unkindly and tilted his head. "Welcome to the House of Industry, Mary. I'm sure Harriet will get you oriented and let you know about all the opportunities we offer here. Have you had any schooling?"

"I like to read, Sir, and am good with accounting."

"And you have an older brother?"

"Yes, Sir."

"But your parents are not living?"

"No, Sir. They died on the route over. My brother raised me."

"As a boy." This was a statement, not a question. He did not hide the disapproval in his voice.

"He was...he was concerned for my safety, Sir."

"Did he have reason to be?"

Harriet was peering at me intently. I had not told her about the incident in the basement. But my reticence was all the answer the reverend needed. He had been living in Five Points then for a couple years at least and no doubt understood the risks for young girls left unattended.

He spoke his next words with genuine warmth. "Well, Mary, we are so pleased to have you. I'm sure you're going to be a benefit to us here."

"Thank you, Reverend. I'm happy to be here and eager to help."

That was the Reverend's secret of his success: he let you know you had behaved badly but that you were forgiven. He made you believe that you had something to contribute, that he was there to help you better yourself.

Something strange happened to me in his office. In that moment, under Reverend Pease's gaze, I wanted to be a child again. I felt tears coming to my eyes. I suddenly felt I had grown up too fast. I thought of my mother, of her true goodness, thought of my father and how he had let us down. I knew right then and there that I wanted to be the perfect pupil, wanted to prove to this decent, hard-working man that I could be respectable and work hard too.

I was ready to be a good girl.

This became my routine: school from 8 A.M. to noon; lunch from noon to one, which I helped set up and clear; sewing work after lunch until 8 P.M., and sometimes later. Sitting so long did not suit me. With James, we might station ourselves outside an office or tavern awaiting instruction, but once we were given an errand, we were off and running. We learned to navigate the city, ate oysters on the street, went down to the harbor to watch the boats, walked bustling Broadway just to people watch, discovered back alleys, rode omnibuses. The island was not so large but it was constantly changing: new construction, new roads, everything pushing north. The Sixth Ward was our home, but we were becoming familiar with other wards too. But when I started with Harriet and Rev. Pease, that all stopped and my world narrowed drastically, as I went from our apartment to Pease's House of Industry and from there, home, where I collapsed in bed only to start it over again the next day. Days were long; time crept by.

School wasn't terrible. My teacher, Miss Clemens, was a tall, brown-haired woman of nineteen, and Protestant, of course. I was part of the group who already knew how to read, so Miss Clemens taught us to diagram sentences for the first hour, then geography for an hour, then math, followed by history. Miss Clemens liked poetry too, though she was more familiar with American poets. She introduced me to the work of Edgar Allen Poe—darkly wonderful. "Annabel Lee" became a favorite; I memorized it and recited it to myself while I worked. Sometimes I read "The Raven" aloud to the other women while we sewed. Then someone complained to Rev. Pease that I was telling frightening and seemingly blasphemous tales. He was kind but firm and provided us a Bible in the workroom to read from instead, which, needless to say, wasn't nearly as riveting as Poe.

The Reverend ate lunch with us and I sat near him when I could. He was tall and slim, his clothes tidy and clean and rather formal but not pretentious. His clean-shaven face had a firmness about it, a resolve.

"When did you arrive in Five Points, Mary?" he asked me one day. We were eating soup with fresh bread, the meal we ate almost every day at lunch. Today there was butter, a real treat.

"Late summer of '46."

"How did it strike you?"

"It was chaos to me, Reverend. Our parents were dead—my brother and I walked down from Canada except for the last part. My brother was just 14. We'd come to America because my father was a ship-builder in Scotland—in Govan on the Clyde—but the work was unsteady."

"What religion did you practice in Scotland?" he asked.

"I was raised in the Kirk, Reverend."

"So I don't have to trouble over your conversion—you're already a Protestant." I nodded and he smiled. I didn't mention that my mother had focused more on poetry than the Bible, or that after her death, I had stopped believing in a benevolent, trustworthy god. Any god, really.

"Do you know, when I first got here in spring of 1850, I couldn't even find a room to preach in that wasn't a grog-shop or a brothel. Finally we did find a groggery and cleaned it out and many people came—children and adults alike. They were a ragged bunch, true pariahs. Some of them were drunk and quarrelsome, some eager for help, but all of them were dirty. I spoke to them as plainly as I could. I reminded them of their innocence, implored them to remember days of virtue and happiness, which I imagined they had known at some point in their lives. I asked them to repent and to accept their Savior. And do you know how it went?"

I shook my head.

"It was a total failure."

"Why?"

He lowered his voice. "The girls listened—indeed, it was those very daughters of shame who broke down and wept openly. And yet what did they do?" I raised my eyebrows in question. "They returned to their wretched homes, drank from the intoxicating cup to drive all pious thoughts from their minds, and continued with their reckless sensuality." His face wasn't bitter as he said this but appeared pained. "Every day of the week and especially on the Sabbath, I entreated them to give up their wretchedness—to no avail." He raised a finger. "Then it dawned on me: they had no escape from their present lives save through the portal of the grave; no homes but their vile dens; no honest work and no one to employ them to do it. For many of them it was accept the wages of sin or starve and watch their children starve. And this after what they suffered in Ireland! That's when I decided to make it my mission to find them an honest means of making a living."

I had finished all my soup and bread and looked at the roll the reverend still hadn't eaten. He noticed and passed it to me. I blushed but took it.

"What I realized immediately is that most people don't want charity—most people genuinely want a means to raise themselves out of poverty. So I found a manufacturer in the city who provided cloth and agreed to stand as security for the materials, and then I announced all week and on the Sabbath that anyone looking to earn an honest living should come to the Chapel at seven in the morning. When I arrived, thirty-five women were there for work. My rules were few: they must arrive to work sober and must make a pledge of total abstinence; anyone lapsing into drunkenness or vice would be discharged. They should attend regularly at some place of worship on Sunday. It was that last part—that 'some place'—that rattled the Ladies' Society. I didn't care where the women worshipped so long as they visited a house of the Lord."

I nodded my head to show my support.

"Yet, after a long day of work, the women would return to their miserable lodgings. And just imagine—many of them were sober for the first time. Before, they'd tolerated their decrepit homes by getting drunk, even when drink itself kept them from bettering their living conditions. It had been a terrible cycle, and now they could see it breaking. But they had to get out of those polluted living quarters. And so, I decided we would also provide lodging. We acquired this house and turned the third floor into apartments for the women, and next year, we're going to add three more houses. This, in fact," he gestured around, "was originally a house of ill-repute if you can believe that. We got the judges and the police to help us take it over, and then—this is the part I really loved—almost all the women gave up their vile professions and stayed on to work and live with us, which just shows you what can happen when you offer people better options. Here they pay $1.25 a week for room and board. We pay them for their labor above this sum and offer them decent clothing too."

I looked around the room trying to imagine the place as a brothel. I peered at the young women, some sitting at their table, some clearing plates, all dressed in long, plain dresses, and tried to imagine which of them had led lives as prostitutes. All of them had been made pure again through hard work and worship. At least that was the idea.

"How do you like the work?" Pease asked.

"The sewing?" I hesitated, wondering how honest to be. He nodded encouragingly, but I could also see the hope in his face, that he had to believe he was transforming lives for the better. "I feel restless sometimes, but it's good work. The women are all very nice."

Pease smiled. "When you feel restless, Mary, just remember that your soul is doing the hard work of cleansing itself. Discipline is its own reward. It might be difficult for you to see how important the job is, how important it is that you are part of our House of Industry. But it is a righteous path. Unlike the one you were on." That firm face again, that resolve. I nodded and thanked him as he rose from the table.

I missed James, missed roaming the streets, getting to know the city and the variety of people in it. But I told myself that Reverend Pease was right, that this was my place now. As he walked away, I looked down at the table and saw that he had left his bowl for me to take to the kitchen, so I did.

As I got to know Reverend Pease, I couldn't help but compare him to my father—or note the contrast. Instead of having moods that were up and down like my father, Pease was one of the most tenacious and steadfast people I'd ever met. He worked tirelessly but steadily. He was agreeable yet firm in his convictions and clear with his expectations—and as long as you met those, you were in good standing with him; you always knew where you stood with him. I appreciated that.

I had not thought of my father for a while. I'd feel a slow boiling anger rise up within me whenever I did, but I had to admit—the Christian preaching I was exposed to at the House of Industry on Sundays caused a shift in how my mind responded to those emotions. I started thinking of my dad with pity—and pity slowly morphed into forgiveness. Even my body responded: my heart, which would usually pound faster when I thought of my dad, could settle into a calm and regular rhythm now. My vision cleared along with my mind, and I began sewing with deft focus and without mistakes. I wouldn't go so far as to say that God had made his way into my heart or that I had accepted Jesus as my Lord and Savior, but something quieter was happening. I was maturing, becoming a young woman. I was able to better understand what had happened to my dad and hence to James and me. It was hard to make sense of, but I felt like I was beginning to accept the hardship I'd been through and even felt gratitude for all he'd done for us. And all this was happening in large part because of the work and stability and religious training I was getting from Reverend Pease and the House of Industry.

That was fine and good, feeling grown up and mature and forgiving and on the right path—as long as I didn't think of my mother. That was one thing I still hadn't managed to pull off: I couldn't sew and cry at the same time.

Now that I was a girl, I gave up my suspenders and button-up shirts; my ratty grey wool sweater that I'd put on every morning and my knickers and derby cap—they all went. Harriet donated them to the mission and replaced them with dresses, with long skirts, with shoes whose heels were small but significant enough that I had to learn to walk all over again. We worked on my posture, on my sitting, on my eating. Girls behaved differently than boys, she explained, and I must be trained. When I asked her why that was, she couldn't answer.

"Just because!" she said. "It's uncomely for a girl to behave as you do. For instance, you use the language of the street."

"What's wrong with that? It's how people talk."

"Well, you should not use vulgar or unladylike language," preached Harriet.

"Like what?" I asked feigning innocence, wanting to hear her speak the words.

"Like the words you use for police —or the word you use for…ladies of the night."

"I'm sure I don't know what you're talking about," I replied.

"They're not pigs or booley-dogs, Mary. They are police officers," she said with strained patience. "And don't substitute molls for women."

"But moll is a certain kind of woman, so it's actually more specific. I mean, the poet does not say 'tree' but 'evergreen' or 'birch.'"

"You're not a poet, Mary. You're a young woman."

"Maybe I aspire to be a poet."

"Then make verse that is more spiritually uplifting—and less degenerate."

She paid attention to everything I said, and everything had to be just so, good and proper. She herself spoke with care, choosing her words slowly and articulating each one. Every sentence she uttered was a model of proper vocabulary and syntax.

But Harriet was good to me, had my best interest at heart, I knew. I also knew that Harriet was happy to get me away from James, away from a life on the streets, away from a life of inevitable drink and tobacco and gambling and fighting—that was what she was saving me from.

Harriet even went so far as to buy me a corset. One dollar and twenty-five cents she spent on it. Went to a shop on Broadway to get it! The ad said it contained "120 bones!" Why *bones?* I wondered. And *whose* bones? I was thick in the middle and the corset was supposed to help give me an hour-glass figure. It poked me and squeezed my lungs. I could hardly bend to sit when I wore it. It made me feel ridiculous.

"It will help you with your posture," she told me, and she was right: it provided substantial discomfort whenever I slouched or relaxed or even breathed too deeply.

Emma's caring attitude didn't change toward me. If anything, she was even more attentive to me. I don't think it was because she now knew I was a girl. I think she knew I would have preferred to have to not become one again. We still napped on the couch together after lunch on school days, with her petting my head until I fell asleep. She invited me to sew in the evening when James went out without me—or rather she would sew and I would read her the newspaper or poetry. Harriet wanted me to read the Bible, but I got enough of that at the mission.

And Liz, now that I turned out to be a girl, saw it as her duty to give me a different education.

"Something you need to know and remember, Murray," she said. She continued to call me Murray, which I loved; also, she knew that it irritated Harriet. "Every cull wants to kiss you or more. The sooner you realize this, the better. And I mean every single one. Even that Reverend you're so taken with."

"Liz! Don't say that."

"I mean it, Murray. If a bloke could get away with it without ruining his reputation or marriage he would—he would if he could. Your job is to be smart about it. And I don't mean be a prude your whole life, but don't trust anyone. Don't fall for some moose face just 'cause he's rich—you'll be miserable and trapped too. Don't fall for the tangle-footed fool who spends all his time at the tavern. Don't tease too much or he'll think he deserves more than he does. Don't take with a married man unless you want to spend your whole life a convenient and never a wife yourself. Give it up too much, you'll be nothing more than a quean and a punk."

I knit my brows in confusion.

"A harlot!" Liz clarified and then continued her lesson.

"If you love him, make him wait. If he's a handsome rabbit, ignore the good looks and just dance, but don't dance a jig if you know what I mean. 'Less you want to end up with a broken leg."

"Broken leg?"

Liz laughed. "A baby but no husband." She narrowed her eyes. "You know how they're made, don't you?"

I shook my head.

Liz then told me in the roughest, clearest terms, not sugar-coating any of it. For so long I had heard sex referred to with so much metaphor or slang that I didn't have a clear picture. By the time Liz was done, I did.

I felt my innards recoil. Was that what the man who snuck down into the basement came to do? What he wanted to sell me into?

I told myself right then and there that I hoped to never experience what Liz had so blatantly just described. Was that the moment when I knew that I would practice, as Havelock Ellis put it, "sexual inversion?"

Perhaps, though I didn't yet know that physical intimacy with another woman was even a possibility.

I saw less and less of James. One evening after dinner, after he and Liz had played a few hands of cards at the table, James left to attend to some business. Harriet, who was sitting in a chair in the corner, spoke without looking up from the sewing in her lap: "I don't think we should continue to have James visit with us here."

"What are you talking about?" said Liz, her voice filled with blatant annoyance. "He's been our friend forever. He and Murray have been coming here long before you moved in."

Harriet continued to sew but looked up, looked at each one of us but her gaze finally rested on Liz. "Some of us are concerned with our reputations. I don't think it looks right having a man come to our house nearly every evening."

The reputation comment was meant to humble Liz but didn't. She went out dancing almost every Saturday and stayed out most of the night, knew all the Irish dances but she was besotted by the black ones—the jigs and break downs—and danced with white men and black men alike. She knew Harriet didn't approve of any of it, especially the fact that Liz slept half of Sunday and always missed church.

"Your supposed piety is what's unbecoming," Liz said. "You think that because you don't dress up or dance or drink or smoke or even laugh that you're better than those of us who do. But are you really living, Harriet? I'll bet you're in love with that Reverend Pease of yours. I'll bet you fantasize about him every night." She got up and twirled around holding her breasts and looking skyward. 'Oh, Reverend,"' she mocked. "'Put the light of the Lord in me!"'

Harriet just stared at her, mouth agape.

Liz said, "The only reason you don't like James coming here is because he doesn't pay a lick of attention to you."

Harriet got up from her chair and walked across the room to the bedroom door. "You're a disgrace," she said. "But we specialize in helping fallen women, so when you're ready, Elizabeth, we'll be there for you. All your sins can be forgiven."

"You know," Liz said to her, "you're not stuck here, Harriet. There are plenty of other souls for you to save in Five Points that might also be able to rent you a room."

This rendered Harriet speechless, and she stared a moment at Liz, but I could see how much the comment hurt her. She might not have been stuck living with Emma and Liz, but she was stuck in her own piety and version of right and wrong. She went inside the bedroom and closed the door.

Liz looked at Emma and me and then burst out laughing.

This battle marked the beginning of a small war, my vulnerable soul at the very center of it.

* * *

I'm in Gallagher's home office, reading him the pages before he gives me a bit of morphine. I need it for the pain, but it also helps me let him examine me and change the bandages. Despite Gallagher's professionalism and genuinely caring nature, it still pains me every time to reveal myself, to show my sex, and my damaged, ugly, angry breasts. I'll be done with them soon enough, but then, they will also be done with me. Dreaded cancer. Well, I was ignorant most of my life, but now I know the quiet, awful suffering of living with tumors, especially when you know they are hastening your demise. Lonely thing, cancer.

I read my pages to Gallagher. I read them to him and then I go home and make notes and changes. Hearing it aloud makes me realize how to revise, how to say it better, clearer, more effectively. I have been a reader my whole life, but to write is something else.

"Those two—Harriet and Liz—they're like oil and water." Gallagher is amused at the fight over my soul.

"Yes, and me in the middle!"

"And yet they both have their merits."

"They both felt they were right."

"Was Liz fairly astute about Harriet's crush on the Reverend?" Gallagher asks.

"That was the thing—Harriet worked with all these poor people, but Liz understood more about human nature, for sure. And yes, I met the Reverend's wife and she was a champion for his cause—and just as tireless as Pease. I think Harriet both looked up to her and also felt tremendous jealousy toward her."

"So who won? Can I guess?" Gallagher asked, preparing the morphine.

"You'll just have to wait."

"Ah, Murray, you've got me on the edge! I can't wait to know how it ends."

"But Gallagher, we both know how it ends."

His face is so crestfallen, I long to take back my words. "I'm sorry," I say to him. "I didn't mean to change the mood or be macabre."

Quietly, he says, "I just wish there was more I could do for you, Murray."

"Gallagher, you're my dearest friend. You're listening—you're helping me tell the story just by being a willing audience."

"I appreciate your trust in me, Murray. You have no idea what it means."

I lay on his examination table and he administers the morphine. It's so wickedly wonderful, so soothing—it's the best I've felt since the last shot. The throbbing in my breast subsides. My mind is at ease. My arms feel so heavy I could not lift them if I tried, but I don't want to try, and that's all right: I don't have to do anything. I can let go, and I do.

Gallagher talks in a soothing voice as he unbuttons my shirt and snips off my bandages.

I'm so grateful for the drug, but even more grateful for this learned, kind friend. The two of them make my cancer—the pain, the loneliness, the fear it ignites—almost tolerable.

Chapter Fifteen

And then it was my thirteenth birthday. James and I were to spend the whole day together doing whatever I wanted to do. I let Harriet know that I wanted the day off and she got approval from Pease. Of course, my pay would be docked for that day, but I didn't care—I wanted to spend my birthday with my brother.

And James was so generous. I told him I wanted to go to see a performance at Barnum's American Museum, but the Broadway Menagerie and Museum was showing live wild animals. He said we could do both—we had all day.

We dressed warmly, as it was January, and cold. Upon leaving our apartment, we headed a few blocks east to the Bowery and found a coffee shop with pretty pastries and cakes displayed in the window. The Bowery was my favorite street in the Sixth Ward: every inch of it was alive, everyone's outfits were varied and interesting, especially the Bowery boys, so dapper with their flamboyant silk hats, fitted pants and colorful shirts. And the women, all painted with their hair done up and their dresses brighter and shorter than what you'd see on Broadway. You could buy anything along the Bowery. There were myriad eclectic shops for clothes, hats, shoes, belts, and socks, shawls and coats and blankets and curtains and kitchenware. It was too much and it was perfect. Beer gardens and saloons were vibrant even in the morning hours. Everyone talking and joking and sometimes yelling and shoving, all of it alive. You could hear Irish tunes coming from the pubs, men's normally rough voices sounding sweet and nostalgic. And not only shops but the streets and sidewalks were filled with vendors selling their wares. The smell of baked pears made me salivate, but I was too full from cake and coffee. James put his arm through mine and I felt like his girl. We had made it: We had survived our childhood in Manhattan.

There'd been a snowstorm a couple of weeks prior and though the skies were clear and cold for my day, the ground was still littered with patches of dirty white. On Bayard Street, James hailed a carriage and I could not believe it.

"Get in!" he said with a grin. "I want to show you something," he said. He told the driver to go to Broadway.

What a difference. So many of my days and years were spent in Five Points that I failed to remember at times that the rest of the city wasn't so crowded and chaotic. Broadway was so wide and the buildings and people so genteel, it seemed a different world. We passed Grace Church at Broadway and 10th. There were manors and mansions and hotels, but farther up, the street was less developed, and we saw fewer houses and people. Then over to Sixth Avenue and up to 40th Street, where what came into view took my breath away. I had heard of it, this Crystal Palace, but I couldn't imagine the exhibition in my mind and didn't really believe it existed. But here it was before us.

"The dome is 123 feet high," said James. "It's got 1,800 tons of iron, more than 15,000 panes of glass." The building itself was massive and spanned almost two blocks. James paid the driver a whole dollar and we disembarked from the carriage, with me almost tripping as I was looking not at the ground but at the beautiful structure before us.

"Can we go inside?" I whispered.

James laughed. "Yes, and don't worry—we'll still have time for Barnum and the Menagerie."

James paid for our tickets. Saturday was apparently a busy day and more than a thousand souls sought the site along with us. The light that shone through the glass panes in the ceiling and sides indeed made the place look like a palace. Marble statues of Greek Gods surrounded a beautiful fountain. But the exhibit's focus was more the new than the old: all the marvels of the industrial age were featured: a giant section of a telegraph cable that spanned the distance between London and Manhattan. This I could barely wrap my brain around—the idea of something being conducted through that cable that would allow communication between these two continents. There were sewing machines and daguerreotype cameras; steam-powered presses. People milled about, some of whom were so elegantly dressed, so obviously cultured, that for a moment I felt ashamed of the plain, awkward dress that had been donated to me, and the mismatched bonnet and cheap purse and shoes. I felt my poverty and struggle, felt that I had them on display for all to see. But I also knew there was something so much larger than myself here—industry, history, art, and architecture—a worldliness I had known little about.

People knew this place was important and you could feel it. And suddenly the little pockets of Five Points that I inhabited—our little tenement and Pease's mission—felt small and insignificant indeed. I did not know what my place would be in the world. Would I be a seamstress for the next forty years? I had no desire to marry a man and have his children; even the thought of that made my belly churn. But what would I do? Who would I be? How did I fit into this exhibit, into this city? My work suddenly seemed so meaningless and petty and boring. I felt I had been limited, but here before me was beautiful possibility. It hurt to look at it, to imagine so many prospects. Up until then I had not: I had been content to follow instruction rather than to blaze my own path.

And here was my brother beside me, a man now of twenty-one. And he was tall and thin, unlike me, and incredibly strong. Seen in his shirt sleeves at home I saw the sinewy strength of his arms. His hair was brown, like mine, his eyes hazel, his clothes rather simple and yet well-made. He tended to wear the same colors and style every day without much variation. He certainly wasn't a dandy but had a confident style and quiet knowledge about him. And yet he was quick with a laugh. I saw the that he was becoming a man in the world, and I was proud of him. He had raised me, taken care of me, and I was grateful.

I was starting to feel myself choke up and wiped at my eyes.

"Magnificent, isn't it?" he asked. "Though it makes me feel rather insignificant."

"I know what you mean."

We walked toward the exit together. James approached a carriage but I pulled him back. "Let's just walk," I said. "It's been so long since we took a long walk together."

He smiled. "We might miss the Barnum show."

"I don't care. I just want to stroll with you."

So we did.

I asked James what was going on with work.

"You know that for the most part, the Republicans detest the immigrants, right? Maybe that's too harsh a word, but the rhetoric they use make it sound like all the Irish Catholics coming here are ruining the city."

"And the Democrats? They're Tammany Hall, right?" I weighed in with what little I knew to keep the conversation going.

"Yeah, they side with the immigrants, and basically control the Sixth Ward—which is Five Points, as you know. And the grocers, the saloonkeepers—they pretty much run things."

"Like Sweeny?"

He nodded. "Like him. I mean, men are creatures of habit, go to the tavern every day, they go to the grocer, and talk, but they also listen. And the saloonkeepers and the grocers—they've got their eye on what's going on, whether it's with jobs or the election of the next alderman. And if you like the saloonkeeper, if you like the grocer, you're going to trust him. Or you're going to at least pretend to go along with what he says."

"Why?"

"In the case of the grocer—say he recommends you vote a certain way and you don't and he finds out about it. Next thing you know you're getting the smallest, most rotten potatoes from the bin or sourest milk or the oldest herring."

"And who wants that?" I said, to interject something. I had been holed up sewing for years while James had learned the political ropes. Men did politics, ran elections, doled out jobs, made more money, ran the city. Women sewed or worked as domestics—cooking, cleaning, caring for someone else's children—for wages that would barely keep them alive and forever keep them poor. And woe betide them if they had their own offspring to care for as well. The only hope was to land a man, hopefully one who was worth a damn. It seemed a dreadful fate, all of it.

"There was just a primary election to see who the Democrats are going to run for alderman. The voting happened at Dooley's Long-Room—remember that place? We delivered messages there together on occasion."

"Oh yeah!"

"Well, it's a primary, right? So you might expect some logical debate. But instead, both sides just bring their gangs—these are the biggest, fiercest men in Five Points—and they fight it out. Whichever side has the most men standing by the end of the night wins the primary."

"Do you have to fight?"

"No—thank god. It's brutal. I saw one man bite another man's ear off."

"Oh!"

"I've been working more closely with Sweeny. He's more brain than brawn and knows that I am too. I mean, I can fistfight, but these guys bring clubs. Sweeny's smart, though—he knows how to get the thugs to do his bidding. Then Sweeny and I figure out the patronage."

"What's that?"

"Who's going to get what in exchange for the vote—like jobs."

I was glad to be hearing more about James's work, but I also noticed an ice cream shop and pointed to it.

James laughed. "You want ice cream? Even on a cold winter day?"

"Well, the walking warmed me up."

James didn't share my sweet tooth. It's true we'd already had cake for breakfast and now I wanted ice cream for lunch, but meals at the mission were so plain and repetitive. I knew I was supposed to be grateful, but oh, the sameness of it…

I got vanilla and strawberry both and James got lemon.

Afterward, we headed to see the animals at the Menagerie. It was one of the best days of my childhood.

He took my hand as we walked, and as we strolled down the street hand in hand, I hoped everyone thought we were sweethearts.

Chapter Sixteen

Two years passed, during which I continued my humdrum routine. There was no time to get in trouble, as nearly every waking hour of every day was accounted for. Harriet had dedicated herself fiercely to the Temperance Society and asked for my help with something regarding it every day. I helped her prepare for meetings or went door-to-door letting people know about the Society and preaching temperance. We often weren't treated kindly. I did not like disturbing people in their homes, but Harriet claimed it to be the most effective way to spread the word.

Then one Sunday found Emma and me lounging on the couch just talking, time that was now more precious since she'd taken a job as a domestic with a Protestant family she lived with during the week. Saturday nights through Monday morning she returned to the apartment. She said she would be too lonely if she didn't see her friends, especially me, which made me feel like the most special person in the world. Harriet had gone to her mother's to have dinner; they were getting along better now, even though the Ladies' Society still claimed to be at odds with the humanitarian approach of Reverend Pease. Emma and James and Liz and I had had lunch, and it was like old times without Harriet trying to read the Bible to us all afternoon and making James feel guilty that he was in an apartment full of women.

Emma lay back and put her feet up on the table and I rested my head in her lap. She pet my hair as we talked. Liz and James got into a game of poker since Harriet wasn't around, and played for money.

I was about to drift off into a nap when Emma said, "I have something for you."

"For me?"

"Yes."

She reached to the side of the couch and pulled out a package wrapped in plain brown wrap and handed it to me, failing to suppress a mischievous grin.

I took my time pulling off the wrapping paper. I stared at the green book in my hands and at its title embossed in gold letters on the cover: *Leaves of Grass.*

I opened it and found myself looking at a photo of the author, a man in a baggy, light-colored shirt, open at the top, his hat cocked on his head, his beard prominent but trimmed, his eyes both wise and playful, one hand on his hip, the other hand in the pocket of his loose, patterned trousers. Cocky, inviting, spirited—a man who looked comfortable in his own skin. Such were my impressions of Walt Whitman before I'd ever read a word of his poetry. There were 12 poems in all. I started reading the first one, "Song of Myself," aloud.

I celebrate myself,
And what I assume you shall assume,
For every atom belonging to me as good belongs to you.

As I read on, I was transported into a New York where all of us belonged, each and every one of us—and not only belonged, but were connected, one with the other, so that the fate affecting any one of us affected all of us, so that joy that sprung forth from one soul touched all souls. He united us in our humanity while at the same time rendering each individual unique and special. And not only humans, but animals and minerals too: buzzards, rocks, oceans, and mastodons, snakes, and elk and razorbilled auk (I had never heard of a razorbilled auk; I felt my mind exploding with images and places and things). It felt impossible and perfect at the same time.

Long enough have you dreamed contemptible dreams,
Now I wash the gum from your eyes,
You must habit yourself to the dazzle of the light and of every
moment of your life.

Long have you timidly waded, holding a plank by the shore,
Now I will you to be a bold swimmer,
To jump off in the midst of the sea, and rise again and nod to me and
shout, and laughingly dash with your hair.

Can you imagine what those words meant to me? It was an invitation to live, to be fully oneself, to delight in one's surroundings, to drink in life, to celebrate its fullness. I had loved my Wordsworth and my Burns and would never forsake them, but here was a poet for me—for me in America, in New York City. I, merely fifteen years old, already felt like I had lived a lifetime: I had lost my true love—my mother; I had known struggle and heartbreak and confusion. I'd been slowly finding my way, but when I read Whitman's words, I felt a rush of understanding, of compassion and passion culminating within me. That's what it was—he had taken his years and observations and feelings and experiences and had served them up in this crazy, capacious poem. I even found answers about God here. Because Whitman did not renounce God, but saw him everywhere, in every object, and yet still saw *himself* as more wonderful! Delightful blaspheme!

Never had I felt such energy or hope. When I read the last words of the poem two hours later—*I stop somewhere waiting for you*—Liz and James were no longer at the table with their card game, but had lain down on the floor and were listening with their eyes closed. Liz looked satisfied, as if Whitman had confirmed what she long felt to be true. Emma beamed at me, entertained by my reading and pleased that I was so pleased. I didn't know whether to cry or laugh. I wanted to go run the streets, to test them out with this new vision, to see the city anew through Whitman's eyes.

I wanted to be free, though I didn't know what that meant. I wanted to be my best self, though I didn't know what that meant yet either.

Whitman was not didactic about it:

Not I, not any one else can travel that road for you,
You must travel it for yourself....
You must find out for yourself.

I wanted to be bold and brave as Whitman—no, as *myself.* Because he believed in me, believed in all of us, saw us capable of so much love and compassion and happiness. But it wasn't only about pleasure and joy; he encouraged the acknowledgement of the suffering of others—not to turn a blind eye or ignore it, but to really witness it and take it on as one's own. If everyone is connected, then when one being suffers, everyone suffers.

I do not ask the wounded person how he feels, I myself become the wounded person.

How would I have to live if I lived with such openness, empathy, and vulnerability? To experience so much exaltation and so much suffering, and to not turn away from any of it? That's what it would mean to be fully alive. It was as if I were taking a first step on a very long and exciting journey. I marked this as one of the most important days of my life. Never before had I experienced that much optimism, energy, zeal, and ecstasy about being alive, and I owed it to Whitman, and to my dear Emma.

I embraced her and kissed her cheek and she laughed and kissed me back.

Leaves of Grass became my Bible. I memorized passages and recited them to myself or to anyone who would listen.

"Why should I pray?" I would suddenly call out. "Why should I venerate and be ceremonious?"

Harriet became increasingly bothered. The book was dangerous, according to her. And I agreed—it was. It was dangerous because it thrilled me and made me want to take charge of my own life. It gave me faith in myself. Why should I obey anyone or anything? Why should I bow down? I should rise up! If there is goodness in me and I recognized that goodness in myself and others, why should I cower and submit? Harriet and Reverend Pease were preaching humility before God....They preached that the only worthy life was one of strict discipline, teetotaling, and hard work. But to what end? What *was* the meaning of life? All these questions and controversies had been brewing in my head, and now I had an answer that rang truer to me than all others. Because the answer to the meaning of life might now come from sewing all day, or ascetic sacrifice, or devout worship. But what if I discovered the meaning of life while loafing and observing a spear of grass?

I felt my soul rising up in joyful rebellion. It drove Harriet crazy. It amused Emma. It delighted Liz.

I decided to change my schedule so that I could work fewer hours and take off Saturdays. Instead of studying all morning and working all day until evening and coming home and eating and falling asleep, I told Harriet that I just wanted to sew from 8 to 6. That gave me enough time and energy in the evenings to be able to do whatever it was I wanted to do, like take a walk with James. Rather than books and a cramped school room, my education would come from observing the city and from being with my brother and others.

I could not understand how people lived in the interior of the country, surrounded by land, land, land. Water surrounded Manhattan—the East River on one side, the Hudson on the other. The bay tunneled out to the sea. I got to know my way around Five Points again: Monroe Hall on Centre; Patrick Kelly's Saloon on Bayard; Alack's on Orange Street—a spectacular dance hall run by a black family on Orange Street (Liz's favorite)—Con Donoho's Grocery; the Tombs Prison (the outside, anyway); and of course, the Bowery. Then the street names changed—Orange became Baxter; Anthony became

Worth; Cross became Park; Little Water became Mission Place—but it didn't really matter: everyone knew the streets not from their names but from their location and from the businesses and tenements and markets that lined them.

I had seen the Old Brewery demolished in 1852 when the Ladies Home Missionary Society bought it. I heard the new mission cost an astounding $36,000 to build. Rumor had it that the workers found human bones in the walls, which didn't surprise me. I still dreamt about the time James and I went there. I felt bad though for the droves of people ousted from their apartments. If there was one thing about the Old Brewery: it might have been a dark, dank and disgusting rat-hole, but rent was cheap!

Reverend Pease's House of Industry was thriving and ever-expanding. Pease had started with teaching the women sewing, but eventually he'd added training in tailoring, millinery, and straw work. The Ladies' Mission might have been saving more souls, but Pease was providing a means, however humble, for people to feed the bodies their souls inhabited. In the end of December 1853, he bought a farm—sixty four acres to be exact—with the goal of selecting the smallest and feeblest children in Five Points and sending them there to live and work, sustained by land and fresh air. He offered me a job there—to help feed, bathe, and educate the children. I would earn $3 a week—would not even be charged room and board, he said. But I could not leave my beloved James and Emma and Liz. I couldn't imagine leaving the city, either, for though the countryside was bucolic and wholesome, it also sounded boring and lonely. I had become a true denizen of Whitman's "Manahatta."

Pease increasingly saw the city as a source of vice and evil, but my new bible and poet taught me otherwise, and I longed to explore and know even more of it. I wanted expansion, vision, experience. Whitman saw the city as full of life, whereas Pease saw it as full of vice. He thought the only redemption was through toil; he wanted to corral the women and children—hide them away in workrooms or classrooms or farms.

Of course, I was not naïve to the city's detriments. After all, I had worked with women whose husbands beat them every night upon returning from the saloons. I had seen children who had not bathed in months, hair full of lice, bodies crawling with vermin. I had seen faces hollowed out by hunger, had seen grown men throw bricks at one another; had seen a black man beat up for walking with his arm around a white woman. I saw poverty that robbed its victims of dignity. Five Points had been my main experience of New York City thus far. But Whitman's poetry taught me to find beauty in the struggle and see the potential for the city, and it gave me hope for myself and my brethren. But even as James and I tried to improve our lives and work toward eventually leaving Five Points, I also knew that we were never going to be the gentry, never going to hobnob with the upper classes; we would never attend Grace Church or shop on Broadway or own a house on Fifth Avenue—that wasn't what we were aspiring toward. And it seemed to me that those people were out of touch with the struggles of most of humanity. I took a clue from Whitman who wasn't high-minded and literary and out of reach. He breathed the same air as the worker.

Something else was changing for me and the impetus came in part from Whitman's poetry. One Saturday evening after dinner, Liz and James left to go dancing. Harriet had long given up on her moralizing and let them be. I was on the couch with Emma and trying to recite her "Sleep Chasings" from memory as she did her sewing, but I couldn't get past the line, *The sisters sleep lovingly side by side in their bed...*

What came next? The men or the mother?

I got up and started across the room.

"Where are you going?" asked Emma, looking rather alarmed for some unknown reason.

"I'm going to run down to my place and get *Leaves*."

Emma shook her head at me silently, her eyes wide. Harriet had her nose buried in the Bible. I looked at Emma who stared at me wordlessly, imploringly. She glanced quickly at Harriet and then back at me and shook her head again.

I sat back down, baffled.

"Tell me the line again that comes before the sisters," Emma said. She put her hand on my leg gingerly, tenderly. I recited,

The married couple sleep calmly in their bed, he with his palm
on the hip of his wife, and she with her palm on the hip of the husband…

"I love that image," Emma said. And then I suddenly understood that Liz and James were not dancing at all, but were in our room, in James's bed, pretending to be married, their hands tenderly touching each other's hips.

I remembered another part of the poem and said aloud:

My hands are spread forth, I pass them in all directions,

I would sound up the shadowy shore to which you are journeying.
Be careful darkness! Already what was it touch'd me?
I thought my lover had gone, else darkness and he are one,
I hear the heart-beat, I follow, I fade away.

Harriet looked up, her visage taken over by a sour look of distaste. "Those poems are simply unclean," she said. "And you do yourself a disservice by storing them in your brain." But she didn't move from her seat and I continued to remember lines. Emma had stopped sewing and was listening. Her hand was still resting on me.

"The sisters sleep lovingly side by side," I said again.

Harriet didn't look up but said, annoyed: "You already said that line."

Emma and I looked at each other and laughed.

That night I could not sleep. I did not confront James or Liz, but I rather relished the thought of them in his bed, and as I lay there staring at the ceiling, I put a hand on my own hip and imagined a lover. I put my hand on my thigh where Emma's had been, and whispered these words:

I am curious to know where my feet stand—and
what this is flooding me, childhood or manhood
—and the hunger that crosses the bridge
between.

And then I let my hand slide upward.

* * *

Oh, those days, of discovering one's body and desire, a rooted thing, this need for pleasure, and Whitman to aid in overcoming the shame the preachers so deftly instill. It was self-discovery. It was addictive. I did not imagine ever sharing it with another, of sharing my discoveries, of sharing my body.

The loneliness in me now stems in part from that loss, of my skin on Celia's skin, of her arm around my waist at night, hand resting on my breast before disease wormed its way in. Her lips on my lips.

Chapter Seventeen

On my sixteenth birthday, January 1, 1856, Liz dressed me up, but first kicked the coarse striped muslin dress I wore on a regular basis to the side of the room.

"Sorry," she said with a smirk. "I'm just so sick of that thing. If you're going to dress like a female, Murray, at least make it count."

Liz and Emma had bought me a second-hand velvet green dress on the Bowery. It fit so well, especially around my rather wide waist. Though I had grown a bit in the last couple of years, I really had no bosom to speak of. But the dress was a miracle! I had to wear a corset with it, which they helped me button, and the dress squished together my small breasts and gave me cleavage. Liz lent me a silk slip which felt wonderful against my bare legs. The dress was a bit long and Emma immediately pinned it and set to hemming it. Their enthusiasm was endearing—and made me feel loved.

When Harriet entered and saw the goings on, we all paused, prepared for her wrath. She observed the scene for a moment: Emma on the couch with the dress draped over her lap, me at the table in her bra and underwear and slip and stockings but nothing else, Liz behind me with pins in her mouth and a brush in her hand trying her damnedest to do something with my pathetic hair—and Harriet didn't scowl but smiled!

"Does she have shoes for the dress?" Harriet asked Liz.

"We hadn't gotten there yet."

"I have something that might work."

Harriet went into the bedroom and we heard the squeak of her trunk. She emerged a moment later with a pair of brown leather boots, worn but wonderful, and laced halfway up the calf. They had a small heel that would be comfortable to walk in.

"Someone donated these at the House," she said, meaning the House of Industry. "I knew they were your size and so I took them for you. Happy birthday, Mary."

"Thank you, Harriet!" I exclaimed. I put them on and they were perfect. Liz finished my hair, which she had pinned up off my neck. Then Emma handed me the dress, which I put on, and brought me a hand mirror. I barely recognized myself. I looked like another person entirely. My eyes were sultry, smudged with kohl; my lips a shiny red. It turned out I did have cheek bones, which Emma kissed, looking pleased. Even Harriet looked content, though I could see her struggling with her innate disapproval.

"Come on, Murray. We're going now," Liz said. "You girls want to come?"

"Where are you going?" asked Harriet.

"The Vault at Pfaff's on Broadway and Bleecker."

"The bohemian beer hall!"

"That's right—we're going to see if we can spot Walt Whitman. He's been hanging out there, I heard."

Now Harriet couldn't stop herself. "Don't forget your commitment to temperance, Mary. It's not just the hard stuff, but beer and wine too."

"Did I make a commitment to temperance?" I asked.

"You did if you want to remain at the House of Industry."

Now Emma spoke. "Oh, Harriet, I'm sure the girls are just going to see the place and get out on the town. She can have a Coca-Cola! I'm staying here to finish some sewing. You and I can keep each other company."

I shot Emma a grateful glance. Liz and I put on our coats and scarves and gloves. I almost didn't put on my hat—I didn't want to mess up my hair!—but when we got outside, the night, with its star-filled sky, was very cold.

I had always scoffed at women I saw walking the streets, shivering in their dresses, while the men accompanying them were warmly clad head to toe. I wasn't going to be one of those silly women, a slave to fashion and beauty; I put on my hat.

We walked quickly, me filled with excitement and emboldened by my costume. I was someone else, finally. I could transform.

Pfaff's was subterranean. We opened the hatch in the sidewalk and Liz headed down the stairs with confidence and not until she was near the bottom did she realize I was still at the top, overcome by terrible shyness and fear. I wanted nothing more than to be at home on the couch, reading Whitman with Emma sewing beside me—not risking meeting the poet in person! I didn't think I could descend those stairs and face anyone, let alone him.

Liz walked back up the stairs and took my hand. "Come on," she said. I took a deep breath and we started down together.

Music and cigarette smoke wafted up the stairs. Halfway down the stairs, the room came into view, windowless of course, but wonderful. How many people were there? Forty? Fifty? The room was packed with patrons sitting in chairs, standing at the bar, smoking, dancing, talking. Tables were covered with ashtrays, bottles, cups. I wasn't sure where to stand or where we would find room or where we were supposed to go. People glanced at us but didn't stare, thank goodness. I was self-conscious, but I was also telling myself not to care what anyone thought. Liz had heard that Pfaff's had become a gathering place for poets, musicians, actors, journalists, and playwrights—the idea of which both delighted and intimidated me. We went to the bar where Liz got the bartender's attention, and the next thing I knew, she put a pint of beer into my hand.

"Cheers," she said and clinked my glass. "Happy birthday, Murray."

There was a little guilt in that first sip. I had never drunk beer or any alcohol. I wrinkled my nose and Liz laughed and said, "Bit of an acquired taste, I guess." I had acquired it by the third sip and within minutes the pint glass was empty and Liz had ordered us another.

I loved the feeling overtaking me: I felt funny; I felt free. Indeed, everything became amusing to me, and I was no longer worried—about anything. Even though I was becoming quite intoxicated fast, I felt absolutely alive. The past disappeared and the present took on a dream-like quality. I could see myself moving through time moment by moment, and Murray and Mary became just monikers. I was myself, in my skin, not boy or girl. I finally understood the reason for the packed saloons, why the beer at the end of the workday had so much pull. Was this feeling what the temperance people were up against? It suddenly felt like a battle that would surely be lost.

We took our fresh pints and walked around the room. There was an opening in the wall, and inside was nothing more than a long table around which about a dozen people sat. We stood near. A woman at the head of the table seemed to dominate the conversation. She had short, wavy hair, and droopy eyes that made her seem irreverent.

"That's Ada Clare," said Liz in my ear. "She's an actress. Isn't she lovely?"

Ada Clare was not only lovely, but confident. She had the attention of everyone sitting around her. Then as my eyes swept around the table, I saw him and grabbed Liz's arm.

He was sitting at the other end, his hands folded neatly around a coffee cup in front of him. His beard and frumpy hat were a dead giveaway, but what struck me most of all was how quietly he was observing his friends. *This was Whitman?* His poetry was so boisterous, a virtual celebration of the body and soul, but here he was not speaking a word, only a hint of amusement on his face. No one was even paying attention to him, not that he was seeking attention.

"Let's offer to buy him a drink," said Liz.

"No!" I yelled too loud and was mortified when everyone at that table, including Whitman, looked at us.

Ada Clare cocked her head and said, "Why don't you join us?"

Liz took my arm and essentially planted me next to my poet.

I was afraid to look at him, so close were we seated.

"How's the ale?" he asked me.

I looked down at my pint, my second one, now half drunk, both the glass and myself. I had appreciated the strange feeling of social ease I felt with intoxication, and yet sitting near Whitman, I longed to be lucid; I wanted my wits about me and feared I'd lost some of them.

"I don't have much to compare it to since this is the first time I've had beer. Tastes a bit like liquid bread, and I relish bread."

He nodded and lifted the mug to his mouth and drank long. When he finished and wiped his beard, which was trimmed short, he said, "Best coffee in town."

"Oh?" I said dumbly. "I actually feel a little guilty about the beer. I work with Reverend Pease at the House of Industry and he doesn't look kindly on those who imbibe."

"In Five Points?" he asked. I nodded. "Temperance Society supported him in that endeavor."

"Yes," I agreed, "but even before that he railed against drink. All those who work, study, or worship there must commit to teetotaling."

He cocked his head at me. "Where's that leave you?"

I blushed and didn't answer. Where indeed? I had seen lives ruined by it, had seen lives improved when it was forsaken. But I also saw the liveliness of saloons and pubs such as these. Perhaps this was where real life unfolded, not in the chapel. But then, here was Whitman drinking just coffee, albeit the city's best.

"I wrote a novel in '42," said Whitman. "*Franklin Evans*, or *The Inebriate*. About a man who loses everything—his job, his marriage, his dignity—because he drinks too much."

"The Reverend has a copy of it! I'm sorry, I haven't read it—I didn't know it was you. I'll read it—I'll read it tomorrow!"

"Don't bother."

"Sorry?"

"It's not very good. I prefer poetry now."

"A friend gave *Leaves of Grass* to me for my birthday and I immediately read 'Song of Myself' aloud to my friends and brother. I was spellbound, Sir. I'd never read anything so perfect. Every poem in the book is wonderful." I was so galvanized, I had to resist citing passages to the man from his own work.

"Then stick to that. Don't bother with the *Franklin Evans*. It took me awhile to figure out what I wanted to say. And instead of punishing a man for what I thought he was doing wrong, I wanted to create a narrator I could admire for living right."

I must've looked confused.

"What is it?" he asked.

"I'm sorry, that idea is so strange to me. I just assumed that Walt Whitman and the person narrating the poems were the same."

He looked at me a long moment and then said, "What's your name?"

"Murray," I said, without hesitation.

He shook my hand with intention and said, "Well, Murray, the narrator did say, 'I am large....I contain multitudes.' I have a feeling you do too."

He let go of my hand and stood. I looked around at the people dancing, and for the first time realized that some women were dancing with women, some men with men. Whitman spoke again: "You can be yourself here."

When I looked up, he and another man, who appeared much younger, were walking away from the table arm in arm.

Ada Clare noticed, and, pausing her conversation with Liz, cried out to him, "Walt, you can't leave. When you go, we lose our credibility."

He smiled at her, tipped his hat, and left.

I drank coffee for the rest of the night, from his cup.

Liz and I walked home arm in arm that night, both of us elated. Ada Clare loved that we lived in Five Points, had told Liz that she and her friends despised the new millionaires, all flaunting their rich houses and carriages and jewelry and clothes. They detested snobbery, which made us so happy. One thing was certain: we weren't snobs!

"Ada Clare talked about how New York City wants to eat everything in its path, how some Manhattan developers wanted to annex Brooklyn and fill in the East River with gravel to connect it to the island and pay for it by charging an arm and a leg for the real estate it would create," Liz said. "She talked about how uppity the bourgeois are as they stroll the grand promenade of Broadway, explained the asinine ritual of people dressing up in their finest to show off to each other but how they don't even acknowledge each other. She prefers the Bowery where everything is 'unruly but real,' as she put it."

I was pleased to hear that, as if it vindicated our working-class existence.

"She said she and a group of rowdy friends will go to Broadway just to act wild and uncouth, just to annoy the wealthy. Wouldn't it be fun to join them?"

"Yes!" I said, but really, I couldn't picture myself doing that at all.

Liz had learned something else from Ada Clare about Whitman. "The poor man—his poetry doesn't support him. He's published in a few journals, but *The Atlantic* isn't publishing his work. Ada said that her friend Henry Clapp—the man sitting at the end of the table wearing a red bow tie?—that he's starting a journal and that he'll publish all of them: Whitman, Ada herself, and all their writer friends—'all the bohemians.' That's how she put it."

We walked on, leaving the more affluent neighborhood behind us as we neared the Sixth Ward. All the rich families had moved above Bleecker, and all their formerly pretty homes that had housed just one family had been turned into tenements, each now with dozens of immigrants. Pfaff's was on the border between those worlds.

I liked the sound of "bohemian," though it seemed like a concept too exotic for me to achieve. But then I thought of Whitman, how his calm repose and coffee-drinking surprised me. I wondered who and what I would become. Would I be able to choose for myself, or would society choose for me?

I would be a girl and a boy. Was I contradicting myself? Very well, I would contradict myself.

There was nothing wrong with that, in Whitman's mind.

After all, I contained multitudes.

I started going regularly to Pfaff's. I would work all day at the House of Industry, and all day I would tell myself that the work was good, that I was making at least some money, that it was the wholesome environment I needed, that it should be enough, that I wasn't going to Pfaff's that night. But even as I walked down Mulberry Street toward home, through the crowds and filth and muck, I could feel a shift in myself. As soon as I left the confines of that building, I felt liberated; even as I breathed the fetid air, I felt free, and I'd feel my stomach flutter in anticipation of heading to Pfaff's that evening. Who would be there? I was both terrified and thrilled at the prospect of sitting at their long table, anxious that Henry Clapp would challenge me with some witticism, and I'd have to think quick and respond or get flustered and be too embarrassed to return to their table ever again.

But I was drawn to them, drawn to them all. Ada Clare had her "Thoughts and Things" column in the paper, and since I'd started reading it, I knew that she practiced her ideas out on the group first. On what subject would she pontificate tonight? Would Whitman be there, drinking his coffee? And if so, with which dashing man would he leave? Sometimes it was the same one for weeks on end, and then suddenly he'd choose another from the covey of handsome culls.

I still just observed, was ever-observing. I took my cue from Whitman and was moderate: I drank a beer when I got there, which relaxed my social nerves, but drank coffee thereafter. I wanted to keep my wits about me. I sat quietly for the most part, looking, listening, soaking it all in. The contrast from what I saw during the day at House of Industry was almost shocking. Could two worlds be any different?

Liz would get me from my apartment after dark. I didn't go to hers because I didn't want questions from Harriet, who would of course disapprove. Pfaff's was supposed to be a one-time thing on my birthday, after all. But I couldn't stop—couldn't get enough.

Liz took me to the dance halls too. Sometimes James and Liz and I all went together. But even though Liz had given me hours of lessons, I was still an awkward dancer. I became too conscious of my cumbrous limbs, too painfully aware of myself.

"Don't care what other people think," Liz would tell me. Easy for her: she was a long-limbed, graceful, and sensual dancer, thrilling to watch.

But she was somewhat mistaken about me caring what other people thought. I cared what I myself thought—and when I danced, I didn't feel natural. I saw the way people like Liz moved to the music, how dancing ignited something in them—the music inhabited their body and soul. For me it evoked only my lack of grace. Hence, I soon abandoned the dance halls and reserved my nighttime outings solely for Pfaff's.

Liz and I set off, but only after she helped me get ready. I couldn't manage the corset alone, which made me feel like a helpless child who could not dress myself. I put on the same green velvet dress—still my only fashionable one—and the low-heeled boots Harriet had given me—if only she knew how often I used them! I forewent makeup. I also realized I didn't like the way the corset and dress created cleavage by cramming my breasts together, so I put on one of James's frocks over it and on my head his leather cap. My outfit, like me, a kind of hybrid.

It was warmer one evening in March when we entered Pfaff's hatch and descended the narrow staircase, our hands, hot from walking, were cooled by the narrow metal railing. I breathed in the familiar aroma of cigarette smoke, sawdust, lager, steak, coffee, and a hint of privy, the House of Industry far, far away.

It was my turn to treat, so I bought Liz and myself a lager and we toasted. I turned to take in the room. Sitting there at the long table was Ada, her short dark hair just one aspect of her boldness. I had learned that she had a child out of wedlock, that her neighbor watched the boy so she could be there most evenings. It should have been scandalous, but of course in her usual audacious way, Ada Clare wrote about it, preempting whatever gossip might spread. She was 24, eight years older than me and so much wiser to the world.

Liz nudged me and tried to quell her own enthusiasm but couldn't. "He's here," she said.

I knew she didn't mean Whitman, which would have delighted me, but rather Fitz-James, who was in his 20s, rakish and bad, the cockiest, funniest, most irreverent member of Henry Clapps' rag-tag bohemians. Liz was mad about him. He was a writer, and wanted fame and fortune, mostly so he could blow it on his friends, treat everyone to a round, or seven.

"He's got a black eye again, the left one this time," I observed.

"I know," Liz swooned, not taking her eyes off him. Then he turned to Liz and winked. I would have blushed and turned away, but Liz winked back. He raised his glass to her and she raised hers in response. Then he waved her over.

"Come on," said Liz, and tugged on the sleeve of my brother's frock. My heart was thumping as it always did as I approached that little room with the long table that could seat more than a dozen. It was surrounded by stacked wine casks, and a cloud of cigarette smoke hung above. The ceiling was lower here than in the main room, creating a hazy, intimate cave. Henry Clapp was, as usual, at the head of the table; Ada sat to his right, and next to her, a few people I didn't know and then Fitz-James on the other end. Liz sat without hesitation. I was learning not to be scared, or rather, I was trying very hard to ignore the fact that I was. But I wanted a place at that table.

I stood before them and waited until Ada Clare noticed me and then I tipped my hat to her. Not without delight, Ada Clare said, "Oh, I love it, I just love your hat. May I try it on?"

I sat across from her, frighteningly close to Henry, who could hurl a verbal dagger if the mood struck him.

"What's your name?" Henry asked suddenly. He had never really acknowledged me.

"Murray," I said. I wanted it to be true—wanted Murray to be my name and who I was. Maybe in Pfaff's it could be.

"And what is it you do with your days, Murray?"

I considered lying, but instead told the truth. "When I was a boy, I ran errands with my brother for Peter Sweeny."

"When you were a boy, huh? And what about now that you're a girl?"

"Or something in between," interjected Ada, amused. She lit a cigarette, blew smoke into the already fumy air, and turned her attention back to me.

"For the last few years I've worked at the House of Industry with Reverend Pease."

Now they both looked amused. "You don't say," said Henry. "Still hocking Temperance to Irish drunks, is he?"

"Insists on it—for those who want schooling or work anyway."

"Let this be done," Henry sang out. "Let the people see that all the ways of Reform are ways of pleasantness, that all her paths are peace. Show the people this, prove to them how perfect is the harmony between the essential principles of true Reform and the divine life of Jesus; and ere long you shall see the people flock to our cause like an army of birds." He paused and in his normal voice, added, "Or something like that."

Ada Clare laughed and looked at me. I smiled but didn't really know what to make of his sermon. "He believed that hogwash at one time," Ada said. "Then Henry Clapp went to Paris and met the bohemians and sat in their cafes and drank their whiskey and smoked their tobacco. And it was so much fun, so much more interesting than the pious existence he'd been living and preaching for years, that he brought back those bohemian ways to New York City—and here we are. Now instead of temperance, he practices intemperance."

"It is often remarked that 'poverty is the parent of intemperance,'" he continued in his preacher's voice.

"Are we poor because we're drinking, or are we drinking because we're poor?" Ada intoned. Then she looked at me again, her head cocked to one side. "Do you miss being a boy?" she asked.

"Yes," I said without hesitation.

"What do you miss?"

"Well, for one thing, wearing pants."

Ada Clare nodded. "Women might wear just pants if men didn't insist they wear dresses." She took a drag off her cigarette and then continued.

"The truth is that the fashion of dress the male sex urge on us—and which we accept—is not only disfiguring, but cruel and unhealthy. When women propose a sensible outfit—like bloomers, for instance—men reject the proposal, often with brute force. They must try to remember, if the superiority of their minds will allow them, that the bloomers have been worn only by old and ugly women, but let the young and lovely have a chance at it for a month or so and I would like to see where male logic would be at the end of it."

I nodded, barely understanding. She took another drag off her cigarette, blew the smoke toward the ceiling and then continued her agnostic sermon: "The attempt to disguise the shape of the woman by hanging innumerable heavy skirts about her hips has been disastrous to her health and spirits. All women remember with horror the weight they were expected to suspend from their hips and shoulders a few years ago—such weight seeming to devitalize those delicate organs, without which the world could not exist. The blessing of the crinoline cage can't compete with bloomers, which at least allow a woman to exercise. So yes, I understand you, Murray, and your penchant for pants."

This diatribe from Ada Clare would be published two days later in her column, almost verbatim.

Later that evening, I met a woman at the bar when I went to refill my coffee.

"Hello," she said. I had seen her there before but we'd never spoken.

"Hello."

"Murray, is it?"

"Yes, but how—"

"I'm Sybil," she said and shook my hand, holding it for a few moments. "Your skin is so soft."

I blushed but it wasn't because of her comment. It was because of the way her hand touching mine made me feel, an awakening, a tremor, a longing.

I walked home alone that night as Liz had stayed with Fitz James. My mind was abuzz. I felt myself transforming: a slow, exciting metamorphosis, as if Pfaff's was my chrysalis, and I might eventually emerge, something authentic and magnificent, and fly away, finally freed.

Over the next couple of years, I gradually forewent bonnets for caps, bloomers for trousers, heels for brogues—at least when I went to Pfaff's. They all knew me, had watched the transition, but no one ridiculed me or made me feel odd. In the morning, I continued to don my old muslin dress and head to the House of Industry, but when the day was done, so was my feigned femininity, and I put on my preferred male attire. Dressed as a woman, I felt deferential, respectable, obedient. I knew my duty—to sew all day—although more recently I was trying my hand at hat making, as my stitch-work was not and never would be up to par and never earned me more than two dollars a week. Dressed as a man, on the contrary, I felt content, confident, even daring.

I asked Reverend Pease if I could help clean, mend, organize, and distribute the donated clothes and shoes. The Reverend and his wife were extraordinarily effective at getting people to donate to the House of Industry, and it helped that *The New York Times* was a fan of Pease and his wife and encouraged donations, both monetary and sartorial. Dozens of shoes came in every day from richer people all over the city, most with much life left in the them. I would clean and polish them, fix the ones that required repair if I could, prepare them to be given to the poor and needy. But I had a motive beyond just helping: I was building my own wardrobe from those donations. Oh, I could have pilfered from James's closet, and sometimes did, but he was long and lean and I was not. His pants were too tight on me and I had to cuff them at the bottom. His feet were like his body, long and narrow, and so his shoes didn't fit my small wide feet at all.

I didn't take much. At first I probably looked like a miniature Whitman because his easy, unpretentious style was one I admired, but then I went for more flair: a waistcoat, a shirt, an American tie, a pair of silk gloves, black boots, a printed handkerchief. I had started to pay attention to clothing for the first time in my life, really, and was a bit obsessed. I could sit in Pfaff's for hours noticing people's clothes, thinking about what looked good and what didn't and trying to understand why. So I filched items from the House of Industry, and if I couldn't use them returned them to be donated. But I gathered enough that I could, once home, try on different outfits to see what suited me. And since I possessed at least passable sewing skills, I could tailor the clothing as needed.

One ill-starred night, I dressed and went to Pfaff's. There, I saw pretty Sybil standing near the bar, sipping a lager and observing the room. She was somewhat of a regular at Pfaff's but not part of Clapp's clan. I ordered the one pint I would drink, and when Charlie Pfaff himself, who was tending the bar that night, put it into my hand, I turned to her and said, "Cheers, Sybil."

"Cheers to you, Murray," she said and tapped her pint glass against mine.

She was 20 years old, one year older than me. She wore a pretty but simple sleeveless dress that showed her graceful body and pale, freckled arms. Then, perhaps emboldened by those first tipsy sips of beer, I did something impulsive: I reached out and touched her shoulder and rain my fingers down her bare forearm to her hand. To my surprise she grasped my fingers. It might have been a simple flirtation, but I felt as if a candle burning soft inside me had suddenly become a torch. I willed my hand not to shake or perspire.

Our beers finished, she asked me if I wanted to dance. I nodded, not trusting my voice. She led us to a corner of the bar and put her arms around me and in that moment, I was so grateful for the time Liz had devoted trying to teach me at least some modicum of rhythm. We swayed with our bodies linked, and I could not even say what music was playing because I couldn't hear anything, my heart was thumping so loudly in my own ears. I looked around the room. Whitman was there, talking to a younger man with whom I knew the poet would leave that night. He caught my eye and smiled. I was almost as tall as Sybil, or would be if she weren't wearing boots with heels. I turned my face away from Whitman and sought Sybil's neck, which smelled of yeasty bread and beer, smoky and sensual. I breathed it in as she moved her body closer. Then I kissed her neck, little gentle pecks, felt her soft, moist skin on my lips. I could have stayed like that for hours, swaying with Sybil, kissing her lovely skin.

Sybil gave a little moan in my ear and I felt a stirring in my pelvis. I sank into her, our bodies melded. I continued kissing her neck, and then she slowly turned her face toward mine so that I was kissing her cheek, and then her face was in front of mine and she was looking into my eyes.

"Kiss me," she said. "Kiss me, Murray."

And I did—I kissed her lips and then kissed them again and again. It was the most exciting thing I'd ever done, kissing a woman's lips for the first time. For a moment it was as if nothing and no one else existed in the whole world. I felt obliterated, gone, without identity. The kiss awoke something in me that had lain dormant my whole life. There it was, finally happening. I wanted to keep kissing Sybil, wanted to lie down with her and kiss her whole being. I wrapped my arms around her more tightly and her body melted against mine. She kissed me back with equal passion, her soft tongue between my lips.

Something compelled me to look around then, which broke the spell.

There on the stairwell glaring at me with disbelief and unmistakable disdain was none other than Harriet, and from the look on her face, she'd been watching us the whole time.

To her credit, Harriet didn't make a scene. She didn't pull me out of Pfaff's; she didn't march me home. She just looked at me with utter disappointment and disgust, and then left. I stood there a moment. Sybil was oblivious until she looked at my face.

"What's wrong?" she asked. But it was too late. I had been hypnotized by our dance, enraptured by the moment. I had not seen myself from the outside—dressed as a bloke, kissing a young woman in a bar—until Harriet's eyes bore into me. Then I saw myself from Harriet's perspective and had to admit, I was ashamed. I had been living one life by day and another by night, and the two were so different, so incongruent, that it made me feel split in two. The Civil War had not yet started, it being only 1859, but it would have made a perfect analogy for the battle escalating inside me. The question of which side was more righteous, of which side deserved to win wouldn't be determined by me, but by Harriet and Reverend Pease. I knew that. I also knew that when I left Pfaff's that night, I wouldn't be back.

"I have to go," I said to Sybil.

I left her warm body and her confused, rejected face, which hurt my heart, and walked to the stairwell. From there I took in the room. I made myself imagine it as Harriet saw it: nothing more than a dirty basement filled with smokers and drinkers, men speaking intimately to other men, women kissing as they danced. But for a moment I let myself see it as what it had been to me: a wonderful place with a sawdust floor, wine casks lining the walls, a faint smell of toilets and yeasty lager, simple tables and chairs that allowed people to gather and converse. I saw Ada Clare throw her head back with a raucous laugh, saw Henry Clapp lower his gaze about to fire a caustic verbal cannon, saw dapper Fitz-James O'Brien, who suddenly broke into some Irish song. I saw Whitman at the end of the table, tucked back, his cup of coffee at his lips. His eyes found mine. I raised a hand to wave goodbye, and he raised his mug. Then I tore my eyes from that beautiful, brilliant man and forced myself up the stairs to ascend, more miserable with every step that took me from that magical place and back to reality.

I barely slept. The next morning was Sunday, and while I didn't usually go to Sunday service, I dressed in my plain muslin dress, an act of atonement, and walked to the House of Industry. Harriet was there, of course, sitting up front. I stayed near the back. The room was filled with rows of simple wooden chairs, about forty people in attendance. I found an empty seat. When the Reverend began speaking and looked at me, I knew he knew: Harriet had revealed my secrets.

"Every day you must choose," his voice rang out. "Sin or salvation, the choice is yours. But you must make the decision and stay steadfastly with it."

His sermon ranged in topics from the detriments of drink and the need for temperance to the folly of sin. He talked of sunshine as a cure for the dark sin shadowing one's life.

"All of us, every parent, worker, and teacher among us, should behave as followers of Christ. Temperance works through the spirit of emulation. We continuously influence others and must be a force of good in our example. Social drinking causes great danger and demoralization for all—the laboring poor, the recently-arrived immigrant, the already destitute, the women working at home or in grocers, ladies under pressure of the claims of modern society. There is excessive drinking in your homes, in your grog shops, and in your taverns. Let yourself not be an additional drinker, but let yourself be a shining example of self-restraint."

Here his eyes settled on mine. I looked down.

"Drink costs not only money but lives. Three-fourths of our crime, pauperism, and lunacy are attributable to drink. And females are not immune. Female intemperance constitutes a new reproach and danger. The greater the danger, the more the need for watchfulness." Harriet turned her head and looked briefly at me after the Reverend said those words, as if her spying were vindicated by them. "We must work to perfect ourselves, as He is perfect. Sin brings with it bondage; with sin you sell yourselves. And this bondage speaks only to our lower nature: it is bondage to the devil, and it increases his power evermore; it may, in fact, never end."

Here he raised his Bible and read from it: "Know ye not that the unrighteous shall not inherit the kingdom of God? Be not deceived: neither fornicators, nor idolaters, nor adulterers, nor effeminate, nor abusers of themselves with mankind, nor thieves, nor covetous, nor drunkards, nor revilers, nor extortioners, shall inherit the kingdom of God." His eyes left the page and again sought mine. "The best pleasures of sin are fleeting—they always fall infinitely below the joys of religion. And when that ephemeral pleasure evaporates, as it always does, what is left in its place? Grinding tyranny, disease, mental and spiritual woe, even death."

I thought of Pfaff's, of the dance I shared with Sybil, and even though Harriet's reproach had made me feel regret and shame, I struggled to see how that sensual joy—how that carnal desire—could lead to despair or death.

I knew Pease's sermons, however, and knew that he would not end on a dismal note, but would, in fact, offer an opportunity for redemption. And so he did:

"Leave sin and enter the garden and see its delight. The Church is that garden. Eden was lost by the first Eve; but yours awaits! The sweet-smelling flowers you'll find there surpass all other earthly delight. Come stroll, and watch the flowers spring forth, warm yourself in the rays of the sun, cultivate the garden of your soul. Find the essential sunshine."

He paused dramatically, leveled his gaze upon me.

"We must have sun. Without the purity of its light, what becomes of plants and trees? They sicken and degenerate. The hayfield is proof of this. It is much the same with human beings. Health demands sunbeams. As sunshine is needful to the body, so is purity to the soul. Pardon yourself of your sins and vow to seek the sun."

When the sermon was finished, we shuffled into the dining room to eat. I sat alone, apart from all, but when I looked up from my soup, I saw Reverend Pease approaching. He sat across the table from me, no soup, not even disappointment, just a determined gaze.

"I've been thinking about you, Mary. The city can be a corrupting influence. I think you'll find that some clean air and hard work will cleanse you and avert any further...misdeed." I felt myself nodding.

"Many children are living at the farm right now waiting to be adopted, and their numbers increase by the week."

The increase came, I knew, not just from parents who willingly gave up their children, as those were actually quite few. But as of late, the Reverend had grown bolder and had been seeking out those parents he thought were not on a wholesome path and attempting to convince them that they didn't deserve to raise their children. He could find them better homes, he assured them, in the countryside of the Midwest, away from the depravity of the city. So persuasive was he that some parents gave him their children, and of those, many came to regret their decision and would demand the return of their children. Few succeeded.

"You're to go to the farm, Mary. We need your help there." It was many miles north of Manhattan near the Westchester County village of Eastchester. I had never been there.

I thought of my brother, of how he'd recently been accepted as a volunteer for the most renowned fire squad in Five Points, the Americus "Big Six"—led by none other than William Tweed, future corrupt boss of Tammany Hall. I thought of Sundays with Emma. I thought of Liz and our outings to Pfaff's. A small part of me believed that the pleasure I experienced there was indeed unholy. That pleasure raised a tumult in my soul: it both titillated and terrified me.

But Pease's displeasure and disappointment in me was a powerful force, and in that moment, his eyes did not leave mine. His face was kind but unwavering and conveyed one single message—that he knew best.

I knew I didn't want to go to the farm.

I also knew I would.

*   *   *

Writing those words immerses me in that time. I wake in the morning earlier these days, and though it's been relatively warm for October, the mornings are chilly. I make coffee if Minnie has slept in, take Walt out to relieve himself, and then make a fire for warmth and comfort. I get back in bed with my pen and paper and write for a few hours. I like to be lucid when I write. When Walt begins to look at me longingly, we get up and take a stroll up to Gallagher's office for my daily dose of morphine. We might stop at Pratt's. I've been reading less since I've been writing, which is a tough sacrifice. One of the things that makes me saddest about my time winding down on this earth is how few books I have time left for. Must choose wisely. Must finish writing.

This morning, I'm still in my room, the smell of smoke reminding me of all the late falls and winters of my life. The winters on Pease's farm were particularly lonely and bitter cold. I went to that rural outpost, exiled from everything and everyone I loved. I hated being there, hated being away from Emma, and Liz, and especially my brother. For two long years, dull life in a dreary dress and old coat. There was so much work, never-ending chores from dawn to dusk, and more than a dozen children at any time to take care of. So it wasn't the sunshine that absolved my sins. It was drudgery of labor that seemed to never end.

The children, my charges, were an ever-changing group: most were adopted at some point, usually sent off to far-reaching places in the nation I would never see, farms in Minnesota, towns on the frontier. Then others arrived from the city. It was my job to keep them clean, to give them chores, to teach them to read and write. I did not get too close, as they were gone before I could, and I would never hear from them again, never know their fates. I could only hope that Pease was right, that they would have a better life, that their new family would not just clothe them and feed them but also love them, welcome them into the fold of the family. I hoped they were not abused or mistreated in any way but had no way of ensuring that.

One thing and one thing only gave me pleasure during that gloomy time. My brother wrote letters to me. We had been living together our whole lives, and since we could not converse daily when I was residing at the farm, he wrote me at least one a week. I saved the letters in a box, which I fish out from under the bed. I open this one and read it:

Dear Murray,

How are you? Everything is fine here, and I'm relishing the work on the fire squad. We put out a fire yesterday that started on the top floor of a three-story tenement. No one was hurt, thank goodness. It's terrible when people get trapped, as they sometimes do, and even worse when they jump to escape the flames. William Tweed is captain of us—he calls us the Big Six. Sweeny helped me get on with them—he and Tweed are well-acquainted. Tweed is a massive specimen, rowdy and funny, and all the men like him. We compete with other fire squads to see who can get to the fire first and put it out. Tweed drives our silver pump engine like a madman through the streets, day or night.

We're all missing you terribly, Murray—Liz, Emma, and me. I don't get to see Emma much since she works at Miller family's house all week, and recently Liz moved in with a man named Emery, whom she met at the black dance hall. That's what you've got to love about Liz—she is not afraid of a scandal and does what she damned-well pleases.

Well, Murray, I'm off to bed since I will likely be woken within a few hours for a middle-of-the-night fire. I get a bit of a kick thinking of you with all those little ones, since—and don't take this the wrong way—you're one of the last people I picture tending children. But they are lucky to have you.

Yours,

James

I have not looked at the letters for years, and I'm surprised by the visceral effect. To have the paper in my hand that he touched, to see the letters he formed with the pen, to see his signature, moves me in a way I didn't expect.

I find the letter he wrote to me after seeing Abraham Lincoln speak. He launched right in, hardly a salutation or greeting, he was so excited.

Murray,

Abraham Lincoln spoke at the Cooper Institute last night. Frankly, I was a little worried about attending and being seen since Lincoln is candidate for the Republican party—the Democrats, as you probably know, are supporting Stephen

> Douglas for president. But I'd been hearing rumors about Lincoln and had to see for myself.
>
> He was so tall, almost gangly—and how he spoke, Murray! Well, he's probably the smartest man you've ever heard give a speech. And yet his words are deceptively simple—no highfalutin rhetoric, just spare prose that's both logical and moving. He encouraged us to not capitulate to the South. He reiterated that slavery is not a right, and oh, how the men cheered, including me. It was infectious, incredibly persuasive.
>
> Of course the Irish are all talking about their fear of freed slaves coming to New York and taking their dismal jobs for even lower wages—that's what I'm hearing, and the overall sentiment is not good. But what the Irish are forgetting is that they have one advantage the freed slaves will never have: their faces are the same hue as the rich men in power; whereas the poor, freed slave will always have the color of his skin, and that is enough to make a target of the shallow, ignorant, fair-skinned folk who are going to fear and despise him no matter how good his intentions or what he has suffered.
>
> Liz told me that Emery came here from the South—did you know that? I don't know if he is an escaped slave, but she said he has been through horrors. They are living in a tenement basement near the dance hall on Orange. Liz said they have to be careful. Even though New York doesn't have a law banning miscegenation, it doesn't mean they're not making themselves vulnerable to other people's meanness.

I remembered how proud I felt of Liz, being with Emery despite how others might judge and even threaten her. Did I compare it to my own situation—to the act that had led me to that farm, the act of kissing a woman? I was still questioning my own morals—or rather, I felt others questioning them and that made me doubt myself. It was the reason I didn't stand up for myself, that I could not bring myself to rebel against their judgment of me—because I wasn't sure about it. Oh, I was sure of the feeling, but I didn't know if that feeling was something unclean, a dirty lust, something that I should avoid or ignore or resist through penance and prayer.

I may have not believed much in God, but I still argued with myself. I still believed I had a soul, and Harriet and Reverend Pease essentially taught me that it was tarnished because I kissed a woman and dressed as a man (but also that the hard work and sunshine there on the farm might redeem me). And then there was Liz, always bolder than me or any of us, defying the rules of society and living with Emery on her own terms.

I continue to read:

> Lincoln talked about Alexander Hamilton as one of the most outspoken critics of slavery. Hamilton was abandoned by his Scottish father and orphaned when his mother died—and yet he made it in America—in fact, he helped *make* America. What if I could make a difference like that, Murray?
>
> At the end of his speech Lincoln said, "Let us have faith that right makes might and that in faith, let us, to the end, dare to do our duty as we understand it," and you could see it, Murray—the whole room was aglow with approval, ignited by this idea, made so clear, that slavery is wrong, that it must not be expanded into new territories, that it must end in the South, without the Union being dismantled or destroyed.

I had never heard my brother so passionate.

The day before the Cooper Union speech, Lincoln visited the House of Industry! Harriet sent a letter to the farm about it, writing how pleased Reverend Pease was to have Lincoln praise his work. Apparently, the Sunday school teacher asked Lincoln to say something to the children, so he told them of his own poverty as a youth, of his toes poking out of holes in his shoes, of shivering in the cold. He told them there was only one rule: to always do their best "and they would get along somehow." Harriet wrote that Lincoln's eyes were filled with real tears when he said it.

Enough writing for today. Walt is looking at me longingly, and I can no longer ignore the pain pulsing in my breast. My bones have healed from William Reno's attack, but his attack on my chest inflamed the tumors' wrath.

I see that Minnie is out when Walt and I emerge from the bedroom. I feel so damned melancholy this morning. I know what's to come and I don't want to think about it.

Outside, the street is a bustling. I am losing track of the days, but it must be a weekday, as omnibuses fly down the street and carriages trample the fresh horse shit in the road, releasing the earthy pungency. Walt pulls on his rope and goes into the road so he can pee on the pile of manure. Farther up, I see that Platt's is closed—she's posted a sign in the window. I'm surprised since I can count on one hand how many times she's closed during the weekday since I've been going there. I'm feeling even more dismal now, so I decide I'll walk up to see Johanna Meyer at her newsstand on West Tenth and get a *New York Times* at least.

Johanna is talking with customer, though she nods and smiles at me before turning back to him. I pick up a *Times* and leaf through it. A little article on Anna L. Adamson, a writer in Chicago, catches my eye for some reason. I've never read her work, though apparently she was the daughter of the editor and publisher of the Saratoga Sentinel and engaged in her own journalistic and literary pursuits. But she is now dead. Her sister found her in her room, apparently suffocated from gas leaking from an open jet. The death was accidental, the sister assumed, since the bedroom door was slightly ajar.

That is it, just a brief paragraph. But it plants the seed of a compelling idea. I leave a dime on the counter and go without speaking to Johanna and begin to walk toward Gallagher's office.

Chapter Eighteen

I had garnered a good feeling about Lincoln from these two accounts—the one from my brother and the one from Harriet.

Then the news trickled in: South Carolina seceded from the Union, and then Mississippi, Florida, Alabama, Georgia, Louisiana, and Texas. They formed the Confederate States of America. Lincoln was sworn in as president March 4, 1861, and a little more than a month later, South Carolinians attacked Fort Sumter and the country fell into war. It was all hard to believe. James wrote to me that any Five Pointers who had considered fighting for the Confederacy (there were some) now abandoned the thought. Everyone was ready to volunteer to fight for Lincoln, including James. And everyone thought it would be a simple, fast war—over before it really began and easily won.

I suppose I was jealous, stuck on the farm taking care of children—teaching. feeding, cleaning, and disciplining them. Why couldn't I go fight with James? I knew nothing of war. I think most of us didn't have any idea what the war would mean, the carnage it would cause. At that moment, all was principle and zeal.

James joined the 42nd Infantry, the "Tammany Regiment" under Col. William D. Kennedy. He wrote me from Great Neck, Long Island, where he was stationed for a month. Then he wrote from Washington, and then Maryland, short notes scribbled in haste to let me know where he was. Then he wrote in early October that his regiment had been assigned to Stone's brigade, Army of the Potomac.

And that was the last I heard from my brother.

The telegram arrived to the farm, delivered by one of the teachers from the House of Industry, come to take my place. James was apparently in Bellevue Hospital after being injured in the Battle of Ball's Bluff in Virginia. I gathered my things and left without saying goodbye to the children.

All the way to Bellevue my mind raced frantically. *James, James, James* I repeated in my mind, a desperate incantation. I cried and then made myself stop. I didn't know how to prepare for seeing him. Should I bring him something? I had no idea as to his condition. The carriage took forever, the over-worked horse clopping along with little gumption. I considered jumping off it and running the way there. It was warm for October. I could feel sweat dripping down my sides under my scratchy cotton dress, stupid thing with all of its layers—and for what? My mind could not settle on one thing. My heart beat in my chest until I thought it would burst. We finally arrived and I leapt from the carriage's cabin. I could see the East River flowing by, dimples on the cool water lit by sunshine. I ran into the hospital's darkness. The miasma theory, that infection was spread through the air, seemed almost plausible. The combination of heat and stench on the inside conjured a sickly hellhole. I found a nurse and asked where I could find James, explaining, "He was hurt in the Ball's Bluff fight." The words sounded absurd, but the nurse gave me a look of true sympathy, and, pointing to a stairwell, told me to go to the second floor.

"So many of them," the nurse said. "Mr. Lincoln thought it would be easy."

On the second floor, there were rows and rows of beds with young men. I saw a man in a black suit standing at a bedside. The person on the cot, his head covered in a bandage, had just one closed eye exposed.

I said, "Excuse me Sir, I'm looking for a patient named James Anderson."

"Murray!" A hushed voice called from the other side of the room. I looked up and saw Liz and Emma seated at a bedside. They stood as I crossed the room and embraced me. I was terrified to look at the face in that awful bed, but when I did look down at James, I let out the breath I'd been holding: he was alive.

My eyes tried to take him in quickly from head to toe, but instead of a full leg on his left side, a bloodied, bandaged stump stuck out from the covers. Where his knee and calf and foot should have been, emptiness. Liz covered the appendage with the blanket and put her hand on my arm.

"He was shot in the lower thigh, Murray," she said quietly.

I finally let my eyes settle on his face. His skin was ashen, damp with perspiration. His lips were dry and cracked, open just enough to let out a raspy breath.

"James," I said more loudly than I meant to. The man at the other bedside cleared his throat. I saw my brother's eyelids flutter, or thought I did. "James, it's Murray. I'm here." But he did not open his eyes.

Everything was quiet save for the occasional moan coming from one of the beds, sheets rustling. James, though, was still. Too still.

"I got here a couple of hours ago," Liz said. "The nurse told me that his leg was amputated in a field hospital. She said that he had anesthesia for the operation—mercifully."

But so much for mercy. The leg was now infected and the infection was spreading, as if that miasma, floating through the hospital corridors, had made its way to his bedside, in through those dry cracked lips, and had settled in to do its bidding.

I watched my brother's shallow breath rise and fall in his chest. I held his hand, which seemed too weathered for his twenty-seven years. What had he been through? What had he seen? I stroked his damp face, grey with infection, and kissed his cracked lips.

It wasn't helping.

Finally he opened his eyes and looked at me.

"James," I said. "I'm here."

His lips parted and I thought he would speak but he didn't. His chest, which had been rising and falling with his belabored breath became still though his eyes still bore into me. Emma touched his face and gently closed his eyes. I wrapped my arms around him and began to weep.

"Murray…" Liz said.

"Leave us alone!" I sobbed.

My brother, my shepherd, my beloved James, was dead.

I cursed Lincoln's war and the men and women and children he sought to free. I would have enslaved all of humanity to have James alive, would have given my life if it meant he could have lived. I lay there for a long time thinking about how I could end my own existence and join him. I understood once more the need for a heaven, the believer's only consolation when death visits—that loved ones shall be united in a celestial kingdom. My rational mind knew it was nonsense, but I also wondered if there were something—some realm where James was now that he had left this diminished shell of a body behind—and if I could find him there. After all, he was the last of my immediate family, and I was now truly an orphan. It seemed that he was my only real connection to this Earth. Without him, I was unmoored.

I fell asleep under his arm, exhausted by grief. Then a nurse pulled me up with a firmness I couldn't argue with, said something about making funeral arrangements so that he wouldn't go to Potters Field.

Emma was sitting in a chair nearby and came to my side, took my hand, and I let her. She led me away from my dead brother.

She and Liz helped me bury him. Sweeny sent his condolences and $200.

Afterward, I shut myself into our place in Five Points, the place we had shared for years. I sat among his things, smelled his clothes, put on his shoes, touched with reverence and pain every single little item he had left behind: a wool cap he wore in winter, a leather-bound diary, a pen, suspenders, the two poetry books we had brought from Scotland.

I found his knapsack under his bed. There was a note to me in it, as well as money—more than a thousand dollars. It was everything James had saved over the last several years.

> Murray,
>
> If you are reading this, then my fate has been sealed. I am sorry I cannot be here for you anymore. I will miss this life, and more than anything, I will miss you.
>
> *For thou art with me here upon the bank*
> *Of this fair river; thou my dearest Friend,*
> *My dear, dear Friend; and in thy voice I catch*
> *The language of my former heart, and read*
> *My former pleasures in the shooting lights*
> *Of thy wild eyes. Oh! yet a little while*
> *May I behold in thee what I was once,*
> *My dear, dear Sister! and this prayer I make*
> *Knowing that Nature never did betray*
> *The heart that loved her….*
> *If I should be where I no more can hear*
> *Thy voice, nor catch from thy wild eyes these gleams*
> *Of past existence—wilt thou then forget*
> *That on the banks of this delightful stream*
> *We stood together…*
>
> Be true to yourself, Murray, whatever that may mean. You're strong; you're my little fighter.
>
> Yours Always,
> James

I finally understood the poem.

Days, then weeks passed. I ignored Liz and Emma's pleas to help me. When they knocked on my door, I wouldn't answer, and if they kept knocking, I shouted for them to go away. I did not return to the House of Industry.

Despite my brother's encouraging words, I did not feel like a fighter—I felt like nothing. A deep despair settled on me, a low-pressure front that moved in and stayed for a long, long time.

* * *

Gallagher arrives late morning as promised. I have been writing all morning and now read the last few chapters to him.

"I'm sorry, Murray. That must've been so terrible for you. I can see what James meant to you."

I nod. "The anesthesia really was a miracle, though. Imagine amputations before it: the patient had to be held down, often by a loved one, as the surgeon sawed the limb off as quickly as possible, the goal being ten seconds or fewer, as the patient writhed and screamed and bled."

Gallagher shakes his head. "I remember reading that Charles Darwin trained to be a medical doctor but couldn't do it because of the brutality of surgery. So he opted to travel the world as a naturalist instead."

"The infections, though…"

"Yes, as that was before Louis Pasteur's germ theory had taken hold, before Joseph Lister promoted sterile surgery."

"True," I say. "During the Civil war, no one cleaned instruments before or between operations. The same bloody saw used on one soldier would then be used on another. Doctors and nurses didn't even wash hands until all the amputations were finished, finally washing away the accumulated blood of so many."

"Your brother's death devastated you," says Gallagher. He will let me divert for only so long to talking about objective things, like science and medicine, before getting back to the heart of the matter.

"For years after his death, I spoke to almost no one except for the most pedestrian interactions. In fact, those years were so dark, I barely remember them."

And yet, the days were so long—days on end, one after another, of droll, tedious existence. It was a bother even to breathe. I had no will to live and yet by some miracle didn't die though I wouldn't have minded if I did. I started smoking tobacco just to have something to do to pass the time. Sometimes I smoked all day, rolling one cigarette after another until my throat felt raw. Then I would go out and buy something to eat—just something to fill the emptiness, but nothing satisfying or tasty like a baked apple or ice cream.

"I wanted no pleasure, no health, no joy. I didn't read poetry, hardly read at all."

"How did you live?"

"You mean financially?" Gallagher nods. "Well, thanks to James, I had plenty of money to live on, if living it was."

I let breath into my lungs, put food into my mouth, barely bathed. I used the privy. I went back to using a chamber pot so I wouldn't have to greet people at the outhouse. The less humanity I had to interact with the better, and when I did see people, I offered them only my frigid, unfriendly countenance if they tried to speak to me. Never would I have acted in such a way in my youth, but gone was the feistiness I'd felt, the delight in the challenge of the day, the impetus of living—it all disappeared. Even in the dullness of my work for Reverend Pease, I still felt a joie de vivre, still loved life. But that left me when James left the world.

"Losing my mother and even my father was heart-wrenching, but I had been young and still had James.

"Emma and Liz would not suffice."

"No. They tried to reach me. I shut the door in their faces so many times they finally stopped coming by. I'm ashamed of that now. But I was not myself. They were stubborn. But I was not budging either."

"They knew how hurt you were but they couldn't save you from it."

"No, they couldn't. You can't save someone who doesn't agree to be saved. I know that. I was either going to get through it, or not. But for years—years!—it seemed I just woke, emptied my bladder and bowels, smoked, ate just enough to stay alive, and slept."

"I'm curious to see what brought you out of it, as something did."

"Yes, I'll write about that next."

He gives me morphine. When the syringe enters my skin, I let myself wonder what it would be like if this were my last shot.

One last dose.

I'm not ready for it.

Not yet.

Chapter Nineteen

If I was alive at all, during that time after my brother died, I just wanted to be me, and not allow others to name me and identify me, to dictate how I should behave, what I should wear, how I should live. But really, I was just stumbling through bleakness. I wondered about my grip on reality. Everywhere I looked, I saw darkness, sadness, pain. This state of the world—of reality—was confirmed for me again and again, the awfulness of life and existence, it's ruthlessness and lack of meaning.

July of 1863 was deathly hot. A terrible heatwave befell the city, making normal folk irritable, and the ornery turn evil. Though I was hardly reading the newspapers at this point, or anything for that matter, I still went out to buy tobacco and a morsel of food on a daily basis, and I heard people talk. At the newsstand, there was a group of men arguing about a draft.

"Lincoln's running out of men—thinks we should fight his war."

"Three-hundred gets you out of the draft."

"You know any got that? I've not seen three-hundred in my lifetime."

I figured it out, little by little, through overheard conversation. I thought of my brother, of the zeal with which he enlisted and ran to the slaughter. I didn't care about the men—didn't care what happened to anyone, not even myself. But having the ability to buy your way out of fighting didn't seem right either. Who's worse off? The poor, always.

I understood their frustration and I could feel the tension mount with the coming draft. Groups of Irish men gathered on the stoops of tenement apartments. They gathered in pubs, their numbers increasing in size, their grumbling becoming louder. As they drank, their meanness came forth. It was fear, yes. Fear that freed slaves would take their jobs, fear that they too would be killed as so many thousands had. Stories had poured in of so many dead on the battlefield, their bodies buried in mass graves. It wasn't glorious. With some battles, death was almost certain. Their lives had been hard—they'd nearly starved in Ireland, had survived the coffin ships, had lived in the city's poorest conditions for years. And now they were facing a draft—a draft that a richer man could buy his way out of. It was a gross injustice.

Their response to it was not only unjust, however. It was despicable, unforgiveable. But mean, sweaty, poor, scared, struggling men become something awful when they form a mob. They can lose any semblance of morality. They can lose their humanity. And that's what happened.

Saturday, July 11, began innocently enough with a protest. I watched as they marched down Mulberry. By nightfall, those protesters were drunk, and when the sun rose on Sunday and the oppressive heat set in, their numbers had grown to four or five thousand. They were seen carrying bricks and other weapons. They began to loot stores. When Sergeant Finney of the third precinct tried to stop them from entering Brooks Brothers, he was beaten on the head and body with clubs and then one of the looters shot him in the hand, blowing off two fingers.

When I heard they were coming for colored people, I snapped out of my fugue. I thought about Liz and Emery. I had not been to their basement apartment, but I wanted to find them, help them, hide them, protect them if possible. The mob was heading toward Sullivan and Thompson Streets, the tenements occupied by blacks. The mob was a terror, a heaving, brutal beast, bent on destruction and death. Someone lit a tenement on fire and when a black family ran out, they were swallowed by the crowd, beaten senseless, including two children. I was unarmed. There was no stopping anyone. Shots rang out. I feared the family shot dead.

I heard some people were taking shelter in the Eighth Precinct Station-house and hoped Liz and Emery were among them. I did not want to be around the mob—did not want to witness them hurting anyone and not be able to stop it. I cowered back to my apartment and locked the door.

The details of the stories told in the *New York Times* over the next few days are too harrowing to repeat here. Black men, beaten and lynched. Apartments burned. Children stabbed with bayonets. A colonel who tried to intervene was stripped and beaten, dragged through the street with a cord around his neck, his face mangled. A mother at home nursing an infant, was shot through the heart; the baby died too. The Colored Orphan Asylum on Fifth Avenue was attacked, and though most of the children managed to escape out the back before the mob burned it to the ground, one child died.

On Thursday night, troops arrived from Gettysburg to stop the madness, but by then, more than a hundred were dead, including eleven black men who had been brutally murdered, hanged, burned.

The *New York Times* thanked the fire squads:

> *The firemen of this City deserve the heartiest thanks and gratitude at the hands of the citizens of our metropolis. Notwithstanding the fact that they have run great risks in attempting to extinguish the conflagrations kindled by the mob, they have been fearless and prompt in the execution of their duties, and have worked untiringly to save property from destruction. The citizens cannot be too grateful to this highly useful class in our community. They deserve the best thanks and gratitude of all true law-biding men.*

I imagined James, had he not died in the war, being one of those valiant firemen trying to save the city. But me? I just holed up for those days, listening to the clamor of the firetrucks as they rushed to save buildings, to the pleas and screams of those getting beaten, begging for mercy, to the howls of sorrow from those who saw their loved ones maimed or killed, useless, as I was, to everyone.

That's what those years represented to me: I saw them through a lens of war, violence, death, and my own cowardice. If I read the paper at all, I went straight to the "City Mortality" section. In October 1865:

> *The deaths in this city during the past week numbered 476: 113 men, 77 women, 161 boys, and 125 girls, being an increase of 54 as compared with the previous week, and of 108 as compared with the responding week of 1864.*

Causes of death? Bronchitis, cholera infantum, infantile convulsions, croup, diarrhea, dysentery, typhoid fever, bowel inflammation, lung inflammation, teething, consumption, dropsy, infantile marasmus, heart disease. People drowned, or died of old age or premature birth. They were strangled. One individual committed suicide by "cutting of the throat."

I lived on, not even really wanting to.

I took odd jobs, often with the city, "abating nuisances." I removed night soil from outhouses. I hauled away dead cows, hogs, dogs, and other small animals from the streets. In a normal week, the city removed one-hundred sixty-six dead horses from the city limits. They were so large and heavy, we had to wait until they decayed so that we could remove the horses in pieces.

I remember walking in Five Points, smelling something especially putrid in the air. As I turned the corner at Cross Street, I found myself looking upon a horse lying on its side in the street. As I approached, I saw that not only was it dead, but it was gutted, bleeding into the street. Three children played tug of war gleefully with its innards.

Every morning was unwelcome, every day a sorrowful burden.

And yet I lived on.

Part Three

1870 - 1900

Chapter Twenty

Then one day, years after my brother died, I was walking down the street and passed a bookstore window. What I saw displayed inside it stopped me in my tracks: a new edition of *Leaves of Grass*. It was January 1870, just past my thirtieth birthday, and it was cold. I'd spent my twenties miserable, lonely and broken-hearted, though not destitute: the money James had left me and the bit I'd earned from the odd jobs had sufficed to keep me sheltered and fed. I stared at the book through the window, thought of Emma buying the first edition for me when I turned fifteen. I felt inside my pocket for money. Then I went inside the shop and purchased the book. I had not bought myself a book since before James died. I took it home and made a fire and read it and read it and read it.

What I found was a different Whitman, just as I was different. The war had devastated everyone, including the poet. How to reconcile the grief?

Tears! Tears! Tears!
In the night, in solitude, tears…
Not a star shining, all dark and desolate,
Moist tears from the eyes of a muffled head;
O who is that ghost?

I could see Whitman's face as I read the poems, his quiet smile, hand around a coffee cup.

In a poem called "O Me! O Life!" I read:

The question, O me! So sad, recurring—
What good amid these, O me, O life?

And then the two lined "Answer":

That you are here—that life exists and identity,
That the powerful play goes on, and you may contribute a verse.

It was a question I had asked myself so often over these years. What was I living for? What was my purpose? Who was I? What verse could I possibly contribute?

Gone was Pfaff's. All that wit and charm and drink and laughter gone. When the war didn't end quickly, Whitman had volunteered as a nurse, had visited the wounded in hospitals, had seen terrible suffering and had nearly lost hope. I wasn't the only one. He felt the desolation, the heartbreak, even the uselessness…and still found a reason to go on. That's what I found in Whitman this time.

I began to walk the city again.

I'd been wearing my loathsome dresses for years, punishment for my worthlessness. But exonerated and re-emboldened by Whitman once again, I let myself put on James's pants, which I cut and hemmed, wore his coat and hat.

A few weeks later, on Sixth Avenue, I came upon a different bookstore and went in. The young woman working there seemed friendly, said that she had just opened the shop and asked my name.

"Murray," I mumbled, not quite ready yet to accept goodwill or invite conversation.

"Well, Murray, Sir," she answered, "if you're a fan of poetry, I've got a lovely selection just over here."

I looked down at the Wordsworth volume I was holding in my hands and then stared at the back of her head as she moved toward a tall shelf of books. I was not mistaken—she had called me Sir.

I looked down at my brother's pants, at the tiny boots on my feet, at the jacket whose sleeves I rolled to fit my arms, which were of course smaller and shorter than James's. She had called me Sir—she thought I was a man. And I felt a flicker of something that had, by then, become quite foreign to me: joy.

I do not know what poetry books she showed me, but I had no money on my person anyway. I told myself that I would be back, though—I would buy books from this wonderful woman who had seen me as a man. I looked up at the sign outside her shop so I wouldn't forget it. In the window was a hand-painted sign on a large piece of wood: Pratt's Bookstore.

I walked around town, even veered over to Broadway to strut with the rest of the crowds. I felt energized, alive. My mind flicked from thought to thought, my eyes darted from face to face. I looked in people's eyes to see how they met my gaze—to see if I could decipher whether they thought me a man or a woman. I realized that the first thing *my* mind settled on—quite unconsciously and automatically—was the sex of the person I looked upon. It mattered not age—from children to the very old and everyone in between, the very first thing I thought was, "That is a woman," "That is a boy," etc. The only time my mind couldn't decide was with a young babe in a carriage, and that's when it struck me: the baby is born with no sense of its sex—it is just a pure, newly-conscious being. But society—others—would designate the sex and thus what dress and behaviors would be appropriate for the assignment.

I had been walking the streets but with my eyes downcast with what I'd hoped was a "get-the-hell-out-of-my-way-and-don't-try-to-talk-to-me" demeanor; but now, with this new identity, I looked into the faces of those walking toward me and an astonishing thing happened. The men barely looked at me and when they did, they seemed to quickly assess me: if I appeared as a man, I was a small one and posed no threat—easily dismissed. But here was the shocking thing: some of the women not only looked at me but smiled. And in a few of their smiles I saw something that might have been friendliness or more—curiosity, maybe even a flicker of interest.

What had happened in Pfaff's all those years back: girlhood-me kissing Sybil, who knew I was a female dressed as a boy. But this was different. These women looked at me as a man.

It was utterly intoxicating.

I was Murray again, but this time, I would not only claim the name, I would embody the man.

I began to study men—their gestures, their gait, their voices. I found myself making small adjustments in my behavior and dress. If I was going to go around as a man, I needed more clothing. But I didn't have to go to a tailor—I could sew my own clothes. My breasts were quite small but I bandaged them anyway. I cut my hair shorter, about shoulder length. I practiced speaking with deeper voice, but that was tedious and too unnatural. I would sound like I sounded. I knew that if people made up their minds upon first looking at me that I was a man, that they would likely remain convinced—or so I hoped. I didn't care for smoking anymore, but I bought a pipe, mostly to use as a prop. I bought a coat that was even larger than my brother's and hemmed the sleeves so it wouldn't look ridiculous. I bought new shoes for my petite feet. Every interaction I had with people told me they believed I was a man—they didn't second-guess themselves. My confidence grew.

There was one difficulty. In Five Points where James and I had lived for years there were many people who knew me as a female. If I was really going to try to pull it off—pull off being Murray again—I had to move to another part of the city. I started packing. I gave away my dresses—just donated them anonymously to the Ladies' mission rather than the House of Industry. I told the landlord I would be leaving at the end of the month. He didn't care—an Italian family of six would rent our little apartment as soon as I moved out.

The neighborhood was in transition: Irish were no longer arriving by the thousands. They had established themselves in New York City—had become firefighters, police officers, business owners, politicians. The democratic machine, run mainly by them, was gaining power. Almost all of them had gotten their start in Five Points, but most had since moved uptown. Not as far uptown as the Republicans, but they had moved to different wards, leaving Five Points available for an onslaught of new immigrants. Around the ward, the Italians were already opening grocery stores, restaurants, bars—and their cuisine was unquestionably superior to that of the Irish!

The trickiest thing about leaving Five Points? It felt like leaving James. It was where we'd landed together, where we came of age, where we grew up. Our little shack behind the outhouses might have appeared dark and dismal to an outsider, but it's where I lived with my brother all those years, sleeping side-by-side in our little closet. He was the last person I spoke with before I went to bed, the first person I saw in the morning. There we had made our tea together, cleaned our bodies, taken refuge.

And Five Points—and its taverns and grocers and food carts and back alleys and endless tenements—it was our neighborhood, our home.

After some searching, I found an apartment on Bleecker. No more view of outhouses—this one was on the third floor and had a window that opened to the street. It was already furnished with a bed, a dresser, a small table and two chairs. There was a small wood stove, though I didn't expect to prepare much food. In New York, it was easy to find good, cheap fare from street carts or inexpensive restaurants—no need to cook for yourself if you weren't inclined. I missed the home-cooked meals I'd had with Emma and Liz and Harriet, but never had any gumption to create them like that for myself (I had not had supper with them since my brother died). But with the little stove in my new apartment, I would make coffee or tea, maybe a simple soup.

I considered seeking them out and saying goodbye to them, but they too, had already scattered: Liz, I heard, was still living with Emery, though in a different tenement; Emma was full-time as a domestic now, and living with the family; Harriet had moved into a room at the House of Industry. Plus I was dressing as a man now, and didn't want to raise suspicions. But it hurt to leave without thanking them for the friendship all those years—indeed, they had been like sisters to me—and it pained me to leave without saying goodbye.

I hired a carriage to move my things in one trip. After it was packed up, I went back to the apartment one last time and stood in the doorway. James and I had no idea how life would turn out for us when we'd moved into it, but despite the uncertainty, I'd felt secure with him by my side.

I felt tears welling up in my eyes. "Guidbye wee hoose," I said in my Scottish voice, and before the tears could fall, I closed the door and walked away.

I had read that necessity is the mother of invention. It's true I felt best dressed in men's clothing—that the prospect of being a man, in dress, manner, and heart, excited me and satisfied something in my soul. But there was another element that compelled me to the endeavor: after so many years of hibernation, even living as frugally and simply as I had and allowing myself almost no pleasure, my savings were nearly gone. After paying a month's rent of $15 on my new apartment, I had $72 left to my name.

I sat down with the new landlord to sign the lease. It was minimal really—she only cared about the money, in having someone who could come up with it every month, and, as most renters included several family members, she seemed pleased to be renting the room to just one individual. Although I had introduced myself as Murray, I wasn't prepared to fill out the first blank on the renter's form: my full name. I stared at it. When I saw that the landlord, who was older and whose husband had recently passed away, was waiting for me to finish filling it out, I searched my mind frantically. I couldn't put my middle name—Margaret—and wanted to distance myself from my given name, Anderson. I almost wrote James for my middle name as it was all I could think of. But then I thought of how James had admired Alexander Hamilton, and so I wrote Hamilton for the middle name. Now—for a last name? I racked my brain; I was beginning to perspire. She was watching me with suspicion now. I had to write something. I looked up at her, my hand paralyzed, pen hovering above the page, and instead of meeting her eyes, I shut my own, trying to think of a name for myself. I saw Sweeny in my mind's eye, but the name was too conspicuous. I tried to remember other Tammany Hall politicians James had spoken of. The landlord cleared her throat. I opened my eyes, looked down at the paper and forced my hand to write H-A-L-L for the surname. I figured I could change my name later if I didn't like it.

But I did—I loved my new name.

And so, on November 13, 1870, on a cool, breezy fall day in New York City, Murray Hamilton Hall officially came into being at the tender age of thirty.

Chapter Twenty-One

So I was broke, or about to be, and the prospect of it terrified me. But far more terrifying was the prospect of returning to women's work. Going back to ten to twelve hours a day of sewing or childcare—well, it all sounded awful. I would be a perpetual pauper, at least until I married a man. His lowest wages would still be ten times greater than my own, no matter his profession. Yet the thought of marrying a man, of lying in bed with him every night, turned my stomach. It would be lying, a bigger, worse lie than my masquerade.

I had lived on my own for years and wanted to continue to do so. But soon I would need employment—a job! How was I going to make money?

I thought of James who had built his career with Sweeny and the Tammany Democrats. Of course I couldn't seek out Sweeny—he might recognize me even though it had been years, but maybe I could find a way.... I thought about James and me waiting outside Sweeny's tavern, patiently hoping for any task that might allow us to prove ourselves. And I knew where I needed to go. I got on my coat, put my pipe into my pocket, and walked out into the night.

The Bleecker neighborhood was new to me, which was perfect. It simply had a bit more breathing room than Five Points: the tenements were interspersed with nicer apartments and shops and eateries. There were food vendors and carts, but not as many, not so much cacophony. There were fewer drunks, prostitutes, and hooligans.

Ah, but it did have taverns, which was what I sought. I spied one on the ground floor of a five-story apartment building, and, walking past, glanced inside. All the chairs were occupied by men, a few rounds of poker in play. The dimly lit place seemed perfect for a first foray. The barman was tall and bald and had a pale, ruddy complexion and a friendly demeanor.

I approached the bar and stood before him. "Whiskey, please," I squeaked out, forcing myself to make eye contact.

His answer shook my core: "Madam, I'm sorry, but we don't serve ladies."

I felt my heart in my throat and for a split second considered running out. I was already being outed as a charlatan. I contemplated my future, sewing all hours of the day for a pittance.

Then I reached for my pipe and filled it with tobacco. Before I lit it, I nodded at him and said, "That's good to hear. Man needs some peace in his life." I heard a chuckle from a nearby table. My reputation was on the line. Not just my reputation—my life. I willed my hand steady and lit the pipe. I blew smoke toward the bartender and then said, "Sir, you're not the first to mistake my delicate, good looks with a feminine essence." I put my hands on my belt buckle and began to remove it. "However, I'm happy to display my manhood, though I may risk appearing indecent, and worse: instilling envy in yourself and your fine customers." I heard more laughter and someone yelled out, "Let him show it, McSorley!"

"All right, my mistake," he said grinning. "But I still can't serve you whiskey."

"Still not convinced?" I began to unbutton my pants.

"It's not that. It's just that I only serve beer here."

It was my turn to grin. "Then I'd like a beer." I buckled my belt and sat back down on a barstool.

McSorley poured one from the tap and put the pewter mug in front of me. "This one's on me," he said, and toasted me with his own mug. "And help yourself to the tobacco." He pointed to a large dish of it at the end of the bar. "That and the raw onion and cheese sandwiches are always on the house."

"Thank you kindly."

"Good ale, raw onions, and no ladies," said McSorley. "That's our motto."

He began wiping the end of the bar. My heart was finally calming and I took in my surroundings. A light layer of sawdust covered the wood floor. A string of wishbones from chickens and larger ones that must have come from turkeys hung down from the ceiling. A sign hung above the rear barroom: *Be Good or Begone.* On the walls were what seemed like a haphazard display of worn horseshoes and old dried up starfish and seashells. There was a portrait of Abraham Lincoln and next to it a framed letter from the *New York Herald* from April 15, 1865, the day after the president's assassination by John Wilkes Booth. I remembered then when Henry Clapp had asked me if I'd ever seen Edwin Booth play Richard III or Iago. The best, Clapp said. Then his brother, John Wilkes, killed Lincoln in his box at the theatre. Instead of superb acting, that becomes your legacy. My brother was killed in Lincoln's war; Edwin's brother killed Lincoln. Such sad, sad losses.

One wall featured several portraits of horses along with more horseshoes.

"You like horses?" I asked McSorley.

"Got a barn 'round the corner where I keep mine, 'long with his companion."

"Companion?"

"A nanny goat," said McSorley. "Everyone, including a horse, should have company at night."

Just then a woman walked in—a real woman. Her dress was tight, her blond curls pinned up to reveal a long, thin neck. Her painted eyes and lips meant business. She approached the bar, took me in, and then stood next to me so that our arms were touching.

Before she spoke, McSorley bowed at her and said, "Madam, I'm sorry, but we don't serve ladies."

Her face clouded over with indignation. She left.

"Man should have company at night," McSorley said. "But not when he's enjoying his beer."

"Amen." We toasted again.

I felt the tug of frustration and indignation for the woman's rejection and yet was so relieved that I had successfully posed as a man and was able to stay. I had been accepted into the club, and an exclusive club it was.

A man at the poker table looked over at me. "Would you like to deal in?" he asked.

I wasn't prepared for that. I knew a bit about poker from watching Liz and James, but I myself had never played. My heart started pumping again. "Sure," I said. I sauntered over, not wanting to appear too eager. The other men looked up briefly from their hands, nodded.

"What's your name?" asked the one who had invited me. I noticed he was a bit of a dandy—his black hat was high quality, and he wore a silk floral scarf about his neck. He was thin, too. Elegant hands.

"Murray. Murray Hall."

"Murray. I'm Charlie." He shook my hand. A good handshake, not too delicate, not trying to prove his masculinity. I took note. The other guys didn't introduce themselves or make conversation, but neither did they seem unfriendly.

Their round ended and one of the men won the pot, satisfied.

"Let's deal in Murray," Charlie said. The man dealing nodded. "You Irish?" Charlie asked.

"Scottish," I responded. I was going to tell him that I had been here since I was six, that I had grown up in Five Points, that most of the people I knew growing up were Irish, but I caught myself. That is one thing most men have mastered: the art of reticence. Again I took note.

Everyone threw a nickel in to ante, so I did too, and willed my hand to not shake, willed my nervousness to not show. The gentleman to Charlie's left—I was sitting to Charlie's right—dealt everyone five cards. I watched the men to see what they did. Charlie picked up his five cards and whistled with exaggeration. He looked at me and winked. He must've noticed my trepidation because he said, "So we're playing draw poker—we're going do one round of betting and then you can trade out as many cards as you want—so if you got a pair but not much else, you might hang on to the pair and take three new cards, see? If you've got nothing and want to try a new hand, just give Keegan your five cards and he'll deal you five new ones. Then we've got one more round of betting."

I was grateful to the bottom of my heart. He could've made it a point to ask if I knew how the game went but instead he just explained it clear as day. We played. I lost almost every hand, but I didn't care. I was paying for an education, and little did I know then that it was one that would serve me the rest of my days. My best moment came when I stayed in with nothing—just a king of hearts—and swapped out four cards for four new ones. The new hand wasn't much better, or so I thought, and I considered folding but stayed in anyway, even after the fellow to the dealer's left raised everyone a quarter. I wanted to be a good sport without appearing gullible. When we showed our cards at the end, I said, "All I've got is a king high."

Charlie looked down at my cards laid out in front of me and hollered, "That's no king high, captain. That's a flush!" All the cards, including the king, were hearts. That beats your straight, Danny," Charlie said. "And that means this pot is yours." He scooped the money toward me. "Nicely done."

I was elated, not just by winning the pot, but because I had ventured out into the world as a man, learned poker, and successfully bluffed the barman and the others, including my new companion.

I fell into a routine, not an unpleasant one, of meeting Charlie at the saloon every evening. It wasn't a set meeting—we didn't plan it, and if one of us didn't show there was no explanation demanded or supplied.

I spent my days reading, sometimes at Pratt's, and although I relished the quiet and contemplation, I looked forward to the evening, to entering that place where I was beginning to be known, the place where, after a few visits, I'd developed a rapport with everyone, including the owner, John McSorley. Some afternoons, I found him just around the corner from the tavern where he kept his beloved horse, Leo, in a small barn. McSorley would groom him there on slow days. Leo was a dappled Bay, McSorley explained, pointing out the dark-colored circles of extra-rich reddish brown on Leo's massive, sleek body. The original owner brought the horse from Denmark—Leo was a Danish warmblood—raced him for three or four years, and then sold him to McSorley. He showed me Leo's diagonal front and hind socks, pointed out the white mark on his nose, which he referred to as a snip. Leo would melt his giant head with his black mane against McSorley's chest when he scratched the horse's neck and chin.

I was afraid of Leo at first when he lurched at me with his nostrils flaring. But McSorley explained that Leo was simply looking for a snack—so I took to slipping a few sugar cubes in my pocket if I would be strolling by. He would shake me down for that sugar cube and then nibble it right out of my hand, his large teeth tickling my palm. It took me right back to Scotland, to feeding apples to the horses in the fields.

Thousands of horses walked the streets of Manhattan—workhorses that rarely lived more than two or three years. They taxied people, pulled trolley cars, ferried carriages through the snow-filled streets in winter. I had thought of them as labor, I admit, and not until I saw McSorley lovingly brushing Leo and speaking to him in a soft, kind voice, did I recognize the animal as a sentient being. I'd never seen a man so smitten with anything or anybody as McSorley was with that horse—they loved each other. You could see it was mutual.

I shared with him my Five Points past, a version in which I had never gone back to being a girl. McSorley, too, arrived there as a youth, with the exception that he actually had parents. He told me his father opened a grog shop next to a brothel, told me he was exposed at a youthful age to that world of vices. I nodded. I knew all too well that world.

"My father was smart, though," McSorley went on as he brushed Leo's side and back in long strokes. "Like any successful peddler of vice, he didn't partake himself. He was a good businessman, tried to stay on good terms with the other saloonkeepers, and didn't take sides in politics."

"That's rare for Five Points."

"I took the lesson to heart. He died when I was almost 19, and with his savings, I opened my place and was eventually able to buy a horse." He didn't look into my eyes when he said this, but into Leo's.

Charlie, I learned, had a different story.

If I arrived at McSorley's before him, I'd order and beer and talk with McSorley and then when Charlie arrived, he'd clap me on the back, grinning, and yell, "Murray!" as if I were a long, lost friend. McSorley would pour him a beer and we'd toast. Then we'd either join a poker game or start one.

But one day he arrived looking almost gloomy. He pat me on the back, but his grin was forced, or just sad. McSorley poured him a beer and we toasted. There were no poker games happening so I asked if he wanted to start one.

"Let's go sit," he said. McSorley handed him a deck of cards and we took a table near the back. Charlie began to shuffle but didn't deal.

"How was your day?" I asked him.

He looked at me, cocked his head. "You know I was born in New York—I told you that." I nodded. "You've probably never been to Paris or London," he said. I shook my head. "As a child, we traveled to Europe many times, to wonderful places. We attended the theatre, the museums, the symphony. I loved music and learned to play piano, flute, violin. I had daily lessons in drawing and painting from renowned artists. We had a gorgeous study with hundreds of books. We lived in a big, beautiful house on Fifth Avenue with lovely gardens and ate delectable food every day."

"That sounds like a dreamy childhood."

"It was fantastical. But it ended rather abruptly when I was 19."

I thought of McSorley—how his life was also altered at that young adult age. "Did your father die?" I asked.

"No. He caught me in bed with a man—the family accountant, actually."

"Oh," I said. I thought of Whitman and wondered if Charlie had read him. "And he was upset."

Charlie laughed, and it was a sardonic laugh, but not to make me feel bad. "Worse than angry, Murray. He was *disappointed*."

"What did he do—what did you do?"

"Well, he fired the accountant. And then he said I needed to get married, that he had a bride in mind for me."

I thought of someone trying to force me to marry. I found myself shaking my head.

Charlie smiled. "That was my response too—I refused the offer, of course. And so he threw me from the house and disowned me." He took a big sip of his beer. "No allowance, no inheritance. He gave my mother strict orders not to help me, though she did secretly help me to get an apartment and to furnish it."

"What did you do—how do you support yourself?"

"Well, we entertained businessmen and politicians regularly at the house, and so I came to understand my father's politics over these dinners. He is, of course, a very well-heeled Republican. So I did what I thought was appropriate: not only would I wholly accept myself and flaunt myself as the splashy fop I knew I was, I would become a Democrat and work for Tammany Hall."

"You work for Tammany?" I practically spit my beer. I had to admit, it was the perfect retaliation.

I had $38 left in my savings, but my conversation with Charlie sparked an idea, and the next evening I asked him if he could help me get a job. We were sipping our beers. McSorley was in the back making onion sandwiches.

"What kind of experience do you have?"

The question momentarily stumped me. Why hadn't I anticipated it? I couldn't say sewing or teaching or taking care of children. I said, "My brother and I used to run errands for Peter Barr Sweeny when we lived in Five Points."

He looked at me, eyebrows raised. "You mean the city's chamberlain? The Boss's right hand man?"

"The Boss?" I asked.

"Surely you've heard of William Tweed?" Yes, but I only knew him as the foreman on the Big Six fire squad—not as a "boss." I did remember reading about him here and there in the *Times*, but I hadn't paid much attention. Poetry interested me more than politics. "Man, where have you been for the last decade?" Charlie teased.

"He was a Five Points fireman."

"True, but then he became alderman. He had a gang tougher than the Bowery B'hoys." I remembered what James had told me—how primaries were physically won with fights in barrooms. "Then he got elected as a Tammany Sachem."

"Sachem?"

"The name Tammany comes from a native leader of the Lenape tribe, Tenamend. The original founders liked the name and adopted some of the lexicon—like, Tammany supporters are referred to as 'braves' and the meetings happen at the 'wigwam.' Tweed puts on a big Indian headdress at election time, which I'm sure makes those natives turn in their graves. Have you ever seen him in person?"

"No. But I heard he's big."

"He's over six feet tall and weighs about twenty stone. And he rose in the ranks fast. Sachem was a big enough deal, but then he was elected to the Board of Supervisors. And Tweed is everyone's friend. People love him—even the Republicans don't hate him, mostly because he gives them jobs. And now he has this little group of four referred to as the Ring."

"Who else is in it?"

"Oakey Hall, the mayor. Everyone refers to him as Elegant Oakey—he went to Harvard for law, writes articles, hosts literary discussions in his salon. He's the perfect face for Tammany, and the perfect contrast to gregarious, obnoxious Tweed. Then there's Richard Connelly, clean-shaven, tall as Lincoln, and always donning a stovepipe hat and gold-rimmed glasses. His nickname is Slippery Dick, which would be a rather enviable name if it didn't suggest subterfuge."

That made me grin. "And the fourth is Sweeny?"

Charlie nodded.

"What's his reputation?"

"He's the brains of the group." That did not surprise me, as that's how James described him. "They say he comes up with the Ring's plan and Tweed uses his connections to implement them. For instance, in the 1868 election, Sweeny knew that if they could get the immigrant vote, the Democrats would win."

He explained how Tweed got State Supreme Court Justice George Barnard to naturalize thousands of immigrants every day before the election—how they naturalized more than 40,000. Tweed promised them housing, food, jobs—he even promised them money for Catholic schools so they wouldn't have to attend the predominately Protestant public schools.

"He got their vote all right," he said. "And they accounted for more than a third of all the voters in that election! The Republicans weren't too happy about it—all those immigrants naturalized just before the election—six hands on a Bible at a time."

He took a sip of beer. I was riveted.

"Then there were the repeaters. On election day morning, Tweed's henchmen would gather fifty men in a saloon, feed them whiskey and send them out to vote again and again. Some were able to vote twenty-five times."

"Wow. What about the ballots?"

"Well, who do you think's counting them? Tammany men do the tallying! And if any Republicans try to oversee the ballot boxes, Tweed just sends him men to intimidate them. Or he bribes them. That works too—it's always an option. That is something Tweed is proving: no one is too righteous to resist the almighty dollar."

"So what do you do for Tammany?"

"I get to know the constituents in my district. I secure them with clothing, food, housing, or jobs—basically build their loyalty to Tammany. On election day, I make sure people vote. I count ballots—make sure we get the votes we need. And by helping Tammany, I get paid and can support myself, and the Republicans, the party my father wants to win—well, they lose."

"That must be very satisfying."

"It's something," he said. "But even though he's corrupt, a lot of people would argue that Tweed's doing good things. By funding the parochial schools, the Irish Catholics are going to fall over themselves to vote for him. He's widening and paving Broadway, which pleases the wealthy. He's pushing for the Central Park project and wants to build a bridge to Brooklyn. Some people say he's a visionary, but really it's the whole Ring that's behind these projects. Have you seen the new Courthouse?"

"Yes. It must be the most opulent building in all of New York City."

"That was the Ring's doing. They set a budget of $350,000. Last I heard, that building cost the city more than two million. Nobody fights it, though, because a lot of people are getting their pockets lined. Well, I shouldn't say no one fights it. Here," he got up. "Come with me and I'll show you something."

We took the last sips of our beers and I followed Charlie outside and up the block to a newsstand. He picked up a copy of *Harpers Weekly*, flipped through the pages, found what he was looking for and handed me the magazine.

There on the right-hand page was an illustration, a cartoon showing a large man with a maniacal clown face. He was accepting a handful of money from a gentleman in pantaloons who was kneeling before the Public Treasury safe from which he was removing bundles of money. The clown was handing over the money to people on the street, one a young child beggar in rags, another a man in a coat and top hat; behind him is a line of others waiting for their handout. The clown is saying, "*Let's Blind them with this, and then take some more.*"

"That squatting, mustachioed gentleman handing over the money to the clown is your Sweeny of course. I told you he was Tweed's right-hand."

I thought of him, how he took us under his wing, gave us jobs, and continued to help my brother once I was whisked off to the House of Industry. I didn't want to believe that Sweeny was corrupt.

"What's that mean?" I asked, pointing to the ribbon on the front of the clown that read "$15,500 Diamond."

"It refers to the 10.5-carat diamond solitaire stickpin Tweed likes to sport."

"The signature—*Th Nast*—who's that?"

"Thomas Nast," said Charlie.

"He made drawings during Lincoln's campaign, didn't he?"

"Yes, some say he helped get Lincoln re-elected in '64. But he's been making cartoons about the Ring for a while now."

I had a decision to make. It was January 14, 1871. I had just turned thirty-one and was near broke. My only skills were sewing, hat-making, teaching, and childcare, all professions that, because they were women's work, barely paid. I could *not* go back. I needed a job and yet had no skills and no capital to start a business or the know-how to make one succeed. I had no formal education. So the answer was clear: I would work in politics.

I would try to make myself useful, even if it was to people who lacked scruples. That's how much it meant to me to remain a man: I would sell a bit of my integrity if it meant that I didn't have to put on a dress ever again.

It meant I could not blunder.

It meant no one could find out, ever.

* * *

Later I learned a thing or two about Thomas Nast, a wild coincidence. Like me, he was born in 1840, and like me, emigrated at age six. The difference lay with our fathers: Nast's was a talented musician, a trombone player, who joined the New York City Philharmonic. Both his parents were cultured. What a difference that can make in who or what you might become. All these stories I was hearing of how these men's fathers influenced their lives.... It seems that if your father owns a grog shop, you might go on to have a successful tavern; if your father is a musician, you might go on to have a career as a well-paid artist. And if your father is a man with a drinking problem whose bad decisions end both his life and your mother's, your opportunities are not erased entirely, but they are greatly diminished. Maybe that's one of the reasons Charlie and I got along: both our fathers had let us down. I tried not to feel sorry for myself, but sometimes I couldn't help it.

But now, near the end of my life, I see those struggles so differently: they made me the man I am today. Yes, man.

Even as every day seemed to start with deception, with literal covering up, moving through the world as Murray felt right to me, felt like a true existence.

The stakes were so high.

They still are. I do not want to face an outraged public, and I certainly don't want to face a disappointed—or worse, disgusted—daughter.

And so if fathers have so much influence on their child's life, what will mine be on Minnie's? I've tried to spare her from the jungle, but if struggle makes us stronger, what am I really sparing her from? But I also learned that too much fear and struggle and desperation can make you mean.

It can make you do things you'll regret.

Chapter Twenty-two

Charlie was just shy of six feet, thin and strong. I spent enough time with him to know he ate only one meal a day. Long lashes framed his beautiful blueish green eyes. His hair was sandy brown, naturally wavy, especially on humid days. When I first met him, he wore a handle-bar mustache and sideburns, but he shaved it one day, telling me that he had tired of the whiskers, that my smooth skin inspired him. I blushed when he said this and turned away. No one saw me as often, as closely, or as clearly as Charlie did. I was aware that I was taking a risk being his friend, but he made my life bearable, less boring. Worth living.

He wore a different silk scarf every day from a collection his mother salvaged for him (she knew, as most mothers do, that her son would practice sexual inversion—as Havelock Ellis coined it—before Charlie himself knew it, he told me). When he was exiled from his home, she brought him all his clothes, most of which she had helped him shop for and buy on trips to London or Paris. And so he had a different outfit every day, fashionable pieces with flair. Clothes fell perfectly on his thin frame. He could wear anything and didn't mind not blending in. In fact, he preferred not to and had the audacity and charm to pull it off.

His temper could sting if you weren't on his good side. Fortunately, I was. I didn't know why he liked me; he just did. He had a playful, no holds barred approach to the day. He loved photography. For some time, he had used a daguerreotype, and then a wet plate camera, but his mother had gotten him one of the first dry plate cameras—and he wanted to use it every day. He was so disarming he could photograph anything. He knew how to behave in any setting—was equally comfortable in a drawing room of a Fifth Avenue mansion as in the back alley of Five Points' worst tenements. Soon I was not only finding him in the evenings but joining him around town by day as he set up his camera and took photographs.

It had been years since I explored the city so much, not since earlier times with James. I had missed a decade holed up and heart-sick. The city had undergone so much change during those years I'd been a recluse—it might have been impossible to get my bearings but for some lasting monuments, like the spires of Trinity Church. There were hundreds more ships in the East River, dozens of new shops and mansions. The new courthouse, of course.

One afternoon we met on Bleecker Street. Charlie was dressed in fitted black trousers with suspenders, skinny black boots with shiny silver buckles, a red silk shirt, a scarf printed with red roses, and a tall silk hat. He led me down the block to an organ grinder—an Italian boy who could barely hold up the organ box. A monkey with a tiny top hat and bright red and gold outfit danced in front of the crowd. Charlie set up his tripod and took his photograph when the monkey was relatively still and then held out a coin. The monkey took it and squealed, jumping up and down, and then delivered it to the upside-down hat in front of the boy.

"The Padrone sends them out," said Charlie. "That's one interesting thing about the Italians being the new arrivals…most of them don't speak English and to find jobs and housing they don't necessarily turn to Tammany—they rely on their Padrone. They're crammed into the tenements even worse than you all ever were. And think about it—those tenements were relatively new in the late 40s and 50s, but now they've housed sweaty, filthy bodies for years, the walls marred with soot from cooking, the ventilation worse than ever. But I'm always conflicted when I give these boys some coins. I mean, if they make money, the Padrone will continue to make them hustle, but if they don't, they probably get beaten. And the organ box probably weighs more than fifty pounds."

I wondered how they made money at all. At first they were a novelty, but now there was a grinder and monkey on every block.

We walked over to Broadway, past Tiffany's, A.T. Stewarts, Lord & Taylor, R.H. Macy's—places Charlie used to frequent that I had never entered. We crossed over to Fifth avenue and Charlie stopped us in front of an enormous house, three stories tall, with arched windows. It was surrounded by an ornate metal gate.

"That's my house," said Charlie. "Or, it was my house before I was forced to leave it."

I took in the stunning fortress.

"Before I left, my father said to me: "You're no better than the Irish nigger shit infiltrating this city."

I winced at those ugly words, put my hand on his shoulder. "I'm sorry, Charlie."

"It's O.K."

I thought I saw a shadow of a person in the second story window, but when I looked again, it was gone. Charlie had been rejected, cast out, because of his sexual proclivities. *We are the misfits*, I wanted to tell him. *We risk everything—exile, rejection, abandonment—to be who we are.*

Instead I said, "You want to go get ice cream? I'll buy."

He laughed. "Murray, you do love your treats."

The ice cream parlor my brother and I had gone to so long ago was still open, and I ordered lemon flavor in memory of him. I never thought I would want to live again, that I would be able to enjoy life at all when I lost James, but thanks to Charlie, I was starting to.

That night, we played a few hands and drank a few rounds at Pete's, which, unlike McSorley's, allowed both whiskey and women. At one point Charlie leaned over to me and said, "You've got an admirer."

A quiver of women was gathered at one table. I recognized one of them but couldn't remember from where. Then it came to me—she was the woman rejected from McSorley's that first day. She was looking at me, then looked away, and then back. I smiled and returned to the poker game, but couldn't concentrate and glanced again. Her dress, though my least favorite color—lavender—was cut to reveal her supple shape. Her lips were a dark red, her cheeks rouged as well. Her look suggested more than mere friendliness. I felt something stir in me that I hadn't allowed myself to consider for years.

"She's pretty," I said.

"Her name is Mollie," Charlie said. "And she charges."

Later I fell into bed alone, thinking of Mollie and her lavender dress—and removing it. I allowed myself the fantasy, knowing that any other option was an impossibility. That night I had sensual dreams, soft sheets, my body intertwined with another, legs between legs, skin on skin, wet soft lips meeting. And I was with a woman.

I had ignored that part of myself for a very long time, the part of me that had been so thrilled by kissing Sybil. The kiss had upended my life—I'd been caught and banished because of it. That's what I had learned by allowing myself to do it, to feel it, to want it.

The risk was too much. I would have to settle for my own dreams, my own fantasies, my own hands. And never be touched by anyone.

As I was not yet gainfully employed, I accompanied Charlie wherever he went, and his forays were never disappointing. Ah, to have a friend again after ten years of self-imposed solitude! He was always equipped with either a sketchpad and coal or pencils, an easel and paints, or his new camera. And when we found something interesting, we'd settle in for a while so that Charlie could make a record of what he was seeing. He was the most creative person I had ever met besides Whitman, but while Whitman captured the city in words, Charlie preferred photographs, drawings, paintings. Nevertheless, I brought Whitman or other books along and would read aloud to Charlie while he worked. When he was making art, he often wanted to hear stories or poetry, to not always have to keep up a conversation.

He had always been artistic, he told me. But it was not until he was rejected by his father and stopped caring what people thought that he was able to create every day.

"Before that," he told me, "I was a pleaser. But you cannot make art if you're trying to please. You can only make meaningful art when you are absolutely true to yourself."

I had been a pleaser with Reverend Pease. What would it mean to be true to myself? Could I be true to myself if I wasn't wholly honest with others? Was this—being Murray—my truest self?

One day I went with Charlie to Central Park. He explained that though Olmsted and Vaux had designed it, it was the Irish who had built it, landscaped it, planted the hundreds of trees, did all the back-breaking work to shape it into what it was, acres of bucolic paths, placid ponds, romantic bridges, ornate fountains, an ice-skating rink for winter. Then the upper classes—Charlie's father among them—had fought to ban the dirty Irish from it. Horse and carriages traveled its trails. Like Broadway and Fifth Avenue, it became yet another arena to flaunt wealth, which is not as enjoyable if the lower classes are lurking about with their drunken picnics and unruly, unkempt children.

Charlie spotted a couple on a bench sitting close together. The man appeared wealthy, the woman much less so, but she was younger and very attractive. I watched as she put her face near his as if to kiss him and then pulled away. They spoke quietly into each other's ears and laughed. The man took her hand and gazed into her eyes while they said nothing—then he kissed her hand. Charlie set up his canvas and began to paint them from some distance. I opened *Leaves* and began reading aloud "Song of the Open Road," one of Charlie's favorites:

Afoot and light-hearted I take to the open road,
Healthy, free, the world before me,
The long brown path before me leading wherever I choose
Henceforth I ask not good fortune, I myself am good-fortune.

Henceforth I whimper no more, postpone no more, need nothing,
Done with indoor complaints, libraries, querulous criticisms,
Strong and content I travel the open road.

And then a few lines later I read:

You road I enter upon and look around,
I believe you are not all that is here,
I believe that much unseen is also here.

Charlie asked me to repeat those last lines, so I did. He kept painting. He was rendering the woman's hat, the flowers in it, with quick flicks of the paintbrush. I loved his style. He worked quickly and didn't try to be perfect or even realistic. He said that if he tried to, he wouldn't paint, wouldn't enjoy it.

"What do you think Whitman means by that?" he asked.

"By what?"

"By the 'unseen.'"

"I'm not sure."

He continued painting but asked, "Do you feel your brother around you?"

I hesitated then shook my head. "I don't believe in God."

Charlie paused his painting and peered at me. "That's not what I asked you. And these are different matters. I'll bet the God you reject is the one Man created. It was Man who put Jesus on the cross after all—and what an image to worship! Who wants that? You reject Man and his churches and hypocrisy and bickering and feuding. I'm guessing that's what you don't believe in. You reject the idea of an almighty man sitting on a throne in the sky, dictating what happens in our lives, taking mercy on some while crushing others. And why is it always a He with a capital H?" Charlie paused his diatribe, poked his brush into a can of water before continuing. "I'm talking about something very different. Whitman sensed the unseen, felt it. Have you?"

"Yes, I've felt it."

"And how does it make you feel?"

"I feel comfort," I said, "but also a yearning that hurts. And when I dream of him—of James—it's so real, it's like he's visiting me. But when I wake up, I feel empty, despondent even. As if I've lost him all over again."

"Could you accept the visit as a gift? I mean, maybe there's an unseen we can't explain. Maybe that's where James is. Not heaven—not anything that requires good deeds to inhabit—but something, something unseen except in dreams or deep meditation."

He resumed painting and I thought for some time about what he had said. After a while, the man and woman rose from the bench. They spoke in low voices for several minutes. He took her hand again and kissed it and then departed from her and began walking down the path toward us. He nodded to Charlie as he passed and then instinctively turned around to look at the painting. There was a fountain next to the bench, and Charlie could have easily been painting that, but his focus was of course the couple.

The man stopped. He was well-dressed in a wool suit and tie, an affluent style you'd expect to see on Broadway. Charlie was wearing a button-up shirt, slim and fitted, and his signature scarf du jour, chartreuse that day. I was in my over-sized coat.

"That's quite good," the man said.

"Yes, I know," said Charlie. This made me grin.

"But why make a painting of us?" His obvious suspicion suddenly made me realize that he might be married—and not to the young woman. I looked down, and of course saw a wedding band.

"I painted it because you two make a lovely spectacle. 'All seems beautiful to me,'—isn't that Whitman's line later in the poem, Murray?"

"Yes," I said.

"I love to capture moments of human nature on display, and what is more beautiful than an illicit dalliance? I found her coquettish response to your advances created the perfect tension: a kind of quintessential model of desiring of that which you can't have—or at least shouldn't. "

The man's face was turning red, his jaw set. "I'd like to buy the painting." He reached into his pocket, pulled out several gold coins. "Here's six dollars." The man thrust the fist of money at Charlie, who looked amused.

"My art isn't for sale."

"Everything is for sale."

"That's what you all think. I grew up with men like you."

The man pulled a billfold from his wallet and peeled off several bills. "This is fifty dollars."

Charlie had begun putting his paints away. The man huffed audibly. "You're being unreasonable. Why spend the time making something if you aren't willing to sell it? This is more money than you'll make in month."

Charlie continued to put away his easel. The painting was lying on the ground. The man threw the bills on the grass and reached for it.

Charlie tackled him. It happened so quickly that I gasped, not unlike a woman might. But they weren't listening. Charlie had him on the ground, a penknife against the man's neck. The man's eyes widened with fear.

"Do you know what I am?" Charlie asked him. "Well, do you?" The man didn't answer but shook his head, though just a bit since the penknife was pushed into his flesh, making a deep indentation.

"I'm Irish nigger shit." Charlie poked the knife more firmly against the man's neck. "And I'd kill you before I'd accept your money."

Charlie got off him, walked over to the painting and held it up, looking at it with satisfaction. The man lay there, holding his neck.

Then Charlie walked over to him with the painting and leaned it gingerly against the man's prone leg. "But if you like it so much, you should have it. Consider it a gift."

I was jolted by this experience and felt the blood pumping in my veins and my heart thumping, but Charlie walked away perfectly calm. As if nothing had happened, he began telling me about Seneca Village, the community of blacks—nearly three hundred—who owned property where the park now stood. They built houses, schools, a church, had good fishing in the Hudson, clean water. It was a refuge from the bustle of Lower Manhattan. Black men couldn't vote in New York unless they owned $250 worth of property, and Seneca Village made that possible for many. But the families were ousted with some compensation so the park could be built. Eminent domain, the legislature claimed: for the public good. And it was true, the park was that. But it came with a sacrifice.

"Even though most of them gave up their homes and community so the park could be built, those black men were not even allowed to work on it."

He recognized injustice perhaps because he himself had suffered loss at the hands of the wealthy who so often determine our fates without concern of the consequences. He was artistic, philosophical, and as that day demonstrated to me, capable of violence.

He became a true friend. When summer hit and I continued to wear the heavy coat that was too large for me, Charlie didn't ask why. When he jumped into the East River to cool off, he didn't question why I didn't join him. Sometimes I thought he knew my secret, but he never confronted me.

While he took photos of ships in the harbor one afternoon, I read him a sexy part of "Song of Myself." Of course, I knew that Charlie liked men, liked them the way Whitman did. I read:

Through me forbidden voices,
Voices of sexes and lusts, voices veil'd and I remove the veil,
Voices indecent by me clarified and transfigur'd.
I do not press my fingers across my mouth,
I keep as delicate around the bowels
as around the head and heart,
Copulation is no more rank to me than death is.

He threw back his head and laughed. Then he said the poem reminded him that he had to take leave of me, that he had an appointment at a bathhouse.

"Don't you have a bath at your apartment?"

Again, he laughed. "You and I are so similar, even in our differences," he said. When I looked at him confused, he added: "I'd invite you, but trust me, Murray, it's not your cup of tea."

Charlie always wanted adventure, and I would agree to any excursion he suggested since they always proved interesting: a ferry trip over to Brooklyn to share a steak and a bottle of Bass at the Phoenix; ice skating in Central Park; a stroll on Coney Island. One afternoon we went to Long Island Sound, ate oysters at Fulton Market, washing down their buttery brine with Milwaukee lager.

Later we went to see one of Barnum's shows. Like Whitman, Charlie loved all of Manhattan. I showed him where James and I lived in Five Points. I told him all about my brother.

Charlie was friendly with almost everyone, unless you were trying to buy his art or push your weight around with money. We visited different bars and saloons; he knew so many kinds of people—police officers, judges, lawyers, bondsmen, reporters, firefighters, and especially politicians.

One day we stood outside Delmonico's on Union Square and watched as New York's elite sauntered in for a mid-day meal. These were some of the most moneyed people in New York City, Charlie told me.

"I'd be surprised if my father doesn't show up, but since today is Wednesday, he's probably lunching at Astor's. He comes to Delmonico's on Tuesdays and Fridays for turtle soup and champagne. He and the rest of them—you can't imagine how terrified and disgusted they are by the hordes of immigrants entering this city—this country—with their diseases and ignorance and poverty." A carriage pulled up in front of the restaurant and an older couple emerged.

"The old rich keep having to move their mansions farther and farther north," Charlie continued. "They don't even like the newly moneyed—the up-and-coming. Old wealth is different, very different. Or so they believe. Look at Tweed, the 10-carat diamond stickpin he wears on his lapel. He wants to make up for having been raised in Five Points. But you never escape Five Points. Because people with old money, like Samuel Tilden who runs the state committee and made his riches as a railroad lawyer, well, he'll be nice to Tweed's face during meetings. But you think he'd endorse Tweed's membership into the Manhattan Club? Tweed is the 'shabby rich'—he'll always be trying to prove himself. He can shop for his wife at Tiffany's, can buy diamonds that costs thousands, but they're never going to fully accept or respect him."

I thought about Five Points, about all those people who came here to better their lives. Wealth wasn't the goal as much as survival was. But for Tweed, I could see that he hoped wealth would gain him acceptance, even admiration. He'd never be one of the upper classes, but that wouldn't stop him from trying. I didn't need to be. As Charlie made me see—it would be out of reach even if I got a lot of money. But I would need a job soon. I still needed to support myself.

Rather than Delmonico's, Charlie and I ate at chophouses on Bleecker or Houston. I came to like kidney pudding, against all odds. It was more palatable than haggis, at least what I vaguely remembered of haggis. Sometimes we went to Dolan's next to the Tribune building—the reporters lunched there. Actually, everyone would eat there—journalists, businessmen, conductors. Though I never saw him there, it was a place Whitman would have loved—a culinary gathering of the working class and the well-to-do, an egalitarian eatery. One day we saw the inventor Thomas Edison there eating a piece of five-cent pie. The railroad developer Jay Gould, one of the richest men in New York, was there one day having a steak. Charlie and I usually opted for a ten-cent bowl of beans with a side of ham or corned beef. Coffee and cake were an extra ten cents. I often splurged, since I couldn't resist dessert. Charlie just drank his coffee and talked to me while I indulged.

I went to Charlie's apartment one morning at his request. When I arrived, I saw that it was a larger place than mine, a corner apartment on the fourth floor, two bay windows on either side. He had beautiful furniture too, including a divan whose emerald green upholstery looked like silk. His paintings and sketches and photographs covered the walls. It was part living apartment, part art studio. He was in the kitchen making us coffee.

"This is such a nice place," I said.

"My mother found a way to make sure I have some creature comforts, despite my father's desire to cut me off. It's all just furniture we were storing anyway, stuff that was supposedly too out of fashion for the mansion."

"This carpet is lovely." It had bold geometric designs in red, yellow, and hints of green that somehow complemented the couch, a Victorian settee. It all looked very stylish and put together and not at all out of fashion, a concept I could hardly grasp, especially about furniture.

"Isn't it? It's Caucasian." I gave him a confused look. "From Turkey," he added, and handed me a coffee.

"Thank you," I said. "Thanks for inviting me here, Charlie."

"We're going to get you a job today," he said. "I invited you here so we could embellish your outfit."

My heart jumped involuntarily. I was wearing pants and boots, a white button-up collared linen shirt—more cream than white. I was not going to try on different clothes—I was not going to take off my coat.

But it turned out he didn't expect me to. He just opened a drawer and rifled through it, pulled out a few ties, one with navy and green stripes and the other red with little black and white flowers.

"You just need a little color," he told me and approached with the ties. He started to put the first one—the striped one—around my neck. We were closer than we had ever been—he was touching my neck and tying the tie in a knot just under my chin. I could smell his cologne, hints of wood, tobacco, and citrus. His face was inches from mine and I was afraid to look into it. He kissed men, I knew he did; and I was afraid that he was going to kiss me and I didn't want him to. But when I looked up he was just grinning his Charlie grin and holding up a hand mirror.

"How about that?"

I looked and saw he was right—the one little detail added much to my bland outfit. I had been trying to disappear, I think, but the tie gave my outfit some flair. I liked the tie, and it made me feel confident rather than conspicuous.

"Wear that one today and you can take it home along with this one. If you like them, I can take you to Brooks Brothers. But we're going to have to wait until you've got a job because they're not cheap."

"I couldn't possibly take them!"

"I have ten more in this drawer. And they suit you." Charlie gestured for me to sit at his little table under the window, which was open. It was summer, and though it had been hot and humid for days, a little breeze came through. It was my first summer wearing my coat and I thought the heat might kill me.

"Now we're going to practice smoking cigars," Charlie said, handing me one. "I know you sometimes smoke cigarettes and pipes, but cigars are different—they can be the perfect ice-breaker. You're going to carry matches in your pocket so you can light a gent's cigarette or cigar when it would be the polite thing to do. Now, I personally think cigars are disgusting, but a lot of men smoke them, right? So if you decide it's a prop that works for you—and I think it might be—you want to learn how to use it in a way that doesn't make you sick."

And so for the next hour, I practiced leaning in and lighting Charlie's cigar and he lit mine. He taught me how to puff on it so that I didn't actually inhale. He taught me how to stub it out. He said that good cigars were a good investment and gave me a box of Cubans—La Rosa Havana, Superiores—to put in my coat pocket. The box was beautifully decorated, very colorful, with gold coins and blue ribbons, a large pink and red rose held by a delicate female hand. My own female hand did not betray me. Though small, yes, my fingers were rather stubby and not at all like the long, elegant fingers of the hand on the cigar box. I kept my nails chewed to the quick, not as part of my trickery, but because I had always chewed them.

When Charlie felt satisfied that I was prepared, we left his apartment. I felt a little nauseated from the cigars but was grateful for the time he was taking with me.

"We're going to head to Union Square," he said. He wouldn't say anymore. I realized that it was one of the first times I'd been with him out and about in the daytime that he wasn't carrying his satchel of art supplies or camera.

As we approached the Square, he pointed to a gorgeous new three-story building with arching windows and elaborate brick work. The grounds were immaculately landscaped.

"Behold the Tammany wigwam," said Charlie.

We entered the massive hall and were met by a life-size wood carving of a Tammany brave. The floors were polished marble. It must've cost a fortune, I thought, and whispered as much to Charlie.

"Your pal Sweeny has an office here. This is the meeting place of the higher ups of the city—Tweed, Connelly, Sweeny, and Mayor Oakey. This is where it all happens."

How far Sweeny had come from his saloon in Five Points.

"We're not going to talk to Sweeny, are we?"

I had no idea if Sweeny would remember my brother or me or if he knew why I stopped working with my brother at the age of twelve, when my girlhood revealed itself on that fateful day. I was just glad I was not menstruating at that moment. My menses weren't due for another week. Sometimes the cramping kept me in bed two whole days.

"It wouldn't be possible for us to get a meeting with Sweeny. We're looking for an assemblyman—George Plunkitt. He knew my father from back in the day, and when I came to him last year, he hired me for the election."

We entered a room filled with smoke and men in top hats. Charlie headed toward a man with a thick mustache seated alone at one of the tables. Another gentleman was standing near him but seemed about to take leave since they had just shaken hands. I looked around and noticed the wonderful floor-to-ceiling bookshelves with what must have been thousands of books. I would have been happy to just sit there all day reading through the titles. But Charlie was already speaking to the man.

"Mr. Plunkitt?"

The man nodded and reached out his hand. "Charlie, how are things going in your ward?"

"Quite good, Sir. And more of our own people are arriving now that the Republicans are taking leave and heading farther north of the city."

"I'm glad you see the potential in that," said Plunkitt. "And who's this?"

"This is my friend Murray Hall."

Plunkitt nodded again, took me in. Meeting someone for the first time was always the most fraught moment.

"How do you do, Sir," I said and reached out my hand which he shook.

"You're Irish?"

"Scottish, Sir. I arrived in Five Points in '46. My brother and I got our start running errands for Mr. Sweeny just after that."

"Is that so? And where's your brother now?"

"He enlisted and died in the Battle of Ball's Bluff, Sir."

"That's a damned shame. That war took too many of ours."

I wasn't sure if he meant Northerners or New Yorkers or immigrants or Democrats—and I didn't ask.

"And what are you here to see me about today, you two?"

"Murray's looking for work, Sir. Understands how our elections…function."

"Does he?" he gestured to the chairs. "Well, sit down then, and let's talk." We pulled out the heavy wood chairs and sat. Plunkitt pulled a box out of his coat pocket and offered us a cigar. Charlie declined, but I thanked him and took one and then Charlie subtly nudged me. I pulled the matches out of my pocket and willed my hands not to shake as I offered to light Plunkitt's. He let me, puffed away on it. I had to resist the urge not to wave the smoke away from my face. I lit my own cigar. Even if I wasn't inhaling, I felt ill from practicing and terribly nervous sitting before this prominent man in whose hands the fate of my employment seemed to lie.

"I'm sure you understand something about elections, Murray, but elections are only part of it. Tammany has done a hell of a job gaining control of this city and we're not about to let that go. We've got new people coming here every day from different parts of the world—Germans, Jews, Italians, Irish, and, like yourself, Scottish. We've got freemen coming up from the South who can vote now thanks to the 15th Amendment. You know about the districts?"

"Yes," I answered. Charlie had briefly explained how the city was split up into not only wards but voting districts. I didn't understand it entirely, but I thought it might make sense eventually.

"Each captain of the election district has an important job. It's not just to get people to vote Tammany on election day; it's to know each and every one of the potential voters in that district—as many as you can. You gotta know 'em by name. You gotta go to their christenings, to their funerals. When they get married, you'd better send a gift and not a cheap one either. If their apartment building burns down, you'd better show up the night of the fire—and not just to offer sympathy but to be at the ready to put them in shelter for the night and find them permanent housing."

I nodded. I knew he wasn't offering me a district captain job, but I wanted to show understanding. I also suddenly realized my ambition to be one someday.

"What do people want?" he asked.

"Jobs," interjected Charlie.

"That's right. You got to be so connected that you can sniff 'em out. Is there construction going on? Does someone need a bookkeeper? If you can provide a job, you will earn a vote. From accountant to bootblack—know your voters' trades and who needs that position filled. I can always get work for a deservin' man. I make it a point to keep track of jobs, and it seldom happens that I don't have a few up my sleeve ready for use. I know every big employer in the district and in the whole city, for that matter, and they ain't in the habit of sayin' no to me when I ask them."

He paused and took a drag off his cigar, as if to see if I would interrupt. I didn't.

"And there's something else," he continued, pointing his cigar at me. "Don't go putting on airs. Now you have good clothes for the job. You don't want to be dressing fancy but neither do you want to be wearing rags. Make the poorest man in your district your equal." I nodded.

Plunkitt then leveled his eyes at me. "You like books? You educated?"

"I don't have a formal education, Sir, but I am rather self-taught. I love to read."

He frowned. "Well, forget the books—you don't need 'em. There's only one way to hold a district: you must study human nature and act accordin'. You can't study human nature in books. Books is a hindrance more than anything else. If you have been to college, so much the worse for you. You'll have to unlearn all you learned before you can get right down to human nature, and unlearnin' takes a lot of time. Some men can never forget what they learned at college. Such men may get to be district leaders by a fluke, but they never last…"

Here I tried to reiterate that I'd never been to college, but Plunkitt talked over me.

"…a lot of talk about the Tammany district leaders bein' illiterate men. If illiterate means havin' common sense, we plead guilty. We ain't all bookworms and college professors. If we were, Tammany might win an election once in four thousand years. Most of the leaders are plain American citizens, of the people and near to the people, and they have all the education they need to whip the dudes who part their name in the middle and to run the City Government. We've got bookworms too, in the organization. But we don't make them district leaders. We keep them for ornaments on parade days."

I nodded again, and again he leveled his gaze at me. "So you want to be an ornament or you want to do some real good for Tammany and yourself?"

"I want to do good for Tammany, Sir."

Plunkitt tapped the ash off his cigar. "Don't be quotin' Shakespeare. He was all right in his way, but he doesn't know anything about Seventh District politics."

It was Whitman I could quote to him, but I would keep poetry to myself, just another thing I had to hide. "Yes, Sir."

"Where do you live?"

"Bleecker, just off Sullivan."

"And Charlie, you're still on Houston?"

"Yes, a block down and a block over from Murray."

"So you're still serving the Eight Ward. Murray, you'd be in the Fifteenth, which is run by a very capable man by the name of McTaggart—Patrick McTaggart. I want you to go see Patrick. He has lunch at the De Soto on Bleecker, just near you. Know it?"

"The English chophouse?"

"That's the one. You'd think as an Irishman he would disdain English food, but he can't get enough of it—says he would eat broiled kidneys every day if he could. I wouldn't put it past him if he does. Go see McTaggart. Tell him I gave you this— "

Plunkitt fished a billfold out of his pocket and counted out a hundred dollars and handed it to me.

"Tell him I gave it to you to get you started. Ask him what you can do for him—tell him that I gave you an advance and that you're ready to dedicate yourself to Tammany. He'll have something for you."

Plunkitt stubbed out his cigar, indicating that our conversation was over. I extinguished mine too, and trying to hide my shock that he'd just handed me one hundred dollars, simply shook his hand with genuine gratitude.

Charlie put his arm around me once we were out of view and squeezed my shoulder.

"Congratulations," he said.

I let out the breath I'd been holding. "Thanks, Charlie."

"Absolutely."

We were about to leave the wigwam when I spotted Tweed coming down the hall. I had never seen him in person, but he was unmistakable from Thomas Nast's cartoons! He was a giant—over six feet tall and at least three hundred pounds. He was laughing and patting a dark-haired, mustachioed man on the back. And that's when I recognized him: Sweeny. He looked much more serious than Tweed, sullen even. Tweed had on a fine suit but was wearing a bright Native headdress—red and white and black feathers stuck out from his already tall head making him appear a foot taller; he had a hatchet in his hand and began chanting and dancing around.

"Looks like Tweed's preparing for the fourth of July Tammany parade," said Charlie in my ear.

It was difficult to believe that this was my new boss, and that this jovial, ridiculous, obnoxious giant, was, according to Thomas Nast in *Harpers* and the editors of the *New York Times*, responsible for robbing the city blind.

But I couldn't concern myself with the corruption of Tweed or the Ring. I had a hundred dollars in my pocket, an amount it would have taken me nearly an entire year to earn with a woman's wages.

I found McTaggart at the De Soto on a Friday where Plunkitt said he would be. He turned out to be Scottish, not Irish as Plunkitt assumed. When I told him I was born in Govan near the Clyde he was thrilled. He himself was born in Edinburgh. I told him about the hundred-dollar loan from Plunkitt, that I was available to start working the Fifteenth district.

"Sit down and eat," he said. "The broiled kidneys are top notch."

I ordered a plate of them from the counter, and sat back down with him. He got down to business, launching immediately into a description of a typical day as I choked down the small gravy-soaked turds, making every effort I could to appear to be enjoying them.

"Last week around 2 A.M., I was woken up by a bartender ringing my doorbell. Wanted me to bail out his boss, a saloonkeeper arrested for violating the excise law—he was selling on a Sunday. I furnished bail and got back to bed at three. At 6 A.M. I was roused by some fire engines passing the house. I got up, went to the fire to help out. You see, fires are the perfect vote-getters. Tenement was all burned up, so I took everyone who managed to get out to a hotel, got them clothes, fed them, and arranged for temporary housing until they could get back on their feet. Two hours later I went to the police court to look for my constituents—of course I find some. With a sweet word to the judge, I secured discharge for six drunks and paid fines for another two. I worked it all out."

He paused to fork a kidney into his mouth. "Then I went to an Italian funeral down at the ferry and an hour later to a Jewish funeral. Afterwards, at 7 P.M., I went to headquarters to attend a meeting of election district captains where each of us submits a list of all the voters in our districts and reports the general attitude toward Tammany, like who might be won over and how they could be won—who's in trouble and how to help them. Then I went to an Irish wedding reception and danced and gave a nice gift. I didn't get to bed until midnight."

I raised my eyebrows to convey how impressed I was. "Quite a day."

"The reason I'm telling you this is so that you understand what goes into this work. It's never monotonous, that's for sure. Here's your part: Read the obituaries. Show up at fires. Go to the weddings and the funerals. Make friends. Be helpful. You got people who need jobs, come to me. We'll find them a job. Make sure your constituents know you and know they can rely on you. And when election day comes around, you'll lead them to the polls, and there will be no doubt in their mind how to vote."

"Yes, got it."

"And check in with me here every Friday. We'll see your progress and make sure you have enough funds to do your work."

McTaggart was rather dapper in a slim fitting shirt with a tie, no jacket because it was a sweltering day. I'd kept my heavy coat on during lunch. He eyed me and asked whether I wasn't miserable wearing a large coat in the terrible heat. My heart hiccupped. He seemed to perceive me as a man, but the coat raised suspicion. I pulled it around me tighter and gave a slight shudder.

"I'm always cold, Sir."

"Poor circulation," he pointed his fork at me. "Broiled kidneys. They're a cure-all."

I pulled out my box of cigars and offered him one, which he accepted.

And just like that, I had a job.

I became fascinated with learning everything I could about Tweed and the rest of "The Ring"—Mayor Oakey, comptroller Connelly, and of course, Sweeny. The *New York Times* ran stories almost every day about them, and Thomas Nast's cartoons in *Harpers* almost always targeted Tweed. The *Times* and *Harpers* were somewhat anti-immigrant, often portraying newcomers as ignorant inebriates too easily swayed by the corrupt Democrats.

Of course, I saw both sides—the drunkenness but also the desire to better oneself. I knew enough stories of Irish who had escaped the famine only to live in filthy poverty here. Some tried to raise themselves out of it and succeeded; others drowned their shame and pain in a bottle of whiskey—or more likely in a bucket of whiskey from a grogshop. I saw all these contradictions, and noted the power of Tammany and their willingness to help immigrants for the price of loyalty and a vote. Many of their lives were devastated by disease, poverty, hunger, loss of dignity, loss of loved ones. Tammany was the safety net that caught them before they succumbed to sorrow and helplessness. I saw rich Republicans whose disdain for the poor was blatant in the scowls they offered them; to them, the poor weren't actual human beings but carriers of disease, spreaders of degradation—not people with ambition or dreams or hopes. It took money to school and house and hospitalize and, yes, bury immigrants, and the Republicans saw them as a drain. I saw many lives improve because of Tammany—including my own.

And Tammany didn't just help individuals. As Charlie had pointed out, many felt the city was being transformed under Tweed for the better. He ordered the construction of sewers, saw to it that people had clean water, gas, paved streets, parks, art museums, schools. The *New York Times* claimed that all these city contracts were bloated and corrupt, but no one seemed to pay too much attention—at first. Everyone was excited to see the improvements and each of these jobs employed hundreds of men.

And the Ring managed all of this—and lined their own pockets—without raising taxes! How? They sold bonds, mostly to people in Europe. But those investors started to see the rants in the *New York Times* and were getting nervous, wondering about the investments they'd purchased with the Rothchilds as their brokers. When Tweed's daughter got married in June of 1871, the party and outfits were so elaborate, the newspapers all talked about it.

The *New York Times* reported:

> *On the bride's bosom flashed a brooch of immense diamonds, and long pendants, set with three large solitaire diamonds, sparkled in her ears. Her shoes were of white satin and diamonds. Mrs. Tweed was richly attired in*

salmon-colored silk, elegantly trimmed with deep point aiguille lace. She wore splendid diamonds. Mr. Tweed himself wore black evening dress, and a magnificent diamond flashed on his bosom.

All that ostentation—all that display of wealth. I thought of what Charlie said about Tweed being the shabby rich. The wedding presents alone were worth $700,000.

But with Nast's pictures and the editorials and daily attacks from the *Times* and other papers, the image of Tweed began to shift, though no one had been able to offer hard evidence about where the money for all these parties and diamonds was coming from.

And so I began another double life: leisurely mornings, I read the *Times* and *Harpers* as they took on Tweed and the Ring, but afternoons and evenings found me doing whatever possible to secure a regular salary from them, usually teamed up with Charlie, whose knowledge and support proved invaluable.

If you judge me, then judge—I'm unapologetic. What else could I have done? I saw no other way to survive, none that I could live with, anyway. People with money and homes and investments and stock and full bank accounts like Charlie's father have luxury and security. Those of us who live on the fringe do what we can to get by, despite the dissonance that may thrum in our conscience.

July 12, 1871 was hot as hell, but Charlie and I had work to do. When I met him that afternoon, he was reading the paper, looking concerned.

"What's going on?"

"The Orangemen Parade is going to happen today after all."

"What's the parade for?"

He folded the paper. "Well, according to the *Times*, it all stemmed from 1690 in Ireland when William of Orange, a Protestant, defeated the English Catholic King James II. So the Irish Protestants—they refer to themselves as the Loyal Order of Orange—use the day to rub it in the face of the Irish Catholics that the Protestants won—and not to forget it."

"There are far more Irish Catholics than Protestants here."

"Yep. And apparently, there's a clash every year—with last year the worst yet. *Times* said five people were killed and more injured. And the two sides *know* they're going to clash—the Catholics said they're going to stop the parade, one way or another. So Mayor Oakey said no march this year, but Governor Hoffman just announced yesterday that the Protestants can march—said it's a matter of free speech."

"And the governor's decision trumps the mayor's."

Charlie nodded. "Hoffman has his eyes on the presidency as the Democratic nominee. He's got Tammany backing too. He wants to be his own man, wants to be the hero of this thing: defender of free speech, protector of the protesters. He's calling in extra police—even the National Guardsmen. Still it could get bad."

"Bad like the draft riots? They were in July too when it was hot as hell." *If only we could blame the heat for the hate in the hearts of the mob.*

"Heat seems to make these things worse. And I heard Catholics looted the city armory this morning looking for guns."

"Should we attend?"

"Of course," he answered and held up his camera box to show me.

We headed to Eighth Street. A large throng of Protestants, perhaps a couple hundred, were already marching, their large orange flags swaying back and forth. They were singing, but the words were too muffled for me to make out. Double the number of the Orangemen marchers were the police, their long rifles either by their sides or perched upward at an angle. Tension was in the air and mounting: all along the avenue, men, women, and children—Irish Catholics, one had to assume—lined the parade route. The men yelled obscenities at the marchers as they passed by, while the women and children threw trash at them. The Protestants sang louder.

Suddenly I saw a brick fly down from a rooftop, smashing into the ground in front of a marcher. Then several stones and another brick. At Twenty-sixth Street, the marchers were blocked from moving forward by a militia of hundreds of Irish Catholics armed with bats, bricks, and guns. Charlie and I were coming down Twenty-fifth Street going toward the parade on Eighth when we heard a loud *pop* that I might not have even noticed if others didn't follow, along with screams. Havoc ensued, bullets flying. Charlie pulled me toward an alley. I followed him as he started to climb a stairwell. My heart raced and my body shook as I followed him up. The stairs opened to a rooftop, and from there, we carefully peered out, where I watched with horror as armed militiamen fired more bullets into the unarmed crowd of marchers.

The haze of smoke rose toward us and I smelled peppery gunpowder, and when that smoke cleared, I saw a terrified mob attempting to scatter, madly trampling the unlucky souls prone on the ground. Those who remained were either dead or dying—dozens of bodies lined the street. The moans of those downed by bricks or bullets I would not soon forget. Three militiamen repeatedly kicked the body of a marcher, even after his screams had ceased.

When I leaned farther over the roof so I could see just below us, my eyes fell upon the body of a young girl, her bright orange dress splayed on the sidewalk with limp limbs emerging from it, her brain exposed, head half gone.

I turned to look at Charlie. He had set up his dry plate camera on its stand, the lens aimed down the street.

"What's strange is they believe in the same God," said Charlie. His voice was not sarcastic at all, but rife with sadness. He took the photograph. Then he pulled me back from the edge.

More than one hundred people were killed. In the paper the next day, Tweed was quoted saying that it was "impossible to tell who was to blame." He refused to attribute the violence to the Irish Catholic thugs; after all, they were his people, his constituents, his employees, his helpers, his biggest supporters.

Chapter Twenty-three

Now that I was working, I had a bit more money. I went about, my guise unsuspected and newly improved with Charlie's sartorial contributions—the colorful ties—and I grew confident. And with this confidence came a perk I had not anticipated: more women began to pay attention to me. I found that women appreciated the most elementary gestures: I looked them in the eye, gave them my full attention, made them laugh. I was not handsome. I was short—especially for a man. My clothes were too big. My voice was higher than I wanted it to be. I had perhaps one singular advantage: I knew what it felt like to be a woman, and so I might have had a better sense of how a woman wanted to be treated. I listened. But more important even than my listening, I knew when to be aloof—and how aloof. No woman fancies an obsequious sap.

Charlie and I were hanging out at the Jackson club with other Tammany men, a younger crowd of mostly young Democrats. Jimmy O'Brien, an Irishman who'd been alderman and sheriff, was there at the bar, and I could tell he was talking about Tweed. I overheard him exclaim, "Tweed's reign will not last forever." I wondered what he knew.

One of the men invited us to a table and the cards were dealt. At some point in the game Charlie nudged me and nodded toward the door. I turned and caught sight of Mollie with a couple of other women strolling in, all in sexy dresses with plunging necklines, painted faces, dark eyes, pale cheeks, red lips. Mollie's hair was up off her neck again. She looked at me and I held her gaze an extra moment before I turned back to the game. The ladies went to the bar, stood a few feet away from our table. I won the hand and collected the pot, and then I walked up to the bar and told the bartender that drinks for Mollie and her friends were on me.

"You must be good luck," I said to her. "In you come and I win."

She cocked her head at me, raised the corners of her shiny red lips. I went back to the table to resume the poker game. A few moments later she came over to our table and stood behind me. I felt her presence and then she put her hand on my shoulder, so lightly and softly it made me dizzy. The other guys looked at her then back to the game. I couldn't see her expression. Her hand remained on me. She could see my cards: four hearts and a club. I gave up the club and was dealt a new card, not the one I needed. I raised anyway; I was bluffing, yes, but felt emboldened with Mollie behind me. I raised and everyone bailed out except for a handsome fellow, a little rough, younger than me, early twenties. He raised a whole dollar; I met him. Turned out he was bluffing too but his bluff was better than mine—he had a pair of twos. I had a king high, not the flush I'd hoped for.

"Not so lucky after all," she whispered in my ear, sending chills down my side.

"I don't know about that," I returned. "Maybe I need something like a rabbit's foot to rub. Have you got a soft foot?"

She sat in a chair near me, put her boot on my lap. I unlaced it slowly and removed it, setting it to the floor. Underneath she had a stocking. She undid something under her dress so that I was able to slip the stocking off with my hand and behold her foot. Her beautiful, pale toes pressed into my fingers, which I ran down the length of her foot to her heel. It was the most sensual moment of my life up until then. My stomach dropped, my heart pounded.

"I think it'll do," I said with feigned nonchalance. I nodded to Charlie to deal. I got a pair of aces and bet on them. But a smug shadow passed over the handsome guy's face—something I hadn't seen when he was bluffing and I so I folded when he raised.

He had a full house—two jacks and three sevens. "It seems I might even be bad luck for you," she said, and slipped back on her stocking and boot.

"The night's not over," I said and dealt the next hand. Mollie got up and joined her friends at the bar.

I was drinking whiskey on top of beer. Someone started belting out "Goodbye Liza Jane," and soon almost everyone was singing along. At one point Mollie and I danced. I bought her and her friends another round of drinks. The handsome guy danced with Mollie but when she caught my gaze, she rolled her eyes.

Charlie came up to me. "Are you taking her home?" I shrugged. "Don't forget that it might cost you," he said.

"Oh, I'm not going to pay," I told him.

He laughed and clapped me on the back. "Oh, you always pay, Murray, even if it isn't with money."

We eventually stumbled out of the club. I held her hand as we walked down the street. "Where do you live?" I asked her. "I'll take you home."

"Where do *you* live?" She squeezed my hand. I could not take her to my place, could not run the risk. But if you have ever been intoxicated, waking down a dark street in Manhattan with a pretty woman who wants to go to your place, you know how I felt. Logic said no but everything else in me wanted her in my bed.

Inside my apartment, I lit two lamps. The alcohol I'd drunk had emboldened me and so I leaned her against the door and kissed her neck. She took my face into her hands.

"Your skin is so smooth," she said. In her heels, she was taller and had to bend down to kiss me. I tried not to think about how many men she had kissed. Her tongue was soft. I could taste the peppermint from the penny candy she'd been sucking. She pushed me backward toward the bed and I sat upon it but she remained standing. Then she slowly removed her boots and stockings and dress. She stood before me in her underclothes, and then, looking me in the eye the whole time, removed those too so that she was totally bare, just her skin aglow in the light of the lamps.

For more than a decade I'd had no intimate human touch. I had never seen a woman naked besides my own unappealing, stout body. Mollie was lovely, her skin pale and almost translucent. She was a little too thin—her rib bones shone on her torso. If her small, supple breasts could speak they would say *good morning!*—quite a contrast to my taped-up lumps that were ordered silent. She had a sexy self-assuredness to her, a playful way she stood and moved her hips and raised her bony shoulders and tilted her head. I was staring at her with my mouth agape. She looked amused, satisfied that I was so taken with her.

"Your turn," she said, and when I realized she meant to take off my clothes, I shook my head.

"Oh, come now," she said. "At least take your coat off."

I was so stupid and reckless with drink and desire, I nearly did. But a remote part of my still-functioning brain knew that I could not take off my clothes. I knew, too, that she thought I was a man, and that her finding out that I wasn't would put me in a dangerously vulnerable position. I didn't know her, after all. I didn't know her, but I wanted her. And what I wanted was basic, primal: I wanted to touch that skin. A thought occurred to me.

"Let's play a game," I said, and grabbed a pair of suspenders from the dresser. "I'm going to tie your hands behind your back."

She giggled. "What are you going to do to me?"

"Well, you'll just have to trust me," I said. "Because once your hands are tied, you don't get to do anything, but I get to do whatever I want." It was an act of bravado, but I was shaking as I wrapped the suspenders around her wrists and bound them.

"Oh…I guess I'm helpless now," she said and rubbed her naked backside against me. I felt my pelvis drop, felt wet and dizzy. I had no idea what I was doing or what was going to happen next. But she was submitting to me—I was safe to explore—and sexual instinct took over.

Her tied hands and bare ass pressed into me. I wrapped my hands around her. I touched her mouth and she caught one of my fingers and sucked it. I felt her breast, her skinny ribs, felt the hair of her pubic bone, slipped my wet finger she had sucked between her legs, felt her writhing against me, thought I would lose my mind. She groaned. I led her to the bed and pushed her down onto it, onto her back, her hands beneath her making her back arch.

"You don't get to watch," I said, and took up a scarf Charlie had given me. I blindfolded her. Her grin told me she was game.

There she was, naked in the candlelight, on my bed, a dream. I tentatively leaned down and kissed her mouth again. She kissed me back, her tongue eager in my mouth. Then I kissed her neck, and then her breasts. I ran my tongue around her nipple. She arched her back more. I thought of Whitman, who understood flesh and appetite. I kissed and sucked her, and without rush, explored every inch of her. I was nervous, so nervous I could barely contain my trembling. And then, a miracle, my tongue was in and out of her, and I stumbled upon something that made her twist and moan. Before I knew it she had wriggled her hands free and was holding my head and cried out.

She pulled her blindfold off and looked at me, still panting.

I felt myself blush and lay down by her side. I pulled the covers onto her and rested my hand on her chest, felt the rapid beat of her heart steady slowly, felt her breath in my ear settle down, felt more relaxed than I had in years.

And then I blundered.

I fell asleep.

Erotic dreams. I was swimming in the East River; the bright sunlight bounced off the water making it hard to see. I climbed the ladder out of the water and sensed that I was naked, revealed. But when I looked down, I saw that I was a man, a beautiful, strong man. Mollie was there treading water and called to me. I dove in, swam to her, and without effort to stay afloat, our bodies intertwined. I could feel her hands on me under the water, a thousand hands touching my manly shape. I roused from sleep, confused and still intoxicated. Then I realized: my coat was unbuttoned, my pants were off, and Mollie's fingers were inside me.

I lay there stunned, terrified, in awe of what I was feeling. I didn't want to move. I didn't want her to stop. Fear gave way to titillation, something I'd never experienced by another's hand. I was melting. I couldn't speak—there were no words in my mind. I couldn't flee, couldn't resist; indeed, I didn't want to. I was turned inside out. I stopped existing. In and out, up and down, such perfect rhythm, like music, the beat faster and louder, thumping in my ears. Blood was coursing through my veins; my heart was going to ignite. I could no longer control my thoughts, could no longer rationalize. Language had disappeared. I couldn't remember the past or imagine the future. My whole body moved with her hands. I heard moaning far away and it occurred to me that the sounds were emerging from deep inside me. The only words that came to me were *Don't stop, please do not stop*, though I said them only in my mind. She wasn't stopping. The music played on, that gorgeous melody and rhythm. My body disappeared. My back arched. Somewhere a star exploded and rained down light on my dark life.

I slowly recovered my senses and breath; I journeyed back to the present, but it was a reluctant journey: my secret was out.

I finally opened my eyes to find Mollie looking at me, grinning like an incubus.

"Good morning," she said.

"Hello," I said, but my voice cracked. I was shy and terrified, my bravado decimated.

"Wonders never cease," she said still grinning. "I had no idea."

"Are you angry?"

She laughed. "Angry? No—I think it's marvelous. I've never been with a woman. I shouldn't be surprised, frankly. I don't know when some bloke took his time with me. I guess I'm the one who should pay you."

"I think you just did." I said and felt myself blush. I was tempted to tell her that was my very first time…but I did not. I did not know whether I could trust her. I felt the delicateness of the conversation. It could go badly and I needed it not to.

"How long have you been doing this?" she asked.

"Doing what?" I asked, but I knew what she was going to say. I just wanted to hear how she would word it.

"Pretending to be a man."

"Quite some time."

"Well, you had me fooled. Had all of us fooled."

What did she mean by that? Was my secret no longer safe? I felt myself about to panic, to plead with her. I felt myself about to cry. I willed myself to be cool, to be centered.

"No one knows," I said quietly.

"*I* know," she said, and I felt the weight and power of those words. My entire fate was in her hands. The moment of intense intimacy was over, and I felt awkward and terribly vulnerable.

A thought occurred to me. "Who do you live with?" I asked.

"There's usually four or five girls in our room. That and two beds. But we share the rent."

"Why don't you move in here?"

She sat up and looked at me.

"Here?" She looked around. My place was fairly spacious, and the bed was bigger than a single. "Why?"

"I like you."

She crossed her arms and looked at me skeptically. "I have to work, you know. I need to have money."

"I'm making a pretty good salary these days with Tammany—more than I need." It wasn't necessarily true, but there was potential with the job. And if I lost the job—if I lost it because my sex was revealed—I wouldn't have any money coming in. Everyone would know. I imagined I could even be arrested. I'd lose my friends, my job, my apartment. I'd lose everything.

"Are you serious?" she asked, her arms still crossed in front of her.

I looked around then and noticed the sunlight pouring through the dirty window. I didn't necessarily want to live with anyone. Part of me wanted my life to return to what it was before, but that no longer seemed plausible. Another part of me wanted to re-experience, over and over, the mind-blowing pleasure we'd given each other.

"I'm serious. I would love it if you moved in with me. But you can't tell anyone about me—can't tell my secret."

"I won't," she said, but the tone was not exactly reassuring. It was as if I had read her mind and caught her thinking about who she could shock first with the news.

It was a Saturday. Three days later she moved in with me.

And I admit, I fell for her.

Chapter Twenty-four

Mollie, Mollie, Mollie. Eating with Mollie. Drinking with Mollie. Sleeping with Mollie. Kissing Mollie. Her body was the universe. My eyes, my mind, my own body awakened from the confines of my own myopic version of the world. I felt that I only existed before but had not *lived*. Now, everything was feeling, delight. Anything seemed possible.

For weeks, we didn't leave each other's sides. I fell out of Charlie's life and into hers. I barely worked. Mollie and I went about town, ate oysters, saw shows, went to Coney Island. We were ravenous for each other when we returned home, and sometimes didn't even wait until we were. (Mollie made me privy to her own lascivious secret: the indecent bliss of dark theatres).

Understand that I had never fallen under the spell of sex, had never known its draw, its power, its ability to drain reason from its victim.

The sharing of our bodies led to a sharing of everything else: I told her everything, all my past, all my secrets and fears. I told her about my mother and Scotland and James and my father and Reverend Pease and Emma. I told her about Pfaff's and my first kiss and how I was discovered and sent off to the farm. She told me about growing up on a farm herself in Pennsylvania with her Mennonite family, how awfully boring it was, how the women were to be obedient to the men, how the women dressed plain and could not wear makeup or dance—and how God forbade drink.

She escaped that dull fate and came to New York, and, like me, she found that most of the work available to women was repetitive and domestic and didn't pay much. So she found a different kind of work.

She knew what men wanted. It wasn't too difficult, for the most part, to make a living providing it. She wasn't proud of it, she said, but she wasn't ashamed either. She liked to make herself beautiful, liked that she could make money and pay her rent and afford to buy dresses and shoes (all the jewelry she owned had been gifts: several strings of pearls, an ivory broach, a ruby ring, delicate gold earrings with tiny diamonds). She liked men well enough and found that most of them wanted companionship and some affection. The actual sex was fairly easy, she said—and often over almost as quickly as it began.

Of course, now that she and I were together, she would stop—at least I assumed she would. We didn't talk about it, didn't talk about much after that initial outpouring of our souls. We just stayed together day and night. The newness of being with a woman excited her. And I suppose I understood things about the female form and what might please it.

I found that nothing delighted me more.

I took the hint about the gifts of jewelry and went to Union Square and stood before Tiffany's. The building itself was five stories tall and magnificent. Inside, I mulled around the glass cases displaying jewelry but also watches and clocks and silverware, too embarrassed to ask about prices. I finally inquired about a silver ring that was etched with three stars whose centers each contained a small, modest diamond. I paid the exorbitant price and late that evening, presented it to her.

"Oh, it's so pretty and simple," she said. "Are you trying to make an honest woman out of me?" She sat on my lap and put her arms around me.

Her question threw me off—I had not been thinking that. I did not want to hurt her feelings or ruin the moment. But neither did I want her to get off my lap. "Well, I suppose we can't make it official…"

"I'll settle for unofficial." She kissed me.

I knew nothing about love. I knew nothing of relationships. I knew only sensual bliss, which had been mostly absent from my entire life. I had never been happier. I slipped the ring on her finger and we fell back onto the bed.

So that's how it happened. I, Murray Hamilton Hall, had a wife. We'd have no ceremony, no party, no wedding dress, no legal papers. All we had was a ring and a wild act of consummation.

The next day we sat on a bench in Central Park watching a mob of sheep graze. I thought of the woman with the man—the painting that Charlie had done. We weren't committing adultery, though some would consider our union immoral, even despicable. But Mollie and I were in love.

I took out my *Leaves of Grass*, turned to the page I'd marked and read the words I'd been dreaming all night of reading to her:

FAST-ANCHOR'D eternal O love! O woman I love!
O bride! O wife! more resistless than I can tell,

the thought of you!
Then separate, as disembodied or another born,
Ethereal, the last athletic reality, my consolation,
I ascend, I float in the regions of your love O man,
O sharer of my roving life.

I looked up at her with anticipation only to find a forced half-smile.

"Sorry, I'm not much of a fan of poetry," she said. "Never really understand it. Can't they just plainly say what they want to say?"

I admit, I felt my heart wilt.

A month went by, then another. I hadn't checked in with Patrick McTaggart at the chophouse, and a dreadful feeling rose up in me when I looked in my wallet. I had almost no money left. I had a box under my bed with two-hundred seventy-five dollars—all my savings since I did not trust banks. I would have to dip into that money to pay the rent.

Mollie always hinted about wanting little gifts when we were out and about. She would find something in a window, go into the shop and inquire, and then I knew I was in trouble. Whereas my hat cost two dollars, the one she picked out cost five. Five dollars! At first I couldn't help myself and willingly bought her the little treasures she coveted—I wanted to please her so badly. But the money was running out.

"Women's clothes are more expensive," she shrugged. "They're finer, prettier. And the fashions change all the time. You can't expect me to wear the same hat I wore all last year."

I told her I needed to go see Charlie and check in about the upcoming election. She frowned but said she'd wait for me. She didn't knit or sew or read or cook—I didn't know what she would do to entertain herself. I told her I expected to be gone about an hour, two tops.

At McSorley's, I found Charlie at a poker table. We hadn't seen each other for some time. He looked at me, a knowing look, a little disappointed perhaps, but he gestured for me to sit down. He dealt me in.

Sitting there I realized what a good friend Charlie was and that I'd missed him. I had fallen under Mollie's spell—willingly of course. She was my first lover, after all. But I'd neglected my friend.

I bought us each a beer. We played a few hands and I won the pot and bought us another round and then later we left to get a whiskey at Pete's. Afterward we got an Italian hot cake on Bleecker, and I thought that I should go home, but Charlie said we should go down to the East River and check out the progress on the Brooklyn Bridge. In truth, I didn't want to say goodbye to him yet.

When we arrived, we stared out at the massive granite posts that would eventually support a span that would link Brooklyn to Manhattan. The bridge was in its early construction, and I could not imagine that it could be completed, that people would cross it, that P.T. Barnum would parade a herd of twenty-one elephants over it to prove to people that it wouldn't collapse. But that night with Charlie, construction had barely gotten underway.

"I'm going to go bust if I don't get back to work," I said to Charlie. "Especially if I'm supporting two people."

"You're doing that?"

"Well, I don't really want Mollie going back to her…job. And I don't know if she has any other marketable skills."

"None that would compete with those wages, anyway."

We were silent for a moment.

"Are you falling for her?"

"I don't know. We don't always have a lot to talk about, but we have a good time."

"She's not the literary, philosophical type?" He grinned at me. "Maybe it's her other skills you fell for."

I felt bad, suddenly, talking about her like that.

"She's fine," I said. "I'm going to head back."

Charlie was still looking out at the river. "Election is in two months. You might check in with McTaggart, tomorrow being Friday."

"I'm probably fired."

"Doubt that. But jump back in and give this election your all. 'Lest *you've* got other marketable skills?"

This time I grinned and shook my head. To myself I thought, *None that I am ever willing to use again.*

"Then I'll see you this week," said Charlie. "Don't be a stranger."

The next morning, with Mollie still asleep beside me, I forced my mind to turn to McTaggart, to work, to Charlie, to the election. I got up quietly, dressed, and slipped out. I would get a coffee at the corner and read the papers. Newspapers didn't interest Mollie, and when I tried to read in front of her, she kept talking to me, not understanding or caring that I was trying to concentrate. At first I found that constant attention endearing, but then I realized I just wanted to read a few minutes in silence. She wasn't a reader, wasn't good at occupying herself, and sometimes I found myself having a hard time keeping up the chatter.

I picked up a *New York Times* and paid the paperboy the four cents. The date was July 22, 1871. It appeared that after many accusations and allegations, the editors finally had evidence against Tweed and the Ring. The headline read, "The Secret Accounts: Proofs of Undoubted Frauds Brought to Light. Warrants Signed by Hall and Connelly under False Pretenses. The Account of Ingersoll and Company." There was a list, a very long list. On it were things like $55,795.15 paid for furniture between January and February 1869. Then another bill for furniture $39,844.68 paid just a month later in March.

It was incredible. The grand total for Ingersoll was $5,663,646.83. And that was just Ingersoll—just one company's payouts! Of course, the company didn't receive that money, the *Times* explained. That was just what was recorded in Connolly's books. The company received money for their actual invoices, a few thousand dollars all told. The rest went from the city's coffers straight into the pockets of Boss Tweed, Mayor Oakey, Connolly, and of course Sweeny.

I looked up and saw a crowd swamping the newspaper boy—what a look of marvel on his face to not have to hawk papers all morning. He couldn't get them into people's hands fast enough. He was pocketing handfuls of change. Everyone wanted to know about the Ring.

At the lunch hour, I went to find McTaggart. The *Times* reporting proved to be advantageous in the sense that he didn't seem to realize just how long I'd been out of the fray. All he said when he saw me was, "Look who the cat dragged in," but then he started ranting about the *New York Times.*

"They've got nothing on Tweed," he said, swinging his fork back and forth. He poked at his broiled kidneys but didn't eat. "Nothing."

He was clearly agitated, but in denial of the ramifications the article could have.

"Ingersoll invoices indicate more than five million," I ventured.

"It's a lie. I don't know how they got those figures, but they're made up. They've been critical of him for years—they've never liked Tweed. They've always backed the Republicans. But we've got an election coming, and we're going to show them both."

"You think Tweed will win?"

He looked at me. "It's our job to make sure he does. Isn't it?"

"Absolutely."

A week later, on Saturday, July 29, 1871, the *Times* published a pamphlet with all the information they had compiled. Payouts to the Ring totaled a staggering $12 million. Their secret was out.

Tweed reportedly said, "All the clamor of the newspapers is of little importance. There's not one scarcely worth reading—in fact, most of them are never read at all."

Well, people were reading them. The pamphlet immediately sold out of its first run and more had to be printed.

When confronted by a reporter from another paper, Tweed responded with a challenge: "Well, what are you going to do about it?"

That was the question on everyone's mind.

The damning evidence trickled out bit by bit every day, but Tweed's supporters didn't waiver. Publicly, I was one of them.

On the evening of September 22, he arrived to twenty thousand people filling Tweed Plaza. Charlie dragged me there for the spectacle. Tweed approached the podium and stood silent several minutes, seeming to soak in with great pleasure the cheers and whistles and flying banners of his supporters. Then he spoke, his voice loud and confident: "At home again, among the friends of my childhood and among their sons, I feel I can safely place myself and my record, all I have performed as a public official, plainly before your gaze. Reviled, traduced, maligned, and aspersed, as man had seldom been, I point proudly to my friends to prove my character and ask only for a full, free, impartial investigation into the official acts of my life."

He yelled his conclusion: "But no man can do justice to himself standing outside and fighting against those who control the public press. I expect my friends to stand by me to meet this untrue and unjust charge."

The crowd erupted, thrilled with his single-minded persistence, his unwavering denial of wrongdoing, his confidence. The press would call them uneducated derelicts, thugs, brutes. In turn, they would dismiss the evidence in the *New York Times* as exaggerations and falsehoods. They believed that Tweed understood them, fought for them, and respected them. And they would reciprocate.

And there I was among the cheering throng.

I had a job to keep, rent to pay, a "wife" to support.

And as I saw it, no other options.

Chapter Twenty-five

I had once said to Mollie early on that she didn't need to wear quite so much makeup. She was naturally pretty, I told her. That wasn't a lie—but the real reason I discouraged her from makeup was that it made her look like a harlot. That's what she looked like, after all, when I fell for her. That's what she had been, after all. Now, if she was with me, I wanted her to appear beautiful but wholesome. Walking down Fifth Avenue I noticed women, especially the wealthier ones, and how little makeup they wore. Their cheeks were rosy only with health; their eyes bright. They looked refined, and if they had makeup on at all, it was subdued.

But she shrugged off my suggestion, and in fact, had me buy a little vanity at which she could sit and concoct and apply her makeup and brush and style her long hair for hours.

It was shocking how much time and energy she put into it—and money. She would ask me for what seemed like an exorbitant amount and then go out to the druggist, returning an hour later with soap, cream, and a dozen other ingredients she'd mix into jars and tall glasses. The alchemy of vanity.

Mollie had some freckles, which I found to be her most charming, sweet feature, but she applied a homemade mixture in an attempt to bleach them out of existence. She sat at her vanity dressed only in a slip, applied heavy foundation of rice flour that made her skin paler than it was. She unscrewed a jar of cream colored with carmine—rouge for her cheeks and lips. She sprayed her face and clothes with rosewater; she mixed soot with oil and drew dark, unnatural lines around her eyes.

I watched her paint her face, carefully, taking her time, precise and confident. She sipped a glass of sherry as she made herself up. For several years, most of her adult life, her time, focus, and energy were put toward getting men to desire her. But now when she finished, she sighed. All that skill and precision and effort—and for what? She had nowhere to go. Maybe we would go to dinner, maybe Pete's for a nightcap. But I knew it wasn't the same.

Those years had shaped her mind, her attitude, her habits, her life, even her friendships—and then I was there, discouraging her from seeing her old friends. I was afraid of her spending time with them, of them gossiping and getting her to spill the beans on her new beau.

It became a cycle. She acted bored and restless and asked me for money so she could go shop. Once, I complained about the amount of money she was spending and suggested she get a job—a different job.

"Doing what, may I ask?" she scoffed. "Make three dollars a week as a hat girl? Sell flowers on the street?"

She had a more profitable product to pawn. All Mollie had known was men's desire and their willingness to pay to have it satisfied. At first she seemed relieved to not have to work, but her independence had been diminished, and indeed the very thing that gave her life shape, meaning, purpose, power, and money had been removed from it.

What made it worse was that she watched me make money with Tammany, saw that there was money to go around to those who worked for the organization, who were connected. And all men.

All men except me, and I was getting away with it.

She admired it at first but then, like her getting kicked out of McSorley's that first day I saw her, it only served to remind her of the limits of her sex. She was forced to leave the tavern because she was a woman, whereas I fooled them and had been able to stay.

We did have this in common: our lives had been one sacrifice after another due to our sex. But with my successful charade, I'd evaded the limits of womanhood. My secret kept a bond between us but also alienated her, isolated her. And yet, we settled into our lives, and I sometimes imagined we would be together forever, a thought that comforted me at times and at others, dragged down my spirit. I had decided to stay with her, to keep her close. I didn't know what would happen if she ever went away from me—and didn't want to find out.

One evening I arrived late, expecting Mollie to be asleep. She wasn't there. My heart began to pound so hard I thought I could hear it. Where was she? Was she gone for good? No, I saw her things there, her suitcase still in the closet, her makeup on the dresser. Then I heard her laugh coming from somewhere outside our apartment.

I went into the hall, heard again her high-pitched titter, and it occurred to me that I had not heard her laugh for a long time. The apartment just across the hall from mine was occupied by a man named Oscar Barrett and his wife Margaret—they had recently moved in, and we'd introduced ourselves. I put my ear to the door and could hear the muted voices of two women, one of them undoubtedly Mollie. I didn't hear the husband. He was a German who worked for a printing press, often late into the night. Margaret was a dull woman with a large, fleshy cheeks and beady eyes. Her face at rest suggested she was an unhappy nag. I felt sorry for the husband. I could see why his work consumed him.

I knocked. "Mollie?"

Margaret opened the door, just a few inches, peered out at me with those suspicious, ratty eyes.

"Well, look who's decided to come home." Her breath reeked of schnitzel and lager. Mollie was sitting at Margaret's table, crushing out a cigarette into a bowl. She looked up at me but didn't stand.

"You ready to go?" I asked her.

"Margaret and I were just chatting," she said. "She has so many interesting stories to tell." She raised a glass to her lips and finished the contents. "The time just flew by. Is it late?"

"Around one-thirty," I said.

Margaret was still standing stupidly at the door. Finally, Mollie stood up, walked to Margaret, and kissed the woman on the cheek. "I had a wonderful time talking with you," she said, and though I knew Mollie must be exaggerating the affection she felt, Margaret's big cheeks bulged with pleasure. "We'll talk again soon," Mollie said and winked at her. Then she walked past me and into our apartment.

"Goodnight Mrs. Barrett," I said and tipped my hat, but she was already closing the door.

When I went into the apartment, Mollie was already getting into bed.

She didn't speak to me, so I didn't speak either.

It was the first night we didn't kiss or touch or even talk, and I lay there awake for more than an hour thinking without thinking, teeth grinding, heart thumping fast in my chest.

A little more than a month later, I read the surprising news in the *New York Times*: Sheriff Matthew Brennan, Tweed's friend, had arrested him. Instead of jail, Tweed was allowed to stay at his son's luxury hotel, in a suite with several rooms. Judge Dowling was also staying there. It wasn't exactly jail. And despite that, there was still an election, with Tweed's name on the ballot, in November!

Charlie and I had our work cut out for us: of course it was our job to make sure the men in our districts voted—and voted Tammany. Nevertheless, just in case, we had extra Tammany votes tucked into a secret compartment of the voting box if the election looked too close. We were in charge of our district's paper ballots, which we printed and gave out to voters who came and put them in the voting box at a designated place. The voting box itself was two feet long and a little more than a foot wide and painted a sanguine blue, but the genius of the design was the false bottom and false side, so that the person in charge of counting the votes could flip the box over and have the winning Tammany nominee's votes at the top, with a few of his opponent's ballots thrown in for good measure.

On election day, one thousand dollars were handed out to each member of the General Committee—extra incentive to make sure Tammany won. Fifteen hundred to two thousand extra "deputies" were hired by Brennan—indeed the same sheriff who'd arrested Tweed—under the guise of making sure no one interfered with people trying to vote, but really their job was to arrest anyone who might try to stop the repeat voters and immigrants from voting. Those Tammany-hired deputies even arrested some Republican vote-watchers on election day morning.

The tactics paid off. Because despite the criticism piled on Mayor Oakey (in their exposé, the *Times* called him "despicable" and "a slave"); despite the mounting evidence that the Ring, with Tweed as leader, stole millions of dollars from the city; and despite Thomas Nast's unceasing campaign to reveal their deception and corruption, William Tweed, despite being on house arrest and with help from Tammany henchmen, including Charlie and myself, was re-elected as New York's state senator in November. A win that I, albeit in a small way, helped secure.

Tweed kept his job and I kept mine.

To say I felt discord in my soul that day would be an understatement.

Since my private life wasn't thriving, I focused obsessively on the news. And the news over those next couple of years did not disappoint—it was wholly engrossing. I read the *New York Times* every day and every new issue of *Harpers*. Every conversation at every tavern in New York City was dominated by the Tweed.

He had been arraigned on criminal charges December 1871, a month after winning the election, but he wasn't convicted until November 1873, when he was sentenced to twelve years in prison. Unbelievably, he still had unyielding support from some of his followers who staunchly and stubbornly, despite mounting evidence of his wrongdoing, defended his honor. Who knows whether they truly admired the man or simply did not want to admit they'd been wrong—or some combination thereof.

But for a brief period, an even more interesting, albeit seemingly tangential, story caught Charlie's and my attention: the case of William J. Sharkey. I didn't know it at the time, but it was a story that would eventually affect my life and more importantly, the life and fate of a different William.

William J. Sharkey was a handsome devil, rakish and impetuous, and head of a gang. He resided in the Eighth Ward, and Tweed, recognizing Sharkey's brawn and influence, lured him into the Tammany fold, assigning him little errands and of course procuring his help on election days to intimidate and cajole. Sharkey proved useful and was even nominated to Assistant Alderman, but it didn't come through for one reason or another, and the Ring abruptly dropped him. So Sharkey went back to old ways of gambling and stealing and managing his gang. He opened a faro bank and lost $4,000.

He was getting desperate, feeling surly, when on September 1, 1872, he entered a saloon known as "The Place," and recognized a man named Robert Dunn, whom Sharkey had supposedly lent six-hundred dollars to, money that hadn't been paid back. Witnesses said the two had been friends, known to joke around and lark about together. But after many drinks, Sharkey began to belittle his indebted pal, demanding repayment of the loan and calling Dunn all kinds of vile names. Sharkey finally pulled out his Derringer pistol and pointed it at Dunn, insisting on a fight. But Dunn didn't want to fight, didn't even like guns, and then Sharkey's pistol went off.

Dunn slumped over the bar. A witness said they heard Sharkey say to Dunn that he did not mean to shoot him and then he ran from the saloon, and Dunn, having been shot in the chest, died a few minutes later. There was a trial, and Sharkey was convicted of murder in the first degree and sentenced to death by hanging.

But those details were not necessarily what made the story so riveting for Charlie and me. What surprised us and everyone was what happened to Sharkey in The Tombs.

The *Times* referred to him as an "inbred scoundrel"—a pickpocket, diamond thief, gambler, murderer, and wife-beater. But he had a dedicated girlfriend, Maggie Jourdan, beautiful and apparently refined. She visited him every day in The Tombs, and the keepers were quite taken with her, as she was not the customary visitor to the prison. She apparently sold all her diamonds and most of her wardrobe to provide Sharkey with money, even though he had apparently abused her repeatedly.

On November 19, 1873, Maggie Jourdan arrived at The Tombs just after ten in the morning and was given the standard red ticket pass and then visited Sharkey at his cell on the second tier. At half past noon, a Mrs. Sarah Allen, the wife of a burglar in Sharkey's gang, entered the prison, obtained her red pass, and then talked with Maggie Jourdan at Sharkey's cell before going to visit her own man, a prisoner named Flood. A few minutes after one o'clock, a female dressed in a black dress and jacket, a veil covering her face, approached the keepers at the main door, handed over her red ticket pass, and walked down the street. One of the keepers said he watched as the woman boldly jumped onto the Bleecker Street trolley while it was still moving—and was surprised by the woman's agility.

Maggie Jourdan left a few minutes later after surrendering her red ticket to the keepers, but when Mrs. Sarah Allen—Flood's wife—went to leave, she claimed to have lost her ticket. The warden was alerted and the alarm sounded. Inside Sharkey's empty cell, his mustache was discovered in a glob of shaving lather.

William Sharkey escaped to Cuba and was never heard from again.

"Sharkey might be a scoundrel," Charlie commented, "but what an escape. Disguising him as a woman was brilliant."

I thought the same thing. Sharkey's disguise only had to last a few minutes, though.

Chapter Twenty-six

In 1873, a recession began that devolved into a depression. It was hard to say what caused it. Northern Pacific Line went bankrupt. Fisk and Hatch folded. The stock market plummeted. Banks stopped issuing credit. Thousands became unemployed. Some blamed Tweed and the Ring's corruption, but Tweed's ardent supporters blamed his enemies.

Charlie and I were well established by then with Tammany, but we had few jobs to offer. People grew desperate. Crime rose.

I was walking down Bleecker one day when I felt a hand go into my coat pocket. I turned and saw a woman running away from me. I reached into my pocket, checking for my watch and chain. They were gone. I gave chase, and, spotting a police officer ahead, yelled, "Stop her!"

When he turned our way, I realized that the man in blue uniform was Patrick McCabe. He reached out and grabbed the thief, stopping her in her tracks.

"She took my watch," I said, when I caught up to them. McCabe pried it from her balled up hand and told her she was under arrest.

At first, I felt the indignance of having been robbed and the satisfaction of justice being served. But then I saw how terribly thin she was. She looked at me with wide, frantic eyes that seemed to be pleading with me to spare her.

I wanted to tell McCabe to let her go. But I didn't.

What stopped me? Appearing too soft in front of him? He was an acquaintance but would become my friend. He would become police chief eventually. On that day, he was a member of the New York City Metropolitan Police, whose job it was to stop crime and I had helped land him a criminal. He arrested her.

It was a terrible moment for me. I understood all too well the woman's desperation—she'd probably lost the job that provided just meager wages anyway because of her sex. She probably didn't have a brother to care for her—a brother who taught her early not to steal. But then there was me: stealing elections to survive. Both of us were committing crimes, though hers was riskier and less lucrative.

I remember that she was sentenced a week later. I looked for it in the paper every morning, and then there it was. I tore it out to save:

> *New York Times* Jun 10, 1873, Court of General Sessions *"Two colored men, named George Duryee and John Johnson, indicted for the larceny of fifty-four yards of carpet from Sarah Whaley, No. 53 Amity-street; George Hause, indicted for stealing a gold watch from David T. Thomas, No. 16 Second-avenue, and Mary A. Monahed, alias McDonald, indicted for the larceny of a gold watch and chain from Murray H. Hall of No. 106 Sixth-avenue, all pleaded guilty to attempts at grand larceny, and were sent to the State Prison for two years and six months."*

In an effort to appear manly, strong, and unyielding, I had essentially sent a distraught and destitute woman to prison for two and a half years. Sometime afterward when reading Karl Marx, I read the quote, "Crime is a function of class struggle," and I thought immediately of that poor woman.

Oh, the things that will haunt us...

Even though Charlie and I had fairly solid jobs, we had to work more hours during the recession just to make ends meet. Tammany's reputation suffered from Tweed's arrest and conviction. I was gone from home more, which irked Mollie. Money was tight.

Every day brought more evidence of a collapsing economy. How far would it fall? People I knew lost their jobs. Some had to move their families from nice apartments to tenements; still others from tenement apartments to squalid vermin-infested basements. Some slept on rooftops, some found shelter in jail. Most begged and camped on the streets, dreading the approaching winter. Every week I wondered if I—if Mollie and I—would be thrown out on the street as well. But Mollie didn't necessarily share my worry; she only saw that I spent more time out and gave her less money.

She grew cranky. As I said, she was not capable of solitude and unwilling to take on work that she thought beneath her. I reminded myself who she was when I met her, a woman who liked attention, who liked to dress up, go out with other women to meet men, to dance, flirt, drink. Her life with me was dull, and she no longer made an effort to hide the fact that she was bored. Her resentment that my work took me out into the world grew and grew. She was not domestic, and when I returned from work, I came home to a messy apartment. Even if I cleaned and tidied in the morning before I left, I'd later find my efforts undone. She didn't do the laundry or sweep or make the bed or tidy the place at all. Most evenings when I got home I'd find her in bed smoking or eating chocolates or both, or visiting with Margaret, drinking beer and eating schnitzel.

I wondered: What was she telling Margaret?

It seemed to me as time went on that our wild cravings for each other had been sated, and what remained? At first when we fought, we made up with unadulterated passion. Later we just fought, not bothering to make amends.

I had no experience with relationships, of how to navigate that unruly sea of emotions, mine and another person's—and yet I had everything at stake. When she fell asleep at night I would lie there wondering what she was capable of. I had bared my soul, and the betrayal of my secret would mean my very downfall. The thought was devastating. Everything I had worked for, everything I had created, was at the mercy of Mollie.

She had never been terribly intelligent, but I began to see her as dangerous. Where in the beginning I pleased her because I thought I loved her, now I tried to appease her out of fear.

One night when I came home late to our apartment we fought with extra intensity. She was drunk. I wanted to be but no longer dared to let my guard down around her.

"You're out with other women—I know you are. Trying to prove your manliness," she said.

"You're mad," I interjected.

"…but you're no man—and certainly not man enough for me."

These words struck my core. I knew they were true—that she had grown increasingly disappointed in me. I understood how she felt all too well. I hated my womb for producing blood. I hated the breasts I had to bandage. I hated that I couldn't be a man. And she hated me for it too, which made me spite her.

"Not only are you mad," I spat the words at her. "You're a petulant moll."

Her face revealed her shock, but I was unrepentant. "You're a spoiled mab, a harlot. Maybe I'm not enough for you but guess what? You're not enough for me."

I walked out, slammed the door.

It was stupid to say those words aloud even if I'd been thinking them for some time. I had kept her close for one reason: I didn't trust her to keep my secret. I'd made a deal with the devil. Now I was reneging.

I felt my heart racing as I entered McSorley's.

As soon as he saw me, Charlie asked, "What's going on? Is it Mollie?"

He was a true friend and knew me well. I hesitated and he looked more closely at me. Finally I answered.

"She knows a truth about me, Charlie. And if that truth is revealed to the public, my life will be ruined."

His expression didn't change but he nodded slowly, taking in the information. And suddenly it occurred to me: Charlie knew—*he knew!* I realized that he'd probably known all along and had never said anything, never confronted me.

"What are you going to do?" he asked.

"I don't know. She spends a lot of time with our neighbor Margaret. She's jealous of me being out on the town and apparently sick of me. We're fighting a lot."

"Break-ups cause rancor. Rancor can lead to mean, revengeful behavior." Charlie understood it was a delicate situation. "Want a beer?"

"Yes, please."

He came back with two glasses and sat down with me again.

"I feel trapped," I said. Then I remembered what Charlie had said: you always pay, one way or another. To his credit, he didn't rub it in, didn't tell me he'd told me so. "Is that why you avoid relationships and just attend the bathhouse?"

"Well, it is much easier," he tells me. "And more fun. No lady bird to support—or gentleman bird, in my case. Not that society would tolerate a union with my beloved if I had one."

We sat there drinking our beer. Then Charlie said in a low voice, "I've got a friend in Five Points."

I looked at him, confused by what seemed a non-sequitur.

Charlie took a sip of beer and looked at me. "He happens to have some very hungry hogs."

When what he said sank in, I looked at him like he was mad.

That was madness.

Chapter Twenty-seven

Time passed. One day I read Henry Clapp's obituary in the *Times*. After preaching and practicing temperance for so many years and then rejecting it after his time in Paris and founding his clan of bohemians at Pfaff's, Henry Clapp died drunk and penniless at sixty years old. I knew Ada Clare had died the year before, after being bit by a rabid dog. She never made it to forty.

I tried to ignore my feelings about Mollie. I stayed out late and she was usually in bed asleep when I got home. I would slip into bed, careful to not even brush against her, and make sure I woke before her in the morning, when I would slip out. I slept in my clothes. I didn't change the bandages on my breasts for weeks on end.

I continued to follow the news about Tweed, buying the *Times* every morning when I left my apartment to read about his arrest and the legal proceedings—he was serving time at the Ludlow Street Jail. Charlie and I talked about it every night at McSorley's.

And then one day, shocking news: Tweed escaped!

Later, the *Times* used interviews and Tweed's personal diaries to piece together the full story. A fellow Ludlow Jail inmate, a convicted bank robber named Bliss, befriended Tweed. Every day when they went out to the yard to take their exercise, they talked. Bliss convinced Tweed he could help him escape, and though Tweed initially laughed at the thought, the more they talked, the more Bliss convinced him that he could make it happen—for a price.

There was a six-million dollar case against Tweed, but because it was considered a civil case, the sheriff agreed to let Tweed go home on occasion to take care of his affairs. On the night of the planned escape, December 4, he was allowed to go to his house attended by two keepers. There he saw the sign that all had been arranged—he had only to give the keepers dinner and plenty to drink. When he excused himself to wash up, he instead grabbed a coat and hat and was out the door. A wagon was stationed outside, and its driver took him across the city toward North River, where a rowboat awaited. Tweed rowed to the Jersey side and disembarked not far from where Alexander Hamilton was killed by Aaron Burr.

From there he was driven away from the river to a dilapidated house in the countryside where he was to hang tight until passage to Spain was arranged. When he finally got hold of a newspaper, he beamed at how he, William Tweed, dominated the news—column after column! He passed the long, lonely wait by reading about his own saga.

A few months later, the next leg was ready: they moved him to a fisherman's hut half a mile from Fort Wadsworth, where a little sailing schooner was outfitted for the journey. Tweed's two-hundred eighty pounds boarded with three others, and they sailed precariously down the coast to Florida. There, Tweed stayed with a guide, Mr. Hunt, with whom he fished and hunted every day—what adventure! Before long, they departed for Cuba, only to land without visas and be arrested. Tweed's real identity was still unknown, however, and he befriended his jailers. Soon, they allowed him to board the Carmen and sail on to Spain.

It did not end well, however. The forty-two-day journey to Spain was long and monotonous, and Tweed was so seasick that he lost one-hundred pounds. Upon arrival, he was quarantined, but then a policeman recognized him—from Thomas Nast's drawings in *Harpers Weekly*! He was extradited to New York, handed over to the sheriff, and sent back to the Ludlow Street Jail.

I had mixed feelings about this. I even found myself rooting for him at times, hoping that, despite his awful corruption and greed, that he would really escape scot-free. I imagined him on every leg of this journey, having left behind his beloved New York City—his family and all his friends, just wanting to start over, to not be trapped in prison. Perhaps I was living vicariously through Tweed. Perhaps I also longed to believe that escape from a predicament of my own making was possible.

Chapter Twenty-eight

By 1876, the economy showed signs of improvement, or at least there was more optimism in the air. But things were not good with Mollie and me. She spent every evening at Margaret's, and if I came home, I went to bed and pretended to be asleep when I felt her lie down and smelled her rank breath of schnitzel and cigarettes. Most nights I stayed out with Charlie until late.

McTaggart offered me the chance to run an employment office in Midtown, at Twenty-third near 6th Avenue. It was a relatively large apartment with a front room that would serve as the employment office. But Mollie wasn't sold on it.

"I don't want to move," she said, as if that settled it.

It was odd, but though we no longer shared an intimate relationship, we had grown used to living together. I feared a breakup for obvious reasons, but I think she stayed with me out of habit and inertia.

"It's in a nicer part of town—and it's a bigger apartment with more space for both of us. You can have your own room."

Now this seemed to persuade her—she understood the implications. She also knew that if she left me, she'd be destitute, would have to resort to her old ways, and share a room again with several women. Over the ensuing years, she had aged and let herself go. Her prospects would not be good.

But I also knew that her reluctance to move had to do with Margaret, that Mollie would not know what to do with herself if she couldn't just saddle over there every night.

To put an end to the discussion, I gave her a handful of money and told her to go shopping. She took the cash, left in a huff. After she'd gone, I threw our things into wooden crates: toiletries, towels, her makeup and jewelry, my books. I hailed a carriage, loaded the things up, and rode over to our new apartment. I paid the driver a handsome tip to help me unload.

The Midtown neighborhood was indeed lovely—stately brick homes with facades covered in ivy, a stretch of mature shady trees. Two doors down, on the corner of 23rd and Sixth, the majestic five-story Masonic Temple loomed. Its construction, slowed by the recession, had finally been completed the year before. George

Washington had been a member, along with John Adams and Ben Franklin. Later that year, the nation's first ever cremation took place there. Christians came out in droves to protest, calling it Pagan and blasphemous.

The crosstown horsecar line ran by the apartment—I could catch it to get down to my Bleecker neighborhood—to meet Charlie or McTaggart—or to get anywhere south of Midtown.

And the apartment was much bigger. It was on the first floor, and the front room, which would be the employment office, would hold a desk and a couple of chairs and bookshelves. There was a small living room and a kitchenette, a good-sized bedroom, a smaller sleeping closet, and a basement for storage. I would offer Mollie the bedroom and take the office and sleeping closet for myself.

I took the horsecar line back to the Bleecker Street apartment to wait for Mollie. She arrived seemingly jovial, but when she looked around at our apartment and saw her things had been moved, she said, "I didn't think you meant we were moving today!"

"Yes—we're moved."

She dropped her shopping purchase, a wrapped box from a dress shop, and said, "I'm going to go say goodbye to Margaret."

I was tired of their acquaintance—and nervous about it. I grabbed her arm. "Just come with me to the new apartment."

She yanked away from me but stayed put.

I told myself to stay calm, tried to make my voice gentle. "I'm just eager to show it to you—I know you'll like it. The neighborhood is part of the Ladies Mile shopping district—tons of shops all within walking distance of our place."

She hesitated a moment, looking around. I wondered if she was going to say something about the apartment, if we should say a goodbye to it. I looked at the bed, where we'd revealed ourselves to each other years before. We hadn't shared affection for a long time. I thought of trying to kiss her, trying to rekindle something that had dissipated, like fog clearing from a landscape. But instead of a lovely sight, when our fog cleared, it just unveiled two not very nice people, bent on survival, their hearts hardened. Familiarity had bred contempt in us.

I put my hand around her waist, trying to be gentle, wanting to be received, seeing if we could maybe mend. She looked at my hand and her gaze followed up my arm to my face, which she met with unhidden disdain. She looked at me like she had had eaten a bite of broiled kidneys, which she despised.

And I knew right then and there that I would never be able to change that look, that she would never come around, and that I wouldn't either. It was just a matter of time, I knew. For now, she would stay with me out of convenience and I would stay with her out of fear.

As we left our old apartment for good, she hesitated outside of Margaret's apartment. I was grateful when she kept going—I didn't want to argue. And I personally hoped I would never see Margaret and her beady, accusatory eyes ever again.

The new neighborhood was indeed much more affluent than our Bleecker Street one, and it seemed to motivate Mollie to care again about her appearance. Her habits of dress and makeup worked to her advantage among grog shops and taverns—there she was something—but in our new Midtown location, she looked poor, cheap. Like a prostitute, I'm sorry to say.

Nonetheless, we simply could not afford the nicer dresses she wanted from Lord & Taylor. If she had been a seamstress or even had modest sewing skills, she could have made herself more elegant clothes. My own skills were rusty, and anyway I didn't like to sew. But she wouldn't learn. She had found a way, in her old life before me, to afford nice things. She missed them—the things. She might have even missed the work.

When B. Altman & Company opened a massively large, luxurious department store a few blocks down, she spent all morning preparing. She made herself up with red lips and pink cheeks. She curled her hair, pinned twists of it atop her head. I knew she wanted to show off her neck; though thicker now, it was still her most attractive feature. She'd asked me to help her with her corset. I did, and once she shimmied into her tight dress, I bit my tongue. Not only did it plummet too much in the front—not so much sexy as tawdry—it pulled at the seams, bulging with her new girth. She frowned but didn't change out of it. Then she gave me a saccharine smile, void of love, and held out her hand for money. I put a few bills into her hand, and she tucked them into her corset—her old habit—and left the apartment.

I was alone, finally, a treat, though the too-heavy scent of her musky perfume lingered, an olfactory residue to remind me that though I was in a new apartment, I was not free.

A few hours later there was a knock on our apartment door. Odd, I thought, since we had just moved there, and who would be knocking? I had not opened the employment office yet. Maybe a friendly neighbor coming by to welcome us?

I opened the door and there stood a police officer. I recognized him but didn't know his name. "Yes?"

"Are you Murray Hall?"

"Yes."

"And your wife is Mollie Hall?"

"Yes—just what is this about?"

"Well, Mr. Hall, seems your wife was caught stealing merchandise from B. Altman and Company early this afternoon. She's being held at the Jefferson Market Courthouse."

According to the police report, she stole a comb first, and then emboldened by her success, tried to also pilfer a pair of lace gloves. By then she was being watched, and when the clerk said, "Madam, you're going to have to come with me," she refused. She then tried to run from the store but her dress was tight and as she shuffled to the entrance, her high heel caught on the threshold and she fell, splitting her dress in the rear. She lay there, exposed, ankle twisted, surrounded by well-heeled customers—it was opening day and the store had drawn a massive crowd. Then a policeman was summoned and, humiliated, she was taken to the courthouse, which had a holding room in its basement.

I spoke with the judge and paid her bail of forty dollars, which seemed like a lot of money considering the crime. I had the money, but if I didn't, I would have had to go to a bail bondsman and pay a substantial fee to have him front the bail. Otherwise, she would stay in jail until her case could be heard and she was sentenced—and I considered that, considered punishing her in that way. But Mollie had suffered enough embarrassment, and so not only did I use my connections to get her released, I made sure before we left that the case would be dismissed. I thought about the woman who stole my watch, the two years she would serve in prison, and again I felt that pang of regret.

Mollie was released and emerged, limping heavily from her injured ankle. She was wearing an over-sized coarse muslin dress, something a milkmaid might wear. I imagined it's what she would have worn if she still lived on the farm where she grew up in Pennsylvania, milking cows every morning. Her ripped dress was draped over her arm.

I suppose I expected her to be grateful; after all, I had come to her rescue! But her face was grimaced with indignation and anger. I wondered if, out of pride, she was trying not to cry. I had a moment of tender feeling toward her.

"Let me help you," I said, and tried to take her arm. But she pulled it away from me.

"Don't touch me," she said as she hobbled away with determination.

"The horsecar line is this way," I said, pointing toward Sixth Avenue.

She stopped, her back toward me. When she turned and looked at me, it was with utter contempt. "I didn't used to have to steal," she said.

"I gave you money."

"I used to make my own money—didn't have to ask anyone for anything." I thought of the collection of jewelry she had when I met her, gifts from men.

She took a step on uneven ground and nearly fell. I grabbed her and she held on to me reluctantly, her jaw was set as if she were making up her mind about something.

After Mollie was arrested, she stayed at home in the apartment more than she had in our last place. Without her friend across the hall, she became as snarly and bitter as a caged animal. She had no one to complain to about me anymore. She began putting on even more weight, stopped washing her hair, no longer put on makeup. If she did go out, it was to purchase chocolates, a gallon of gin, cigarettes. I found myself staying out even more just to avoid her.

One night, after a couple of months of living at our new apartment, I came home around eleven, expecting her to be asleep—at least hoping she was—but she wasn't there. I listened in the hall to see if I'd hear her. Nothing, just the sound of a baby wailing on the third floor and a horse clopping by on the street. The apartment was quiet and empty, but rather than relish the solitude, I felt myself tensing up, my heart beginning to pound.

Where was she?

I poured a glass of whiskey to steel my nerves. Then I heard the tap of footsteps coming up the hall. The door handle turned and Mollie stumbled in.

She shrugged off her coat and let it fall to the ground. She was squeezed into the lavender dress that no longer flattered her. She looked around and caught my eye, frowning deeply. I saw that she was heavily made up, her lipstick smeared. Then I got a whiff of her—of the telltale schnitzel and lager and cigarettes—and I knew where she'd been.

"So how's Margaret?" I asked her.

She was swaying slightly, but tried to straighten up.

"She knows," she said, crossing her arms in defiance.

My heart skipped a beat. "What do you mean she knows?"

"She knows—I told her, told her everything."

I shook my head. "No you didn't." I continued to shake my head no, as if denying it would make it less possible.

"Yes, I did," she was slurring her words; the "did" came out more like "din" but I understood too well what she was trying to say.

I stopped shaking my head and stared at her. "I think you're lying."

"I'm going to tell other people too. Murray Hall"—she said my name with vitriol, not addressing me but speaking in a snide voice as though she were referring to someone else—"thinks he can get away with anything. Friend of the downtrodden. Get those beggars to vote and if the ballots don't add up, make it so that they do. 'Cept for one thing: *He* is a *she*."

At this she threw back her head and laughed, a mean cackle. I could feel my face darkening, my hands balling into fists. She continued her diatribe. "Think you'll still be allowed in McSorley's when he finds out? *I'm sorry, Madam, we don't serve ladies,"* she added with derision. "Think the Tammany boss will still let you run an employment office?" Then she smirked, her bitter face balling into one nasty sneer. "You'll be back to sewing garments, maybe hat-making if you're lucky."

I walked up to her, raised my fist. I thought I might kill her with my bare hands. She looked at me with spite, unflinching.

"Not man enough to do it, are you?"

I shoved her to the floor.

"I didn't think so," she yelled from where she lay. "Not man enough!"

Afraid of what I might do, I stormed out of the apartment. It was a little more than a mile to McSorley's, and I ran the entire way. The streets were relatively quiet. I prayed Charlie would be there.

He was. I had never been so desperate, and so grateful, to see my friend. He was at a table with two other fellows playing poker, just like the day I met him. I approached and he looked up at me, deep into my eyes. He turned back to the poker hand and said, "Boys, it's your lucky day: I fold." There was a rather large pot in the middle of the table, a pile of coins with a few bills on top.

He pushed back his chair and stood up. "You all right?" he asked quietly. I shook my head. "Follow me," he said, and headed for the door.

He walked around the corner to the barn where McSorley kept his horse, Leo, and the nanny goat. They were asleep there in the darkness, settled into some clean hay.

"What's going on?" Charlie asked.

"I don't know what to do." I was wringing my hands and began pacing nervously back and forth in front of the stable. "She's told Margaret, our old neighbor, told her…my secret." I couldn't say the words aloud. "She said she's going to tell everyone."

Charlie looked at me, his gaze tender and steady. Then he nodded slowly. He was calm and deliberate when he spoke.

"You'll stay at my apartment tonight. Tomorrow is the Salvadori's wedding. You're going to buy a gift for them when the shops open in the morning. Go to a few different places and take your time—make sure the shopkeepers speak with you so that they'll remember you if they're questioned later. At six you'll head to the church and then you'll attend the reception—say that you're there in my place. And stay until the festivities end: you are not to leave until the party's over. And don't sit in a corner—I know you don't like to dance, but dance. Drink and celebrate. That's your cover. When the wedding ends—probably at dawn if it's a typical Italian wedding—you can go back to your apartment."

"What about you?"

"What about me?" Charlie put his hand on my shoulder. Then he added, softly: "Do you want this taken care of?"

"I don't know. No. Yes. God, I don't think I have a choice." Sweat was itching my head and I reached up to scratch it. I wanted to jump on Leo, ride far away. "What are you going to do?"

Charlie put his apartment key into my hand, which he clasped with both of his, holding them for a moment. He squeezed and let go.

Only when he walked away did I remember his comment about his friend in Five Points.

Those hungry hogs.

In Charlie's apartment that night, I lay atop his bed, sinking into his duvet-covered blanket, the fluff and softness more comfort than I could stand. I stared wide-eyed at the ceiling, willing myself to sleep, but I couldn't. I must stop him, I thought. I must intervene. But I just lay there paralyzed trying not to imagine what might be happening. After several hours, I finally got up, lit lamps, and made coffee.

Charlie's flat was as tidy and stylish as I remembered it. I thought of Mollie's and my apartment. She put no care into it, her stuff strewn about, her makeup and bottles of perfumes and creams all disheveled, no order to anything. She never made the bed, and even if I did—if she were out of it by the time I left the apartment—she would be back in it again, blankets in disarray.

Here at Charlie's, even the corner where he had an easel set up was organized. A small table held a row of half-used tubes of oil paints, bottles of turpentine, a stack of rags, a few jars with various sized paintbrushes, all neatly arranged. I turned to look at the canvas. It was a man, in repose on Charlie's green divan. He was looking directly at the viewer, naked and vulnerable, pale white skin, dark, wavy hair down and relaxed, just brushing the tops of his shoulders. The young man wasn't smiling but neither was he passive. His chest seemed hairless, his pink nipples small, his torso thin. His penis rested on his thigh. His lips were soft and pink but his eyes were intense, bold, daring me to look, to see. Most nudes were of women, painted always by a male artist. It was jarring to see one of a man, and even though I was not attracted to men, I found him beautiful.

I lay back down and was finally able to fall asleep.

I went to the wedding the next day. I brought a gift—I'd gone to three shops where I'd made my presence known and finally settled on an embroidered tablecloth. That evening, at the start of the ceremony, the bride arrived spectacularly on the back of a tall white horse. Her family came separately in a carriage fit for royalty. Even though they weren't wealthy by any means, no amount was spared on the wedding; the Padrone saw the value in funding a wedding the family could be proud of, which in part left them forever in debt to him.

I toasted with champagne, and despite my nerves, ate a delectable meal of several courses—pasta, veal parmesan, chicken cacciatore—and imbibed wine throughout. I danced. At midnight there was another feast—an entire buffet of cheeses, salads, fruits, desserts—and then I saw it—an entire roasted pig, an apple in its mouth, its menacing dark eye sockets staring at me. I drank some Vichy and bicarbonate of soda and willed myself not to vomit.

In the early morning I walked back to my apartment, lucid and nervous despite drinking all night. I climbed the stairs and reluctantly unlocked the door. I called out Mollie's name. No answer. I looked around, saw that half of Mollie's clothes were gone from the closet, including her suitcase. It all felt surreal. I felt faint and stepped over to the bed and had sat down on it when I saw on the bedside table a piece of stationary, which I picked up and read:

Dear Murray,

I'm tired of living in New York City and have decided to move back to Pennsylvania to live with my family. I don't wish you to come look for me, but I DO [underlined three times] *wish you the best.*

Yours Truly,

Mollie

The note was hastily scribbled, obviously written under duress.

For a moment, I allowed myself to believe it, pictured her packed up and boarding a train back to Pennsylvania where she would begin again on her family's Mennonite farm, humbled and repentant, eager to atone for her sins. The delusion lasted just a brief moment. Then I sat on the bed and began to cry.

At first they were tears of regret, of shame, of anger, of sorrow. But when I finished crying, I let out an extended exhale, a long sigh that embodied one single emotion: relief.

A week later I received a brief letter from Charlie.

Murray,

I'm halfway to San Francisco—heard they have better bathhouses there. Strong and content I travel the open road, though I will truly miss you, friend.

Take care of yourself.

Charlie

Thus, in one week's time, I had condemned my "wife" and lost my best friend. I had chosen myself over both of them.

Mollie might not have been the best person, but she certainly didn't deserve her end. But the loss of Charlie was just awful. Because of me, he had done something beyond his nature; he'd done it *for me.* And now he was gone, self-exiled, and I would never see him again.

I was racked by guilt and sadness, in shock at the lengths I would go for self-preservation.

Chapter Twenty-nine

I went back to my reclusive ways. I vowed not to get close to anyone again, neither man nor woman. No more close friends and certainly no more lovers. I'd learned my lesson—I knew what intimacy wrought.

I threw myself into work. My employment office was up and running, with people coming by every day for jobs. After my experience with Mollie's arrest and bail payment, I realized it could also be worthwhile to become a bondsman. Judges were demanding outrageous amounts for bail, and while a wealthy person would have no problem coming up with the money, poorer folks who couldn't post bond would have to sit in jail until their case was heard, which could be days, weeks, sometimes months. If they had a family at home and lost that income, there would be no food and no money for rent. The family could become even more destitute—and the worst part was that the jailed person might be found innocent or the case eventually simply dismissed.

And though Tammany provided work, the organization also demanded its people pay dues. The bottom line was that I needed to make more money.

I continued to meet with McTaggart, attended chowders, played poker. For all intents and purposes I was functioning, congenial, productive, even, on occasion, downright chummy.

I was so lonely, however—empty and utterly alone, no nanny goat to see me through dark nights. I had only to remind myself of the precarious, unhappy years with Mollie to realize that the sadness I now felt was worth it. But I was not at ease in my soul. I began to drink much more and when I was drunk, became surly, and started fights. I gambled with higher stakes. After risking everything to maintain my secret, it seemed I now flirted with being discovered, as if I were bent on destroying myself.

I passed an occult shop one day, a strange shop tucked away in an alley off the Bowery. The owner was Brazilian, from Porto Alegre, she said, speaking in broken English with a heavy Portuguese accent. What drew me into the shop were the string of shriveled fetuses strung in the front window, and when I pointed to them, she said they were from goats and added something about Santeria. Inside the shop were hundreds of candles burning at all sorts of altars. The smell of incense filled the shop.

In the back, my eyes fell upon a human skeleton laid out on a table. I stared at it, mesmerized. The right arm was missing from the ulna down, as well as three toes on the left foot. Most of the teeth were still there, frozen into a macabre grimace. There was a bit of still-decomposing skin around the nose. I couldn't tell for sure since the skeleton was prone, but it looked to be about Mollie's height.

I purchased the skeleton, and the store owner folded it into a large box and secured it with twine.

"*É uma mulher*," she said. "Woman." Then she said something like, "*A alma ainda está presa nos ossos.*" I looked at her quizzically. "The soul stuck in bones," she translated, waving her arm over the skeleton, as if beckoning that soul to emerge.

I took the skeleton home, laid it out on my bed and reclined next to it.

Yes, Mollie's height. I wrapped my arm gingerly under that willful skull. I tried to mentally walk through every moment I'd had with Mollie, starting with that first sight in McSorley's, when she was ousted while I got to stay. I forced myself to imagine her horrific end. The bones seemed to glow in the night's darkness, pulsing next to me. I slept, tormented by nightmares.

When I awoke, I folded the bones back into the box and took it down to the basement.

Later I hired a man, Arthur Hughes, to clean my apartment (I liked hiring a man, he was desperate for work and so I offered him housekeeping, which most men thought they were above), and gave him very few instructions before I left him alone to clean my place: *Don't look in the box in the basement.* Then I left.

When I returned, the apartment was clean, but Arthur Hughes was gone. He did not show up to clean for me the following week.

So Mollie stayed with me, what I imagined to be her bones in my basement, haunting me, and I allowed myself to be haunted.

I deserved it.

Chapter Thirty

When I read of Tweed's final demise in the *Times*, I felt unexpectedly moved. Apparently, Tweed's daughter visited him at the Ludlow Street Jail on April 12, 1878. He had spent four years as a prisoner there, in a modestly furnished room, suffering from what the newspaper referred to as "a complication of diseases that must have been far more painful to him than any physical tortures the State could inflict." It was almost as if they were finally taking pity on him.

That night, Tweed was increasingly restless and complaining of a great pain in his heart. The next morning his doctor was summoned to the sickroom, and in the last minutes of his life, Tweed said to him: "I have tried to do some good if I have not had good luck. I am not afraid to die. I believe the guardian angels will protect me." Just before noon, his daughter left to go out and get him his favorite ice cream, but he died before she returned.

Tweed's death was the topic of every newspaper I saw and conversation I heard in the coming days. I learned from one of his obituaries that though three generations of his family were born in America, his ancestors harkened from Kelso, Scotland, on the Tweed River.

He was the master of graft as well as voter fraud. His influence on New York City was massive and unforgettable and enduring, but he had been brought down by Thomas Nast's illustrations in *Harper's Weekly* and by the editors of the *New York Times*. In the end, not even the judges he put into power could save him. The reformers rejoiced—corruption had been exposed and Tweed had gotten what he deserved. Tammany could, and indeed would, repair its reputation. Life would go on. I would still have a job.

I only hoped that when my time came, I would not die in a jail cell, alone. Unlike Tweed, I did not believe in guardian angels that would protect me.

I was in my employment office at 292 Sixth Avenue when I heard a knock at my office door. It was early November 1879, what would prove to be an extremely cold month.

"Come in," I called out. I had no appointments until later in the morning and was not expecting anyone.

The door opened and there before me stood our old neighbor. If I were blind I would have recognized her from the aroma of schnitzel, cigarettes, and perspiration that wafted in when the door opened. Beady eyes, scowl, and stench. I could not think of one person I'd rather see less.

She looked determined, pursed lips. She exhaled audibly through her nose. She had gained weight. Her hair was dull, greying, and her jowls sagged. She was wearing a large, floral dress, no doubt meant to camouflage her extra pounds. She took off her gloves, exposing red, swollen hands. For a moment her name wouldn't come to me but then did.

"Margaret Barrett," I said. Not good day or welcome or sit down—no way.

"Murray Hall," she said and crossed her arms in front of her torso. "Or should I say Mary Anderson?"

So this was it, a moment of reckoning. I did not let my face change, willed it not to. But my eyes must have flickered ever-so-briefly with fear or dread because she looked satisfied.

"I don't know what you're talking about," I said with dismissive nonchalance.

She offered a conceited smile. I saw that she was missing an incisor and felt grateful for my own full set of teeth.

"Of course you do. Mollie told me all about you—about how you came from Scotland in the 40s. How your parents died on the way. All about the brother who raised you as a boy—until you were found out. How when he died, you reverted to your godless ways. How does no one know, I wonder? How do they not suspect? I mean, look at you—no whiskers, barely five feet tall. Those tiny feet. Your voice."

I was beginning to twitch.

"And that dear Mollie, your 'wife'. What happened to her? She told me you threatened her. What happened to her, *Mary Anderson*?"

I spoke, hoping my voice would sound unafraid. "Why are you here?"

"I want justice for Mollie. But there's no bringing her back, is there?"

I thought of Tweed, his famous words: *What are you going to do about it?* Instead I said, "You want money."

"Yes, I do. And I think $5,000 will suffice. For that amount, I'll take your secret to the grave."

"And if I don't pay it?"

"Think of all the people who will be fascinated that the Tammany captain rigging elections isn't even allowed to vote—because he's a woman." She was growing bolder, her voice low but threatening. "And wouldn't the police like to know a few details. Your wife disappears and you're exposed as a liar, a sham. You could face prison time for your masquerade alone, but you'll probably be investigated for her disappearance."

"Mollie went back to Pennsylvania."

Margaret shook her head. "I contacted her family. She never arrived."

I considered this and tried to shift the topic. "Where's your husband?"

"He's still working the press. And no—he doesn't know. But he will. Everyone will if you don't pay."

She placed a notecard on my desk. "This is the address where I work. Come to the basement door tomorrow. I'll expect you between two and three."

I read the card: No. 37 West Eighteenth Street.

When I looked up, she was leaving the room, her large derriere rounding the corner, but her foul aroma lingered.

My mind was racing and I willed myself to think clearly. I had about $1,000 in my savings. I thought I could get an advance from McTaggart, maybe five hundred.

That coercive crow. How dare she?

I looked at the card again. Tomorrow between two and three.

The next day I took the trolley up 6th Avenue to Eighteenth Street and walked the few blocks to No. 37. The money bulged in my pocket—the thousand from my savings, which was everything I had, along with five hundred I had borrowed from McTaggart, no questions asked. I wasn't entirely sure what I was going to do.

When I got to the door, I rang the bell. Margaret Barrett answered, looking satisfied and smug, but when I offered her the $1,500, she shook her head.

"Five thousand or I tell," she said.

I did not like that answer. I could feel something inside me being bent so far that it was about to break. As if moving in water, I slowly folded the bills and put them back in my pocket. From my other coat pocket, I withdrew a pocket-knife and calmly opened the blade. I held it up and it caught a gleam of light. And then that bent thing inside me snapped.

I lunged toward her and stabbed her in the stomach. She screamed. I stabbed her again and again, jabbing the knife into her corpulent gut. She fell back, slumped against a wall in the hall, a small pool of blood forming in front of her.

I squatted down and put the knife to her neck and whispered in her ear, "If you tell anyone, I will cut your husband's eyes out and feed them to you." I wiped my penknife on her dress and put it back into my pocket. "And if he goes to his grave before you, it will be your own eyes you'll eat if anyone ever finds out."

When I turned to leave, I saw a police officer running toward us, summoned by her screams. I recognized Tim Connors, whom I'd played poker with many times.

Inside the Jefferson Market Courthouse, I stood before Justice Flammer, whom I knew from Skelly's. He set the bail at $1,000. I tried to give him the money, but he said I had to fix it with the District Attorney. I found him, paid my bail, and was released. Margaret Barrett was in the hospital and was unable to appear in court.

A reporter came up to me and asked a few questions. This article ran a couple of days later.

> *Murray Hall, who keeps an intelligence office at No. 292 Sixth-avenue, was before Justice Flammer, in the Jefferson Market Police Court, yesterday, charged with having assaulted Margaret Barrett, a servant at No. 37 West Eighteenth-street, and stabbed her five times with a pocket-knife, inflicting severe though not dangerous, injuries. The wounded woman is now at the New-York Hospital, and is prevented by her injuries from appearing in court, and Patrolman Connors, of the Twenty-ninth Precinct, who arrested Hall, told the magistrate that Margaret, before being removed to the hospital, told him that Hall rang the bell at the basement door of her employer's house, and when she answered the summons he asked for Dr. Quackenbos. She told him that the Doctor did not live there, and he then pushed his way into the hall-way, and drawing the knife, shouted 'Now I've got you,' and stabbed her five times. The prisoner said that it was all the result of a mistake. He went to see Dr. Quackenbos, but got into the wrong house. He said that he had difficulty with the woman in his office some time ago.*

New York Times City and Suburban News
Nov. 11, 1879

Nothing came of it, no jail time—not even probation. And coincidentally, I never had a problem with Margaret Barrett again.

Chapter Thirty-one

I had fooled everyone, had managed to keep my job, supposedly had the life I wanted, yet I had become a miserable person. Self-preservation had come at too great a cost.

I continued with Tammany, built up my bond business, and played poker with acquaintances every night. I drank myself into a stupor so as to not think, only to wake like clockwork at 3 A.M., lonely for my brother and Charlie and Emma and Liz, sweating out the booze. Images of Mollie, alive, dying, and dead, tormented me.

I attracted women. Sometimes I would buy one a drink, even stroll about town with her arm in mine, but that was it. No one was going to get in ever again.

What was I living for? What kept me alive?

I suppose it was habit. Even the most wretched souls feel the compelling pull of animate existence. I kept waking every day and so I kept living, but deep down my soul was empty and my heart ached, and I feared—indeed I knew—that this was it. This feeling of meaninglessness, and the thought that I was a cruel, violent, selfish person, would carry me to my grave. I didn't have a god in my life to beg forgiveness, so no one heard my sins, and no one forgave.

I remember when the Brooklyn Bridge opened on May 24, 1883. It's unveiling only made me miss Charlie more as I recalled the night we stared out at its foundation. It was built by the Irish, just like Central Park was, but it was opened on Queen Victoria's birthday, which felt like a slap in their face. The Irish boycotted it, but that didn't stop the celebration.

I watched from shore as Clipper ships sailed underneath it, fireworks exploded above it, and thousands promenaded across it. A week later, twenty thousand people were on the bridge, which was swaying and creaking in the wind. Then a woman tripped and panic ensued. Somehow twelve people got trampled to death, including a few children. Progress always came at a cost: something or someone would be sacrificed to achieve it.

I remember walking across the bridge the first time and looking down at the murky, turbulent East River below and wondering if I should jump.

One night I was arrested at the Iroquois Club. I had just popped in to pay my dues and play a hand of poker but was arrested instead—the charge was straw bonds. My bond business had been going fairly well, though as with my whole life in politics, I saw the unfairness of it and still endeavored to use it to my advantage. Bail amounts were set randomly depending on the whim of the judge, with practically no rhyme or reason it seemed, and some of them were outrageously high, Eighth Amendment be damned. Maybe the judge was having a bad day. Maybe he didn't like the look of the person.

It was a money-making venture, a revenue generator for the police who arrested the person, for the judge, for the bail bondsman. If a person didn't want to rot in jail until their trial, they posted bond. If they didn't have the money, they came to someone like me. I charged a fee, usually ten percent, so the higher the bail amount, the more money I pocketed. But I had to put up collateral, show that I had money or capital, like property, to back the bond. A straw bond was a bond that had no backing; it was a metaphor for my life: I presented a façade and tried to pass it off as the real thing. But a straw bond, like me, was nominal, worthless.

Survival meant risk; survival meant fooling people. I was successful for a long time. My canard worked until it didn't.

Teddy Roosevelt had been courted by the reform Republicans and offered the position of police commissioner. He launched a campaign to clear corruption from the police force and the courts, which at that point mostly employed Tammany men.

The man who arrested me was O'Reilly, a new officer, born in the United States, but descended from Ireland. He had a bushy head of hair and a freckled, boyish face, and seemed nervous and apologetic when he came up to me just outside the Iroquois.

"Murray Hall?" he asked.

"Yes…"

"You're under arrest for issuance of straw bonds."

I said to him, "Oh, come have a drink with me at Skelly's before you haul me in." I knew plenty of the boys would be there, maybe even Skelly himself.

To my amazement he relented, cocked his head to one side and almost grinned. "All right," he said. "But just one drink and then to the courthouse. And you're treating."

"Of course!"

Indeed, Skelly was at the bar, and when he saw the situation, he had someone run back down to the Iroquois Club and rally a few politicians, including Joseph Young, one of Senator Martin's lieutenants. Young and Skelly were nice enough to accompany Officer O'Reilly and myself to the Jefferson station, where Skelly posted bail for me. Then we went back to his bar and all had beer and whiskey and then to Teddy Ackerman's on the corner where I had some wine. I admit I was extremely intoxicated—I never liked to mix wine and beer—but when they said I should go home, I refused.

"I should've just thrown him in jail in the first place," said Officer O'Reilly as they were trying to wrestle me out of Teddy's.

That irritated me, so I turned and punched O'Reilly in the face.

He arrested me again, and indeed I did spend the night at the Jefferson Street Jail. I was supposed to be sentenced to The Tombs the next day, which made me downright nervous: I had heard of judges sentencing bondsmen to several years in prison for straw bonds. But to my relief, Skelly and the boys showed up first thing in the morning and squared it with the judge, which meant that, all in all, I spent only five hours in jail and was passed out for most of it. I was released, but instead of going home, I went back to Skelly's and bought everyone a round. They all boasted of the "storm cloud draping" under O'Reilly's left eye. I knew I must've gotten him good since the knuckles of my right hand were swollen and bruised.

I was acting recklessly, but I also figured that the arrest and night in jail solidified my manhood—that no one would ever doubt my manliness after that.

I was wrong.

Chapter Thirty-two

A knock at my office door late one morning. Trouble always seemed to start with that. Again, I wasn't expecting anyone.

"Come in," I said.

The door opened slowly, and a woman looked in.

"Sorry to bother you," she said. Kind eyes—that was the first thing I noticed.

"There's no bother," I said in a voice I barely recognized. She came through the door then, a sizable woman, much taller and more robust than me. She had on a thin coat, but her hair was curled with some care. No discernible make up. She looked healthy, smiled at me, a real smile.

"May I?" She gestured at the chair in front of my desk.

"Please."

She settled in, placed her pocketbook on her lap.

"What can I do for you?" I asked.

She looked at me curiously. I reached for my cigar, held it in my fingers for a moment. Then something odd—I didn't light it. Let her be curious.

"I'm looking for a job, and I wonder if you could help me," she said with affable directness. "I wasn't sure where else to go. I've been checking the classifieds every day, but I haven't found anything suitable. We had lunch at a chop shop today, and the owner suggested your office. I'm Celia, Celia Richards." She held out her hand.

"Murray," I returned. "Murray Hall"—and then I reached across the desk and shook her hand. I felt our mutual softness. She must've felt it too because she peered down at our interlocked hands. I knew I only had a few moments to erase her doubts and solidify my maleness in her mind. Again, I thought I should light my cigar, and again, I didn't. "Where are you from?"

"I arrived here from Bangor, Maine—Penobscot County—in '79, but I was born in Jackman. I come from a logging family."

"Jackman off the old Canada byway?"

"Yes, that's it."

Now I smiled. "I passed through there when I was a child." I pictured James walking a few feet ahead of me on the road, the mountains surrounding us, covered in trees, the burbling of the river. But my nostalgia was interrupted by the sight of a fast-moving shadow swishing by, crossing the partially opened door.

"Hello?" I called out.

"Imelda Richards," Celia said firmly. "You mind your manners and wait patiently!" She shook her head. "Sorry, that's my daughter. She's…spirited. Well, that's a euphemism for it, anyway."

I laughed. "Would you like to come in?" I called out to the daughter.

She popped her head in the doorway, a dark-haired, pale-skinned girl with an unabashed grin.

"So you're Imelda," I said.

"I prefer Minnie," she replied. "And you're Murray."

"Murray Hall," her mother corrected. "Manners, please." I noticed that Celia didn't say Mr. Hall.

"How old are you, Minnie?"

"I'm six."

It was 1886. I did the math in my head. Where was the father? Celia had been in New York City since her daughter was born? "I was your age, Minnie, when I arrived in New York City with my brother, James."

"And with your parents as well?" Celia asked.

Now that was a question I had never been asked in this office.

"No." I shook my head. "My mother died en route from Scotland, my father when we arrived in Grosse Isle."

"And so who raised you?"

"My brother, actually. He was only 14 at the time, but he took care of me."

"That is so sad your parents died," Minnie said with real emotion. "I don't know what I would do without my mother." She looked as though she were about to cry. I suddenly felt like I could too.

I cleared my throat, and fingering the cigar, asked Celia, "Where do you and Minnie live?"

"We're in a tenement on Canal Street, but we don't want to continue staying there. It's not a…not a good situation. We're hoping to find better lodging, but to do so, I need to make a bit more money. Right now I'm working as a domestic and Minnie goes to school. But her school day ends before my workday, and I haven't found someone reliable to keep an eye on her."

I nodded. So they were in the northern border of Five Points, probably the only affordable situation in the city for a single mother.

What other options did she have? Another tenement or maybe John Bremer's Hotel? But both were places you wouldn't want to stay long term.

I thought of my apartment, the extra room. The room Mollie had occupied. The part of me that was tempted to mention it was silenced by the part of me, the rational part, that was hell-bent on survival. I had been living alone for years. Well, alone if you didn't count Mollie's ghost. But there was something about Celia I liked. Her honest face. Her forthrightness. Her bold, energetic daughter.

"The rental situation is difficult, for sure. Let me ask around to see if there are any positions available for you and a better living situation. What work interest you?"

"Well, I've done bookkeeping. I can cook and clean. I prefer a schedule that would allow me to be with Minnie after her school day ends, but I realize that might not be possible."

I nodded. It was a Thursday. "All right, well, why don't you come back in a few days? Say, on Sunday? Maybe Sunday…after church?"

"Oh, we don't go to church," Minnie chimed in. "Mama thinks church is—"

"That's enough, Imelda," Celia interrupted and stood up. To me she said, "Sunday morning would be perfect. Say 10 o'clock?"

"Yes, fine."

"I'm grateful to you…" she paused and looked at her daughter and then back at me. "So very grateful to you…Mr. Hall."

Then she shook my hand again. I thought I glimpsed a hint of mischief in her eyes, and it seemed to ignite something in me—a rush comprised less of fear than titillation.

I went into my apartment after they left. I pulled back curtains, opened windows. I found a few crates and began clearing things out, mostly bric-a-brac I'd unintentionally collected and stored over the years. I went into Mollie's old room. Her vanity still stood there, covered in her little bottles and jars, now caked with a fine film of dust. I put them all in the crate. I opened a wooden chest to the smell and sight of her clothes. I carried the chest out to the street and set it there. A junkman would grab it—or someone for whom it would have value. Back inside, I picked up the vanity and then set it back down. Maybe…maybe it would be a useful thing for a young girl. I knew what I was doing and yet did not let myself think of it. It was ridiculous to consider, utterly void of reason. I kept cleaning.

For three days I fussed over the apartment. I discarded a broken chair and replaced it with two good ones so that there were three around the table. I cleaned out the ashes from the stove and wiped the walls. I hung hooks and washed the windows. I swept. I cleaned my office and threw out old newspapers. *Bookkeeper*, I thought.

I kept the skeleton. I did not deserve to be rid of it. I didn't deserve any reprieve from loneliness or remorse.

But when Celia and Minnie returned promptly at ten on Sunday, I was so pleased. Again, the handshake, the pocketbook placed on her lap, the warm smile. Only this time, I did light a cigar. Minnie stood there in a pretty navy dress. I could see that she was trying to be good and hold her tongue and keep her hands folded in front, but then she fidgeted, scratched at the white bow in her hair. Her mother gave her a firm look, and Minnie stared straight ahead, suppressing a grin.

"I haven't found any work for you yet, unfortunately," I said. I didn't say that it was because I hadn't bothered to look. "But I do have an extra room you could rent."

"Oh no," Celia said but she was smiling. "We wouldn't want to inconvenience you."

"Why not, Mama?" said Minnie, and I laughed.

"It's vacant right now, cleaned out and ready to go. I'd rather rent it to someone I've met rather than have to advertise it and deal with whoever shows up. Be nice to make a little rent money. I'll make it affordable for you and keep asking around and see whose hiring and for what. In the meantime, you could help me keep my office in order. I could use a bookkeeper."

"That's too kind of you."

Minnie piped up: "Well, it's kind, Mama, but it's not so kind that we can't accept it, right?"

Celia shot her daughter a stern look of warning, but I just laughed again and then said to Minnie: "The way I see it, it's a good deal for all of us. Now, are you tidy? Do you make your bed in the morning?"

"Oh, yes," the girl said.

"And do you like to read?"

"I love to read."

"And do you know how to cook?"

At this she shook her head. "No, not yet. But Mama makes the best bread and soups."

"No bragging, Imelda."

"You do, Mama." And here the child could not help herself and bent down and wrapped her arms around her mother's neck and kissed her cheek.

I felt a pang of something so buried it me it was like hearing a whisper inside a deep cave. I was Minnie's age when my mother died, and I was seeing, I was witnessing before me, a daughter's unabashed love for her mama. And I could see that Celia loved her and wanted to keep her close and see her thrive. I stubbed out my cigar. I could feel Celia watching me and when I looked up, I saw that hint again of something in her eyes, that puckish look. Did she know or even suspect? I sensed she did. Also, would she move in with a man she barely knew—and with her daughter? She trusted me so quickly. But could I trust her?

I knew I was complicating my life by inviting them into it. I didn't care.

As I said, I was feeling reckless. Maybe I was tired of beating myself up, tired of loneliness, tired of lying.

They moved in. Celia proved to have a keen eye for keeping the books, for organizing my office and records, which was not at all my forte. She tidied and swept and organized. She did the shopping and the cooking.

In the evenings after dinner, Minnie would go into their bedroom to read and Celia and I would sit down together and have tea and talk. Early on, she was frank with me: I learned that she had a brief and not very pleasant time with a lumberjack in Jackman, Gregg Hawkes.

"He was not a good listener," she said and then added quietly, "and he was physically stronger than me."

When she learned she was pregnant, she decided to leave without telling him.

"I couldn't go, however, without saying goodbye to my mother, but it was a mistake. She betrayed my trust and told my father. He insisted I marry Hawkes, threatened to reveal my secret."

She told her father she would go speak with Hawkes the next morning but instead left in the middle of the night for New York. She doubted Hawkes would follow her. He hadn't.

But Celia was alone in the city, hardly any money to her name. She landed in Five Points, of course, still the cheapest lodging in town. She found work at a grog shop, cleaning and stocking and selling. The owner allowed her two small potatoes from the bin every day and a little milk. She feared for her livelihood and that of the child she might have. She knew in New York that abortion was legal until the quickening—the moment the woman felt the fetus move in her, around four to five months.

"But my quickening came early," she said. "And I knew once I felt that flutter inside me that I would give birth. But I also knew that it was almost guaranteed that my life—and the baby's—would likely be awful, nearly impossible."

A child would limit her possibilities, would require more money and resources than she had for herself. But she was also so lonely in New York City, and she felt that whatever was growing inside her was keeping her alive, tethered to the earth.

"Without her," she said, "I might have just slunk into the East River one night and floated away." I knew that feeling all too well.

I was spellbound by Celia, by her misfortune and courage and openness with me. I thought my life had been difficult, trying to fend for myself. Then add another person—a baby!—and the fact of being a woman, living as a woman, that is, and a mother on top of it! I thought her extraordinary.

Because she was.

Minnie attended a public school down the street, and afterwards, came to my office to say hello and would stay on and read.

I lent her my Wordsworth, but soon I took her to Pratt's and bought her Lewis Carroll's *Alice's Adventures in Wonderland.* I read to her sometimes or she read to me, and I helped her with the words she couldn't pronounce as my mother and James had done with me. I bought her more books, anything Pratt recommended. *Little Women* by Louisa May Alcott became her favorite. We read it four times, and she cried every time Beth died, while I forced myself not to.

I still went to Skelly's, though I kept my poker games shorter and felt calmer and more content than I perhaps ever had. I felt no obligation to Celia, just a yearning after a few rounds of drinks and cards to get back to the apartment. If I arrived in time, she might still be awake, and I could converse with her a few moments before we said goodnight.

One evening I arrived having left Skelly's after just two rounds of poker and one beer. When I walked in the door, Celia was there on the sofa in the living room reading a book by oil lamp, her face serene. She looked at me, gave me her warm smile.

"You're back earlier than usual," she said. "Everything all right?"

I just stood there, looking at her for a full minute.

"No it's not," I finally said.

She raised her eyebrows. I took a deep breath. "You see, I love that you're here when I come in. I—I love coming home to you."

"Come here," she said.

Though I crossed the room slowly, my heart was racing. I stopped at the other end of the sofa. She patted the space on the cushion next to her, and I sat. She took my face in her hands and looked me in the eye. I hadn't been in proximity to another human being like that for years. My heart was beating so hard, I was sure she could hear it.

"I love being here with you, Murray," she said. She leaned forward, her hands still cradling my face.

"No," I said but didn't pull back. "I'm not—I mean, you don't know…what I am."

"Oh, I know," she said, and kissed my lips.

We held each other in my bed, both of us naked as the day we were born.

"Tell me everything," she said.

We talked into the night, until I got to Mollie. Then I just clammed up.

Finally, I spoke.

"There's something you should know," I began. "Something you deserve to know." We lay facing one another, the light of the lamp illuminating her face: fresh and honest and kind and open. She was stroking my arm with her fingertips.

"Yes?"

I turned away from her and stared at the ceiling, agonizing over what to tell her. If I revealed my violent ways, she might not want to stay—and who would blame her? But to withhold the truth didn't seem right at all.

"I lived with someone, a woman…"

"Yes, Murray?"

"She threatened to reveal me…." What else to say? How to defend the indefensible? "I—I would have lost everything."

She was quiet but when I looked at her, she was still looking at me with that same kind look. I forced myself not to look away. "I did something terrible."

"It's all right," she said, and resumed stroking my arm.

"What do you mean it's all right?" I sat up.

"I know my heart and my mind, Murray, and I trust both. I do not perceive one ounce of evil in you, not one bit. I see someone who fought to survive. I see someone deserving of love." She sat up too and took my hand and held it to her heart. "I trust you. I trust you, but more importantly, Murray, you can trust me."

And then I wept. I'm not ashamed to say it. Celia held me, until the tears stopped coming and then I still cried. She kissed my wet cheeks.

Celia slept in my bed that night and every night thereafter until she died.

Chapter Thirty-three

The Statue of Liberty's hand holding the torch was plunked down on the edge of Madison Square Park; she was still awaiting the funds for her plinth. Joseph Pulitzer made an appeal in an editorial for donations to finish erecting the statue. People would stroll by, see the arm sitting there, giant yet forlorn, and feel compelled to give money. I, myself, was not immune and gave fifty dollars. The campaign worked, and by spring 1884, the first stone of the plinth was laid.

She was finally completed in 1886. New York City got her majestic lady that would welcome newcomers into the country and old-timers back from their journeys, broken chains at her feet marking an end to bondage and tyranny. Celia—big, bold, kind, righteous, and majestic—had liberated me. On the day of the Statue of Liberty's dedication, October 28, 1886, I asked Celia to be my wife. She said yes.

I told her I would love Minnie as my own daughter.

"You already do, Murray," she said. "It's one of the reasons I love you the way I do."

We moved to a different apartment between 17th and 18th Streets, a fresh start—we left the past behind. I didn't bring the skeleton.

We decided to wait to tell Minnie about my sex until she was much older. It wasn't fair to expect her to keep a secret of that magnitude. We didn't want to confuse or burden her.

I didn't really realize how having a daughter would change my life. When she called me Dad for the first time, almost shyly, I looked at her with amazement. Then I pinched her nose and pretended to eat it. It became our daily game.

We took Minnie to see PT Barnum's circus, took her to the theatre. I saw the city afresh through a child's eyes. We rode the El trains all over because Minnie loved them. Coney Island delighted her. I wanted to work and not gamble too much because I wanted to make sure we'd have money to do things with her.

Celia didn't care for trinkets or even diamonds. Although we were two women living together raising a daughter, which was taboo, perhaps even illegal, Celia was a proper person—she believed in manners and decorum. She was moral and fair. She didn't like buying things just to have them and show them off—that made no sense to her. If she bought things, they were practical, well-made, durable. She valued craftmanship, not decoration.

When I asked her to be my wife and presented her with a small diamond ring, she said we would take it back to the shop and exchange it for two simple gold bands, one for each of us.

"If we have money left over after we buy our rings, we should take a trip to Niagara Falls," she suggested. "A honeymoon."

"I love that idea. I haven't been out of the city in years."

"And Murray, we don't have to bring Minnie, you know. It could be a trip for just the two of us if you like. We can leave her with someone we trust."

But of course we brought Minnie. We were a family.

The three of us walked across the suspension bridge above the falls, all 825 feet of it between New York and Ontario, Minnie utterly fearless. Celia clung to my hand. We stopped in the center, mist spraying our faces. I closed my eyes and thanked a nameless god for my happiness. When I opened them, Celia was staring out at the falls, a look of awe and amazement on her face. I put my arm around her, and we held each other, the roar in our ears, and looked out at the rushing, cascading water and then at each other for a good long moment. I tried to freeze it in my mind, memorize it, make the feeling last forever.

It was a magical time.

On Minnie's eleventh birthday, Celia and I decided to let her stay home from school. It had taken some convincing for Celia, who already felt like I spoiled the girl. We let Minnie sleep in, and when she emerged from her room, rubbing her eyes, not fully awake, Celia and I were sitting at the table.

"Happy birthday, Minnie," Celia said. She walked to her mother, sat down on her lap and Celia embraced her. Rather than envious, I felt a vicarious twinge of warmth. Though I loved Minnie intensely, I had made a conscious decision not to be too physically affectionate with her, mostly out of fear of her detecting anything but also to respect her.

She looked at us, brushed her dark hair to the side out of her face and said, "Aren't I late for class?"

"Your father has somehow convinced me to let you take the day off from school today—thought an adventure was more proper for an eleven-year old than a day of sitting at a desk in a classroom."

Minnie beamed at me. I took the present I had sitting on my lap and placed it before her.

"Happy birthday," I said. Pratt had wrapped it with a pretty green bow.

She took her time unwrapping the gift: three books by Jules Verne: *Journey to the Center of the Earth*, *Twenty Thousand Leagues Under the Sea*, and his latest: *Around the World in Eighty Days*. She clapped her hands and started paging through them, which pleased me to no end.

"Your imagination can take you anywhere," I said to her.

She stood and came round the table, put her arms around me and kissed my cheek.

"Thank you, Dad," she said. I felt joy flood my cells. She brought out a filial tenderness in me that no one else did. I poked her in the ribs, and she laughed.

"Go get dressed," I said. "We have our own adventure planned for the day. Jules Verne doesn't get all the fun."

We took the ferry to Coney Island and then the train to the Brighton Beach Bathing Pavilion. It was early September, still warm. I had on my large coat, as usual, and sat under one of the tents, while Celia and Minnie, dressed in their bathing dresses and hats, went down to the water. I heard Minnie squeal with cold and glee and felt happy. She ran back to the tent.

"Dad, you must join us."

I had one of the Jules Verne books open on my lap, feigning concentration.

"I prefer to read," I said, waving her away.

But I didn't. I just didn't have a choice, of course.

"Just your feet then! Dad, you have to feel the ocean!"

She squatted before me, took off my shoes, pulled off my socks, and rolled my pants. Then she took my hand and pulled me to standing. I walked down to the shore, the cool sand under my feet and between my toes. Celia was standing there, her head cocked to one side. She was grinning at me, but there was a touch of sadness in it. That's what love was I had realized: a look of total understanding and compassion that didn't require words, someone knowing exactly how you felt—and caring.

Minnie had my hand. The sun was lower in the sky now that it was the beginning of fall, but still bright, almost blinding. The ocean was green and blue and grey and white. A wave lapped to the shore, covering my feet. I felt utterly alive.

Later we went on a carousel, Minnie on a camel, I on a zebra. Celia watched us. This was before amusement parks would start operating there—just a simple, enchanting carousel, going around and around to the music. Pure, simple happiness.

Back in Manhattan, we strolled, exhausted, past a pet shop. Minnie saw a crate of puppies in the window, and like a fool, I let her go in and see them.

She picked up one of the pups, a minuscule black and tan thing, and held it to her. She snuggled the tiny mutt into her neck, and it licked her face. She was grinning ear to ear.

Hence, Walt.

Oh, how I fell for this silly animal. The feeling made me think of McSorley, how he groomed and cared for Leo every day, how caring for that horse was part of his daily life, the affection it bred in both of them.

So it was with Walt. Because although he was supposedly Minnie's dog, I cared for him, took him on walks, fed him, cleaned up after him, gently chided him when he chewed nearly everything he could get his puppy teeth on. I procured bones for him from the butcher, but he seemed to prefer to gnaw on everything else—shoes, pencils, newspapers, chairs. He slept pegged to her side, but I was the one who woke in the middle of the night to his soft whining, took him outside so he could relieve himself, and then tucked him back into bed again with Minnie. By day, I walked him all around the city to wear him out, often ending at Pratt's bookstore, where he would fall asleep on my lap as I read.

My bond business grew steadily with Celia's help. We had a little money saved, but always there were expenses. Unlike Mollie, who was petulant when I didn't give her extra money to spend, Celia was thrifty, always looking for ways to save or stretch a dollar. In fact, we saved enough to invest in two vacant lots.

Then one day, someone I posted bail for didn't show up for his hearing. The bail had been set at $900, and I had put up the two lots we'd bought as security, but we'd made a mistake, apparently, and rather than in both of our names, the properties were in Celia's only.

The reformer judge—part of Roosevelt's corruption cleanup—issued a warrant for my arrest.

An officer knocked at our door. I knew him from Skelly's. He was nervous, I could see.

"I'm so sorry," he said. "Don't worry, Murray. We'll get it squared."

"It's all right, man. We've done the paperwork—it's just a misunderstanding. You're just doing your job."

But when I went before the judge at the Jefferson Market, he was unrelenting, and sentenced me to The Tombs prison. I thought I might throw up.

I had no idea how long I would be there. Again, I knew of others receiving long sentences for straw bonds. But this wasn't a straw bond—Celia would never do that. It was a mistake in our paperwork. And this wasn't a night in the Jefferson Market Courthouse holding jail—this was prison. It would be the ultimate test of my resolve, of my ability to finagle an existence as a man, something I'd been able to pull off for years.

I was worried. It wasn't just the awfulness of losing my freedom—that was certainly one level of it—but obviously, my biggest concern was being found out, losing my livelihood, my existence, everything I had built and protected for years. Not to mention that I now had something more precious to me than anything: a family.

The Tombs, which had been known for many years as City Prison, took up an entire city block, bordered by Leonard, Franklin, Elm, and Centre. I had read that the man who designed it had modeled it after an ancient mausoleum he'd encountered on a trip to Egypt. The Tombs was damp, which made sense, as it was built where once stood Collect Pond, a deep and seemingly bottomless spring-fed freshwater lake. It was built for far fewer prisoners than it ended up housing, and so conditions there for most inmates were not good—cells meant to hold one person had two or three. How would I share a cell? It was impossible. I'd be found out in no time.

The main entrance to the prison was on Centre, up very steep, dark stairs that led to a portico surrounded by four stout columns. The prison for men was inside in the center of a large courtyard; a bridge connected this building of 150 cells to the outer building, forming a kind of catwalk. It was known as the Bridge of Sighs, and rightly so, as it was where the gallows were placed during executions. People were hanged in The Tombs until 1889, at which time death by electric chair replaced hanging and the executions were moved to Sing Sing. (Death by electricity was supposedly more humane, though I read horrific stories about it; in some cases, the ordeal lasted more than eight minutes, and on more than one occasion, a person had to be electrocuted twice.)

Even though executions were no longer happening at The Tombs when I got there, I knew that more than fifty people, almost all men, had been hanged there. This dark place with its locked cells and history of death was a stark reminder of society's power to remove freedom—and life—if one broke the law, and was caught, and convicted. Or wrongly convicted (this seemed to happen fairly regularly, according to the *New York Times*). If I were implicated in Mollie's death, this is where I'd likely spend the rest of my life—or I'd be put to death in Sing Sing.

I was brought to the Police Courts there at the prison and waited my turn for the Special Sessions, which meant my case would be looked at by three justices, rather than the General Session, which called for a jury. I knew from my business that sentences were harsher in the General Session, and so that gave me hope.

There were three cases before me. The first was a man with what looked like a broken arm who accused a watchman of throwing him down the stairs of a hotel. The watchman, however, convincingly claimed that the man was drunk and fell himself. The justices quickly dismissed the case.

The next was a case against an old woman who had supposedly stolen liver pudding from a German butcher. Since neither of them spoke English an interpreter delivered their case.

"When did you first see the liver pudding?" the lawyer asked the woman.

I was amused despite my nervousness. A detective came in and presented a basket with liver pudding in it, which all three justices smelled, one after the other. Then Justice Gardner, Scottish like me, asked the German butcher, "How do you know this is your pudding? Aren't there twenty thousand other such livers in the city today just like it?" The case was dismissed, though the smug look the old woman gave the butcher made me sure of her guilt. I half expected her to stick her tongue out at him.

Next, a woman with her head wrapped in numerous bandages went before the bench. She accused a man of beating her and pointed to a large, mute fellow. Justice Gardner told her to unwrap her bandages.

She did so reluctantly, revealing a perfectly preserved head without a scratch. Case dismissed. Her supposed attacker didn't bat an eye; I'm not even sure the dumbbell knew he'd been accused.

My name was called. I took a breath and prayed silently that my case too would be summarily dismissed. I went and stood before the justices, hoping my face looked impassive and yet cooperative—and didn't reveal the terror I felt in my core. The Court Reporter explained the case: I had issued a bond with the security being a pair of two properties that were supposedly not in my name but in Celia Richards'.

"In September this year," I explained, keeping my voice professional and calm, "my wife, Celia F. L. Hall, transferred the St. George's Crescent property to my name. We filed the paperwork properly, so I'm not sure why the transaction wasn't recorded."

Justice Morgan, who sounded American, said that until the paperwork was sorted out, I would be serving time in the ten-day cell. My heart sank. Was this to be my reckoning?

An officer led me from the court and down the hall where I was asked by a keeper if I would like a prison uniform. I could keep on my regular clothing, he explained, or have my wife bring extra garments—even extra food and reading material if I wanted. She was allowed to visit with me, too. I opted, of course, to keep my own clothing, including, and especially, my over-sized coat.

The communal cell, aptly referred to as "Bummer's Hall," was about sixty feet by twenty feet and housed about twenty-five men—mostly vagrants, pickpockets, drunks, and disorderly persons; their cases would be heard in the morning. The windows were set too high to look directly out of; with a glance, I caught sight only of November sky, a dreary grey that day. There were two stoves set at either side of the room, and indeed, I was relieved at the warmth. A bench ran the perimeter of three sides of the cell; the fourth was of course a barricade of iron bars and a locked barred door.

I sat on the bench. I had nothing to read, though I was not sure I would have if I did; it seemed like something that could get you beat up in a place like that. I closed my eyes. I wanted to lie down, but there was only the dusty floor. Some men were gathered in groups; others did lay themselves out on the bench taking more room for themselves and leaving little to others. Some of the men were still inebriated. A couple of them shouted and shoved each other suddenly, and the officer in charge told them to calm down. It was a dismal, yet tense, situation. Then I had an idea.

In my pocket I still had money they hadn't taken from me. I gave the guard a few dollars, asked if I could write a note and have it delivered.

An hour later, Celia arrived at the cell, handed me two decks of cards, a bag of tobacco and rolling papers, several pipes, and matches. We couldn't have a tender moment, but the look on her face showed that she knew exactly how I felt—and the precariousness of the situation. I told her to go to the city records, to get a copy of the deed transfer we filed in September as proof of security.

"I've already done it," she said. "But they won't have the copies ready until tomorrow."

She looked at me with such concern and compassion I felt my heart cracking and told her she should go. She understood.

After she left, I started a poker game that lasted through the night.

Two days later, this article ran in the paper.

> November 17, 1891, *New York Times*
>
> *"Recorder Goff yesterday paroled Murray H. Hall of 145 Sixth Avenue, the alleged 'straw' bondsman, until Monday, when he will furnish $300 bail for further examination.*
>
> *Hall was arrested Friday and committed to the Tombs in default of $2,500 bail. He was charged with giving as surety for bail two vacant lots at Van Cortland Avenue and St. George's Crescent, which, it was alleged, he did not own. He showed to-day that his wife owned the property and conveyed it to him after he had become surety in the police court."*

I only had to spend one night in prison thanks to Celia. So it proved not to be my reckoning but only a close call, one that shook me—shook both of us—to our cores.

Chapter Thirty-four

I was finally promoted to captain in 1893 after helping out with the election and assuring the Democrat's win. With my bonus, we moved to our place on 145 Sixth Avenue, right near Pratt's. A recession hit, and we weathered through it in part by renting out our additional bedroom to Ester and Louise. It felt good to not be so precariously poor after all those early years of struggle and tenement living. Celia and I were in our fifties; our health was top notch. Life was good.

Minnie turned fourteen. She had grown taller than me and was asserting herself—her teacher smacked her knuckles after Minnie rolled her eyes at him (some disagreement they had about Hester Prynne). She was becoming too smart for her own good, but I didn't discourage her. I liked sharing books with her—I bought her Twain and Austen and even Dostoevsky. Well, I bought them for myself too, but I let her read what she wanted, and then we discussed. *Frankenstein* became her favorite book; she read it so many times it fell apart. I may not have been able to give her riches, but I offered her something else: an intellectual life. It was a marvel to witness her growing up.

In 1885, a man named Sigmund Freud published a book called *Studies On Hysteria.* Pratt suggested it to me, and I read it cover to cover in one afternoon in her bookshop. It was one of the most curious books I'd ever read, and it made me furious at Freud, but also at the "hysterical" women whose cases he discusses. I wanted to slap them out of their trances, tell them they were stronger than they thought themselves, that their bodies were rebelling against society's oppression of their sex. The women suffered blindness, paralysis, convulsions. They wouldn't eat. Freud linked it to some early trauma, either real or imagined, and likely sexual. I felt in a perhaps oversimplified manner that if they could only break out of their environs, they would find themselves so formidably strong…but they couldn't even vote yet, and so what *was* society telling them? You're delicate, your moods dictate your day, you're confused, sad, mad; you need to be treated, to rest.

Still, there was one thing Freud seemed to do quite well: he *listened* to the women. He helped his patients go deeper, to pay attention to their memories, to their dreams. He believed that by asking questions and letting the women talk and really listening, that they would heal. In that sense the book and Freud were remarkable. As you can see, I had quite mixed feelings about it. I wondered what a session with Freud would be like, what we would discover about my life, what theories he would put forth. Would he conclude that my masquerade was the result of illness?

I didn't feel ill. At least not in my head.

Then Celia noticed a change in my left breast. Something was inside it that hadn't been there before. And I knew from some of the books I had read at Pratt's that this was not good.

That small knot in my breast focused everything—everything seemed to exist in light of it. For the first time, I could see the end.

It made me tremendously sad, but it also made me experience each and every interaction with Celia and Minnie with a sharper lens. I hated that, the power this small foreign growth inside me had over my life, and yet it made things like having a cup of tea with Celia or walking Walt or reading with Minnie feel precious. I could see things more clearly. I was still me—still Murray—and I would still play poker and drink a whiskey and slap John Bremer on the back and go to the Iroquois club. But I was watching it all now with amazed yet sad detachment. Because it would all eventually end.

Someday, I would cease to exist. I had lost my mother, my father, my brother—and so I should have accepted the fact of *my* imminent demise. But until it was my own fate that hung in the balance, I was mostly removed from death. The idea of not existing had been inconceivable.

I lay closer to Celia at night. We lingered in bed in the morning, just being together, not so eager to jump up and start the day and tackle the tasks at hand. We held each other, and she was tender with me. I could be open, fragile even, in her arms. I could voice my fears. And then I would get up and dress and go out into the world as Murray, emboldened and buttressed by Celia, by her love.

Then on an ordinary day in 1898, Celia got a sore throat, which should have been nothing—a cold that would disappear in a few weeks.

But a fever enveloped her, making her ache with every movement. She moaned. Her glands swelled. I sent for Gallagher, whom we had known for years—he had treated Minnie through her childhood and knew Celia and me well. I saw the look on his face when he examined her.

"She has diphtheria, Murray," he told me.

It wasn't difficult to contract, just another contagious disease. He saw the telltale signs: a greyish membrane that covered her throat making it difficult for her to breathe; it would eventually cover her nose and throat, he explained.

"And suffocate her?" I asked, horrified. I tried to keep my voice low. We were talking in the living room.

"It's a bad case of it, my friend," he said. "If that happens, I could try a tracheotomy to clear her throat. It's been done successfully a few times—I've read about the procedure."

"Anything, Gallagher, that might save her. Please."

She was confined to our bedroom. I was to keep Minnie from her. I thought of my father, not letting James and me near my mother as she died. I remember hating him for that. He probably saved our lives.

"What causes it?"

"A bacterium," Gallagher explained. "Just discovered recently, in fact. Klebs-Löffler bacillus. Two Germans, though I think Theodor Klebs is German-Swiss. They used the technique of staining the bacteria to distinguish it from other bacteria."

They had discovered the bacteria and named it, but there was no prevention, no treatment, no cure.

Her body fought. Her neck swelled and her breathing became even more shallow, fast, raspy. Her eyes looked frightened. I held her hand, wiped her brow with a cool cloth. Gallagher gave her a shot of morphine and tried the tracheotomy, which cleared her throat, but the results didn't last.

On July 7, a day I will never forget, she said to me in a barely audible voice: "You will take care of Minnie."

I nodded and squeaked out the words, "Of course."

"Murray, you must also take care of yourself. I'm not going to be here. Your dog cannot be your only confidante." With this she attempted a smile, but I could see the pain she was in.

She coughed, then whispered, "Your tumor…you must confide in someone. Tell Minnie everything. She loves you—she won't be angry. You can trust her, Murray. She'll take care of you."

"Don't worry—I'll tell her," I lied.

Her nose was dripping, and I put a tissue to it, told her to blow. But she could not. She squeezed my hand. I began to cry. "No, Celia…"

And just like that, she was gone.

Minnie wept and raged and wept more. She was 19 and not ready to lose the mother she loved so dearly. Whoever is? No one. To lose your mother is to have your life forever altered; it was within her body your existence took hold. Even the death of a cruel or even just indifferent mother is monumental. But the death of a beloved mother is a blow to one's heart from which one never fully recovers.

We buried Celia in Mount Olivet, without a headstone, as I was unable to afford the one I wanted. I would save and purchase a good quality one, as Celia would have done. One that would last.

Our boarders, Ester and Louise, came to the funeral. They had appreciated Celia's kindness, her openness toward them, and they grieved. They cooked for Minnie and me every night for weeks until we could function again. I didn't charge them rent that month.

Minnie had begun smoking when her mother was ill, sitting outside the bedroom she wasn't allowed into, killing time by rolling cigarette after cigarette. She became even thinner, paler. Louise, who was warmer than Ester, took to brushing Minnie's hair, and watching them brought me back in my mind to Emma, who cared for me all those years. Women, I observed not for the first time in my life, helped each other. They could be there for each other through hard times.

So entrenched was I in appearing manly, I feared showing anything. I waited until I was alone in my bedroom, and instead of crying on someone's shoulder, I sobbed silently into a pillow, Celia's pillow, that she had slept on for years, and breathing in the scent, I felt my heart and soul irreparably break.

Part Four

1900 – 1901

Chapter Thirty-five

And that is the story of how I got to where I am now: more than two years of mourning that hasn't yet ended; a sandbagging by William Reno that angered and ruptured the tumors already hell-bent on my demise; a daughter who apparently loves me but doesn't know the real me.

What is there left to live for?

There's really only one answer: for Minnie.

I worry about her constantly, worry about leaving her with insufficient money. She knows that unless she marries, she will have to support herself, and she says she wants to be independent. She had interests, ideas about her life, before her mother fell ill: one day she would say she wanted to become a nurse or even a doctor; another day she said wanted to become a writer, maybe put on plays. She will become a suffragist, she said. Or maybe a trapeze artist. But when Celia died, her gumption for life and any of these pursuits waned. She's adrift.

For right now, I live to be with her, so that she doesn't have to suffer another loss, though we both know that with my advancing cancer, she eventually will.

I admit I've have had evil thoughts about William Reno, imagined scenes in my mind where I wreak revenge on him. If I wake up tired and beat down, I have only to think of him beating me up to get my heart pounding, anger and resentment flowing through my veins. It's a distraction—I know that. I have devised plans in my mind where I hire someone to sandbag him, but that seems too easy. I prefer to set a trap, something that will reveal Reno's true scoundrel nature, and see if he will fall for it. He will.

I have been keeping track of him in my own way, and I learned that he has a job as a cook in a diner, which doesn't pay much. I'm sure he wants and needs to make more money. The plan comes to me when I go to Pratt's one day. She mentions that she's caring for her friend's apartment the next street over, on Seventh, feeding their cats and watering the plants while the friend and her husband are traveling in

Europe. Pratt's daughter, however, has just given birth to her first child several weeks early, and it's not clear whether the infant is going to live. Pratt wants to close up shop for a week or more and go to be with her daughter and grandchild—but she feels an obligation to the friend and her apartment.

"We can help out," I tell her. "Between Minnie and myself, it wouldn't be a problem."

"Really, Murray? I'm just not sure how long I'll be gone. Could be a week or a month. You wouldn't need to go every day—just every few days. I don't want to inconvenience you."

But I assure her we're happy to do it, and Pratt, eager to leave that very afternoon, gives me the keys to the apartment and the address.

I go there that evening, and it turns out to be a rather stunning place. A cat meows, comes out of the shadows and presses against my pant. I pet the feline—it's a beautiful specimen—and then another emerges and then another. I wonder how many cats they have.

It's a lovely apartment. The plants are in gilded pots, beautiful leafy things of all kinds. The floors are tiled, which is rare and expensive. The rugs must be Caucasian, as they remind me of the one Charlie had. The furniture is ornate. This is a level far above my station.

Then suddenly I think of William Reno. I don't want to implicate Pratt, but William Reno, I decide, is going to rob this place. He's not going to get away with anything, however. He's going to get caught in the act. That's my revenge, I realize: to send him back to prison!

I will need a few people for the job—and also an officer who's willing to arrest him. They won't be too difficult to line up, not for the right price. I'll have to do my homework, though, and find an ex-con who served time with Reno, someone out now too whom Reno would recognize from the penitentiary. Someone who'd be willing to rob Reno of his last dime.

I feed the cats and water the plants with a pretty copper watering can. I'm smiling thinking about my plan.

That night, I walk to Skelly's with a spring in my step. Life suddenly has renewed purpose. Upon entering, I scour the room for police officers I know and see Patrick O'Henry and John Wadsworth. No, too straight. But then I see Officer Callan playing poker at a table with a couple other men, and I know he's the one. I put in a good word for him on the squad and basically got him the job. He owes me, and I know his salary as a new member of the department is modest. I will both pay him a fee and give him a chance to make a name for himself by catching a robber.

I saunter up to the table and say hello. Callan invites me to buy in.

After several rounds and some profit, I ask Callan if he'd like to join me at the bar for a drink—my treat. When I explain the ruse, he gets excited. He's in, enthusiastically so.

Back at home that evening, I go to my office and look up my own bail bonds records, most of which are in Celia's neat hand. I know Reno spent time at Dannemora. I look for one of my own clients, someone I bailed out who had also done time there. Someone not above doing a job on a fellow ex-con. Again, shouldn't be too difficult if the price is right. I find him—Daniel Hickey.

The next day I pay a visit to a restaurant on 23rd near the Hudson, a place I know is advertising for a cook, and it pays well, more than Reno's current job. I tell the owner he has a favor to do for Tammany: when a guy named Reno shows up to apply, he's to tell Reno the position has been filled—that's it. Under no circumstances is he to give Reno a job, no matter the sob story. I give him a case of wine and a few bills. Celia's headstone will have to wait.

I go to Teddy Ackerman's bar and choose two men I hired previously to help with elections, O'Malley and Fitz. I tell them the plan. They like it, and like the money I offer even more. It's part of their job to make sure Reno knows about the cook's position at the restaurant on 23rd and the specific day he needs to apply for it. Fitz is practically giddy about the scheme, even comes up with the name 'Curley,' though he's bald as a coot. He thinks it's a riot.

After asking around, I find that Hickey is working down at the docks. I go find him—he's gargantuan still, the largest face you've ever seen on a man, deeply lined from hard living and framed with unruly black eyebrows, wiry black hair, and a thick, dark beard with crumbs stuck in it. I make him the offer, fill him in on his role, tell him it's all squared—no risk on his part, only profit. I give him twenty dollars to whet his palate. He's in.

The next few weeks focus my life: I get morphine shots from Gallagher and then meet with Callan, Fitz, O'Malley, and Hickey until everything is set.

Days later, on the date we set, to my amazement and delight, the scheme goes off without a hitch! Reno tries to rob the place and Callan catches him red-handed and hauls him in. It's unbelievable.

When I meet Callan in Skelly's that night, he whoops when he sees me. He's a bundle of energy, talking fast and practically shaking. I pat him on the back and buy us both a double of whiskey. He drinks his down in one gulp. I order him another one.

"Murray, you should've seen him! It was perfect, went off just as you said it would. First, I approached the door of the house, crept up as quiet as I could. It was closed but unlocked. I turned the doorknob careful as could be. I was nervous—you never know what kind of knife or gun the thief might have!"

"True, true." He is young, far from seasoned—so his nerves make sense to me.

"So I open the door, worried it will make a creaking sound and give me away, but it doesn't. And when I poke my head in, I see Reno there in the hall! He's squatted down and I can't tell what he's doing at first, and then when he sees me, he startles, and then I see these creatures scatter—cats! The chump comes to rob the place and stops to pet the cats! But the robbin' was already done, which was the good thing for us. Caught red-handed, pockets full of jewelry and a sack full of all kinds of things, including all the silverware in the house. But petting the cats!"

He said Reno gave himself up without a struggle but cried like a baby.

I get so drunk that night that I fall walking home, split my lip and chip a tooth. I wake up the next day in my bed parched, still in my coat, blood on my shirt. I lie there for a long time thinking about William Reno.

This article runs in the *Times* afterward.

> *Three weeks ago Reno was arrested by Policeman Callan, charged with breaking into the house at 167 Seventh Avenue. He was indicted by the Grand Jury and arraigned before Judge Newburger Wednesday. The Judge remembered him well. When seen by a New York Times reporter, Reno told the story of his downfall after he had promised Judge Newburger solemnly to lead an upright life.*
>
> *"To my bitter disappointment, after being discharged by Judge Newburger, I found it impossible to obtain employment as a needle worker. I knew nothing of machine work, and all the hand workers were women. My years of labor were thus of no avail. The trade I had learned after much toil benefited me none, as I*

> *knew nothing of machine work. I sought employment as a cook, finally, and eventually worked myself up to a $9 a week position. I always tried to better myself, and from all my employers I have good recommendations. I saved in time $68.*
>
> *"If I had wanted to steal, I had many opportunities to carry off thousands of dollars' worth, but I touched nothing. Three weeks ago, I went to Eleventh Avenue and Twenty-third Street to apply for a position at a larger salary than I was getting, and I had my $68 with me. The position had been filled. I was just too late. It was then about 6 o'clock in the morning and very foggy. Walking up Eleventh Avenue, in my disappointment, I met a former ex-convict I had known in prison. He told me a hard-luck story, and I gave him $2 from my savings, advising him to lead an honest life. Another man was with him, and shortly after I was struck from behind and knocked senseless. When I came to, my money was gone.*
>
> *"Later that day, cold, half-starved, and desperate, I met a man named 'Curley,' who took me into a saloon and gave me two drinks of brandy. Then he gave me three keys, described a house in Seventh Avenue, and told me I would get enough there to start my life anew if I only kept my nerve. I was weak, hungry, and my brain was befuddled. I was tempted and fell with this result. I deserve all I will get in court."*

I should feel pleased—after all, Reno had finally paid for the pain and suffering he inflicted on me. I know he's been sitting in prison awaiting his trial because he cannot afford to post bail. And he knows what he's facing—after all, he has spent most of his adult life in prison. I picture him back in a prison cell with this his intricate embroidery. I think of his efforts to find a place in this world, to hone a skill, to make a living doing something lovely but under-valued since it's women's work. If I know the judge, he will probably sentence Reno to another decade in prison. I think of the Marx quote again, about crime being a function of class struggle. "Curley" made the offer, told him about the house, gave him the keys—and Reno didn't resist—he stole, or had planned to. He fell for the trap. The trap I set.

Yes, I should be overjoyed. But Reno's arrest and re-imprisonment make me feel lower than I have for a long time. The hangover doesn't help.

I keep drinking.

A few days later, I'm still in bed. I haven't changed my bandages and I can smell myself: ill, sweaty, sour. I'm quiet with Minnie when she comes in; I refuse to be chipper, even for her, and when she urges me to tell her what's wrong, I snap at her.

"Can't you just leave me alone?" I say. "And take the stupid dog out—he's been whining." I kick Walt and he whimpers, falls off the edge of the bed. She looks at me surprised—indeed, I've never spoken to her harshly. She bends down and pets Walt's head and leads him out. If I were her, I would have slammed the door, but she closes it softly. Her crestfallen face makes me hate myself.

I fetch a fresh bottle of whiskey from my nightstand. She doesn't come back the rest of the day.

I finally stumble from bed. When I open the door, Walt is lying on the floor just on the other side of it. He looks up at me, but I just step over him. I'm in pain, and I want morphine, but I want to kill more than just the pain.

Gallagher is there at his office, reading in his study, drinking a glass of brandy when I barge in.

"Murray, hello."

"Offer me one of those?"

"Of course."

He pours me one and invites me to sit down on the couch. I can smell my breath, my body, my dirty clothes and wonder if he can too. He hands me the glass and I clink his a bit too hard.

"Haven't seen you or heard from you, Murray. How are you?"

"Never better. Did you read about William Reno in the paper?"

"I did."

"Then I guess my work is done here."

"Meaning?"

"I'm ready, Gallagher. Can't live forever."

He looks at me for a long moment. I walk over and refill my glass of brandy myself and drink it down in one gulp.

"I'm afraid I don't know what you mean, Murray," he says. "Are you finished writing?"

"Yes, I'm finished writing the damned story. It's over, Gallagher. The story is ending." I fill my glass again and drink it down. "I'm ready to die."

His brow wrinkles. Perturbed, he shakes his head. "Not like this, friend."

"Just give me the fucking morphine, Gallagher. I can do it myself."

Again he gives me that long, thoughtful stare and then says softly, "I understand how you must be feeling, Murray. But not now. Not like this."

How dare he. I feel my blood beginning to boil. "You understand nothing, Gallagher. You're well—you're not dying," I accuse him. "How dare you wield your power over me!" I pick up a lamp. He's on the other side of the room, still on the couch.

"You should leave, Murray. Go home and sleep it off and we'll talk in the morning. We can come up with a plan, but not like this. Not when you're so angry. And drunk."

I throw the lamp at his head but miss, and it shatters against the wall behind him.

"Leave now, Murray, or I'll call the police," he says with a sternness I've never heard from him. "You're my friend, Murray, but you're not in your right mind."

I slam the door so hard behind me, I hear a painting fall off the wall.

Forget Gallagher. Forget everyone—they can all go to hell. It's where I'm headed and all I want at this point. Hell is all I deserve.

I will find another doctor to help me.

The next day I wake in a horrible state. Sobbing, angry. I feel terrible that I threw the lamp at Gallagher, but even more terrible that I'm still alive.

I call on another doctor I know of, John A. Burke. He has an office on 152nd, but he says he'll make a house call. I drink a little whiskey while I lie there.

Minnie is home, and I hear her let him in. "Where is Dr. Gallagher?" I hear her say, but he knows nothing of Gallagher and says so. Then he knocks on my bedroom door.

"Come in," I call out. I have stashed the whiskey bottle. I'm lying on the bed, my back against the headboard. I pull my coat around me.

"Good day," he says. "I'm Dr. Burke. Murray Hall, I presume?" His voice is too bright for this dismal room.

"Yes, I'm he," I say. We don't shake hands.

"What seems to be the trouble?"

"I'll get right to it so as not to waste your time, Doctor. I'm suffering from cancer."

"What kind of cancer?" he asks, merely curious and not at all compassionate. He's a small man, taller than me but thinner. He appears to have a nervous habit of raising his pince nez to his eyes, even when he's not looking at anything. I doubt he's married, and indeed, no ring.

"Cancer of the breast," I tell him and watch his eyes squinch up. "Men can suffer from it too, I'm sure you know."

"Oh, yes," he says. "Though it's more common in women."

Anticipating this moment, I offer him a cigar, which he declines, so I light mine. "It's not curable," I say. "It's not curable, and I'm looking for some morphine to help with the pain."

"Oh, I will have to examine you before I prescribe that," he says.

I shake my head. "That's not necessary."

"Oh, but it is. I never prescribe medicine without a full examination." Those pince-nez again—it's definitely a nervous habit with him. "You'll have to at least remove your shirt."

I shake my head at him again, then resigned, say, "You know, Dr. Burke, I'm feeling better today and don't think I need any morphine after all."

He's confused, clearly, but bids me goodbye.

A few days later, I'm desperate and call him back to the apartment. After feigned pleasantries, I lay it out for him.

"The tumors are ruptured, Dr. Burke." My whole body is beginning to shake. "You need to just give me the bloody morphine."

He looks at me offended, of course. And he must think I'm an addict with the way I'm behaving.

"I'm afraid that's impossible unless I do a proper examination," he repeats, indignant. He is a tiresome, prissy man. For a fleeting moment I consider bashing in his skull and getting the morphine out of his bag myself. I look around my room. The large glass ashtray would suffice.

"I can't be cured—there's…there's no cure," I say trying to keep my voice calm but speaking through gritted teeth. "Do you understand?"

"I'm sorry but without an examination—"

"Just leave," I say to him. He looks at me, baffled and indignant. "Leave now!"

I need him to go before I do something I'll regret, and lucky for him, he does. I drink enough whiskey to kill a horse, but regrettably not myself.

The next day, another story runs about Reno. He is haunting me. You know the story, so I won't repeat it, except for the final lines, which stab at my heart:

> *"Then he gave me three keys, described a house in Seventh Avenue, and told me I would get enough there to start life anew if I only kept my nerve. I was weak, hungry, and my brain was befuddled. I was tempted and fell, with this result. I deserve all I will get in court, but I wish my people to know that I did lead an honest life after my discharge until I fell."*

I don't think I can live with myself.

I picture the cells in The Tombs, the concrete bed, the cold, the damp. The wizened apple and stale bread they serve with water as a meal. The only exercise a walk around the inside loop, no sunshine or fresh air ever. How the lights go out at night, and you sit there in the dark with only your thoughts—you can't smoke because it's a fire hazard, and you're allowed no light with which to read—or embroider. I imagine the awful boredom and loneliness of those nights. And William Reno is looking at thousands of them.

I think about how he hasn't had a Christmas since before he was 22. I think of his elaborate, and yes, beautiful embroidery, the pride he had in it when he showed it to me that first meeting, how I scoffed, because he was a man. His frustration at not knowing how to work the sewing machines, only knowing what he could create with his hands. The shame and frustration of being poor. How similar William Reno and I are, really. How lucky I had been to have a brother who clipped short my career as a thief when I was just a child and stole that apple. Did William Reno have a brother to discourage him from thieving? A loving mother who taught him to read poetry? Friends who made sure his belly was full with hot food at least once a week on Sundays? Much less a wife, a daughter to love?

Yes, I had felt trapped by history, by my time, limited by sex. I wanted so badly to escape the hand I'd been dealt. William Reno probably did too, wanted to be seen for who he was in his heart, not what outside circumstances had made of him. Learning to embroider all of those years, thousands of days of mastering his craft, thinking himself an artist, only to emerge to an indifferent society who doesn't want original lace patterns made by a man—and anyway, we've got machines for that now. You thought you made something beautiful for the world, and the world responds: You're useless. Reno works, saves, tries to better his lot. Even offers two dollars to a friend who's down and out—an acquaintance I convinced to rob him and who made off with Reno's last sixty-eight dollars. Twenty-two years in prison, finally out, and I, Murray Hall, set him up for failure. All right, it wasn't right for him to take his anger out on me, but if anyone understood temper and desperation, it was I—I who punched cops, and stabbed Margaret Barret, and made my first wife disappear.

No, William Reno and I are more alike than I care to admit.

Every night as I lie down to sleep, I try to drown out these thoughts. I pour whiskey into my morphine-deprived body and pass out. But when I wake, usually at three in the morning when I waddle to the toilet in the middle of the night and then get back into my luxurious bed with its soft, comfortable blankets, it is William Reno's face I see. I dream of Celia, but she's silent, scolding. She isn't proud of me for exacting my revenge. She is disappointed.

I am riddled with guilt and remorse. I try to remind myself of Reno's beating, of how he kicked me without mercy, worsened my tumor, hastened my death. But I cannot clear my conscience of him, cannot not set myself free.

Suddenly I remember another William. What was his name? Starkey? No, Sharkey. I get out of bed, put on my robe and slippers and go up to my office—I had clipped the story of him from the newspaper and saved it. I open a few drawers, sift through the stack of articles I cut out and saved throughout the years.

Ah, there it is—I find it. I re-read it for the first time in years. I think of how Charlie and I marveled at Sharkey's audacity. And I know what I have to do.

Though I know I don't have much time left, William Reno might.

When I arrive at The Tombs two days later, I'm carrying a sack layered with a few items. I announce my name to the keeper, tell him that I'm there to see William Reno. He wants to check the bag, so I open it and show him what's on top: a billy club.

"What's that all about?" he asks.

"What's your name?" I ask.

"Sullivan," he answers.

"Well, Mr. Sullivan, I have a score to settle with Reno. He sandbagged me last year when I wouldn't give him a job. So if you don't mind, I'd like some time with him." I slip him a fifty.

He glances at the bill and grins before shoving it in his pocket. It's more than three times his weekly salary. Then he raises a finger at me. "Don't you kill him—not on my watch."

"Oh, I'm not that merciful," I say. "I want him serve his full sentence." He chuckles and hands me a red card—my pass—and leads me up the stairs to the row of cells on the second floor. Reno is lying down, but when he sees me, it takes him a second, and then he bolts upright, eyes wide.

"Please don't let him in here," he says to the keeper.

"Want me to wait nearby?" the keeper asks me, ignoring Reno.

"No, that's all right. I'll call you if I need to," I say.

He nods. "Take your time. Just lock up when you leave. I'm off in a half hour, but the next fellow will take back your pass."

When he walks away, Reno stares at me a moment then sits back down, looking resigned. I fish through the bag and remove a straight razor, hold it up so that it catches the gleam of a thin band of light shining in from the tiny window to the outside. I think of Margaret Barrett.

"Please don't kill me," says Reno.

"I'm not going to," I say. "But we should shave that beard if we're going to try to pass you off as a woman."

I hold my breath when, an hour later, Reno leaves the cell dressed in Celia's clothes, wearing a wig, and holding my red pass. I hear no alarm, no calls, no scuffle.

I wait another few minutes and then leave, closing and locking the cell behind me. I walk past the rows of cells, see bodies locked in, most prone, some sitting with their head in their hands, some pacing. I wait until the keeper is busy and try to pass.

"Hey—" he calls out. I stop, heart pounding. "Where do you think you're going?"

"I was trying to find my client." I try to think of a name and can only think of one. "Samuel Clemens," I say. "Awaiting trial tomorrow. I'm the bondsman, here to post bail."

"You're in the wrong area, Sir. You need to see the judge in the courtroom if you're going to post bail. Not the prisoner."

I nod, apologize, and walk toward the courtroom. He doesn't stop me and is totally unaware that I have used Mark Twain's real name for my fictitious story.

I am free, but more importantly, so is William Reno. I gave him a ticket from the Grand Central Rail Depot for a train ride to San Francisco, one-hundred-fifty dollars, and Charlie's name in case he can find him; he's to tell Charlie that Murray Hall sent him and sends his regards.

The turmoil in my soul is mitigated by setting William Reno free though not totally assuaged. I still live with the ghosts of regret and loss. I still fear disappointing the living person I love most.

I've recorded the story of my life—but to what end? One problem is that I have not only implicated myself but also Charlie. I spend the next weeks re-reading and typing up what I have on the Remington type-writer Celia had bought for our office. It proves to be a good process: I pare down prose in many places, expand it in others, add more detail, clarify. I change names. I don't use Charlie's real name or his surname. I remove what feels superfluous or indulgent and try to make it more readable overall. But for whom?

For Minnie? For her to find after I'm…gone?

What does it matter, I tell myself. *I'll be dead.*

But it does matter. I think of how deceived she felt when she learned about the cancer—that I had kept it from her. What will happen if she learns that her whole relationship with me is based on a lie? And how will that fact—that she was lied to throughout her childhood—affect her life? Will she ever trust anyone? And what if she doesn't learn about the real me until after I'm dead—when I can't explain it to her?

But here is the worst part of the conundrum: What if I tell her before I die, and she hates me? I risk dying with her scorning me instead of loving me as she does now. How could she still love me when she knows the truth? I could not fathom her contempt.

It would make my entire life not only meaningless, but a failure.

I send word to the two women, Johanna Meyer and Pratt, who have sold me my reading materials over the years—so many newspapers, so many books. I'd like to see them one last time. I want to thank them and say a proper goodbye. Oh, how I will miss reading.

I buy Gallagher two new lamps from Tiffany's and have them delivered. With them, I send a letter in which I sincerely and humbly apologize and ask his forgiveness. I thank him for his friendship and care throughout the years. I understand if he will not see me again.

He shows up the next morning.

I am sober, humbled. He examines me. I'm in pain—I haven't had morphine in a long time, and he knows it. He can also see how far the cancer has advanced. Whether from the cancer reaching my heart or other organs or from infection, I'm going to die soon. And Gallagher knows it will not be a pleasant death.

He gives me a small dose of morphine, and we calmly make a plan for the next day.

For the final dose.

I have to destroy my writing, and yet I find I cannot—*cannot.* I have written my story, told it to the best of my humble ability. I am no Poe, Austen, Twain, and certainly no Whitman. But I have tried to make it palatable, and I have told it honestly; it's written with my heart and soul. I wrote this story in part to show that my life was more than just a masquerade; it is my contributed verse. I admit: I wanted a seat at that table. Whether or not this would have gotten me there, I will never know.

I cannot destroy my writing, but I can ask Minnie to. And I can give her the opportunity to read it if she wants. I call her into my room after Gallagher leaves, tell her I have some things to discuss with her.

She's solemn—she knows my end is near. I tell her about the will, which I officially filed the previous year. She will have about $5,000. I truly wish it were more. We also own this apartment and the two lots in the city. She nods, indifferent to the details of the inheritance. She does not know what all of it means right now, but she will someday soon.

Then I open the drawer of my nightstand and take out the stack of typed pages.

"I want to give you this…this story." I don't know what else to call it.

"Oh, that's what you've been writing all this time?"

"Yes. And I'm not sure how to say this except to say it. I don't want to sound histrionic, but I'd like you to destroy it—the story, these pages. The whole thing."

She looks genuinely confused. "Why?"

I take a breath, as deep of one as the pain will allow. "It's my life, Minnie. But there are things in here I'm not proud of and details that might implicate other people. I wouldn't want them to suffer because I wanted to tell the story of my life."

She nods, slowly, takes this in.

"Few lives are pure virtue, Minnie. But there are things in here that would be quite a surprise to you, even shocking, and most certainly disappointing. So I'm giving you these pages, Minnie, and asking you to dispose of them."

"Why can't you?"

"I just can't. I've…put too much of myself in them. And, in fact…" I was stumbling, trying to get the words out. I put the stack of pages into her hand. "You can read them if you like before you dispose of them. But please—don't feel obligated."

She takes the pages, holds them in her lap. The cover page has one word: MURRAY. She turns to the next one and begins to read.

"No—not now, please! Not in front of me. I couldn't bear it."

"Oh, Dad. I'm sure anything you've done had reason. And how bad could it be? 'The Sordid Tale of the Tammany Bondsman,'" she teases. She smiles, so I do too.

"There's one more thing….Gallagher is coming tomorrow. He's going to help me, Minnie. I'm going to…I'm going to take one final dose of morphine."

Her face darkens. "No, Dad," she shakes her head vehemently as if trying to un-hear the words.

I give her a moment. She looks at me, still shaking her head.

"I don't care how advanced the cancer is—you can't just give up. Why should you leave this earth when you're not ready? You can still live. You can still drink coffee, read books, play poker with your friends."

She looks as if she's going to cry, but she's also angry.

"But all those things, Minnie….I won't be able to enjoy them much longer." My voice is quiet, gentle. "I won't be able to take Walt on a walk or go to Pratt's to read or to Skelly's for poker. I want to leave this world on my own terms. I want to be lucid and not in agony."

"Are you—are you in pain?"

"Yes, yes I am." *More than I've wanted to admit.* "And it's only going to get worse. I don't want to die in a hospital, and that's where I'll end up if I wait much longer."

She finally does start to cry.

"I'm ready, Minnie. I know you might not be ready to lose me, but I have to go. Can you accept that? I know it's a lot to ask."

"All right," she relents finally. "But I cannot be there. I can't watch you die."

I nod. "I understand completely. Gallagher will be with me."

She silently cries for a few moments, wiping tears that fall down her cheeks. I want to tell her that she and her mother were the best things that ever happened to me, that I can die fulfilled only because of them. Instead I say, "Let's have tea and I'll read Whitman to you."

She makes tea for both of us but also brings me a whiskey. I call Walt up onto the bed so the three of us can be together. I read *Leave of Grass* aloud until Minnie falls asleep, something we haven't done for years. I stop after I read the lines: "*I am the poet of the woman the same as the man / And I say it is as great to be a woman as it is to be a man.*"

I lie there wondering if there is an afterlife. Will Celia be there? My brother? My mother? Whitman? I will know soon enough.

I write these, my final written words.

And so I say goodbye.
Goodbye, body and pain.
Goodbye, friends.
Goodbye, books.
Goodbye, good dog, Walt.
Goodbye, daughter.
Goodbye, sweet earth.

Chapter Thirty-six

Gallagher knocks lightly on the bedroom door.

"Come in," he hears and slowly opens it. Murray is sitting in bed, propped up against pillows, Walt nestled against him, his head in Murray's lap. Murray's hair is damp; he appears freshly bathed.

"Hello, friend," says Murray. "I want to thank you, Gallagher. You've been a tremendous support to me."

"The gratitude is mine." He sets his leather bag down on a chair and takes an audible breath. "You know the Hippocratic Oath, right, Murray? To do no harm? If you want this, you're going to have to inject the morphine yourself. But I can guide you."

"You're not harming me, Gallagher. You're setting me free."

"I know that, Murray. We both know that you're not going to get better, that the cancer is spreading, that your pain and suffering will only increase."

"Yes."

"Your affairs are in order?"

"As much as possible. I filed my will last year. I explained it to Minnie last night."

"Did you explain anything else to her?"

"I gave her the pages I've written—the story of my life, as it is. I told her to destroy it, but I also told her she could read it if she wants to."

Gallagher nods.

"Did you see her out there?" Murray asks.

"Her bedroom door was closed, but I think I heard her."

Murray bends down, pets Walt's head tenderly, scratches the dog's neck. "I'm ready, Gallagher."

"You're an extraordinary person, Murray. I truly feel honored that you trusted me with your care—and your secret."

Murray nods, perhaps afraid to speak. Gallagher opens his large satchel and removes a vial of morphine. He unscrews it, puts the needle inside and draws it back, filling the syringe.

"This is an extra strong concentration and dosage. You'll feel nothing; you'll just drift off to sleep, and it will be over."

"Yes. Yes, thank you."

Murray rolls up the sleeve of his left arm, onto which Gallagher places a tourniquet as they have done many times before. Murray pumps his hand until the blue vein bulges under the skin. Gallagher places the needle into Murray's right hand, which is shaking, so Gallagher gently places his hand over it.

"Are you ready?" asks Gallagher.

"Yes."

The needle pierces into Murray's skin and enters the vein. With his thumb, Murray dispenses all of the liquid into his blood stream.

He lies back, takes a deep breath. "Thank you, Gallagher."

"You're welcome, my friend."

Murray closes his eyes and Walt licks his hand, lets out a sigh.

A quiet knock at the door, and then it opens. Minnie enters.

"Is he…"

"Not yet, but close."

Minnie approaches the bed, sits and takes Murray's hand in hers.

She leans down and whispers in Murray's ear: "I just finished your book, Dad." She squeezes his hand. "I love you—and always will."

He tries to smile and squeeze back. He smells her familiar scent of cologne and a hint of tobacco, feels her soft lips linger on his forehead.

Then he drifts away.

Epilogue

Jan. 20, 1901, *New York Times*

The funeral of Murray Hall, the woman who for more than thirty years posed as a man, was held at her home, 148 [sic] Sixth Avenue, yesterday afternoon. There were about twenty persons on the sidewalk in front of the house at 3 o'clock when the body was taken from the house. The burial was in Mount Olivet Cemetery.

Two men and the adopted daughter, Minnie Hall, comprised all of the funeral attendants. For the first time in forty years Murray Hall was dressed in woman's clothes, the garments of her sex.

January 29, 1901, *The Evening Post*

The foregoing is a verdict rendered by a jury in Coroner Zucca's court yesterday. It was rendered only after testimony had been heard bearing upon the strange career of the woman, Murray Hamilton Hall, who for nearly 30 years posed as a man and associated with many politicians without the secret of her sex becoming known.

Coroner Zucca began the inquest by confessing that the case was not one which should ordinarily come before him. He referred to the fact, however, that an estate was involved and its legal disposition necessitated an authoritative establishment of the sex of Murray Hall. It took the jury just seven minutes to settle the question of Murray Hall's sex for all time.

Imelda Hall, the adopted daughter of the mysterious woman who hoodwinked everybody for so long was a witness. She proved to be a slender brunette who evidenced considerable spirit. She showed that she had a mind of her own. Miss Hall answered the preliminary questions in a clear matter-of-fact way. She said that she had lived with her "foster father" since 1885.

"And during all those years you never thought he was a woman?" Inquired Coroner Zucca.

"No, Sir."

"You knew he was ill, didn't you—knew that he suffered from cancer?"

"Yes, Sir."

"How long had he—she, I mean—suffered from the disease?"

"For six years."

"Did you ever hear him say that he had been drugged and sandbagged by a man by the name of William Reno, and do you think that the sandbagging made his disease worse?"

"Yes, I knew that he had been sandbagged," she replied. "But I never heard him say that the sandbagging made him worse."

"Wouldn't it be better for you to say 'she'?" the Coroner suggested politely.

"No, I would rather say he," she said. "He was always a man to me, and I shall never think of him as a woman."

"Did Murray Hall have a doctor?" Coroner Zucca went on.

"Yes."

"Who was he?"

"Dr. Gallagher."

The Dr. Gallagher referred to is the William C. Gallagher who has been frequently mentioned in connection with the case. He said on the stand yesterday that he had attended Hall during her last illness at intervals of the year previous to her death and that she suffered from cancer of the breast.

"When you examined him—her—did you discover her to have cancer of the breast?" The doctor was asked.

"Yes, Sir."

"Didn't you find out that she was a woman?"

"That's a question I don't care to answer; a man can have cancer of the breast."

"When you filed a certificate of death, was she dead or alive?"

"She was dead."

The coroner further asked Dr. Gallagher if he considered that the sandbagging might have hastened Murray Hall's death, to which Dr. Gallagher replied that it might have been an "exciting cause," that it might have accelerated the end.

"Dr. Gallagher, will you tell the jury whether the deceased was a female or a man?" the corner asked.

"She was a female, a woman," Dr. Gallagher replied.

The jury then wrestled with its sex problem, and the foregoing verdict was finally read:

The Coroner's jury, after spending half a day over the inquest into the death of Murray H. Hall and becoming inextricably involved in a mass of the masculine and feminine gender pronouns, rendered this verdict: "Murray Hall came to her death by natural causes. He was a lady."

January 20, 1901, *New York Times*

Dr. John A. Burke of 152 West Eleventh Street was called in to see Murray Hall on Dec. 6. Dr. Burke says he knew Hall by sight for years, but had never attended her professionally. Hall said she was suffering from a cancer of the breast and wanted him to prescribe for her. "I said, 'Take off your shirt,' and took off my coat and rolled up my sleeves preparatory to making a proper examination. She said she felt a good deal better that day and wouldn't have any examination then."

Dr. Burke says he regarded it as peculiar but left, and a few days afterward was called in again. "I asked her how she felt and what her symptoms were, and got all the information I could, but she would not have an examination made and wanted a prescription. I said it was impossible unless I could make a complete examination, but she said she would not have that done, as a cancer could not be cured anyway, and she insisted on the prescription." Dr. Burke says he thought the refusal to have an examination was a piece of crankiness, and that Murray Hall thought a doctor could do as much for a patient without giving an examination. He left and did not give the matter a thought until he heard of Murray Hall's death.

January 27, 1901, *The Anaconda Standard* (Anaconda, Montana),

In going into practical politics joining Tammany, Murray Hall, the New Yorker who for thirty years was known as a man, and who turned out to be a woman, demonstrated one way of solving the woman suffrage question.

January 19, 1901, *New York Times*

I wouldn't believe it if Dr. Gallagher, whom I know to be a man of undoubted veracity hadn't said so. Well, truly, it's most wonderful. Why, I knew him well. He was a member of the Tammany district organization, a hard worker for his party, and always had a good argument to put up for any candidate he favored. He used to come to the Iroquois Club to see me and pay his dues, and occasionally he would crack a joke with some of the boys. He was a modest little fellow, but had a peppery temper and could say some cutting things when anyone displeased him.

Suspect he was a woman? Never. He dressed like a man and talked like a very sensible one. The only thing I ever thought eccentric about him was his clothing. Now that they say he's a woman, I can see through that. You see, he also wore a coat a size or two too large, but of good material. That was to conceal his form. He had a bushy head of black hair, which he wore long and parted on the left side. His face was always smooth, just as if he had just come from the barber.

--New York State Senator Bernard F. Martin

January 19, 1901, *New York Times*,

I knew him well, and I remember that we both worked tooth and nail to get the larger vote. If he's a woman, he's the wonder of all the ages, sure's you live, for no man could ever suspect it from his actions and habits. Why, he had several run-ins when he and I were opposing Captains. He'd try to influence my friends to vote against the regular organization ticket, and he'd spend money and do all sorts of things to get votes. A woman? Why, he'd line up to the bar and take whiskey like any veteran, and didn't make faces over it, either. If he was a woman, he ought to have been born a man, for he lived and looked like one."

--Joseph Young, one of Senator Martin's most trusted lieutenants and an officer of the Iroquois Club, was the Tammany Captain of the district when Murray Hall served in the same capacity for the County Democracy

***New York Times*, 1901**

Not once did I ever suspect from word or action that he was masquerading and was really a woman. I believe that he meant to confide in me and tell me his secret when he sent for me. If I had only suspected I certainly would have gone to see him. His adopted daughter, Minnie, was here this morning. The poor girl is terribly shocked over the disclosure. She said she always believed her foster father was a man, and never heard her mother say anything that would lead her to suspect otherwise.

--Johanna Meyer, who kept a newsstand at 109 West Tenth Street

January 20, 1901, *Davenport Daily Leader* (Davenport, Iowa),

Arthur Hughes, who lives on Sixteenth street, west of Sixth avenue, seems to be the only person in the neighborhood who had any suspicion of Hall, and even his suspicion had nothing to do with the questions of sex. The story as Hughes told it was that Hall instructed him not to go near a large box in the basement when he was cleaning up for Hall. Of course he took the first opportunity to examine the box closely, and he says that he saw inside the skeleton of a woman. He did not explain how he knew it was a woman's skeleton but in telling the story, Hughes shook his head solemnly over his belief that the box contained the body of Hall's first wife.

Feb. 1, 1901, *Bedford Gazette*,

She smoked her pipe, got drunk and went into a fight. Murray was a fine politician, true to her friends, and woe betide her enemies.

March 25, 1901, *Arizona Republican* (Phoenix, Arizona),

New York, March 24 - The will of the woman Murray H. Hall, who was known as a man for forty years was filed for probate yesterday. It speaks of his 'deceased wife'. It was executed on April 8, 1900 in the presence of Louisa Perkins and Esther O'Donnell, both of whom resided at 145 Sixth avenue. The value of the estate, which is small is not given. All goes to the testatrix's adopted daughter. The will runs:

"I, Murray H. Hall of New York City, being of sound and disposing mind and memory and considering the uncertainty of life do make publish and declare this to be my last will and testament as follows, hereby revoking all other and former wills by me at any time made.

First—after my lawful debts are paid, I give devise and bequeath all my property, both real and personal, and wherever situated to Imelda A. Hall, and especially request that at my death the said Imelda A. Hall shall cause to be erected a suitable headstone over the grave of my deceased wife Celia F. L. Hall. I hereby appoint Imelda A. Hall to be executrix of this my last will and testament."

January 18, 1901, *The Pokeepsie Evening Enterprise*,

New York City produces one of the most remarkable cases of the kind on record. By the death of Murray H. Hall on Wednesday night, it was discovered that a woman had passed herself off for a man for thirty years with complete success. Hall had been prominent in Tammany politics, a member of clubs, had twice been married, had done many things peculiar to men, and in appearance, actions, voice, etc., was a man. Death alone revealed to 'his' friends and intimate acquaintances the sex of the individual.

January. 20, 1901, *New York Times*,

We must pass such a bill....We want a law providing that Captains in Tammany Hall must wear whiskers. We don't propose having Tammany ring in women on us in the Twenty-First district.

--Republican Abraham Gruber, leader to the 17th Assembly district, expressing the necessity for a law to avoid any more Murray Hall deceptions

January 18, 1901, *New York Times*

So he's a woman, eh? Well, I've read of such characters in fiction, but, if it's true, Hall's case beats anything in fact or fiction I can recall."

--John Bremer, owner of the Fifteenth Ward Hotel and friend of Murray Hall

About the Author

Melanie Senn was born in Camden, New Jersey—the resting place of Walt Whitman—but was raised in California from the age of 5 by a single mother. She earned her bachelor's degree in Latin American Literature from the University of California, Santa Barbara and subsequently lived abroad in Argentina, and Chile, where she found gainful employment as a teacher and translator. When she finally returned to the United States, she married her pen pal and settled in San Luis Obispo, California, where she earned her Master's in English from Cal Poly. She taught in the English department for many years while raising her two boys, somehow managing to carve out time for her own writing. Melanie learned about Murray Hall while researching a grad school paper on Walt Whitman, which led to years of historical research about Murray's life and 19th century New York City. She's lived on Murray Avenue for more than two decades.

Acknowledgements

I started writing *Murray* before my sons were born. I wrote it while juggling parenting, teaching, running a household, and trying to keep a marriage intact. My sons are now 16 and 17, and my spouse and I have been married nearly 24 years. I turned 50 in 2021 and left teaching to focus on writing and audio journalism and to soak in the last couple of years with my sons at home. I was able to do this thanks to the love and support of my generous spouse. I love my family dearly.

In 2019, I found an agent in New York to represent me in finding a market for Murray. He began making pitches to book editors in February 2020, but we were unsuccessful in finding any takers. We parted ways amicably, and I'm grateful to him for believing in my book. I still believe in it as well, so it's time to put *Murray* out into the world, gatekeepers be damned.

Of the editors pitched, only one questioned whether a "cisgender woman" had the right to tell this story. I write the following not as a defense but as an offering of insight into my own proclivities and motivation: I was always a tomboy. I dressed mostly in my brother's clothes, like Murray, and eschewed what was considered feminine behavior. I was feisty and unkempt. I learned how to fight at a young age and also learned how vulnerable girls are. I worked on my cars, surfed, and eventually bought a motorcycle. The editor knew nothing about me, though she was right that I am not a transgender person. Still, who has the right to tell a story? Isn't the act of writing, the act of imagining, ultimately an act of empathy? Writing *Murray* was challenging and humbling, a labor of love, an honor. The respect, awe and admiration I have for him drove me to tell his story.

Another editor pointed out that there's evidence Murray tried to live as a young man in Scotland, where he was born, but was "discovered" to be a woman and *then* emigrated to the United States. Indeed, my first drafts of the novel took that approach. But other clues led me to consider and imagine a younger Murray emigrating with family, and ultimately, that's the path I chose. I had some bones to work with, some real newspaper articles, mostly from the *New York Times,* that touched on his life; in fact, all of the newspaper quotes I included in the book are genuine. I spent years upon years imagining the rest, but this is, nevertheless, a work of fiction.

I want to thank my old friend Scott Richard, who read the first pages of Murray eons ago and encouraged me on. Thank you to the talented Jenny Ashley for reading the first chapters I drafted—and for years of friendship.

I'm grateful to my writing group—Jim Ringley, Lisa Coffman, and Cindy Myers—for their insight, suggestions, and support. Thanks for reading the entire manuscript on my 49th birthday!

I'm so grateful for Jonathan Ned Katz, whose book *Gay American History* introduced me to Murray Hall more than 20 years ago. An entry of a few pages in his book led to two decades of writing, research, and finally, publishing.

In the early 2000s, there was little discussion about transgender people. When I began writing this novel, I was simply in awe over what an audacious, bold, courageous, self-determined person Murray was. I tried different approaches with narrative voices and pronouns. Fairly soon, I began to think of Murray as *he*. When I was nearing the end of writing and revising Murray for the final time, I spoke to a young transgender man named Syd. At 16 years old, Syd had a double mastectomy and became the first person in his high school to transition. At the end of our long conversation, I told him about the novel and asked him if he thought Murray was transgender.

Syd asked: *Did Murray feel happiest living as a man?*

I said, *Syd, he risked everything to live as a man.*

You already know what Syd answered. The answer was clear: the answer was yes. Syd was one of the kindest, most self-possessed people I'd ever spoken to, and I found myself wanting to share his story with everyone I knew.

For now, I'll share Murray's.

Thank you for reading.

Made in the USA
Middletown, DE
10 September 2024

60128760R00187